MOUNTAIN JUSTICE

Savage was almost livid as he faced the newcomers. "Pilgrims," Savage announced, "you've bought yourselves a load of trouble by coming out here. I'd advise every last damn one of you to go back to whatever rock you crawled out from under."

The five men gaped, and their faces turned angry. Art Victor balled his big fists. He reached in his pocket and pulled out the money. Savage worked up a chew of tobacco and spit on the wad of bills. For an instant, Victor was so stunned he just stared at the brown juice and the greenbacks. Then, with a curse, he dropped the money and reached for the gun stuffed in his belt. . . .

He never had a chance. The Green River hunting knife came up in Savage's hand and its blade ripped through his opponent's belly. Victor's eyes bugged and he lifted to his toes. Savage held him as if on the end of a wire. Nobody said a word as Victor crashed to the ground and lay still. . . .

Also by Gary McCarthy

≈   RIVERS WEST : BOOK 3   ≈

The
Colorado

Gary McCarthy

BANTAM BOOKS
NEW YORK • TORONTO • LONDON • SYDNEY • AUCKLAND

In memory of my father,
whose life began—and ended—beside the Colorado River.

RIVERS WEST: THE COLORADO

A Bantam Book / January 1990

ISBN 0-553-28451-7

Published simultaneously in the United States and Canada

Bantam Books are published by Bantam Books, a division
of Bantam Doubleday Dell Publishing Group, Inc. Its trademark, consisting of the words "Bantam Books" and the
portrayal of a rooster, is Registered in U.S. Patent and
Trademark Office and in other countries. Marca Registrada.
Bantam Books, 666 Fifth Avenue, New York, New York
10103.

PRINTED IN THE UNITED STATES OF AMERICA

OPM   0 9 8 7 6 5 4 3 2 1

≈ AUTHOR'S NOTE ≈

Although Isaac, Nathan, and Matthew Beard are fictional characters, much of this novel is based upon actual historical events. For example, I learned the Ute legend of Spirit Lake while visiting Grand Lake, headwaters of the Colorado River.

The exploration of the Colorado did begin with the assembly of the little steamboat *Explorer* at the Gulf of Mexico and its arduous upriver journey is accurately seen through Matt's eyes. At this point in history there was friction between the Mormons and the U.S. Army, which prompted this expedition. Also, Lt. Ives's overland trek to Fort Defiance was remarkable; the expedition was saved by the Hopi at their mesa city of Oraibi. The Hopi did conduct their early morning prayers as described and Ives went on to help design and construct the Washington Monument.

Mayor John Wesley Powell was also an extraordinary man whose daring exploration of the upper Colorado is well documented. Anyone who has ever visited the Grand Canyon cannot fail to imagine how courageous Major Powell and his men must have been to make that great river journey, always wondering if a giant waterfall might swallow them up around the next bend. Bill Dunn and the Howland Brothers did finally lose their nerve and desert the expedition. They were never seen alive again.

And finally, old Chief Cairnook of the Mojave was killed for helping his captured tribesmen escape into the Colorado River at Fort Yuma.

≈   PROLOGUE   ≈

The tall, broad-shouldered young man working behind the dry goods counter seemed far too big and powerful to be a clerk in a general store. His size was a disadvantage as he moved down the narrow, cluttered aisle. "New beaver traps are fifteen dollars apiece," he said as he easily grabbed the string of traps hanging from a hook almost twelve feet above the new plank floor.

"Damn the price! I'll make that up in one good day, trappin' beaver on the Grand River!"

Isaac Beard believed Jim Savage. Since coming to work in his father-in-law's general store, Isaac had dealt with other mountain men and they all had money, more money than Isaac had ever seen in the hands of St. Louis working men. But once they arrived in this riverfront city, they spent their beaver profits as recklessly as deprived children.

"How many traps do you want?"

"Hell, I want all of 'em!" Savage barked, loud enough to be heard down on the banks of the Missouri.

Isaac figured quickly. The traps would cost $120 and the testy old mountain man was spending almost that much on other supplies. Mr. Wilke would be extremely pleased. There was big profit in supplying mountain men, two hundred percent at least.

"There you are," Isaac said, placing the heavy traps on the counter beside the blankets, the new Hawken rifle, powder, ball, and a Green River hunting knife with its long curved blade of tempered steel. "That all?"

"I want salt and Indian trinkets. Ten dollars' worth." Savage spat a long stream of tobacco juice on Mr. Wilke's new floor. Isaac frowned but said nothing about the tobacco. There was a spittoon handy, and Isaac knew that his father-in-law

1

would be furious if the spittle wasn't wiped up before a lady came through the door.

Isaac stiffened as Everett Wilke walked toward the front counter. Mr. Wilke had small, wire-rimmed glasses that kept slipping down his nose. His narrow face and prominent nose reminded Isaac of a ferret. His magnified eyes behind the thick little lenses missed nothing.

"Good afternoon, sir," Wilke said, his smile quick and without warmth as his mind tallied the price of the supplies piled high on the counter. "Are you being taken care of properly, or can I help you myself?"

Isaac felt his cheeks burn at the insinuation that he was somehow incompetent at a job that required a lot more muscle than brains. At times like this, he struggled with all his might to remain silent. His wife, Catherine, would someday inherit this big general store, and it would be passed on to their son Nathan and any of his future brothers and sisters. The Beards had always been poor but Isaac had vowed that would change in St. Louis. He would eradicate the family's reputation that a Beard was always an outlaw, a cutthroat, a drunk, or a thief.

"Who the hell are you?" Savage snarled.

Wilke's Adam's apple yo-yoed. "I own this establishment. My name is Everett T. Wilke, at your service."

Savage spat on the floor again. He used his new hunting knife to stab a pickle from the barrel and did not appear to notice that his tobacco had spattered Mr. Wilke's polished boots and stained the cuffs of his shiny gray trousers. Isaac didn't smile, though he wanted to.

Turning to Isaac, the mountain man drawled, "You work for this weasel-faced little sonofabitch?"

Isaac managed to say, "Yes, Mr. Wilke is my employer."

The mountain man stared into his eyes. "A big fella like you ought to be ashamed of hisself fer wearin' a sissy's apron and bein' such a toady."

Isaac's thick hands tightened on the beaver traps until the bones of his knuckles were white. He barely managed to say, "Your goods come to $282.50."

Wilke saw a chance to regain his respect. "How does this gentleman know his correct bill without you adding it up on paper? Isaac, how many times do I have to tell you to tally the purchases so my customers know you aren't cheating them!"

A hard knot formed between Isaac's shoulder blades. Pain radiated the length of his spine and his hands shook a little as he gripped a pencil and began to jot down the prices that he knew by heart. He had four complete years of schooling, more than any Beard had ever had, and he knew his total was correct. He knew it and took pride in his ability to add numbers in his head. But Mr. Wilke was watching him and so was the mountain man. It seemed to Isaac that their eyes were nibbling at him like hungry mice. He totaled up the figures, feeling the pain throbbing somewhere in the back of his head. He tried to think of Catherine and especially of Nathan, his three-year-old son, but when he did, he lost his tally and had to re-add the figures. He turned the paper around on the countertop for the mountain man to examine. He was sweating when he said, "Still $282.50, sir."

Savage didn't even glance at the figures.

But Mr. Wilke did. He went over the column of figures twice, his thin lips working in concentrated silence. Isaac saw the man's disappointment. "The figure is correct, sir."

Savage paid his bill with cash money, slamming it down on the counter one bill at a time. "Only ones getting rich in the fur trade anymore are you bastards," he grunted, slipping his new Green River hunting knife under his belt, then scooping up his rifle. He left his traps, blankets, and Indian trading goods behind as he headed for the door.

"Help him carry out the rest!" Wilke ordered. "Don't just stand there!"

The mountain man spat once more on his way out. His tobacco splashed against the side of the pickle barrel and then rolled down to the floor. Isaac, arms laden, followed him out onto the porch.

"Just set it all right down there in a pile," Savage ordered. "I'll be back for it later." The man looked up at Isaac, seemed about to say something, then shook his head and started walking down the boardwalk with the fine Hawken rifle resting in the crook of his arm.

"Wait!" Isaac called. "You can't just leave all this here! Someone will steal it for sure!"

The mountain man continued on, his stride long and swinging as he called, "You watch it until I get back."

"But. . . ." he turned to look at his employer. "Mr. Wilke, we can't let him leave these supplies out here unattended."

"Goods bought and taken aren't my responsibility. You just leave them be and attend to your job. He isn't paying you, I am! And I'll be gone this afternoon."

Isaac breathed a sigh of relief. Lately, Wilke had been taking some afternoons off because of the doctor's orders. His heart was giving him trouble.

"It's for your own good, sir."

Wilke's thin face twisted with derision. "Since when did you start giving a damn about my failing health! You can hardly wait for me and Mrs. Wilke to die so Catherine can inherit this store."

Isaac's face colored with shame because Wilke was right. Otherwise, he would not have put up with working for this man a single day.

"You're nothing but an overgrown opportunist, Isaac. Why Catherine married a man like you will always be a mystery."

"She loves me," Isaac blurted, realizing how ridiculous that sounded to a man like his father-in-law.

Wilke's expression soured. "She could have had any man in St. Louis, but she chose a worthless no-account like you. It sickens me."

Something that had been bending within Isaac snapped. "I wish you'd drop dead right now," he said in a voice that he barely recognized as his own.

"Ah-ha!" Wilke cried. "You've finally said it, said what I knew from the very beginning and I've told Catherine a thousand times. You're an evil man with an evil family background. And if you weren't married to my daughter, I'd have fired you quicker than I could work up a spit."

Isaac clenched the edge of the counter. His heart was pounding, and he struggled to keep from grabbing the man. "And if you weren't my father-in-law," he breathed, "I'd take off this apron and cram it down your scrawny throat."

"You dare threaten me! You *are* fired!"

"So be it," Isaac said, the heat going out of him. He took off the hated apron, wondering what he was going to tell his wife. He had promised her every day of their marriage that he would never lose his temper and provoke her father into a dismissal that would rob his family of their legacy. And now, he'd failed. "Whatever grief you bring to me, you bring to Catherine and your grandson."

"The grief started the day she met you!"

Isaac could not look at Wilke for fear he would strike out in anger. "I've got a couple of hundred dollars of back wages coming."

"Not from me, you don't!"

Now Isaac looked at the man. "Mr. Wilke, I've been working overtime for years. We had an agreement."

"Get out of my store," the older man hissed, "before I call the sheriff. You know he don't think any more of a Beard than I do."

Isaac hurled his apron to the floor. "You *owe* me money!"

"You have nothing in writing. You can't prove a thing in court." Wilke gloated as he moved between Isaac and his cash register. Isaac almost grabbed the man by the throat, but instead he stumbled outside and nearly fell over two men in the act of stealing Jim Savage's new blankets and trading goods. Isaac, already wild with fury, caught and slammed them up against the building so hard that it shook.

The men struggled and tried to reach their guns but Isaac grabbed them by the ears and bashed their heads together. They collapsed to the boardwalk. Isaac pounded their heads together again and again. A woman screamed, "He's killing them!"

Her words penetrated Isaac's rage, and he released the unconscious men. Grabbing them by the legs, he dragged them off the boardwalk, then went back to Savage's supplies and slumped down to wait for the mountain man.

The woman marched up, hands on hips, face working with outrage. "You . . . you ought to be locked up in prison! You almost killed them."

"Get away and leave me be," Isaac said as a small crowd gathered to watch. "All of you, get away and leave me alone!"

The crowd dispersed.

Isaac needed solitude and a chance to think in peace, but that ignorant Jim Savage had expected him to watch over his supplies, supplies that had taken him months of hardship to earn. Dammit, but Savage was a trusting old fool!

Isaac waited for the mountain man to return, partly out of duty, but mostly because he didn't want to face his wife just yet, not until he had some kind of a plan for their now very uncertain future. He knew that the best thing he could do for Catherine and Nathan was to abandon them . . . or get himself hanged or shot dead. That was the only way Mr. Wilke would make things right.

At five o'clock, Wilke locked up his store. He glared at Isaac and said in a voice loud enough for passersby to hear, "I fired you for good! Sitting here waiting to ask for your position back won't help."

"I wouldn't take the job back for double the wages I was getting," Isaac said in a strained voice.

Wilke wagged his finger. "I saw what you did to those two men. You're going to kill someone before long and then you'll hang."

"If that's true, I hope that it's you. It'd almost be worth hanging for."

Wilke paled and scurried away.

It was nearly sundown when Isaac heard a wild shout and looked up to see Jim Savage and another mountain man. The stranger was leading a big mule and was grinning from ear to ear. "Whooo-weee!" he yelped. "Whooo-weee!"

In contrast to his companion's exuberance, Savage appeared murderous. He clenched a half-empty bottle of whiskey as if ready to use it as a club, and when they stopped in front of the general store, he didn't even acknowledge Isaac, but said, "Well, there it all is, Rufus! Everything bought and paid for. Brand new traps, blankets, food, Indian doodads, and trinkets."

"Thankee, thankee!" Rufus exclaimed, grinning from ear to ear. The man planted his moccasins wide apart and stared at the goods, almost beside himself with glee. He was short, but powerful, and his muscular thighs were tightly encased in dirty buckskin breeches. He reminded Isaac of a feisty black bear.

Savage was so mad he had trouble speaking. "If you had any honor, you'd let the debt ride until next summer when I could pay in fur."

Rufus howled with mirth. "Since when has a mountain man got honor!"

"If'n this was the other way around," Savage spat, "I'd let you owe me till the rendezvous."

"Well," Rufus said as he mounted the boardwalk and started grabbing up supplies, "it *ain't* the other way around and I ain't waitin' to collect my winnings."

Savage upended the bottle and drank recklessly as he watched Rufus load his mule. "You're puttin' me out of business! You know as well as me that there ain't no credit left for a mountain man in St. Louis."

"That's a fact. Damn shame, Jim. But we both realize that there's already too damn many of us out there huntin' too few beaver up along the Yellowstone," Rufus said, trying to hide a grin. "I got to do for myself as best I can. Old man, you had your day. It's my turn now, even though you, Bridger, and Ashley's boys didn't leave me a hell of a lot of fur left to trap."

Rufus finished loading the mule and tying everything off with a diamond hitch. "So long, Jim!" he shouted heartily as he led the mule away. "Beaver is waitin' for me out there."

Isaac shook his head and climbed to his feet. It seemed like this was a bad day for a lot of men. Him losing his job, old Jim Savage losing his stake and facing a winter lost in a city. Rufus hadn't any more decency in him than Mr. Wilke.

"Damn your cold heart!" Savage bellowed at the departing figure.

In answer, Rufus turned and yelled back over his shoulder, "Find a city job. You're too old for trappin' and you can't play poker worth a damn! You're just lucky I let you keep your damn rifle, knife, and buckskins!"

Savage lost all self-control. He threw the Hawken to his shoulder, then realized it was brand new and still unloaded. Howling with fury, he began to load the weapon faster than Isaac would have believed humanly possible.

Isaac knew he had to do something to prevent a murder

and subsequent hanging. He launched himself at Savage and just managed to knock the Hawken aside as the old mountain man was ready to aim and fire. The big rifle exploded with a roar. A shower of dirt kicked up in the street, and the lead ball ricocheted through Oscar Widaman's storefront window. A passing freighter dove into the boot of his wagon and his team bolted and ran. People on the street leapt for cover. Rufus and his pack mule sprinted around a corner, heading West.

"Goddamn you!" Savage shouted at Isaac, drawing his knife and springing into a fighting stance. "I'll gut you like an antelope!"

Isaac retreated a step. He had fought men before and had always won, but he'd never faced a wild mountain man bent on opening his stomach. "There's no need for this."

Savage attacked, a screech rising from the depth of his gullet. It was a wild, primal sound that raised Isaac's hair. As the knife swept in toward him, he lashed out and was lucky enough to strike Savage on the top of his forearm. It was a powerful blow and before the older man could recover, Isaac's massive fist came down like a sledgehammer to meet the point of Savage's whiskered jaw. The mountain man hit the ground hard. He rolled over twice and came to rest without so much as twitching.

Isaac took away the man's knife and six-gun and stuffed them behind his belt. He dragged Savage over to a watering trough and dunked the old man's head until Savage began to thrash.

"You cooled off yet?"

"I'm gonna kill you fer . . ."

Isaac shoved the head down again. Savage's hair was long and greasy, and it was easy to get a solid fistful. When the man started to flop around, Isaac jerked his head up again. "I'll drown you if you don't behave."

It almost killed the mountain man, but he choked, "Lemee up, you overgrown sonofabitch!"

Isaac let loose and stepped back. Savage reached for his gun, then his hunting knife.

"I already got 'em," Isaac said, watching the man sleeve water and moss from his eyes. "And you promised to behave."

"I don't hold to no promise I make when my head is held under water."

"You better simmer down and sober up."

"Why the hell should I?" Savage climbed to his feet, hair plastered down the front of his face, almost to his chin. "I'm out of business."

"Maybe. Maybe not."

"What's that supposed to mean?" Savage shook hair from his eyes. "You gonna get Mr. Wilke to stake a mountain man?"

"He won't do it," Isaac said. "But I'm owed some money by him so maybe I will."

Savage lowered his voice. "How much you owed?"

"Two hundred dollars at least."

It was almost a full minute before Savage spoke. "Bein' owed is one thing, havin' the cash in hand is altogether another."

The man was right. Isaac had been thinking all afternoon. There was only one answer and that was to take what was rightfully owed. If a man didn't stand up for what was due him, he wasn't much of a man. "I mean to have my money."

Savage wasn't a bit impressed. "I guess you figure I'm blind or somethin'. Hell, even half drunk it's plain to see he fired you. And a man who fired another man ain't likely to pay him what is owed. That stingy old man will send you to prison."

It was the truth. Isaac swallowed and shifted his feet in the dirt. "I've heard it said a man can make a thousand dollars or more in one good trapping season. Is that true?"

"Why you askin'?"

"'Cause I got no choice but to get my money and go trapping with you." There, he'd said it out loud, put into words the truth he'd been fighting so hard to get around.

"The hell you say! I got enough troubles already."

Isaac started to turn and walk away. "Suit yourself."

"Wait a damn minute!"

Isaac stopped and turned around. Savage looked at him hard and long, as if taking his measure. "Gimme my gun and knife."

Isaac thought it over and then handed them to Savage,

but he stayed close enough to whack the crazy old mountain man.

Savage frowned. "You know anything about trappin' beaver?"

"No."

"I didn't think you would."

"Do you know where there are any left?"

Savage dipped his chin. "You ever heard of the Shining Mountains?"

"Them the Rockies?"

"The Ute Indian part of the Rockies," Savage corrected. "The Utes don't let just anyone in those mountains. I never said nothin' to Rufus or anyone else, but the Ute let me and my friends in to trap. This fall, I mean to start up near Spirit Lake."

"Never heard of it."

"The fact is, Spirit Lake is up near the headwaters of the Grand River. This year, I've been hired to take some other pilgrims up there."

"What's that mean?"

"It means I get cash money to take men like you trappin'."

Isaac wasn't at all pleased. "Beaver are getting scarce. If we take other men, there won't be enough for us."

"Hell, you don't know what you're talking about! Why, there's so many beaver along the Grand they's like locust crawling across a cornfield. You could be rich in two seasons, buy your own damned store instead of grovelin' for the likes of Wilke."

"I don't expect to get rich," Isaac said, thinking about how Catherine and little Nathan would take his leaving for so long. The only silver lining to the cloud was that Mr. Wilke would be shamed into taking good care of them.

"You'd like the mountains," Savage told him. "They grow *in* a man, not around him, to smother his spirit like a damned city."

"I always wanted to see them," Isaac admitted, feeling an excitement build. "I always did."

"Then you'll do it!" Savage yelled.

Isaac took a deep breath. He had no choice, and though he would not tell Catherine and hurt her feelings, he had been pining for years to seek adventure and quick wealth. Clerking under Wilke had nearly poisoned him. Isaac found that he was nodding his head. "Then it's settled. I'll help you."

"You gonna steal from the old man?"

"It's not stealin' to take what is owed."

"That's right, but . . . well, the law in St. Louis might figure things different."

"That's why we must leave tonight," Isaac said.

"We'll need horses, too. Saddles, packs. You outfitted plenty of mountain men. You know what we need."

"I know."

Savage stuck out his rough hand and he was happy again. "You and me will ride back into this town next spring as rich as kings! You can pay Wilke off anything he thinks is still owed and have plenty of money left."

"I won't take more than is due me," Isaac said, "for that would be thievery."

Savage's grin slipped. "That's . . . well, that's right noble of you. Now, while you're doin' all this, I'm goin' to go back to the saloon. I still got a few dollars left to spend that Rufus could not steal. I'll meet you after midnight on the trail west of town."

"I'll find you," Isaac promised.

Savage started to turn away, then he stopped and whispered, "You gonna break down the door or bust in a window?"

"Neither," Isaac said. "He forgot to ask me for my key."

Savage barked a laugh. "That just serves the superior actin' sonofabitch right!"

Isaac gently laid Nathan back down in his bed. "I couldn't bear to wake him to say goodbye," he said to his wife. "You tell him I'll be back next summer and I'll buy him a pony."

Catherine Beard nodded. She was slim, blonde and, tonight, much paler than usual. Even in the lamplight, her eyes were puffy and red from tears. But tears had not changed his mind, and the crying was done. "I will tell him," she said. "And I will tell our new baby."

Isaac had not known his wife was pregnant until less than an hour ago. But outside waiting were two horses and the supplies. He had crossed the line and there was no turning back.

"You'd better go now," the woman said. "You'll need a good head start."

"Talk to your pa," Isaac said, his voice almost pleading. "Tell him I only took what was owed. I'm your husband, the father of his grandchildren! Catherine, you've got to make him see."

"I will speak to him," she said, trying and failing to muster up any sign of encouragement. "But you know how he's always felt about you. This is going to make it harder."

Isaac gently pulled his wife to his chest. As always, she seemed so frail that he handled her as if she were a small bird in his hand. "I *need* to know you understand."

She looked up at him. "I understand you want to go."

"I *have* to go! It's for you, and Nathan and the child you carry."

"Why is it that men always go off telling their women the same things? I've known that you wanted to leave for a long, long time. I saw how my father treated you. It hurt me deeply. It hurt all the time." She swallowed. "I do not hold this against you. I love you. We'll be waiting and praying."

Isaac groaned. Leaving his family was like a knife in his belly, twisting and bleeding away his resolve. "I have to go now or I won't do it at all."

He stepped out into the night. The two horses belonged to Mr. Wilke, as did everything else. But all together, it was not worth what Wilke owed Isaac.

He mounted and found he could not move.

"You go now!" his wife ordered, pulling her shawl close, masking the shine of moonlight on her golden hair. "You go and you come back to us with more beaver than anyone has ever brought back to St. Louis."

He nodded and wanted to say something more. "Your father will take you out of this shack. He and your mother will put you up in the big house. You'll be better off than you were with me around."

Catherine covered her face and began to weep, and before Isaac broke down and wept too, he slammed his heels into his horse and galloped away.

On the outskirts of town, the mountain man emerged from a stand of cottonwood trees. He mounted the horse Isaac had brought for him, then led off to the West. He gave a wild whoop of joy that drifted back to St. Louis and Isaac thought he ought to do the same but he couldn't summon up a single whoop to save his hide.

All he knew for sure was that there would probably be a posse after him by ten o'clock the next morning but it would never catch him. And when he got to those Shining Mountains of the Ute people, he was going to work harder than any of the other pilgrims that Savage was bringing along. He'd outwork them all in order to get rich enough to take his wife and children away and start over again.

No would-be mountain man had ever gone West with more to gain—or to lose—than Isaac Beard.

≈ **BOOK ONE** ≈

≈   ISAAC   ≈

Under normal circumstances, Isaac and the mountain man would have followed the Missouri River to Independence. But with the likelihood of the sheriff and a couple of deputies hunting them, they chose a looping overland trail. This created new dangers. Because white men almost always followed the rivers west, the fugitive pair found themselves in undisputed Indian country.

It was a beautiful land. The lush green tablelands and rolling hills were covered with wildflowers and Isaac would have enjoyed the scenery had he not been continually looking over his shoulder and wondering if he had made a mistake that would haunt him the rest of his life. Mr. Wilke would, of course, try to have him arrested when he returned to St. Louis. The vindictive old man would do anything to keep Isaac from inheriting a profitable general store and reclaiming his family. Isaac missed them terribly. The ache to hold his wife and son was so real that even the warm sun, the magnificent clouds, and the vast blue sky could not raise his spirits.

"If you keep lookin' back," Savage drawled late one afternoon, "you'll never have time to see what's up ahead. You might run into a bullet or an arrow. If you don't start lookin' where yore headin', you'll be a dead man in the high mountains."

"What does that matter to you? If I die, then you'll just take what pelts I have and sell them for yourself."

"The thought has occurred to me, Pilgrim. The same holds true for the others that I'm supposed to lead to the Shining Mountains. I'll bet they're a sorry collection."

Isaac was surprised. "You've never even met them?"

"Nope."

"Then how . . ."

Savage scowled at the memory. "I was broke. Damn cards again. Anyway, it was in Chicago and I was a long way from the mountains and with no money to get back. Hell of a walk. By and by, though, I met a man who made me a deal."

"What kind of a deal?"

"I agreed to take pilgrims into the mountains for a hundred dollars each. I reckon they paid him the same."

"I didn't realize that anyone would want to go. Especially with a stranger."

"Hell, don't you know that them cities back East are full of young men like yourself just itchin' to get out and have some fun. Beaver is money and money will always bring city men a runnin'. Them that paid will be waiting for us in Independence. I'll apprentice the whole lot."

Isaac nodded. He'd outfitted enough mountain men to know that they often took on apprentices. After a year or two, a pilgrim would then know enough to be able to strike out on his own. It was something Isaac himself had often considered, but only in the context of fantasy. Now, fantasy had turned to reality but the price had been too high. "I could have owned that general store some day and had my family, too."

"Ha! You'd a killed him—or yourself—first." They rode on in silence. The mountain man wondered if he had sorely overestimated Isaac Beard with his great size and strength. Savage could still feel a pain in his arm and his jaw where the giant had struck him. But he wondered if Isaac had the grit and the pluck to survive in the mountains. It took more than size and strength to be a mountain man. It took being able to withstand hunger and cold and loneliness. It took survival instincts as keen as those of a wild animal. So many things could kill a trapper in the high mountains. A single mistake and you were dead. And there was something else, too. To withstand the hardship, a man needed to love isolation and the peacefulness of the pines. If his heart was corrupted by city living—the way Isaac's might be—then he was doomed. He might go crazy or else he would become careless until he made that one fatal mistake, a mistake that might easily cost them all their scalps.

Savage knew it would surprise Isaac to learn that he had not become a mountain man until he was well into his thirties.

He was the son of a Tennessee horse breeder. Having had a family of his own, Savage understood that a man might find it hard to leave his wife and child for a spell. But men had to do what they had to do. Savage had gone off to war before heading west. He'd done it alone, too, rode out beyond the Missouri as bold and free as an eagle and sighted his course on the great Shining Mountains that Zebulon Pike had seen in 1806. Savage had found those mountains because they were so damned tall and long that there just wasn't any way to miss them. But most important, he had also discovered his friends the Utes. Best people on Earth, the Utes. Better'n white people, for sure.

The Utes knew how life was meant to be lived. Just being with them in their mountain villages had convinced Jim Savage that living in a city where he was hemmed in by too many people, barking dogs, and bickering neighbors was the way to ruin. Savage knew some people looked down on squaw men. To hell with 'em! Snow Bird was young and beautiful. She loved him and she'd give him sons, in time. One thing sure, she'd never expect her man to kowtow to her father, Kicking Elk. Not the way Isaac Beard's wife musta done.

Savage wished he could tell Isaac about the Ute women and how they treated their men. But he guessed he'd let Isaac see for himself. Maybe it would open his eyes a little. Watching the big man mope over having to leave St. Louis for a piddling year revolted Jim Savage. It made him want to swat him across the ears and wake him up to the adventure that lay in store. "Dammit, quit twistin' your neck around and take a gander up yonder. More buffalo!"

It was not the first herd Isaac had seen since leaving St. Louis, but it was by far the largest and it pulled him back to the present. "There be a million of them."

"It's a mighty herd and that's fer sure. But always remember, where you find buffalo, you stand a fair chance of finding Indians."

Isaac said nothing. He did not want to find Indians. "How far to Independence?" he asked, hoping it was close.

"We'll be there by tomorrow. Pick up some more supplies and the pilgrims, then strike out for the big mountains."

They rode slowly now, and when they were within a

quarter of a mile of the herd, Savage dismounted and slipped a percussion cap over the nipple of his Hawken rifle. He winked. "There's so many buffalo out there, I'm reminded of the beaver in Ute country just waiting to be took."

Isaac didn't believe the man, and it must have showed because Savage added, "The Grand River is so full that we'll all wade through their ponds clubbin' 'em with tree branches. Wait and see, Pilgrim."

Isaac wasn't thinking about beaver but about the buffalo. "Are you going to shoot buffalo?"

"Yep."

"But why! You've already shot more than we can pack on the mules."

"There's always room for some extra smoked tongue," Savage told him. "Day will come this winter when you'll be most grateful for 'em."

"But . . ."

Savage cut him off. "Dammit, I plan to give some to my wife's people. Utes like nothing better than smoked buffalo tongue."

Isaac blinked with surprise. "You're a squaw man?"

"Damn right I am! Anything wrong with that!"

"No." Isaac shook his head. "Of course not."

"I'll bet yore a damned Catholic or maybe a Baptist. Which is it?"

"Baptist." In truth, he went to the Baptist church to please his wife and her family. He'd been raised a Presbyterian and found them considerably more forgiving of a man's weaknesses.

"Them are damned holy people. My mother was a Baptist. Intolerable woman. Drove Pa off the farm with her religion."

"There's nothing wrong with Baptists. It's a strong, God-fearing religion." Isaac would brook no one talking down the Lord's and his wife's church.

"Might be you'll find the Indians have a religion that makes a heap more sense than ours."

"You believe in their religion?"

"Some of it. But I don't want to talk religion none right now. I got buffalo to shoot." Savage dismounted and handed his reins to Isaac, then turned in a full circle, his face slightly upturned.

"What are you doing?"

"Seeing which way the wind blows."

"There isn't a bit of air moving."

"Yes, there is. The wind never stands still. It's like us mountain men."

Isaac was getting mad. They had enough meat and this was hostile country. "I still don't think you ought to shoot any more buffalo. Seems wrong to kill a thousand-pound animal, one as magnificent as that, just for a couple of pounds of tongue meat."

"What I do and why I do it ain't none of your business."

"You're wrong. Rifle shots could bring Indians down on us. You as much as said they might be close to a herd this size. My scalp *is* my business!"

The mountain man cocked one eye shut and gazed up at Isaac. "I do believe the pathetic truth of this conversation is that you are squeamish, Mr. Beard. I do believe you object to the natural sight of blood and guts. Is that so?"

"I find unnecessary slaughter immoral, yes."

Savage scratched himself. "I was a soldier in the War of 1812. When you've seen soldiers blown apart on the battlefield—British or our own boys, no matter—you think nothing of killing buffalo or beaver. Killing is a part of life. Sometimes dying can be a sight easier than living. Just ask any man that gets taken alive by hostile Indians."

He strode off, leaving Isaac to ponder his words. In the few days that they had known and lived together, Isaac had come to realize that Jim Savage was a reasonably intelligent but very stubborn man. And this foolishness could get them all killed. Isaac had no choice but to wait with the horses as Savage went to shoot buffalo.

The first time they had come upon buffalo, Savage had shown him how to stalk the herd by moving in a direct line toward the poor-sighted animals, always from downwind. You could get into rifle range walking upright.

The buffalo herd sensed danger. A big cow threw up her massive head and signaled a warning. Almost at once, the bulls formed a loose defense. But they were still confused, unsure as to whether or not there was any real danger. Before they could make up their minds, Savage reached into his fringed jacket and withdrew the forked stick he carried. The hunter stretched full out on the grass, propped the heavy fifty-caliber percussion rifle across the notch of the forked stick and hesitated only a few seconds before he squeezed off his first, crucial shot.

The big cow who'd first sounded a warning was the herd leader. Savage had spotted her, and now Isaac saw very bright red blood pump from her sides and mouth. The cow collapsed, then thrashed back to her feet. A calf rushed in close, its plaintive cries sharp and distinct. Head down, weaving as if she were drunk, the cow tried to run but her legs moved strangely, and after completing a small circle, she fell again. Isaac swallowed and knew she would not rise a second time. The dying cow kicked her legs wildly while her calf lowered its head and bawled. The other buffalo, frightened by the roar of the Hawken and the smell of blood, wanted to run but, seeing their leader down, stopped and came back to her and the calf, stomping, sniffing, and milling about in abject bewilderment.

Then, a new leader started to run and the Hawken boomed again. The new leader somersaulted head over heels. Its massive head slammed the earth over and over as it tried to stand but failed. Isaac had seen enough. He turned his back on the slaughter and faced distant St. Louis. He pictured Nathan and Catherine and wondered if his new child would be a boy or a girl. Ignoring the rifle fire, he decided that he wanted a daughter, one like Catherine.

The Hawken thundered for what seemed like hours. Isaac stood holding the horses and tried to blot out the sound of the killing. Jim Savage was wrong, and Isaac knew he would not want to eat any more buffalo tongue, not if it was gained through such wastefulness and wanton destruction. Isaac decided the mountain man must have been twisted by war and death. Certainly the man held the value of life in far less esteem than civilized white men. Savage was a throwback to another age when the instinct of hunting and killing dominated man's every action. Maybe it took that kind of instinct to survive in the high mountains. Isaac hoped not. One thing for sure, he knew that it was useless even to attempt to understand the reasoning of such a killing man.

To the east from where he had come, Isaac saw huge thunderheads boiling up into a salmon-colored sky. He wondered if it was raining in St. Louis and if his wife and young son were now comfortably housed with the Wilkes on State Street. Probably. The thought of Catherine and Nathan living in comfortable surroundings did not bring him great pleasure. I am jealous, he thought, resentful that I could do no better. But I will. If ever we get to the mountains and the Grand River, I will.

They rode into Independence the next day and it was nothing but a muddy street, a few stores and saloons, a cafe, and one huge tent with cots renting for ten cents a night. "Ain't much, is it?" Isaac said with some disappointment because the thought of a new city had somehow buoyed his flagging spirits with a sense of anticipation.

"It's as big as any town I ever want to see. What day is it?"

Isaac calculated when he had last seen his wife and added the number of days they had been on the trail since fleeing from St. Louis. "May seventeenth."

"Well, I'll be damned! That's exactly the day I told them to be here and that we'd leave this city."

Isaac would not have complimented Independence by calling it a city by any stretch of the imagination. Outpost would have been a fairer description. The three hundred or four hundred inhabitants were as unsavory a collection as could be found on the Western frontier. Many of them were fur trappers and traders, wearing their skin caps, fringed buckskins, and beaded moccasins. They all carried rifles and knives and strutted about as if they were rulers of this empty land. But there were also hucksters, teamsters, whores, and gamblers. Isaac's first impression was that everyone was busy, but when he got right in among them, he realized that only a few, such as the blacksmith and the wheelwright, were employed in any useful occupation.

Savage claimed that five men would be waiting here to be led into the Ute country under his guidance and protection, and that they had come from far and wide. "Some of you will

die before spring," Savage had told him. "Maybe all of you.
Depends."

"On what?"

"Luck and how fast you learn." They dismounted in the
shade of a tree and Savage handed the reins of his horse and
the rope of his mule to Isaac. "I'll be along directly. Any that
ain't here will get left behind."

Isaac tied the animals to the tree as he prepared for what
became a considerable wait. He stretched out on the grass and
watched the clouds over the leafy branches high above. The air
was humid and the muddy street told him that Independence
had just received a very heavy rain. As the afternoon wore on,
his boredom was temporarily relieved by the sight of two
drunken trappers brawling in the mud, cursing and gouging
each other as they rolled and grunted. Down the street, he
heard shouting and then a single gunshot. The two brawlers,
faces battered nearly shapeless, hesitated for only a moment
before they continued their struggle. At last the fight ended.
Isaac turned to see who had won but they both looked like
losers as, arm in arm, the pair staggered off to the saloon to
refresh their spirits and friendship. Isaac grew sleepy and
closed his eyes. For the hundredth time, he wondered if he
was doing the right thing or if this was all an excuse just to run
away from responsibility. And for the hundredth time, he
reminded himself that either way, it didn't matter. He had set
his foot on a path that had to be followed, wherever it led.

"Hey, Pilgrim, wake up!"

Isaac snapped awake. He climbed to his feet and studied
the five men who flanked Jim Savage. Savage told him their
names. Mack Peel. Paden Tolbert. Andy Davis. Doug Mellon.
Art Victor. Mellon and Davis were several years younger than
himself, the other three his age or slightly older. Only one
struck a bad chord with Isaac. Art Victor was a beefy man in his
late thirties with a blacksmith's arms, an aggressive stance, and
a fist-busted nose. He and Savage both smelled of whiskey.

"Pilgrims," Savage announced, "you have bought yourselves a load of trouble by coming out here. I'd advise every
last damn one of you to go back to whatever rock you crawled
out from under."

The five gaped and then their faces turned angry. Art

Victor balled his big fists. "Old man, you said you alone have exclusive rights to hunt in the Rocky, or the Shining Mountains, as you call them. That's what we paid good cash money for. Is that the way it is, or not?"

Savage stiffened with anger. "That's the way my stick floats, all right. The Utes are my friends. I married one. And if you can keep your big mouth shut and follow my orders, you might, just might, live to see next spring."

"You talk big," Victor said, "but we're paying for more than talk. And how do we know you won't leave us stranded once we are out in the wilderness? Just take our money and leave us to the murderin' Indians?"

"What kind of a white man do you take me for?" Savage raged, his hand moving closer to his knife. "I made a deal and I keep my word on a handshake. All you got to do is to follow my orders."

Isaac believed him. Not even an actor could have faked the outrage on Savage's face. Isaac felt a deep sense of relief. Up until this very moment, he had not completely trusted Jim Savage, but now he felt the man's intentions were honest. Still, one question continued to nag at Isaac, and he figured that this was as good a time as any to ask it and get it settled. "If it isn't the money these men are paying you that is so important, why not take experienced men into the Ute country? They'd probably be able to trap far more beaver. Bring a lot more money than what these men are paying you to come along as apprentices."

Savage was almost livid, but what he said made sense. "After I got the Utes to give real mountain men their blessings, the bastards would clean the river of beaver faster'n you could work up an honorable spit. You pilgrims don't know enough to get along without me for at least a year or two. And I'll pay you a fair share."

"You call fifty-fifty a fair share?" Victor snarled. "We want two out of every three pelts we trap and skin. And that's being charitable." Victor glared at Isaac. "That all right with you, big man?"

"I have my own deal with Mr. Savage," Isaac told them. "This is between you and him."

Victor didn't like that. "But you stand to profit as much as we do!"

Isaac understood the logic, but it changed nothing. He shook his head.

Victor whirled on Savage. "He don't back us, he don't come with us. It don't matter one damn way or the other to me. But we still get to keep two out of three pelts. Is that understood?"

"Get outa my sight before I kill you," Savage spat. "You ain't goin' nowhere with me."

"Now, wait a minute! I paid a hundred dollars back East and I got another hundred in my pocket." He reached into his pocket and pulled out the money. "Here, damn your eyes, take it!"

Savage worked up a chew of tobacco and spit on the man's money. For an instant, Victor was so stunned he just stared at the brown juice and greenbacks in his fist. Then, with a curse, he dropped the money and reached for the gun stuffed in his belt.

He never had a chance. The Green River hunting knife came up in Savage's hand and its blade ripped upward through Victor's belly. The man's eyes bugged, and he lifted to his toes. Savage held him as if on the end of a wire. When the knife was jerked out, Savage stepped back and the man reeled away, already more dead than alive.

"Anyone else want to change the rules of our agreement?" Savage looked eager to use his big hunting knife again.

No one said a word as Victor crashed to the ground and lay still.

"Goddamn good thing," Savage grated. "We leave at first light. If you ain't ready, that's fine with me. I been on flatland so damned long I'm fixin' to get mean if I don't smell the pines soon."

Jim Savage left them gaping at him and then at the body he had left behind. Examining the shock on their faces and knowing it reflected his own, Isaac decided they were all crazy if they followed Jim Savage into the high mountains. Crazy as loons.

≈ 2 ≈

"Psst! Mr. Beard, wake up!"

Isaac opened his eyes and looked overhead at a ring of four faces silhouetted against starlight. "What do you want?"

"To talk," said Mack Peel, the oldest of the group and therefore the chosen spokesman. "We all need to talk."

Isaac sat up and rubbed his eyes. He had not been sleeping soundly. The memory of Victor being gutted would interrupt his nights for a good long while. Besides, it didn't take a lot of brains to guess what they wanted to talk about. "I'm listening."

"It's about Jim Savage," Mack said, crouching down on his haunches. "We think he's crazy and a killer. We're ready to ask for our money back. What do you think?"

"I think that if you've already handed him a hundred dollars each, then you'll have to kill him before he gives it back."

Mack took a deep breath and let it out slowly. "We were afraid you'd say that. Any chance you'd help us?"

"No. If four of you can't handle this, then . . ."

"We don't want to have to kill the man!"

Isaac looked at Andy Davis, a baby-faced kid from Columbus, Ohio, who'd left his father's jewelry business and come out to be a mountain man. Andy was the youngest of them all, and Isaac doubted if he was strong enough for the mountains. He looked like a choirboy.

Paden Tolbert was grim-faced and a man of few words. He had thin lips and a hatchet face. Probably in his mid-twenties, he looked tough and determined. "I ain't givin' up two hundred dollars. I'm going to the mountains, and if he has lied to us, I'll kill him myself."

Isaac looked at the last man. His name was Doug Mellon,

and his hair was as white and fine as corn silk. Doug was a
six-footer, but he was soft and gentle looking. He spoke very
quietly and seemed detached from the others. Isaac had the
impression of a highly educated and intelligent man in his late
twenties, one filled with a certain sense of tragedy. In just the
few hours he had observed the men last night, it had become
apparent that Doug Mellon would be a misfit on the frontier.
He was quite obviously more intellectual than physical, and
Isaac could see by the outline of his packs that he carried books
and writing materials. His poor attempts at humor went over
their heads. He seemed self-absorbed and there was a haunted
look in his eyes. Of all the men, he bothered Isaac most.

"What about you, Mellon? Isaac pushed himself up on
one elbow. "Are you willing to kill in order to get your money
back?"

Doug Mellon shook his head back and forth.

"Then I think you ought to go back home," Isaac said.

"Now, wait a minute," Mack Peel objected. "Doug has as
much right to come as any of us. Why are you telling him not
to come? So you can get more beaver for yourself?"

Isaac's voice took on an edge. "You woke me up and asked
for advice. I'm telling you that Jim Savage won't give you your
money back. He don't give a damn if we go home or push on
with him to the mountains. But he made you a deal and you
took it. So live with it."

"I'm going to the far mountains and I'm coming back
rich," Paden Tolbert vowed. He had long black hair that kept
falling into his eyes. Brushing it back, he said, "There's a farm
I want to buy in Pennsylvania."

"Same here," Mack Peel said. "Only it's in Kentucky and
there's a wife that goes along with it."

Isaac looked at Andy Davis. "What about you? A little
young for this, aren't you?"

The boy shook his head. "I'm nearly seventeen. I been
working hard for my pa since I was eleven."

Isaac did not smile. "You told us your father was a jeweler.
That's not hard work."

Andy stuck his jaw out a little. "Don't matter. I'll hold up
to work and I'll carry my own weight."

They all stared at Doug Mellon. He was the only one who

had said nothing of his past, and it was clear he was not cut out to be a mountain man. "I think you ought to go home," Isaac said, unable to think of a way to help the man save face. "You saw what Jim Savage did last evening. I don't think you want to live with mountain men and Indians. Do you?"

Mellon smiled, his face a mixture of defeat and sadness. He might have been a handsome man had he not been so pale and preoccupied. "I can't go back."

Isaac did not have the heart to ask why, but he knew it must be a hell of a good reason because Mellon was scared stiff. Perhaps the young man would tell them the reason some day, but Isaac doubted it. He wondered if the man also had stolen money and run away. It seemed likely.

"We'd like you to tell us what you know about Mr. Savage," Mack Peel said. "Yesterday was the first time we ever set eyes on the man. You've been with him since St. Louis. Can we trust him?"

"I think so," Isaac said. He knew it would not help if he related the incident between Savage and Rufus Tulley and how it had almost resulted in his own gutting. Besides, to Isaac's way of thinking, Savage could have killed him, but hadn't. "I will admit that Savage is a violent man with a murderous temper."

"We know that. We seen Victor die with our own eyes," Paden Tolbert said in a hard voice. "But I remember that Victor went for his gun first."

"That's right," Isaac said. "And I can tell you this, Jim Savage does know beaver and trapping. He's already told me many things about them. Things that we have to learn."

"Such as?"

Isaac shrugged his heavy shoulders. "How to set beaver traps. How to stay warm and dry in the mountains during winter. How to stalk buffalo and make a stand."

"There ain't no buffalo in the mountains, is there?" Peel asked.

"No," Isaac admitted. "At least not up high. He says the Utes go down onto the Plains to hunt them once a year."

"What about the beaver? Do you believe him when he says they're plentiful?"

Isaac did not answer quickly. He had given that very same

question a great deal of thought. "I believe Jim Savage can take us into beaver country that has never been trapped before. I think he knows this Grand River that runs through the Rocky Mountains better than any white man, better even than Zebulon Pike and his men. I also believe he is married to a Ute woman named Snow Bird and that he has permission to trap on their land. Look closely at the beadwork on his possibles bag, his jacket, and moccasins. I have seen enough other beadwork to know that it is not Cheyenne, Sioux, Comanche, or Kiowa."

"But maybe not Ute, either."

Isaac dipped his chin in agreement. "Maybe not. I go on the assumption that Mr. Savage wants to keep his scalp as much as any of us. I see no reason for him to lie. I think he realizes that other white trappers are going to be coming into the Rockies in the next few years—with or without the permission of the Utes. In my opinion, he brought us in here to clean out the rivers, lakes, and streams before they do. At least this way, he gets a cut of everything. It makes sense to me."

Mack Peel was satisfied and so was Paden Tolbert. Both nodded their heads. Andy Davis followed and Doug Mellon surprised Isaac when he said, "Then we're going, by God! Does anyone have whiskey to toast our grand and gloriously insane venture into the wilderness?"

Peel and Tolbert had full jugs and everyone, even Isaac, shared a drink. It was a crazy hour to drink and Isaac knew that Catherine would be upset if she knew he had violated the precepts of his religion and tasted strong spirits. But hell, he only had a sip and it sort of made a pact between the five of them.

"We'll have to trust and help each other," Mellon said. "Won't we?"

"We will," Andy agreed, looking to big Isaac. "We're all going, mostly on what you just told us."

That bothered Isaac mightily and made him sit upright. "Now wait a minute," he protested. "I don't want the responsibility for anyone coming." Isaac studied each man separately until they nodded with understanding. "If you go or stay, it's your decision. Any or all of us might die up in the snow or get scalped or drown in a river. It can and does happen."

"We're men," Peel said, bringing out a corncob pipe and loading it thoughtfully. "Men got to take chances for what they believe in."

"Amen," Tolbert said with hard conviction. "I don't plan to work on someone else's land the rest of my life. This is my chance and I mean to make the most of it. I borrowed ten dollars from everyone in the family and I sold some of my ma's best things. They're counting on me back in Pennsylvania. I won't come back whipped or empty handed. I either come back with good money—or I don't come back at all."

Isaac realized he felt exactly the same way about it. He hadn't put it into words so blunt and irrevocable, but it was true. He wasn't about to crawl back and ask Everett Wilke for forgiveness and, at best, grovel behind the man's counter or, at worst, decay in a prison.

"Sun will be up in a few minutes," Peel said, watching the stars fade.

Tolbert grunted, but the others said nothing. There was nothing left to be said. Just to do. So the four pilgrims sat huddled close together around Isaac and watched the sun come up over the eastern horizon. Occasionally, Peel and Tolbert took a silent pull on the whiskey. Mellon drank much faster. Nobody objected because he looked so damned worried. But before the sun was high off the horizon, Mellon was drunk and they were amazed to see that he had consumed Peel's jug. Isaac figured that whiskey might be the reason Mellon was so desperate to leave civilization. Whiskey was the devil inside a man who had no tolerance for it. One thing for sure, if there was any way short of applying brute force to get Doug Mellon to stay in Independence, Isaac would have used it.

In spite of Mellon, a peacefulness had come over the men. Each seemed to realize there was no turning back after Independence but at least they had made their pact, and they would stick together. And that way, they would have an even chance of returning next summer with enough pelts to build a dream on.

Two days west of Independence, Savage told them there were rivers to the Shining Mountains they could have followed, but that the chances of meeting Indians were much

greater if they did. So they stayed away from the rivers and
trusted to luck in finding water. It seemed to Isaac a good
trade-off. Besides, the prairie grass was long and lush. It
turned out there were plenty of streams and even some ponds
in the low spots. Their horses and mules grew fat despite the
steady travel and one day stretched endlessly into another
until time lost all meaning on the vast ocean of the plains.

Isaac had heard stories of the great tableland of the west,
of how the wind blew without respite and the grass waved like
seaweed on the ocean floor. Neither he nor the other four
pilgrims could really believe the size of the buffalo herds they
came upon. There seemed no beginning and no end to them.
Nor to the colonies of prairie dogs.

The little critters were a constant source of amusement.
Fat and feisty, a sentinel would stretch up at the first sight of
the riders and bark a warning to its neighbors. At the alarm,
hundreds of prairie dogs would streak toward their burrows.
And no sooner would they disappear than they'd poke their
heads up and chide the intruders for infringing upon their
territory. Isaac saw coyotes and hawks hunting prairie dogs on
the open plains, but almost never did they catch one of the fat
rodents.

Between the animal life and the constant watch for Indian
hunting parties, the days passed swiftly. A routine soon
established itself. Jim Savage always rode a few miles ahead,
and he was their hunter and scout. Though the land was almost
flat, Savage would take advantage of the creekbeds and
depressions and keep his party off the high ground. They
never crossed a ridge unless it was absolutely necessary, and
they never built a buffalo-chip fire at night except when it was
in a hollow or depression.

Isaac preferred breakfast and so did Andy, so that was
their meal for cooking and cleaning up after. Mellon, Peel, and
Tolbert took care of the night meal and the collecting of chips
for the following morning. Everyone except Savage took a turn
at night watch. During the long, empty hours of darkness,
Isaac thought constantly of Nathan, Catherine, and the child
she carried. If it was a girl, he wanted to name her Sarah; if a
boy, maybe they would name him Isaac Junior. Catherine had
wanted to do that with their first, but her parents had raised

such objections that they'd dropped the idea in order to keep peace. They had said Isaac was a Hebrew name and meant "laughing one." Isaac had been shocked to hear such nonsense. He wasn't a Jew and he sure didn't laugh very much. Hell, names meant nothing except to those who gave or received them. Some were easier to say and remember than others, but they were just names all the same. You could call a person any damned thing you wanted to, but it didn't change what they were even a whit.

Five days out of Independence, Jim Savage found a big herd of buffalo grazing on a piece of bottomland. He snaked on his belly to a rise over the herd and shot twenty-three of them before the stand broke and ran away. Isaac knew before reaching the slaughtered buffalo what he'd find, so he held back and let the others gallop on ahead. By the time he arrived, Savage was already instructing them about carving off the hump meat and the tongue. Isaac watched their faces, wanting to read their thoughts. Mack Peel and Paden Tolbert seemed eager enough but Doug Mellon was clearly repulsed by the gore and the sight of death. He wanted no part of the butchery. Young Andy Davis tried to help, but his heart wasn't up to the task.

"We're gonna gorge tonight, eat until we're as round as fresh-fed ticks!" Savage said. "We'll smoke what we can take and leave the rest for the wolves and coyotes."

He glanced at Isaac and, when he said nothing, Savage laughed. "I'm glad that only two of you pilgrims is squeamish. Sure hate to think I brought a bunch of wimmen into the high mountains!"

Mellon blushed but Isaac just turned his head away. He kept remembering what Savage had said about buffalo and Indians being found close together. God could not have made a finer country for both.

That night, they feasted like winter-starved wolves. As usual, the talk ran to what lay ahead and what they could expect to find in the mountains. Savage, with hot grease running through his beard and a little of Paden's whiskey in his belly, was unusually talkative. Until this evening, he seemed to have considered the rest of them beneath him and had stayed apart and aloof.

"Yessir, Pilgrims, you'll love the Ute people! Most likely, their squaws will think you are all mighty fine. Except for you, Mellon, 'cause you're too damned weak and ugly. And you, kid, because you're still a boy."

Both Mellon and Andy Davis stiffened under the cruel insults. Savage laughed obscenely at their embarrassment, but no one else did. The mountain man picked at his teeth with that big hunting knife and tossed a few more buffalo chips on the low fire. "Yes sir, I got me a squaw and she's a good one. Probably about fifteen years old is all and she's plenty frisky for an old fart like me. She likes to tickle my beard and comb it in front of the firelight. She likes that real fine."

Savage leaned over the fire, and the grease glistened on his face and beard. His eyes seemed unnaturally bright and as he worked at his teeth, the knife glittered wickedly. "You pilgrims are gonna have to listen to me when we reach the mountains. I ain't told you this yet, but we can't start trapping until fall."

"What!" Tolbert demanded.

"It's the fur," Savage said. "It has to be long and it don't get long until after the nights begin to freeze."

"What are we supposed to do until then?" Mack Peel asked.

"We hunt, jerk meat, follow the streams and creeks and learn where the beaver be. We got to build a log cabin and cut plenty of firewood. I'll show you how to use aspen sticks and rawhide to make snowshoes. And I'll show you how to use castoreum scent to make sure the beaver come to your traps. Each man will take a different stretch of water. You'll have a trapline to set and watch. Each man will have to be gone on his own for days at a time. That's why you'll need to know how to do everything yourselves."

Isaac interrupted. "How much farther is it to the mountains?"

"'Bout a week if we move smartly. If we kin see Pike's Peak, we went a hundred miles or so too far to the south. We look for a double notch in the mountains with a river runnin' strong down the west slope between a pair of big tabletop mountains. It's just to the north of that we'll find Spirit Lake where the big river starts. But we'll have to climb like you've never climbed before. Oh, I tell you boys it's so damned high up that there's places where the snow never melts and where the trees won't grow. There ain't nothing but this mossy stuff to walk on, and the wind blows cold even in August. And the air is thinner than grass and it'll tucker you out just to walk a few steps."

Isaac could not imagine mountains so high that trees wouldn't grow on them. "Are there beaver in this Spirit Lake?"

"Beaver ain't to be found in still lake water. But even if they was, we wouldn't dare trap a one of 'em. We don't even catch fish outa that lake."

"Why the devil not!" Tolbert demanded. "They special or something?"

Savage looked him dead in the eye. "Because the lake is haunted," he said. "The Utes tell of a time long ago when they were attacked by a big war party of Arapaho. Utes and Arapaho, they's mortal enemies. Always have been. Anyway, the Utes, knowin' they was outnumbered, lashed together a raft real quick and floated their women and children out on Spirit Lake where they'd be safe. But when the women and children saw their men gettin' killed, they began to cry and wail. Their wailin' grew so loud it woke up the spirit gods, and they got angry. Sent a big wind and capsized the raft, and damned if they didn't drown every last woman and child."

Savage poked at the fire, watching the men digest his story before he continued, "They say the lake is haunted by those that drowned. That you kin hear their drownin' cries on the wind. That's why we won't trap beaver there, Tolbert."

"I ain't afraid of spooks or superstitions."

The mountain man's face darkened. "Then you'd best believe the Utes would kill any man trapping on Spirit Lake. Damned fool!"

There was a long silence before Mellon cleared his throat and said, "Mr. Savage, what happened to the Utes that day long ago? Did they all die?"

"Hell, no. They fought like demons trying to win so's they could go out after their drowning women and children. And they won the battle but by then it was too late. The wind stopped blowin' and it was over."

"That's a fine story," Mellon said, obviously moved by the tale.

"Story! Damn you, that ain't no story, it's the truth!" In his outrage, Savage lashed out with the back of his hand and struck Mellon across the face. They all heard his big nose crack and he cried out in pain and covered his face. Isaac moved to help but Savage caught his wrist with one hand and grabbed the handle of his knife with the other. "It's between the misfit and me," he warned. "Don't buy trouble unless you can't get out of its way."

Isaac yanked his arm free. He looked at Mellon, then back at Savage.

"You hit him like that again for no good cause, I'll drive my fist down your throat along with your teeth. You understand me?"

Savage snarled, "The day might come when you'll feel my blade digging into your innards, big man. Yessir, I do believe that day will come."

Isaac was too mad to be afraid. The mountain man had no right to pick on Doug Mellon. He was fed up with watching Savage bully and insult the weaker man. But he would make no more threats against Savage. If the day was to come when they would fight, then so be it. Isaac now had a hunting knife and rifle of his own, and he knew how to use them. Maybe not so well as Savage, but he'd learn and what he lacked in speed or experience, he'd make up for in size and strength.

"I'll take the first watch," Isaac said, climbing to his feet.

Sniffling and blowing his nose to clear it of blood, Mellon shuffled morosely along beside him. Isaac would have preferred to be alone with his dark thoughts but he sensed that Mellon needed comfort. "Go on over to that stream yonder and put your face in the cold water until the bleeding stops," he said.

"I want to thank you for sticking up for me. I don't know why he hit me like that, do you?"

Isaac shook his head. "If it helps, he doesn't like buffalo either."

Mellon just glanced at him a moment before he went away.

Two days later, they heard shooting up beyond a low rise

of hills. Isaac knew the familiar retort of the Hawken, and when the others became alarmed, he said, "It's only Savage hunting more buffalo."

They listened to the shooting for a good half hour. Suddenly, Isaac realized something was amiss. "He's beginning to shoot way too fast."

"What does that mean?" Tolbert asked.

"It means Savage warned me over and over never to shoot more than a round a minute. He said the barrel of your rifle will get too hot and misfire."

They all timed the shooting. The Hawken was firing at the almost unbelievable rate of three times a minute. The echoes of the heavy rifle fire were almost continuous.

"Maybe some of them are charging him right now," Mellon said, his voice hopeful. "Just grinding the mean sonofabitch into the prairie."

"I heard a scream!" Andy whispered, turning his head slightly into the wind. "There, I heard it again!"

Isaac couldn't hear it, but then he had already noticed that the kid had the most acute hearing in the party. "I think we'd better get to him in a hurry," Isaac said. "He's in trouble."

Wrapping the mule's lead rope around his saddle horn and whipping his horse into a gallop, Isaac rode forward as fast as the mule could follow. He gripped his own Hawken rifle and felt a lump of cold dread form deep in his belly. Up until this very moment, he had not realized just how helpless they would all be without Jim Savage. He went racing over the low hills, afraid of what he'd find. Maybe Savage was already dead and maybe there were a hundred Indians just lying in ambush.

Isaac crested a hill, and a chill shot up his spine. He saw dead buffalo, at least ten or fifteen, but he hardly gave them a moment's notice. His eyes were fixed on the Indians. Three were dead, but two more were kneeling over the prostrate form of Jim Savage, who quite obviously was not dead. He was pinned to the earth with a war lance driven through his body just under the apex of his rib cage. The mountain man's feet were flopping around and the Indians appeared in no hurry to dispatch him from his agony as they sawed away at his scalp.

They were so intent on their grisly work that they did not see Isaac until he was almost on top of them. The Indians had

bows and arrows but no time to use them as Isaac drove his
horse into the first Indian and sent him sprawling. The second
warrior hurled himself at Isaac but the stock of the Hawken
caught him flush in the face. His skull popped like the brittle
shell of an acorn.

Isaac came off his horse and the first Indian was back on
his feet. The man had a war club and rushed at Isaac, a terrible
cry twisting the shape of his lips. Isaac regripped the Hawken.
He timed his swing perfectly and again the stock crushed
skull. The wood shattered but the Indian's war club fell
uselessly to the grass. Isaac dropped the broken rifle and
swung around to see that one of the fallen Indians was up. The
warrior had somehow managed to notch an arrow in his bow
and was straining to draw back. Isaac lunged for his broken
rifle, knowing it probably wouldn't fire even if he could reach
it in time. A shot rang out and the Indian grabbed a hole in his
chest and fell over backward.

Paden Tolbert had been accurate from over a hundred
yards. The man from Pennsylvania lowered his rifle and waved
his hand as Isaac hurried over to the fallen Jim Savage. The
man's hair was matted with blood and there was a big red patch
about the size of a pony's hoof that was bare. Savage was barely
alive. Isaac knew better than to pull the lance. He had no
illusions about Jim Savage's chances. Isaac could hear a death
rattle and knew the mountain man was finished.

"Savage!" Isaac called into the dying man's ear. "What can
I do?"

The man shook his head. His eyes fluttered open, and
they were already starting to glaze as his lips moved. Isaac
leaned close and listened very carefully.

Savage's voice was a soft hiss in his ear. "Go on alone,
Pilgrim. Send the others back. Tell Snow Bird . . . tell . . ."

A violent spasm passed the length of the mountain man's
body, and then he lay still.

"Oh, no! Is he dead?" Mack Peel cried, as he and the
others raced up to gather around the body of the slain
mountain man.

"He's dead all right," Isaac said, looking up at the others.

They were all stunned. Like Isaac, they now realized how
their own situations had suddenly changed. "I saw you talking

to him," Mack Peel said, his voice shaky as he stared at Savage's violated scalp. "What'd he say?"

Isaac closed the man's eyes. "He said to go on."

"Are you crazy!" Peel shouted. "We wouldn't stand a chance without an experienced guide!"

"He told me to go on alone. I reckon that was good advice. And I'll take it."

They stared at him as the meaning of his words sank in slowly. Without realizing it, they had come to see Isaac as their own leader, and now he was telling them they should give up and return to Independence while he went on to the Shining Mountains alone.

"I'll be damned if I'm turning back," Paden Tolbert said angrily. "If *you* go, *I* go!"

Mellon, now that his tormentor was dead, seemed to gather some new strength. "Unless you order me not to, I'm going, too, Mr. Beard."

Mack Peel and Andy Davis exchanged anxious glances. It was Andy who said, "Count me in."

"Me, too," Peel grumbled. "Though I think we'll end up frozen or scalped before next spring."

Isaac did not say anything, but had anyone asked him his opinion, it would have been the same as Peel's. They were inexperienced and in wild, unmapped territory. There were Plains Indians all around them, Cheyenne, Crow, Arapaho, and Sioux. But Isaac had no choice and neither did Mellon, so they were going. He couldn't say why Peel and Tolbert were coming along, too. Maybe they just had too much pride or stubbornness to turn back in defeat.

"We'll find his wife's people," Isaac told them, trying to sound more confident than he felt and to come up with some reasonable course of action. He stood up and looked at the dead buffalo. Jim Savage's lust for killing had gotten him scalped. And there might be more Indians close by.

"We've got to get out of here in a hurry," Isaac said. Steeling his nerves, Isaac yanked the war lance from Savage's body. He raised it high overhead, then smashed it down across his knee, shattering the shaft just above the spearhead. He took the bloody point and crammed it into his saddlebags.

Without meeting anyone's eyes, he said, "Let's mount up and get out of here. There's no time to waste."

"But what about Mr. Savage?" Andy was appalled. "Are you just gonna . . . gonna leave him lying out for the wolves?"

"We got no shovels to dig with," Isaac said. "If these Indians heard the shots, maybe some more did, too. I busted up my rifle so I'll take his Hawken and knife. We can settle up on his horse, mule, and other things later."

Isaac waited to see if there were any objections. The Hawken and the knife were almost new while his had been plenty used. He and Savage had argued about that in St. Louis. Isaac had been unwilling to steal new weapons from his father-in-law so he'd taken used. Savage had called him the worst kind of fool.

There were no complaints so he continued, "We'll take his buckskin shirt and possibles bag along with us into Ute country to prove that he was our friend."

"What the hell will they prove?"

"Plenty," Isaac said. "I'll show them the shirt and then the head of the war lance. I'd guess that would be evidence enough that we didn't shoot him ourselves."

Everyone nodded and watched as Isaac used Savage's own knife to cut off his shirt. The mountain man's body looked very thin and white. He seemed much smaller and so vulnerable unclothed that even Mellon wondered how he could have been so intimidated. In beaded buckskins, Savage had seemed half demon, half animal. Bare chested, he looked almost frail and very dead.

"Get his moccasins, damn you!" Isaac growled.

Tolbert jumped to obey. He yanked the moccasins off. "I reckon they'll fit me about right."

Isaac didn't care. He folded up the buckskin jacket and examined the contents of Savage's intricately beaded possibles bag. The bag held ammunition, fishhooks, flint, a small piece of mirror, and some jerked beef and chewing tobacco.

Tolbert had removed his boots and replaced them with the beaded moccasins. "They do fit!" He walked around for a minute before he realized that everyone was staring at him. "No sense in wasting good footwear, is there?"

Mack Peel changed the subject. "All I got to say is that it's a damn good thing Savage told us not to catch any damned fish or nothin' in Spirit Lake."

"Hell," Tolbert snapped, "fishin' is the least of our problems. There ain't a one of us even knows how to trap beaver."

"I do," Isaac said, stuffing the bloodied jacket and possibles bag in beside the spearhead. "I told you once before I've heard it explained a dozen times."

They remembered and took great heart at this bit of news. Isaac understood. When men found themselves in desperate circumstances, even small blessings loomed very large.

Isaac led his men out of the killing ground a few minutes later. They galloped hard to the west, each wrapped in a cloak of fear and desperation. Isaac remembered the mountain man telling him that you couldn't miss the Rocky Mountains. All you had to do was just keep moving west and, sooner or later, you'd naturally run into them.

He had to find Snow Bird and tell her of her husband's death. What tribe of Indians had killed him? Isaac had no idea. But the Utes would know when he showed them the spearhead. All Isaac knew for certain was that the dead warrior had been fierce and brave. He and Savage had each killed two, Paden Tolbert one. It had happened so fast it had been almost . . . almost easy. Unthinking. Instinctive. The way that Jim Savage had lived and acted.

Isaac swallowed hard. He was already in the killing and survival business, and he hadn't even gotten to the high mountains yet.

≈ 3 ≈

Isaac Beard felt trapped by his own desperate circumstances. He had somehow been put in a position of being responsible for the lives of four decent men. It was a burden he did not want. And yet, cold reason told him that someone had to be in command and, in truth, Paden Tolbert, Mack Peel, Andy Davis, and Doug Mellon were followers. Isaac guessed he had won the leader's job by default.

As they rode west, Isaac wished to God that Savage had not been so blood-crazed whenever he'd come upon buffalo. That sickness had gotten him impaled on a war lance, and it was all too likely that the rest of them would get the same. Isaac remembered the mountain man telling him that there were seven or eight bands of Utes, all loosely related, but separate. Some were of the high mountains, and others lived on the lower slopes, both east and west. Savage had admitted he did not know at least three of the bands. That meant that there was a possibility that Ute warriors had mistakenly killed Savage. Isaac could not even imagine how it would go if he presented Savage's wife and tribe with a Ute spearhead. It was a chilling prospect and one he did not mention to anyone in his party.

As they hurried west, the land stayed very flat but it seemed rich. Under a plow, it would produce well. Tolbert and Peel, both farmers, were constantly remarking on the changing colors of the soil and the height of the grass. They acted as if no one owned the land and it was just free for the taking.

One night, they heard wolves howling somewhere out on the prairie and then, around three in the morning, a distant rumble that grew louder and louder until the Earth seemed to shake. The moon broke through the clouds, and Isaac saw a massive cloud of dust created by thousands of buffalo thundering toward them.

"Buffalo stampede!" he shouted, grabbing his boots. "Get the mules loaded up and then saddle and ride!"

Isaac did not have to give the order twice. The buffalo were running south and, in the moonlight, he could see a wall of the beasts that stretched for miles across the western horizon. It came sweeping across the land like a scythe, leveling everything in its path.

Isaac and his men hastily loaded the mules and then left them to run for their lives. The mules proved to be much faster than expected and, though they could not overtake the men and horses who soon raced ahead, they did themselves proud. Two packs slipped loose and some provisions were lost, but no one complained as the ghostlike sea of buffalo raced past for hours until they finally vanished, leaving their dust to shimmer over a horizon turned gold with sunrise.

"Look," Tolbert whispered as the last sounds of the herd died in their ears, "Indians!"

It was true. But the mounted Indians were so far away they appeared little more than specks. Isaac felt a chill, and his first impulse was to run, yet he held his horse in, knowing he and his men would not be seen unless they acted unwisely. "Let's move slow and easy to the west. The buffalo will have wiped out our sign."

It was hard not to drive spurs into their already exhausted animals and put as much distance as possible between themselves and almost certain death. But they all understood and obeyed Isaac's command. By noon, they were miles to the west and out of danger. Still, the sight of the hunting party had heightened their urgency to reach the mountains, which could hide men and animals. Each of them reasoned, both privately and out loud, that they would be safer in the mountains, among Jim Savage's adopted people, the Utes.

It took them four more days to see the outline of the Rocky Mountains and, when they did, none of them were prepared for their incredible size. Isaac and his men stared at peaks that stretched as far as the eye could see, both to the north and the south, mountains that humped and bulled their way up to the heavens like monuments to a lineage of ancient gods.

Mellon put into words the very thoughts that were in Isaac's mind when he said, "A person could get lost and wander forever in those mountains. It must be like another world up there, a world few white men have yet been privileged to see. A world more beautiful and probably more dangerous than anything we can imagine. And glory be, look how they shine!"

Tolbert, ever practical, said, "They're nothing but big piles of rocks and trees. I just wonder how far away the damned things still are from us."

Isaac took a guess. "At least a hundred miles. But it's hard to say. The air out here is so clear it deceives the eye."

"I'd guess they're closer to seventy miles," Tolbert said. "One thing sure, they ain't going to come to us if we just sit here gawkin'."

It was true. They rode on, and their eyes never left the mountains. Every hour, the colors changed as the sun moved across the sky. Early in the day, the Rockies mirrored the bright colors of sunrise, at midday they turned jade and then emerald green, then late in the afternoon, blue, and finally, around sunset, their peaks caught the last rays of the sun and were like a column of torches against the dark backdrop of the Western sky. Isaac had never seen anything so beautiful in his life. Not the fall colors of Vermont or the sunset that rippled across the Missouri River, so that it looked like a rainbow fallen to Earth. And amazingly, the mountains were even more ethereal and wondrous at night when their white-capped peaks glowed luminous in the dark in patterns and shapes that challenged the imagination.

If anything, the beauty and mystery of the Rockies increased as the men rode closer and closer. Isaac felt them drawing him like a magnet, and when he rode into their shadows, he felt as if the silent giants had a spell that no man could long resist. And yet he was inwardly fearful and, though he could not quite find the word for it, he felt intimidated and smaller than a child. He reasoned that it was against man's nature to live so high above the plains, in a place where the air was so thin, the sun and stars so close, and the winters reputed to be so unbelievably harsh. No, he thought, mountains were not made to have men crawling on them. Not even the Utes.

To bolster his own resolve and restore confidence among his men, Isaac tried to remind them of Jim Savage's words. "He said the mountain valleys and canyons were like a mother's womb. They protect you from the sight of your enemies. They feed you with all the game you want to eat, and with wild berries and herbs. He said a man would never go hungry in the mountains and he could live long and well if he was careful."

"He was full of horseshit and we all know it!" Tolbert snapped. "Look at what he did to us! Got himself killed and scalped and all because he couldn't stop killing buffalo even when we had more meat than we could eat all winter. I don't believe anything that old man said."

Isaac turned away in silence. How could he argue when Tolbert was telling them the truth? Savage might have been a mountain man, but he had been reckless and foolish. He had liked to hunt and he had liked to ride far out ahead and be alone. Still, the man had died fighting and he had fought well. Maybe he had gotten old and didn't give a damn about life anymore. Maybe that was why he allowed himself to be killed. They'd never know the answer to that riddle. The only reality was that Savage had promised to take them into the Shining Mountains of Colorado and then show them how to trap the Grand River of all its beaver. Instead, he'd failed and left them in a fix. Isaac did not remember the old mountain man with much fondness.

He knew they had to make a decision. Were they north or south of the notch and the river that would lead them to the headwaters of the Grand River?

"Ought to be pretty easy to find," Tolbert said, also mustering up a confident voice. "Maybe some of us should ride north and some south and . . ."

"No," Doug Mellon said, "I definitely think we should stay together."

Tolbert was not used to Mellon contradicting his thoughts. "Who said your opinion amounted to anything?"

Isaac stepped in. "Doug is right. We need to stick together."

Tolbert bristled. "So where are we, north or south of the notched peaks?"

"I don't know." Isaac took a coin out of his pocket and flipped it high into the air. He caught it and slapped it down on his saddlehorn. "Call it, Tolbert. Heads, we go north; tails, south."

"Heads."

And heads it was. So they reined north and kept moving until they found the crest notch, the river, and the tabletop mountains. Isaac breathed a deep sigh of relief as he dismounted. "That has to be it. Exactly as Savage told us."

He removed his hat and dropped to his knees and recited the Lord's Prayer out loud. Then he said a prayer of his own, for his wife and children, born and unborn.

Andy, Peel, and Doug Mellon removed their hats and bowed their heads in the shadow of the Rockies. Isaac was glad. It seemed perfectly obvious to him that no man could stand up to these mountains and survive unless he had the Lord's help.

They remounted and Isaac reminded everyone that Jim Savage had said there was a treeless pass just north of this spot. Once they had climbed that, they would find Spirit Lake, the headwaters of the mighty Grand River that would provide them with a fortune in beaver pelts. Isaac tipped his head back to the sky and prayed that they would find enough beaver to match their dreams. They weren't hoping for great wealth, just for enough money to buy the opportunity to work for themselves. That's what they wanted. At least all of them except Doug Mellon, whose intentions remained a mystery. Isaac had decided that the only thing Doug wanted was to be left alone—by whiskey and by men like Jim Savage and Paden Tolbert.

They rode one full day north, then attacked the slopes of the Rocky Mountains. Jim Savage's Shining Mountains. The air already seemed thin before they even began the climb, and all too soon they were panting hard. They found a trail, maybe an Indian trail and maybe just one used by game moving to the higher elevations during the summer. The path was narrow and brutally steep but at least it saved them constantly chopping through the manzanita and brush.

The mules, surefooted, sturdy beasts, showed their superiority in the mountains. The horses, fleet and perfectly adapted to the prairie, now stumbled and sometimes even fell to their knees. They balked at turns, which folded right back on themselves, and they had to be spurred and whipped through narrow defiles better suited to mountain goats.

The first night on the mountain, the men ate nothing but cold jerked buffalo meat. After weeks of using buffalo chips, suddenly they had all the wood they wanted to build a fire but there was no strength in any of them to do it. Isaac did not post a watch. They could not be attacked on the slopes of a mountainside. Men fell exhausted on their bedrolls. The starlit sky was brilliant and the air very crisp. Isaac knew it would be cold when they finally reached the peaks. Even on summer nights, it would be damned cold. He wondered if they should have cured buffalo hides for robes or coats. But maybe that would have taken too much time. Isaac knew the hides had to be stretched, scraped of fat, and then rubbed with arsenic and salt even before they were left to dry. That would have occupied them for many days. Too much time, given the threat of the wide-ranging Plains Indians—better cold than dead.

The second day's ascent up the slopes was even harder than the first. The air was thinner, the trail steeper, and very treacherous. Men and animals alike felt their lungs burn and their quivering muscles knot and cramp. It was late in the afternoon when they finally emerged from the thick forest to stand on the naked crown of the mountains, realizing they had passed above the timber line.

The men staggered upward and saw tundra, small rocks covered with purple and blue moss, and a field of tiny yellow and white flowers. A stiff, cold wind blew a rooster tail of snow from the back of a deep pack of melting snow. The ground was mushy, soggy with water that squished under their feet. It seemed as if they were at last at the forehead of the mountain god, and he was gray haired and sweating.

Doug was sweating, too, and when he removed his bandanna from his pocket and mopped his brow, he said, "Just a few hundred feet higher and we're as close to heaven as we may ever get."

Isaac wouldn't argue that fact. And best of all, he knew

that within the hour, they would be looking down at Sprit Lake, headwaters of the Grand River, sanctuary of a fortune in furs.

They went up the last few yards to the mountaintop like a cavalry charge and did not stop until they had slammed through a narrow snowbank and could stand on what seemed like the top of the world, gazing at spiralling peaks jutting up into a cobalt sky for as far as they could see. And less than five miles below them, they saw Spirit Lake, headwaters of Colorado's greatest river.

Isaac dismounted and climbed onto a high, lichen-covered boulder. He shaded his eyes and felt the sharp bite of the wind. He studied the mountains and felt humbled. They will never be conquered, he thought, at best they will only tolerate men. It also occurred to him that he and his party would never survive until spring unless they adapted, and adapted well, to these mountains. Isaac supposed his city-dulled senses would have to sharpen: hearing, smell, everything. Living in the forest, he would need to become a part of the forest.

Isaac returned to his horse feeling small and worried. He felt compelled to voice his fears, for he understood that protecting the four men beside him was beyond his measure. He was not even sure if Jim Savage, with all his Indian and mountain-man savvy, could have done it.

Isaac cleared his throat. He felt he must offer some kind of warning, and yet he was not sure what to warn against, besides the obvious dangers of Indians and grizzly. "When we leave this ridge," he said to them, "it's going to be like another world. One that might kill us before we learn enough about it to survive."

The others nodded, for they too were humbled by the vista, the incredible vastness that lay before them. But Mellon's voice was light, almost gay, when he responded by saying, "The world behind is the real killer. Big cities, moral decay, and corruption. Prejudice and greed. Poverty, disease, and ignorance. Before us is freedom—the Garden of Eden. A place to find peace. To think and see what is real, pristine, and unchanged since the beginning of time. Think of it! Its natural wonders have never even been recorded. Sure, the Spaniards

have long been down in Sante Fe, but they're plundering,
insensitive men, louts bent on little more than subjugation of
the Indians and gaining riches for Spain. What we will be
seeing, we will see with a fresh eye. Before us are species of
birds and animals, plants and fish, that we do not even know
exist!"

"The only animals we care about are the beaver," Isaac
said, slightly annoyed by the man's silly talk.

Mellon looked at him and grinned as if he alone knew
some wonderful secret. It made Isaac wonder if the man was a
little addled by the thin, cold air. This suspicion did not lessen
when Mellon leaned close and whispered for his ears alone,
"You can have my share of the beaver, Mr. Beard."

Isaac moved away. Doug would bear close watching. His
eyes seemed too bright, and Isaac vowed they would have a
talk soon. Perhaps the hard climb and altitude could have this
effect on men. Isaac hoped it was just temporary.

"Mount up!" he called. "Tonight we camp at Spirit Lake;
tomorrow we look for the Utes and the river."

Andy cupped his hands to his mouth and let out a wild
shout of joy. "We made it! Yippeee!"

His words echoed over the mountaintops and then followed the streams that gurgled down between the blue ridges.

They remounted and started down toward Spirit Lake. It
was a difficult descent, for they had to traverse a huge bowl of
loose rock. Back and forth they rode in tight switchbacks,
going two miles to descend two hundred feet. Isaac's horse
kept floundering in the shale so he dismounted and led it on
foot. Each step caused landslides, sending showers of rock and
dust down the mountainside. Finally, they reached the pines
again, and Isaac remounted, his legs feeling rubbery. An hour
later, they tumbled from their horses at the shore of Spirit
Lake and drank deeply of its clear, cold waters. The horses,
sweating and covered with dust, sank their muzzles and drank
their fill, then pawed the water. The mules stood close
together, and their eyelids drooped with contentment.

The men hobbled the animals, then unpacked and unsaddled them before they stripped out of their sweaty and
dust-caked clothes and dived into the still, frigid waters. It
took a man's breath away, and when Isaac had scrubbed

himself clean, he lay down on the long marshy grass near shore
and let the sun dry him completely. He rolled over on his side
and studied the lake, trying to imagine the great storm that
had claimed so many Ute women and children long, long ago.

Just before evening, Isaac shot an elk that had come down
to drink. They butchered him and feasted beside the rippling
waters, seeing huge fish jump and splash as they fed on
mosquitoes and other flying insects. Everyone was in high
spirits, sure that they soon would find and receive the
protection of the Ute people. Isaac fell asleep that night
hearing the sounds of the forest all around him. He wondered
how long it would take to find the Utes. In such a vast domain,
it could take weeks or even months, couldn't it? White men
and red men could pass within a few miles of each other and
never realize the fact. Why, entire cities could be swallowed
up by the valleys, which were like furrows in a field of corn. So
how, he reasoned, would they find the Utes?

The next morning, Isaac awoke just as the sun was starting
to ring the treeless mountaintops. The new day was so still it
seemed as if every living thing in the world was yet asleep. No
squirrels scolded them from above, no blue jays screeched
from the trees. There was no wind moving in the air, and the
only sound that Isaac could hear was a faint lapping of ripples
against the shoreline.

He opened his eyes and then blinked twice before he
realized that the camp was surrounded by mounted Indians.
Tall, gaunt, sitting their ponies with arrows nocked on their
bowstrings, Isaac counted about twenty warriors.

He didn't know what to do. He was afraid that, if Tolbert
and the others awoke with a start, they might be panicked
enough to lunge for their weapons. That would be disastrous.
Isaac slowly reached for his saddlebags and pulled out Jim
Savage's possibles bag with the broken lance stuffed inside.
Dry mouthed, he found the dead man's bloodstained buckskin
hunting jacket and then held both up for the Indians to see.

When they showed no sign of recognition, he shivered,
then rose to his feet. He decided he must get closer to display
Savage's Ute beadwork. Barefooted, Isaac traipsed through
the tall, wet meadow grass. At fifty paces from the impassive
warriors, he stopped and again raised both artifacts. The

thought occurred to him that these Indians might not even be Utes. Isaac began to sweat in the chill air. Finally, the Indians looked to one man, a tall, powerful warrior who wore beautifully beaded buckskins and who carried no bow or arrows but a war lance instead.

Isaac could not help but study the lance and he tried to see if the colored wrappings that bound the flint to the shaft were similar to the decorations on the one that he had pulled from Savage's body. He did not think they were as he laid the hunting shirt on the grass. Retrieving the broken spear, he made a downward stabbing motion toward the shirt and grunted, "Jim Savage. Savage!"

The Indian leader dismounted. His face was angular and painted yellow and ochre. He wore three eagle feathers in his long, black hair and his movements were as fluid as those of a cat. When Isaac met his eyes, he thought he might as well have been face to face with an animal. The warrior spoke to him but Isaac understood nothing. His blank expression caused the leader to use sign language and, again, Isaac stood baffled and bewildered. Desperate and feeling like a man rushing toward a cliff, he again pointed at Jim Savage's jacket and possibles bag. Desperation seizing him by the throat, he choked, "Snow Bird."

A full minute passed before the Indian leader picked up both items and studied them carefully. He took the spearhead and fitted its point through the blood-crusted rip in the jacket. Satisfied, he nodded once. "Arapaho!"

He shoved everything back to Isaac and motioned for him to wake the others. It was time to go.

Isaac was almost weak with relief. "English, you speak English!"

With complete disdain, the Ute leader turned his back on Isaac. He went to his pony and, grabbing the mane, swung lightly onto its back. He gestured toward Isaac's sleeping companions. He was telling Isaac to awaken them and to do so at once. Somehow, he conveyed the message that they would be killed if even one reached for his weapon.

Isaac understood and he was determined to take no chances, so he collected each man's rifle and placed it safely out of reach. The Ute warriors dismounted and took the rifles.

They were very excited about the weapons, and Isaac saw his own Hawken pass to the leader. He despaired, realizing they had to have firepower or they would never survive in the wilderness. But he would worry about that later.

He knelt over Tolbert and shook the man. "Wake up," he said, loud enough to wake them all. "We have visitors. Utes."

Tolbert came out of a dead sleep, reaching for his weapon. Isaac clamped his hand around the man's wrist and squeezed it hard. "We only have one chance at living," he said, as the others roused into drowsy wakefulness that quickly turned into rigid alertness. "Everyone get up, get your stuff together and don't say anything."

Tolbert tried to pull his wrist free but could not, which made him furious. "Let go of me! I want my rifle back!"

Isaac could not believe the man was stupid enough to make a scene. He grabbed Tolbert by the shirtfront and shook him like a rag doll. When the man struggled, Isaac batted the young fool across the side of the head and stunned him.

"You listen to me," he hissed, his voice low and shaking with fury. "You want to get your hair lifted, fine. You'll have your chance. But I'll be damned if you'll get ours lifted, too! Make one stupid move and, if the Indians don't scalp us first, I'll make you wish you were dead."

"Look," Andy whispered, his face the color of alkali, "they're taking our horses and mules!"

"Better the livestock than our lives, wouldn't you say?" Doug Mellon climbed to his feet. "If they wanted us dead, we'd be dead before now." He stepped up to the leader and simply raised one hand, palm open.

"What the hell is he doing?" Tolbert hissed.

"Shut up!" Isaac rumbled, for Doug had begun to make sign language. Isaac could scarcely believe what he witnessed. And, after several minutes when the leader turned away, Isaac said, "Why didn't you tell us you could do that?"

"Long story, not enough time to tell it," Doug said. "Right now, they want us to grab up our packs and go with them to their village. I think we have no choice but to accept their hospitality."

"It's going to be all right then?"

"I hope so," Doug said. "But they're not pleased to find us beside the lake. Not pleased at all."

"Then tell them we'll be moving out."

"I explained that. It's too late. We're to meet their chief."

Isaac did not have to give the order to do as the Indians said. Unarmed and surrounded, even Paden Tolbert had no quarrel with the decision to do as they were told.

The sun rose higher as they marched around the lake and then followed the headwaters of what Isaac was certain was the famous Grand River, called by some the Colorado River. "Look over there," Isaac said, pointing, "beaver dams!"

They all gawked and, sure enough, there were dams aplenty. "This is the one," Isaac said, feeling sure that everything was going to be all right once they met Snow Bird and she understood that they were her husband's friends.

Mack Peel nodded. "Now, all we have to do is figure out a way to live long enough to harvest them."

"We will," Isaac said as he plodded along, his blankets stuffed with provisions and trade goods and everything tied up and roped to his back. "Isn't that right, Doug?"

"I think we'll be fine if we keep our wits about us. If the chief likes us and we mind our manners, I believe these people will treat us rather well."

As if to reinforce that assessment, Mellon began to whistle a gay tune. Isaac didn't try to stop him. It was better to whistle than to fret; it showed the Utes that they were not afraid. Isaac even joined in, and so did the others, except for Tolbert. He was too damned mad to whistle. Tolbert was definitely the one most likely to get them killed.

≈ 4 ≈

They had followed the river for miles and it had already grown deep and strong with snowmelt from the surrounding mountaintops. Everywhere Isaac looked, he saw streams and creeks surging down into the river canyon. And they were all teeming with beaver. He could hardly contain his joy, a joy that was mixed with intense gratitude toward Doug Mellon who, incredibly enough, had demonstrated that he knew at least the rudiments of sign language. He was angry at himself for not insisting that Jim Savage teach him sign language after they left St. Louis.

St. Louis. Isaac took a deep breath and tried to picture Catherine's face as he strode along a shadowed forest trail. But it was Nathan's image that came clearest to him. The boy stood by the Missouri River, looking over the water as a barge full of supplies was being poled upriver. On top of the barge, a mountain man was smoking a pipe. The mountain man was dressed in buckskins and a coonskin cap. He was big and powerful looking, and when the image sharpened, Isaac saw that the mountain man was himself. Even worse, he was laughing and waving goodbye to his son, and the boy had begun to cry.

Isaac opened his eyes and shook his head, wanting to blot out the image. He *would* return for his wife and his son. He would return with a sack full of money from all the beaver he would sell next spring. His wife would be so happy, and they would leave St. Louis forever, perhaps to move farther west where land was free for the taking. Isaac remembered the countryside surrounding Independence. It was good land, with soil so rich that even a man like himself, who knew nothing about farming, could make a fine living, perhaps even leave his children a great deal of property and wealth. Isaac wondered again if he would have another son or a daughter. He had changed his mind and decided that he wanted another son. A farmer needed many sons to help with the work. Farming would be hard, but a better life than working in a general store.

"Look," Andy said, for he was in the lead. "Their village!"

The Ute village was immense. It covered a good twenty acres, though at least half of that area was occupied by Indian ponies of every color and description. Isaac's attention snapped to the tepees, which were about fifteen feet tall, white, with yellow, red, and blue designs and symbols painted on them. Smoke drifted from their top flaps, and the sides were lifted like skirts to allow a breeze to circulate on these warm summer days.

Children by the score came racing out to greet them, their bodies lean and fit. Some of the younger ones were naked, and they were laughing. The older ones stood round eyed and solemn. They seemed to miss nothing and several pointed to Isaac and spoke rapidly.

"What are they saying?" Isaac asked Mellon.

"I have no idea. I know only sign language. But from the way they are pointing at you in particular, I would think it has something to do with your size. You might just be the tallest man they have ever seen."

"Oh." Isaac studied the unsmiling faces of the women. These were a handsome people, medium of stature, slender, and graceful. The women wore beaded dresses, moccasins, and silver, turquoise, and bear-claw necklaces.

Tolbert was staring at the women, too. "Damn," he whispered, "look at that one right there! Ain't she a beauty! There's lots of pretty girls here. I wonder if they favor white skin."

Isaac's anger flashed. "You keep your hands to yourself. Indian women are chaste."

"How do you know that? You ever been around one before?"

"Just do as I say," Isaac said, upset with himself for losing his temper at a time like this, when the entire village was watching.

The camp was full of fierce, barking dogs upset by the strange-smelling white men. One dog in particular, a huge,

gray-coated beast with the face of a wolf, seemed to be the
leader. An old squaw pointed to Isaac and her face reflected
hatred. She hissed something at the gray wolf-dog, and it
rushed forward. Before Isaac could react, the beast's fangs bit
into the calf of the leg. The Indians fell silent and watched. No
attempt was made to stop the dog. Isaac stood immobile for a
second, trying to prove that he was strong. But when the dog
began to worry the leg with its powerful jaws, he reached
down, took ahold of its neck with both hands and throttled its
windpipe. The dog's eyes bulged. Helpless without air, it had
to release its grip. In spite of the fact that the struggling animal
weighed nearly a hundred pounds, Isaac lifted it overhead,
and then hurled it like a rock. The animal struck the hard-
packed ground, then rolled over and over. When it came to its
feet, it ran with its tail tucked between its legs.

The Utes were impressed. They saw blood staining Isaac's
torn pants, and they measured the great breadth of his chest
and shoulders. The old squaw spat at the other dogs and
scolded them until they slunk away. The leader who had
brought them to this village dismounted and made a sign.

"What do they want?" Isaac asked.

Mellon's full attention was on the chief and his own hands
as he made sign. It was clear that he was slow, far slower than
the Ute, but that his movements were precise. "They want us
to empty our packs and show them what we bring for their
people. Then they want us to hand over our knives and any
other weapons. I'm not sure what they want after that."

"They probably want to tie us to a stake and roast us!"
Tolbert growled, his eyes hot with anger and suspicion.

Trying not to limp, Isaac moved closer to the hotheaded
man. "You just do as they ask. Anything else would be
suicide." He looked at the others and said, "Empty your packs
and blankets. Put everything out for them to see."

It took only a few minutes. Mostly, they carried food and
beaver traps. Andy Davis had a Bible, Mack Peel an old
looking glass that one of the Indians immediately confiscated,
and Doug Mellon surprised them all with a stack of journal
paper, writing and drawing pens, and sketch pads.

Isaac saw that the Indians were most interested in the
trading goods. The women were excited by the inexpensive,
but colorful, beaded necklaces, sewing needles, and thread.

The men were more preoccupied with the steel arrow points, fishhooks, and sharpening stones.

An old man came out of his tepee and the camp fell silent, except for the crying babies. Isaac said, "This must be their chief. Savage told me his name was Kicking Elk."

The chief had skin that was wrinkled as old parchment paper. His eyes were a dark brown and watery. He moved slowly, the weight of his years plain for anyone to see. When he stopped in front of the white men, he turned to Doug Mellon and began to talk in sign language.

"Translate for us," Isaac ordered.

"Chief Kicking Elk says that he welcomes the white men who were friends of Jim Savage. He wants to know how many Arapaho we killed."

"Tell him six."

Mellon simply held up six fingers. The chief looked very pleased at this news. The young Ute leader, who had brought them to the village, moved forward into the circle. He handed the chief Jim Savage's possibles bag and then his stained hunting jacket. The chief studied them for a moment, then turned and extended them to a beautiful young woman who stepped forward. She was composed, yet it was easy to see the pain in her eyes.

"Is that Savage's widow?" Tolbert asked in amazement. "Why, she's young enough to have been his daughter!"

"Shut up!" Isaac hissed.

The chief glanced at Tolbert. His brow furrowed and he signed rapidly. Mellon said, "He wants to know what Tolbert said about Snow Bird."

"Tell him . . . tell him that he said she was very beautiful and that he was sorry that she has lost her man."

Mellon passed on the message. The young woman nodded and looked to Tolbert with a sad smile. She bowed slightly, turned, and moved away. Tolbert could not keep his eyes off her. "She likes me," he said eagerly.

Isaac wasn't even listening. "Tell the chief that all these trade goods are for our friends, the Ute people."

"The chief is very pleased. He asks us to stay as guests in his village. He says that our weapons and animals will be returned to us, and he wants to know if we are after beaver."

"Tell him thank-you and, yes, we want as many beaver as we can take between now and next spring."

Mellon repeated the message. The old chief nodded, then shuffled away. The entire tribe turned their backs on the white men and went about their business. Isaac knelt and examined his leg. Just then, the same squaw who had set the dog on him appeared. She knelt at his feet with a bowl of what looked like steaming spinach. Before Isaac quite realized her intentions, she squatted on her heels, jerked his ruined pants leg up to his knee, and then slapped the wad of green stuff against the bite wound.

The poultice was scalding hot, and Isaac bit back a groan. The woman pressed the scalding mass tightly against his torn flesh and smiled up at him as if she were enjoying his pain. Isacc gritted his teeth and felt sweat bead across his forehead. He placed his hands on his hips and said, "Doug, ask her how long I'll have to stand like this."

Mellon tapped the old woman on the shoulder. She glanced up, watched him make sign language, and then shrugged her round shoulders.

"What did that mean?"

Mellon shrugged his own shoulders. "How should I know."

The squaw began to chant. Isaac swore under his breath. He felt ridiculous and feared he might be immobilized by this crone for hours.

After the first few days of wariness, both on the part of his men and the young warriors, the tension disappeared. The Indians were content to live their own life and a good life it was. The women made clothing and prepared the meals. They also were expected to gut and skin the deer, pluck the mountain sage hens, clean fish, and skin rabbits. The men had things quite to their liking. They sat around a great deal and talked or played games, using a kind of dice that they threw on the ground. They did go off hunting every few days, but since game was plentiful, their departures were festive occasions with much laughter and teasing.

"It's a life fit for a god," Mellon said, holding his sketch pad across his knee and drawing the outline of a mounted hunting party as it prepared to leave the village amidst a great deal of clamor and confusion. "But I suspect that it is the women who own all the property and rule the households. That's the way most primitive societies operate. It's called a matriarchal society."

Isaac studied the sketch. It was just taking form but it was obvious Mellon was talented. He was able to capture the excitement, admiration, and even the humor of the children who watched the warriors ride out to hunt. One Indian maiden in his sketch was particularly arresting, and Isaac recognized her as Chipeta, a young Ute girl married to Crow Feather. Chipeta was striking, her eyes were heavily lidded, her lips full and sensuous, and her figure slender but rounded. She reminded Isaac of a beautiful deer, and it was hard for any man to keep his eyes off her when she passed. But there were other Indians who were equally impressive, and Doug had done a remarkable job in capturing their pride and dignity as well as their sometimes impish expressions.

Isaac was very impressed. Being a simple, practical man, he was in awe of people with artistic ability. "I never imagined for a moment we had an artist among us."

"Thank-you, but I'm not an artist. I'm actually a scientist. I'm interested in evolution of species and anthropological theories."

Isaac had no idea what the man was talking about. It must have shown in his expression because Mellon continued, "You see, my father was a very famous scientist. I tried to follow in his footsteps, but failed in Africa."

"Africa?"

"Yes." Doug Mellon sat down. It was a warm afternoon and they were alone in their separate little camp just a hundred yards east of the village. The other men had gone off to swim in the river. "I was interested in the civilizations of darkest Africa. I studied what little is known about those people. Then, relying on my father's reputation, I was able to solicit enough funds to form an expedition. I had a wife and a small son. I insisted they join me."

Isaac thought he understood. "I have a little boy, too. He's only four."

Mellon's eyes grew wintry. His voice fell to a whisper. "We all went to Africa and one day while I was off sketching the veld, our camp was attacked and everyone in it was slaughtered."

Isaac squirmed and looked away. "You don't have to tell me this."

"Of course I don't. But you befriended me and I owe you an explanation. Somehow, I escaped. I don't remember anything that happened afterward for at least six weeks. I'm told I got drunk and I stayed drunk for two years. I lost my self-respect and I tarnished my father's great name."

Isaac was moved. Now that he understood Mellon better, he felt much closer to him. They longed for their wives and sons. The only difference was, Isaac's family was among the living. He felt ashamed of how he had mooned around in the evenings, feeling his own loss. How trivial was his loneliness compared to Doug Mellon's. Isaac said, "So you've come here to . . . to what?"

"I don't know. To escape civilization and find . . . perhaps self-respect. I may return with you to St. Louis with notes and sketches and sell a book on the Utes of the Shining Mountains. Perhaps another on the fur trade and the mountain men. I don't know. Either would be a wonderful story and very successful." He did not look or sound very excited about the prospect but added, "Look at how successful Lewis and Clark were with their published writings. I was captivated by their accounts of life in the wilderness. I heard Mr. Lewis speak at a conference that was standing room only. He and his colleague were famous."

"I don't think you want fame," Isaac said without thinking, and instantly wished he could take back his words. He had no right to make that kind of a judgment. He hardly knew this man.

"Isaac, you are a very perceptive and intelligent man. No, I wouldn't want fame. All I want is to heal the wounds I caused myself and my dear father. That's all."

"No beaver?"

"No. In fact, I'll probably leave you before winter if I have the opportunity to go live with other clans of Ute. I want to get to understand these people. I became well acquainted with one of Lewis and Clark's guides. He's the one who taught me sign language. According to him, it's pretty universal out in the

West. A man won't be able to carry on any deep conversations, but it will get him by."

"Will you teach it to me?"

"I'll teach it to all of you," Mellon said. "It's essential."

Isaac agreed. "One thing I want to know. Were you really so frightened of Jim Savage?"

"Yes. I thought the man was crazy and a killer. I also knew that, if I didn't do exactly as he said, he'd make sure I didn't get this far. The reason I came was because of his friendship with the Utes."

"He wasn't much different from most of the mountain men who come to buy goods in St. Louis."

"Then I'll stay clear of mountain men and let someone else write that book for posterity. I have a feeling I'll get along much better with the Ute people."

"We'll be making forays down the Colorado starting tomorrow, looking up canyons and picking out the best places to set traps. I don't suppose you want to come?"

"No." Mellon sharpened his pencil.

"That's what I figured," Isaac said, watching another hunting party gallop out of the Ute village, trailed by barking dogs and shouting children. "I guess you'd rather draw sketches and talk to the Indian women and children."

That night, with the warriors absent, the camp was quieter than usual. Isaac, Mack Peel, and Andy Davis talked about the next day's journey down the Colorado. They agreed that they would take many side trips up promising canyons to survey the number of beaver that could be taken. They were eager to go.

"Where do you suppose that damned Tolbert is tonight?" Peel snorted. "He's the one that's been chompin' at the bit to explore the rivers. He ought to be here to help plan this."

"He said he wanted to take a walk and do some thinking," Andy said, looking over their own little campfire toward the village.

Isaac hoped that was what Tolbert was doing. He'd give the man the benefit of the doubt but the plain truth of it was that Chipeta had caught Tolbert's eye. He'd been talking about her constantly and had even spent some time hanging around her teepee while Crow Feather was off hunting. Isaac was afraid that Tolbert might have seized this opportunity to visit the young woman while her husband was away. If that was the case, there might be hell to pay when the warrior returned.

"Do you think he might have lied and gone to visit Chipeta?" Mellon asked, seeming to divine Isaac's dark suspicions.

"I don't know," Isaac said, "but we can't just waltz into the village and pull open her tepee flaps so I guess we'd better hope he's got more sense than that. Let's turn in and get an early start."

They doused their campfire and climbed into their blankets. Isaac knew he could not sleep. He wondered what Utes did to an adulterous woman and the foolish man who used another's wife. Maybe they killed them both. He did not even want to consider the penalty. Instead, he thought about Mellon and Africa, about slaves, and how he had felt like one himself during the years he had worked for Catherine's father in St. Louis. His mind drifted back over the years, examining each one like the pages of a book. So many mistakes. So much time lost. But he had a family, and now at last a chance to do right by them. With that thought firm in his mind, Isaac finally drifted into an uneasy sleep.

He awoke in the night to hear a loud scream. Instantly, dogs started barking and then there was a second scream as the Ute villagers rushed out of their tepees. Isaac sat up and the moonlight revealed a strange and chilling sight. Tolbert was backing out of Crow Feather's tent, and Isaac could see that he was holding his side, bent over with pain. He turned and ran through the village toward their camp.

"I hurt her!" he wheezed, falling down beside Isaac. "I didn't mean to, but I hurt her and she stabbed me!"

Isaac felt his stomach knot with dread. "How bad did you hurt her?"

Tolbert didn't answer. Instead, he was pulling up his shirt to examine his ribs. He was bleeding, but the wound was superficial. Isaac grabbed him by the shoulders. "How bad did you hurt her?"

"I don't know. I just hurt her and she started screaming. Woke up everyone."

Mellon swore in anger. "Damn you, Tolbert! You may have sentenced us all to death!"

"What the hell do you mean?" She wanted me. Kept looking at me. I could tell what she wanted. Then when I gave it to her, she turned into a goddamn wildcat. Went crazy on me!"

Isaac wanted to hit the man. "Tell that to Crow Feather when he comes back!"

Tolbert ran his forearm nervously across his face. His right cheek had been raked by Chipeta's fingernails, and his lips were puffy. "I'll offer him something. Maybe my horse. Yeah, I'll take his damn squaw for my horse. He'll be happy to do that, won't he?" He looked at Mellon. "You know so goddamn much about the Indians, you tell him what I'll give for her."

"What if he is shamed and kills her?"

"Then he don't get my horse!"

Mellon turned away in disgust. "You might have to fight Crow Feather. You've shamed him and anyone could see he was proud and jealous of Chipeta. Even so, you might have traded your horse and rifle for the girl, but not after tonight."

Tolbert blustered. "I'll fight him if that's what he wants. I'll kill him and keep my horse and the woman."

Isaac was heartsick. He gazed into the village and saw Chief Kicking Elk standing with his arms folded over his skinny chest. He was staring at them. "Doug, you better talk to the chief," Isaac said.

Mellon looked into the village at the chief standing in front of his tepee. His arms were folded over his chest and anyone could see he was stiff and angry. "Yeah," Doug said, "I better talk real fast."

But when he began to walk to the village, Kicking Elk turned his back on them and went inside his tepee, then closed the flap. Mellon returned with a sad shake of his head. "It doesn't look good."

Isaac slept no more that night. The next morning, he and his men remained in camp instead of exploring the river as planned. No one spoke a word to Tolbert, and his nerves were stretched tight as piano wire. He paced and fussed, and tried to do little things, like sharpening his knife, but it was clear he was so agitated that he could not stick with any one thing for very long.

About midafternoon, the warriors came riding back into camp with a buck and two does tied to the backs of their horses. But unlike before, there was no laughter or smiling villagers to greet them and they immediately sensed that something was very wrong. Isaac saw an old man go quickly to Crow Feather and speak to him. The young warrior's head twisted first to his tepee, then to the white men who waited, almost holding their breath. Crow Feather jumped from his horse and hurried toward his tepee. He disappeared inside and Isaac could only hope he did not kill Chipeta in his jealous rage. His worst fears were realized when he heard Chipeta wail. Her cry ended with chilling suddenness as the warrior emerged and started toward them with the other members of his hunting party trailing behind.

Isaac and the others stepped in close to Tolbert, who looked pale but determined. All his bravado had evaporated. He had his rifle in the crook of his arm and Isaac knew the man would not hesitate to use it against Crow Feather.

"Doug," Tolbert hissed, "you better talk to him or he's a dead Indian! I ain't going to stand here and let that sonofabitch put a knife in my guts. No sir!"

Doug nodded. "I'll tell him we are willing to trade for his wife. It might cost us plenty, but it's our only chance of getting out of this mess. Everyone else keep your hands away from your weapons!"

The Utes came to a halt. Crow Feather stepped forward as Mellon made sign as rapidly as he could. Crow Feather shook his head in anger, and he yelled in Mellon's face before he pointed to Tolbert, then shoved Mellon aside. With a snarl, he drew back his knife.

"What's he saying!" Tolbert shouted. "Does he want to fight?"

"Yes. He wants your scalp and, after he opens your belly, he will cut off Chipeta's nose and give it to the dogs."

Tolbert swallowed noisily and drew his own knife. "He'll go to hell first!"

"Isn't there anything you can do to stop this?" Isaac pleaded.

"No," Mellon whispered. "He is within his rights. The woman has shamed him and she will be cast from the tribe to starve if she doesn't bleed to death or kill herself first."

Tolbert pushed forward. "She's all mine after I kill him. Give me some room."

Isaac, Mellon, and the others stepped aside and, without being conscious of the act, a large ring formed around the two men. In size, strength, and age, they were closely matched. Both were wiry and very quick. Isaac, knowing that he himself was not as agile, was glad that he was not in that ring. Either man could probably have cut him to ribbons unless he could grab them and use the advantage of his size and strength.

The two men circled each other warily. Crow Feather's arm was out in front of him, and his face was blotted with hatred. Tolbert crouched and seemed to wait for the first lunge. Crow Feather feinted with the knife and, when Tolbert jumped back, the Indian dropped and whipped outward with both legs. The move was so fast and unexpected that the Ute's feet caught Tolbert against the side of his left knee. Tolbert screamed in pain and staggered, then lunged at the prostrate Indian. His blade ripped through Crow Feather's buckskin jacket and then buried itself to the hilt in the dirt. Before he could tear it free, Crow Feather drove his own knife upward into Tolbert's throat. The man's body stiffened, and both hands came up to grip Crow Feather's wrist. With blood pouring down on the Indian, the two struggled for a brief instant and then Tolbert collapsed. Crow Feather rolled over on top of the dead man. He threw his head back, lips drawn across his exposed teeth, then howled in triumph. He took Tolbert's long hunting knife, which was superior to his own, and grabbed Tolbert by the hair.

Isaac started to jump for him but Mellon shouted, "No! Interfere and we'll all die!"

"But I can't . . ."

"Yes, you can," Mellon said. "You have no choice!"

The Utes had drawn their knives and were poised to fight. Isaac studied their faces and knew Mellon was right. If he interfered, they'd all be slaughtered. "All right," he whispered, turning away.

A moment later, Crow Feather howled again, and he jumped in front of Isaac holding up the grisly prize before his eyes.

"Steady," Mellon whispered. "Don't move or say a word."

Isaac was shaking. He did not know if it was from fear or anger or frustration. Maybe it was from all three. He had never felt so helpless and outraged. But he held steady, because he had to.

Andy got sick and vomited.

Isaac looked away to see Chipeta coming toward them with her head down. Two shrieking squaws were lashing her across the back, buttocks, and the calves of her exposed legs with willow branches. When she came near, she raised her head and stared at Crow Feather, who was still chanting and dancing. But when the young Ute saw his wife, he fell silent and his expression again twisted with hatred. He advanced toward the beautiful girl. When he stopped right in front of her, he held Tolbert's scalp up before her eyes, and then he smeared the bloody trophy across her face. Chipeta did not even blink. Finally, Crow Feather stuffed Tolbert's scalp behind a beaded belt that Chipeta had probably made for him and raised his knife to her face.

"No!" Isaac could contain himself no longer. "Doug, tell him *I* will trade for the girl. Tell him he can have anything but my traps."

"I should be the one doing this," Mellon choked. "But I can't bring myself to even look at another woman, Isaac! Maybe if she was old, or fat and . . ."

Isaac was shaking with anger. "Tell him, goddamn you! If one of us doesn't stop this, that girl will either bleed to death or be so ugly no man will ever want to look at her. She'd be treated worse than a dog. Am I right?"

"Yes," Mellon whispered. "I'm afraid so."

"Then make a deal. Tell him I want her for my woman."

Mellon turned to Crow Feather and, with swift gestures, he translated Isaac's wishes. Crow Feather seemed determined to disfigure Chipeta at first. Isaac went over and got his horse. "Tell him it's a good horse. Here," he shouted, pushing his new Hawken at the warrior. "Tell him it's his. All I want is my mule and my traps."

Mellon nodded and the dickering went on while Isaac stood a little apart, with his back turned to them all. What the hell have I just done, he asked himself. What the hell else could I have done? But I can still trap beaver. Maybe I can take Tolbert's horse and rifle. But what do I do with the woman?

He expelled a deep breath and turned to look at Chipeta. Her chin was up and her eyes were on him alone. What was she thinking? Look at her face. It shows nothing. Isaac could not imagine how he could ever tell his wife what he had done for another woman. Catherine might understand but, then again, she might not. Isaac vowed he would not take the chance. He would simply turn the girl back to her people and be done with it. At least, he could live with his own conscience this way.

"She's yours for your horse and rifle," Mellon said. "And I'm ashamed I didn't do it myself."

"I'll give her back to them. "

"No!" Mellon's voice was sharp. "You can't do that."

"Why not?"

"Because you would be insulting Crow Feather."

Isaac wanted to shout with frustration. "But I can't keep her. What am I supposed to do?"

"Get her to teach you and the others sign language and the ways of the forest. She can cook. She can do a hundred things that will keep you warm and alive this winter. Take her, Isaac."

"*You* take her!"

Mellon closed his eyes. "I wish to God I could. Maybe someday I could, but . . . but not now. I . . ."

"Never mind," Isaac said. "I understand."

Chief Kicking Elk came to them and spoke a few words. He ended his message by pointing at the white men and then making a sweeping gesture.

"He wants us to leave the village tomorrow morning. He says it has been dishonored. He says we are not to touch Tolbert's body but leave it for the dogs and wild animals. If we do this, he will let us go in peace. He says we can come again in the spring if we will leave his women alone."

They looked deep into each other's eyes. There really was no choice. Isaac realized he must not allow himself to weaken or to look down at Tolbert's body. In a voice he did not even recognize, he said, "Tell the chief thank-you and we will leave as ordered."

It was done. They had been banished. Doug Mellon was leaving to strike out on his own because he had no interest in beaver. And I have a young and beautiful squaw, Isaac thought. God help me!

Morning seeped over the mountaintops to flood across the green forest. Isaac, Peel, and Andy Davis packed their gear and prepared to leave camp. Mellon shook their hands. "I'll leave after I tell the chief again we are sorry for the trouble caused. Watch out for the girl."

"What do you mean?"

"I mean she'll drive Peel and young Andy crazy this winter."

"Oh. Yeah," Isaac said, "I hadn't thought about that."

"Use her as your woman, Isaac. It will save you all kinds of grief. She'd not understand it any other way."

"No goddamnit! I have a wife!"

Doug Mellon stepped back. "I knew you'd say that. Then give her to Mack Peel and let them sleep apart from you."

Issaac didn't want to talk about this. Chipeta was a human being, not some animal to be bartered or passed from hand to hand. "So long," he said, wishing that Doug Mellon was coming with them. "You can always come down the river and find us if you get into trouble or need friends."

"I know that. I just need some time alone."

Isaac mounted Tolbert's horse. He looked over at the girl and offered her his stirrup. She shook her head.

"What does that mean?"

Mellon almost smiled. "It means she will walk behind you wherever you go."

"Damn," Isaac swore softly as he kicked his horse into a walk. He did not look back. He didn't have to. He knew that Tolbert's stiff, blood-soaked body was where they had left it and that the Ute girl was right behind him.

Isaac felt low. In the mountains, nothing worked as a man expected.

Absolutely nothing.

≈　5　≈

They followed the Grand River for the better part of a week, watching it grow in size and power with every mile. It soon became too swift for beaver, but there were many streams and brooks feeding down from the mountains, and Isaac saw beaver dams everywhere. He had worried about Chipeta's ability to keep up with the horses but, even though she walked, the Ute girl seemed tireless. While she never strayed far from Isaac, Chipeta acted as if Mack and Andy did not exist. She communicated only with Isaac, and then in just the simplest of sign language.

Mack and Andy were stung by her aloofness. During the first few days, they tried to be friendly but the Ute girl looked right through them. They soon became angry, but Isaac told them to ignore Chipeta and be glad for her help. And she was very helpful. She gathered wood and wild berries. She butchered the deer they shot, and she did all the cooking and washing of utensils. She was up long before daybreak, and she liked to use the steel fishhooks and bring them a string of trout for their breakfast.

Isaac was pleased by her behavior. Chipeta asked nothing of him, but gave constantly. He would find a deep mattress of pine needles under his blanket at night and his horse and even his mule were curried in the morning. She always seemed to make certain that he got the choicest pieces of meat, and she quickly grew able to anticipate his small needs.

"She's ruining you," Mack growled. "How you gonna square this with your wife back in St. Louis?"

The question hit a nerve, and Isaac's voice took on a rough edge, "That's none of your business."

Late one afternoon, when they came to a long mountain meadow protected on one side by a towering bluff, Isaac figured they had found a perfect winter camp. There were deer, elk, and even moose grazing on the lush grass, and Isaac dropped a fat elk cow. At the sound of his rifle, deer bolted into the trees but the moose walked slowly along the stream as if they had no fear.

While Chipeta dressed out the elk, Isaac studied the craggy northern bluff with an eye for defense against a surprise attack by Indians. The lower slopes were covered with pines and the upper two hundred yards strewn with loose rocks. Isaac noted where a spring gushed from a stand of sugar pine to join the powerful Grand.

"It's a good place to build a winter cabin," he said, pointing toward the spring. "There's plenty of game, fish, and beaver close by. We'll be out of the wind and backed up against a rock wall. There's wood and we can build everything far enough into those trees so that we can see enemies coming long before they can see us."

Mack and Andy exchanged glances. "Seems sort of crowded up in here, don't you think?" Mack said, pulling on the beard he had grown, which made his face seem older and heavier. "I mean, I thought we'd want to build a cabin where it was more open."

"Easier for Indians to spot us," Isaac said.

"Yeah, but we're in Ute country. Old Kicking Elk would never attack us."

"I'm not worried about the Utes," Isaac said. "You both heard the story about the Arapaho and Spirit Lake. Jim Savage warned me that there are other tribes that hunt in these mountains, and that Indian tribes are always warring with each other. The worst thing we could do would be to think we've nothing to worry about from hunting parties."

Mack Peel was still uneasy. "I understand that, but that bluff appears like it's about ready to tumble down right where you're talking about building a cabin."

Isaac glanced up at the rocky bluff. "It's been standing for centuries. My guess is that it'll last another winter."

"Couldn't Indians roll rocks down on us from up top?" Andy asked, craning his neck up to the rim.

"I guess they could," Isaac said, trying to curb his rising impatience.

"I think we ought to move on and keep looking," Mack said.

Isaac turned his head away, not wanting to show his anger. They would not find a better wintering place than this but he wasn't a man to force his will on others. "We'll ride tomorrow. Tonight, we'll camp here and jerk elk meat. Smoke it on green sticks over the fire."

"Let your squaw do it," Mack said. "I'm worn out."

They dismounted and hobbled their horses. Chipeta gathered wood and, within an hour, they were chewing on elk steaks while the Ute woman gathered a quart of wild berries for dessert. Isaac could tell by the way Mach and Andy ate that they were pleased.

"If she's half as good between the blankets as she is rustling up food, you got a gold mine," Mack said, berry juice staining his lips and beard. "When you going to take her to bed?"

"I'm not," Isaac said. "And I'll have you watch your tongue."

Mack stiffened. "She don't understand nothing we say! And if you won't use her like a woman, then give her to us."

"Touch her and I'll break your back like a twig," Isaac said without hesitation. He stared at them both, realizing what he had really said. His voice softened, for he had not meant to threaten them. But he wanted them to understand his thinking. "Listen, the woman is my responsibility."

"She's just a squaw," Andy said in a low voice. "I heard the mountain men say that squaws . . ."

"Never mind what you heard! I'm not interested in that." Isaac looked at the girl. "I won't let her be used. Do you both understand that?"

They nodded.

"There's one more thing we better get straight," Isaac said, knowing they were angry with him and discovering he did not give a damn. "We've followed the Grand far enough. This is where I'm going to winter. You boys can do what you want."

They stared at him. Andy said, "You know we got to stay together, Isaac."

"I know I'm wintering here," he replied. "I hope you'll

both come to see it the same way. The farther we go, the farther we'll have to return our pelts. Come morning, I'm going to start building a cabin right in those trees," he told them.

"What about the Indian?" Mack asked. "She gonna sleep next to us all winter?"

Isaac's cheeks warmed with embarrassment, and yet he understood what an awful temptation Chipeta would be during a long, bitter winter—for all of them. "We'll just have to build her a separate room."

"Might be a good idea," Andy said. "She's just a squaw, but she's godawful pretty. You got a wife, Isaac, and a reason to be true. Me and Mack don't have no one. It's worse for us. And it'll get harder and harder."

"Then you better work yourselves down to a nubbin running traplines," Isaac told them as he rolled over and gazed up at the first star of the night. "Because if you bother Chipeta, you'll come to regret it. We came for beaver and you'd best remember that."

"You ain't human," Mack said, "but you ain't no saint, either. We'll just see what happens before spring. I'm betting we'll all be sleeping with that girl before the snow melts."

"We'll start the cabin come daylight," Isaac said. "We'll have two rooms in it to ward off the devil's temptation. And if either one of you say another word about the girl, I'm going to land right on the top of you. And that'll be a shame because you won't be fit to move in the morning."

Daylight broke pristine and cold. They cleared a site in the woods and, very quickly, Isaac realized that none of them knew how to build a log cabin. Still, it had to be done so they cut the logs, trimmed them, notched the ends, and then stacked them head high, one on top of the other. The logs were so crooked there were big gaps between. Chipeta filled them with mud and moss except for a couple of places that would serve as gun ports. Chipeta's room was only six feet square, and they blocked it into the east corner. It reminded Isaac of a root cellar. Back in St. Louis, a man wouldn't have asked his dog to live in such a tiny, dark place but this was the Rockies. Isaac told himself it was the best they could do for the girl until he found her another clan of Utes and returned her to her people.

The idea of finding another clan had been with him almost from the day they left Kicking Elk's village. It was the only plan that made sense, though he knew that Andy and Mack would not like the idea. The devil with them both. They were not bad men, but they would have no qualms about using Chipeta for their pleasure, then perhaps leaving her pregnant the next spring. That was wrong. A child deserved at least to know who had fathered it, deserved more than to be some half-breed bastard. No, Isaac had decided, Chipeta must be returned to the Ute people. Doug had said that there were seven clans of Utes in these mountains, and Isaac hoped maybe he would stumble on one of them if he ranged out of this valley. It was worth a try, for though he'd never have admitted it, Isaac found himself increasingly attracted to the young woman.

Sometimes, when she was alone beside the rushing river and believed no one could hear her, she sang. Chipeta had a voice that filled Isaac with joy. It was high and full and it told him that she was not unhappy to be his woman. Or maybe he had nothing to do with her singing. Maybe the girl was just happy to be alive and have a nose to breathe through. Isaac reminded himself every day that he would find her a good, handsome young warrior for a husband. Of course, he'd learned enough about Indian ways to know he had to ask plenty for her if she were to be treated with respect. The more ponies she cost, the greater her social standing in the village.

Despite their lack of practical experience, the cabin progressed as well as they might have expected. But, when the walls were up, Isaac discovered that the roof would offer the toughest challenge of all. They'd all seen sod houses, and they considered digging up squares of meadow grass and laying them down flat on the roof, but they were not sure the walls were strong enough to support that much weight. So, in the end, they had Chipeta carefully stuff the cracks with moss, then cover that with a thick layer of pine needles and finally dirt.

When they finally stepped back to appraise their work, they agreed that it was the roughest kind of shack. "It isn't much," Isaac said. "If we had buffalo hides, Chipeta could fix us up better in a tepee. But it'll have to do. Maybe we can make some improvements."

"We'd better," Andy told them, standing back and looking at the cabin. "And I'd say the first one would be to figure out how to build a chimney. Otherwise, all we got ourselves this winter is an icehouse."

Isaac slammed his fist down on a log. "I knew we were forgetting something!"

Mack, always ready to look at the dark side, drawled, "If we started a fire in there now, the smoke would surely choke us to death."

Isaac studied the problem for almost an hour while the other two fretted and debated and Chipeta kept filling in wall cracks with mud and moss. Since they had no stovepipe to run out a wall, it seemed to Isaac that they must either tear off the roof and start all over again, or make a major adjustment.

"The devil with it," he grumbled, walking inside. He set his feet wide apart, reached high overhead and grabbed a couple of roof poles. Grunting, and with dirt, moss, and pine needles falling into his eyes, he pried the poles apart until a wide crack opened up in the roof. "Now we've a place for the smoke to go," he said, spitting dirt and wiping it from his eyes.

The two men glanced up at the gaping crack in the ceiling. "I got me a hunch that a lot of snow is gonna fall down that crack this winter," Mack said.

Isaac was out of sorts and in no mood for any more arguments or complaints. "We can't expect all the comforts of home and nobody said being a mountain man was going to be easy."

"What about a door?" Andy said, peering through the floor-to-ceiling opening in the wall. "The wind will come whipping through this place with nothing to stop it."

"I been thinking about that," Mack said. "And I got an idea."

His idea was to build a solid wall of poles about eighteen inches in front of the cabin's opening to block the wind, then hang a curtain of animal skins over the place where a normal door would fit. "It'll be like a double door. If we just hang a hide without a protecting barrier, it'll flap and blow in the wind and be worthless. I tell you, given the fact that we don't have a saw, a plane, or any hinges, this is the best we can do for ourselves."

Neither Isaac nor Andy was overly impressed, and Mack got angry. "All right then, you boys figure out something better and I'll be happy to go along with it."

Isaac and Andy could not think of anything better, so in the end they set the wind barrier of poles. In the weeks to come, they would accumulate deer and elk hides for Chipeta to sew together and hang over the real doorway.

By Isaac's calculations, the first snow fell on October 2. The temperature plunged to well below freezing that night and every night for three weeks before it warmed a little. They cut a small mountain of firewood and built themselves a hearth in the cabin. But when the snow was falling, the smoke wouldn't go up the hole because of a downdraft. One of them—usually Chipeta—had to tend the fire constantly while another stood by the skin door windmilling a blanket to drive the smoke outside. And there seemed to be no happy medium. They either froze or half smoked their lungs out. The dirt-covered roof warmed up in the day and snowmelt dripped mud that froze again when the sun went down. They built crude cots to keep themselves and their supplies off the ground but they knew that they were in for real trouble when deep winter arrived in December and January.

Still, despite the cold, the dripping mud, and the smoke, they were in high spirits. The beaver were coming into their long winter coats, and Chipeta helped them find what turned out to be a necklace of beaver ponds that chained down from the mountains. They also followed the main river for two days and, even though it was too deep and swift for beaver, it was constantly being fed by lesser creeks and streams that were loaded with the animals.

"Their coats are thick and ready," Isaac said by the end of October. He held up a small bottle of yellow fluid for them to see. "Castoreum. I took it out of Savage's possibles bag before I gave it back to his wife. I figured she had no use for it. We'll have to make more of it before spring. It comes from the glands of a beaver. Savage told me all about it. A drop or two on a stick will draw beaver like flies to honey."

Isaac uncorked the bottle, and they each sniffed it and agreed that it would be hard to ignore by beaver or anything else with a nose for smelling. Even Chipeta wrinkled up her nose and made a face, which caused them to laugh.

"Tomorrow morning," Isaac said. "We start trapping tomorrow morning."

Mack and Andy grinned. They were ready.

All four of them stood in icy water up to their knees as the sun struggled to rise over the eastern peaks. Isaac was shivering and the water was so cold that his bones ached. Chipeta seemed not to notice the cold. She had lifted her buckskin skirt to reveal her lovely ankles and lower legs. Under any other circumstances, the men would have been gawking, but not this morning. They had found a beaver pond that looked especially promising. Lugging two five-pound traps each, they waded upstream so that their scent would be carried away. They were gasping with the cold and slipping in the mud.

"They saw us already," Mack complained. "I could hear them slappin' their damn tails all up and down the line of ponds."

"I know." Isaac opened and set the jaws of his trap. He looked up at Chipeta, thinking maybe she knew something about setting traps, but her face was set with a slight frown as though she disapproved of this. Isaac took the trap chain and moved out a little farther. Taking a heavy stake from behind his belt, he reached down into the muddy floor of the pond and found a large, flat rock. "You've got to drive the stake in deep or a strong beaver will pull it out when the trap closes on his leg." He bent over and seeing no way to keep his chest out of the freezing water, he blindly hammered the stake into the bottom of the lake. When he raised up, his skin felt like ice. "There's got to be an easier way," he reasoned, "but I guess we'll find it in our own good time."

Trying not to shake too hard as the others looked on, Isaac uncapped the bottle of castoreum. "I need a stick."

"What kind of a stick?"

"Any stick. Just make sure it's long enough to poke out of the water a little."

Andy found the stick. He and Mack watched as Isaac poured a few drops of castoreum on one end of the stick and rammed the other into the mud beside the trap.

"My god, man! Your lips are purple," Mack exclaimed. "We can't be getting all wet every time we set a trap this winter! We'll surely die of pneumonia."

Isaac could not argue with that. "Maybe I'm doing it wrong," he said. "I should have paid better attention but I thought Savage would be here to show all of us. Let's set the traps and see what happens by tomorrow."

It took them nearly an hour to set six traps. They put them up at the top of the big pond and along the sides. By the time they were finished, they were freezing and since the wind had begun to blow, they rushed back to their cabin. Chipeta wanted to build the fire herself but she was shaking violently so Isaac gently pushed her aside and got a fire roaring hot. Outside, the wind began to blow harder and snow came slanting off the north rim to drive across the canyon.

Huddled in his blankets and shivering so hard his teeth chattered, Mack was filled with discouragement. "I don't know about this trapping business. Even if we catch six beaver, it sure ain't worth dying of pneumonia."

Isaac had been watching Chipeta. She had only a thin blanket, and he vowed she would be the first among them to have warmer clothing, even if he had to sacrifice beaver pelts to do it. But now, he turned to Mack. "Nobody said trapping would be easy."

"Well, what are we going to do when the beaver ponds freeze over? Bust the ice?"

"If we have to," Isaac said. "I don't know. I never asked Savage."

"I don't think we're going to trap and skin any eight or nine hundred beaver, not if we got to take an ice bath every time." Mack looked at Chipeta. "That squaw is the only thing that could keep us warm."

"Shut up," Isaac warned. "Not another word!"

Mack did shut up, but his eyes never left the Ute girl until, finally, she went into her room and lay down on her bed, just out of sight.

The storm lasted two days, and then the sun came out and

melted a foot of snow off the meadow in just a few hours. They hurried to the beaver pond and, to their great dismay, the long thin sticks tainted with castoreum were gone, but the traps were empty.

Mack panicked. "What happened? There's a whole bunch of beaver in this pond."

"I'm not sure," Isaac admitted. "The castoreum worked because the sticks are missing."

"Well, a lot of good that's going to do! We aren't here to feed the damned beaver!"

Isaac had a strong urge to throttle the man. He was also shivering and miserable. Sick of living in mud and ice after being in the mountains for nearly two months, they still had not caught one damn beaver or earned a cent. Isaac was painfully aware that they were in virgin territory, and a real trapper already would have caught and skinned dozens of the critters while he was still messing around and trying to figure out how everything worked. It was mighty discouraging.

"We'll try it again," he said. "Only this time, we'll stake the traps down in shallow water and cover them with a layer of mud."

"What about the castoreum?"

"We'll do that the same. Shorter stick, of course. Maybe plant it right next to the trap so that the beaver will stand up on the trap to sniff the damned stuff."

So again they set their traps, only this time they stayed dry above the knees and it wasn't so bad. Heartened by a warming sun, they went back to their camp and impatiently waited until the following morning.

"Jesus Christ!" Mack swore when they arrived at the pond again. "Look what happened now!"

Isaac's face was grim as he made his inspection. Of the six traps, four had caught beaver and, in each case, the animals had dragged the traps up to shore and knawed off their feet to free themselves. It was a grisly, depressing sight if ever there was one and it gave Isaac a hollow feeling in his gut. "Let's try another pond," he said, glancing over at Chipeta and feeling her eyes boring into him with strong disapproval. He was sure by now that she disapproved of trapping. Never mind that, she didn't understand. He turned his mind back to the traps and, after a few minutes, he said, "I think I got it figured out right this time."

They again staked down their trap chains but not so deep as the first time nor so shallow as the second. "I remember now," Isaac said. "Savage told me that a trapped beaver will either head for deep water and drown or shallow water where he'll chew himself loose. This morning, we gave him shallow. This time, we stake the chain so he can't keep his head above water. The weight of the trap will drown him."

It worked. The third morning, they had trapped three nice beaver. The animals were thick coated and fat, a couple of them weighing over fifty pounds. They moved up to the next pond and reset their traps. That night, they pelted the beaver, scraped the fat away, and stretched the pelts out on the floor, using pegs. Mack and Andy got mad at Chipeta, who would have nothing to do with the pelts or the carcasses except to cook the tails.

By the end of the week, they had trapped twenty-three beavers and were each hauling ten traps up separate streams. Fortunately, the weather held and, by the end of November, they had over a hundred pelts—or plews as they were called by the fur traders.

Isaac refined his method of trapping and shared the fruits of his experiments with his companions. "Put the big stake out deep and pull the chain until the trap is about three feet under water. Lay it in a cradle in the mud and cover it up nice and neat. Put a little greenery on the stick you scent up with castoreum and it'll draw beaver even faster. Be sure you cover your tracks along the banks. Wipe 'em out with a branch to mask your scent."

By using these techniques, Isaac found he was filling his traps regularly. He never made any attempt to catch all the beaver in any one pond, for he knew that a man did not eat the seed of a future harvest. He did not intend to come back to the mountains again, but then a fella never really could count on anything. Maybe the price of pelts would be off this year and he would have to return. Maybe his father-in-law would demand interest on the debt and he'd have to pay some heavy toll in order to remain a free man. Either way, Isaac figured that the beaver would replenish themselves within a year or two and the mountains would be no worse for his having come and gone.

Isaac worked two long traplines even after the snows grew deep, something he alone was able to do because Chipeta made snowshoes for the two of them out of willow branches and rawhide and then insisted on following him and carrying some of the heavy traps. She would trudge along all day in his big tracks and, though she would not set the traps themselves, she began to use the castoreum. It was the highlight of Isaac's day to watch her nose wrinkle and twitch under the powerful odor. He never laughed or even let her see his amusement, but it was funny. He had seen cats react that way to bad smells and, in some ways, Chipeta was just as animated as any feline. She would watch him set the traps and when she became bored, she would make a spear and attempt to spike fish. She almost never succeeded. But she had fun trying. And she would become so excited that Isaac would have to shoo her out of the water because she'd roil it up so much he feared stepping into his own traps.

"You're a wild, savage woman!" he would yell playfully at her. "Wild and beautiful. I'm going to find you a handsome young buck and trade you for six fine ponies. Hear me!"

Chipeta would smile and make sign language, most of which Isaac could not yet understand.

"A wild woman," he'd repeat as he marveled at how much he had come to depend on her help and to delight in her company. She was half child, half woman. All day long he would talk to her, tell her things she could not understand, things about himself that he'd never told another living person. Things you could say when someone as beautiful as the Ute girl just nodded and smiled without judgment or understanding, only acceptance. Sometimes, he'd even talk about Catherine. She was very different. Of course, how could she be otherwise? Could a man even compare two such women? Isaac didn't think so. They were like creatures from different worlds. Both female, both capable of loving a man and giving him sons and daughters, but that was where their similarities ended.

"I don't think I had better tell her about you," he said one day. "I don't think Catherine would understand you any better than you'd understand her."

Chipeta smiled and nodded. She talked back to him in her own tongue and he wondered what she was saying.

When they returned to the cabin each night, exhausted and half frozen, each man marked his own pelts, for Isaac had made it clear that they should each be rewarded for his own labor. Andy was a workhorse like himself but Mack was much less inclined to exert himself. As Isaac's stack of beaver pelts grew much taller than his own, Mack made excuses and even seemed a little bitter. But by the first deep snows of winter, he resigned himself by saying, "You two are gonna be rich. Me, I'll just be content to buy a small farm and settle down with the missus and children."

Isaac drove himself without letup, but he worried about Chipeta. He had insisted she use the furs of deer and elk to make herself heavy winter clothing: a coat, skirt, and knee-high moccasins, which she greased until they were water resistant. But Isaac knew that their days of trapping were nearly over until the next spring.

What surprised him the most was that he found he was growing very comfortable in the mountains. At first, the trees had given him a slightly claustrophobic feeling, but now he began to feel a certain comfort in the thick forests that hid him from view of potential enemies. He also discovered that the wildlife had its own language and would serve him as an unfailing warning system if only he listened. When a big grizzly came near, he could tell that something was wrong because the forest fell silent. Despite his growing awareness and ease in his mountain surroundings, Isaac always carried a weapon.

The new year found the mountains caught in the midst of a real blizzard. Their cabin was worse than an igloo and the weight of the snow and the roof itself caused the roof poles to sag dangerously. "We need to get out of here before we're buried alive some night when the damn things falls in on us," Isaac said.

The two men looked at him with concern. Then they studied the roof and said nothing.

But Chipeta understood and made it clear that she agreed

wholeheartedly. She beckoned them to follow her outside and up toward the bluff.

"What the hell is she up to?" Mack groused.

"I don't know," Isaac said, as they bucked and fought through the drifts. "But she generally knows what she's doing."

Chipeta led them to a cave. It was less than a mile from their cabin and high enough to offer a spectacular view of the entire meadow. Isaac grinned and pushed inside. The cave was at least twenty feet deep and big enough to hold their mules and horses in addition to their pelts. "We can build a fire back here." He looked up at the roof, which was about ten feet high. It was black. "Looks like someone already had the same idea."

"Hey!" Andy cried. "There's drawings on the walls!"

They hurried over and, sure enough, there were drawings, mostly of deer and men but also a couple of bear and buffalo. "Did your people do these?" Isaac asked in sign language.

Chipeta nodded and her hands moved rapidly.

"What'd she say?" Mack asked.

"She says the drawings belong to the Utes. They were made long, long ago. She said the bear is very special to the Utes. Second only in courage to the mountain lion."

"She said all that?"

Isaac nodded. He was beginning to understand her very well. They spent so many hours together every day on the traplines that it was starting to pay off in his ability to make and read her language. "Yeah, she said all that."

"Humph!" Mack grunted, as he studied the pictures. "If I couldn't draw a deer any better than that, I wouldn't even bother."

Isaac grinned. Sometimes, Mack amused him.

That very afternoon, they moved, put their heads down and into the wind and snow and carried their provisions and pelts up to the cave. The cave was cold but dry, and they blocked out the wind by piling rocks at the entrance. Moving back into the cave, they built a huge bonfire and discovered that it warmed the rocks and, best of all, the smoke just naturally caught in the wind and was pulled up the side of the bluff, leaving them pure air to breathe.

"We should have done this months ago," Mack said,

roasting chunks of beaver tail in the fire. "It would have been better."

Full winter brought a hard freeze. Isaac tried every way imaginable to break the ice and set traps, but it was no good. The ice became so thick that even he could not break through, and the beaver seemed to be content to hole up in their thick lodges for the winter. "Trapping season is over," he told the Ute woman. "We're stuck until spring. Maybe if the weather doesn't get too bad, we can go find some more of your people."

Chipeta smiled. The wind pulled at her raven hair, and her face was flushed and healthy looking. Isaac wished he had Doug Mellon's artistic talent. With her standing close and gazing out at the snowy mountains, it was a picture he would have given almost anything to possess.

January was interminable. Every afternoon, huge storm clouds piled up around the crests of the tallest peaks. The air grew hushed and still, the birds and animals disappeared, and then mighty clashes of thunder would echo from the highest mountaintops. Great bolts of lightning would stab out of the boiling heavens and explode against rock and tree. Isaac saw one tall tree burst into flame and burn like a pitch-covered torch until it was pelted by hailstones. The tree smoked and steamed until the eerie sight of it was obliterated by sheets of driving snow. During those storms, there was nothing to do but take cover. If one of them was out hunting or gathering wood, he went to the ground until the lightning storm spent itself, and then he bucked through snow trying to reach the cave and safety. The drifts were ten, even fifteen, feet deep.

Isaac counted his pelts at least every few days, and their number always reassured him that this sacrifice was worth everything and that he had not failed his wife and son. In spite of a very slow start, he had still managed to accumulate 114 pelts, though a few of them were anything but prime. He had ruined some of his earliest catches by scraping too hard and cutting through the skin. Felt hats could not be made out of pelts with tears or gouges in them.

Andy and eighty-seven pelts and Mack, sixty-three. If they trapped as many in the spring, and got them all to St. Louis, they'd be exceeding their most optimistic expectations.

The horses and mules were a major concern during the

hardest part of the winter. It had been a long time since the grass was green and the animals were thin and rundown. As the snow became deeper, they had to subsist on the bark of the sweet cottonwood trees that grew along the streams and creekbeds. Unwilling to turn their animals loose and risk having them drift for miles stripping trees of bark, Isaac and the others were forced to harvest the trees. This they did by taking axes and cutting off the smooth lower branches and then carrying them up to their cave where they sat around the campfire for hours, shaving off the green bark with their hunting knives. Chipeta never tired of this, though Isaac and the men found they could not do it for more than a few hours at a stretch. Stripping bark was tedious and time-consuming work but they had little choice. Their animals could not have survived the winter any other way.

In mid-February, two things happened, one good, one bad. The good was that the cold weather broke, and a chinook melted snow and turned the rivers, steams, and even the little brooks into raging torrents. The thick ice on the beaver ponds began to thaw and Isaac knew that they would be trapping very soon.

The bad thing was that Mack Peel lost control of himself one day while Isaac was out in the woods. He grabbed Chipeta and tore her skirt, trying to pull it over her hips. The Ute woman clawed his face and got free. She ran out into the forest and, when she found Isaac, he could see the fear and anger all over her face.

"So, it finally happened, did it?" he said. "It was bound to. You're a beautiful woman. I said I'd kill the man who put his hands on you, but that wouldn't be right. I guess what I'll have to do is find your people and trade you for some horses."

Chipeta only understood part of what he was saying, the part that said he was going to trade her for horses. She stiffened, and Isaac saw pain in her eyes. He groaned. "Don't tell me you've come to think I'm an all right fella," he said gently. "I told you about my wife and my children."

Chipeta answered that she did not care about them.

"Well, I do," he said. "And now I've either got to hurt Mack or he'll do it again."

Chipeta indicated that she wanted his Green River knife.

She would cut out Mack's intestines and feed them to the wolves.

"I expect you could. But no," Isaac said, "I've got to find your people. I'd have to do it anyway before I left the mountains. Might as well be before the ponds melt and the trapping begins."

So Isaac led the young woman back to the cave. Mack was waiting, his rifle primed and ready. "Whatever she told you, it was a lie!"

Isaac looked at the man. "No, it wasn't. But I'm taking her to her people. I'll be back before the ice melts."

"You're leaving us!" It was Andy and his face reflected his worry.

"I said I'd come back," Isaac told them. "I'm leaving all my pelts in your care, aren't I?"

They relaxed. Both men knew how much the tall stack of pelts meant to Isaac.

That very day, he paced a week's supply of jerked meat for himself and the girl, and they left the cave.

"You be back soon or we'll trap this country out!" Andy shouted, his voice echoing up and down the canyon.

Isaac nodded. The Ute girl, her expression sad and painful, walked slowly along behind him.

Chipeta knew he would not change his mind about leaving her and she knew where another clan of Ute were wintering farther west on the Grand River. It took them almost a full week to reach the village she sought and, when Isaac met the chief and explained his intentions, the word spread quickly. The next day, he had three new horses, and he felt like a man who'd been kicked in the groin.

"I found you a good man whose name is Running Wolf," he said, standing before Chipeta and trying to memorize every little part of her face. "I told you right from the beginning that I had to do this. You'll be all right here. Any man who'd give three good ponies for a bride has to have serious intentions. Running Wolf has another wife who can help you do the work. He wears eagle feathers, and I'm told that means he's a very brave warrior."

Chipeta's hands moved. She asked what she had done wrong that he should trade her for horses.

"Nothing," he said out loud while his own hands moved in sign. "Nothing at all. Chipeta, you're a good woman. It just had to be this way."

She suddenly whirled from him and ran away, leaving Isaac standing with the entire village watching him. Without a word of farewell, he gathered his ponies and rode back up the river, back to Mack and Andy and the beaver pelts. He was glad now that he could never have sketched her face. He was glad as hell.

In March, they trapped more beaver. Lots more. Isaac worked himself like a man bent on self-destruction, for he no longer took any joy in the mountains. Not without Chipeta. He missed talking to her, hearing her voice, her laughter, and her songs. He missed the way she dipped his trap stick into the castoreum and wrinkled her nose. He missed watching her at night as she tanned hides and made buckskin clothes for them all to replace the rags of cloth that were coming apart. He missed everything about her.

To fill his loss, he spent hours thinking and reminding himself of his own family in St. Louis. He yearned to know if he had another son, or perhaps a daughter. He would put the mountains and the Ute girl behind him forever.

"There's no sense in taking more than we can haul out," he said one night in April. "The beaver are losing hair and we've got all we can carry."

The other two men did not argue. They had been ready to leave for over a week. Snow geese were flying over the mountains. The earth was sprouting with greenery, and the willows were starting to bud. Isaac stood at the face of his cave—Chipeta's cave.

It was time to go home where he belonged.

≈ 6 ≈

At the end of their mountain meadow, a blood-red sun fired the eastern sky, and Isaac paused to watch an owl glide silently to rest in a towering pine. He hesitated, not even sure why. When the others also stopped and looked at him questioningly, he said, "Go on. I'll be along in a few minutes."

Andy and Mack nodded. Their animals were loaded with beaver pelts, and they made no sound as they tread over a carpet of pine needles.

Not wishing to be left behind, Isaac's horses and mules stamped their feet impatiently but he paid no attention. He squared the pack containing his very best furs on his own back as his eyes ranged across the meadow one last time. He missed nothing now, not the deer edging out of the forest or the old moose that liked the sweet new grass near the riverbank. Not the eagle whose offspring were testing their wings up high against the bluff or even the inquisitive brood of raccoons that would soon be exploring their cave.

He could not see their cave back under the bluff and behind the stand of pines, but it was fixed forever in his mind. In fact, he could see nothing to indicate that he, Mack, and Andy had lived in this wild, incredibly beautiful sanctuary for an entire winter. They had left their priceless beaver traps, their axes, and tools in the ancient Indian cave. Perhaps some future trapper would find those things and use them well. Maybe they would even save his life.

In a few years, the poorly constructed walls of their cabin would tumble down and rot. In a few years more, nothing would be left to indicate that three white men and a beautiful Ute Indian girl had lived there and trapped these mountain streams. The beavers would replenish themselves, the elk and deer would forget the sound of a rifle. The meadow would be as pristine as it was the first moment he had seen it.

Men could change the valleys and the plains, but not the mountains. The mountains were too harsh for women, too barren for farming, too cold for children and livestock. Isaac was glad the mountains would never change. He had come to respect them even more than rivers, and he had always loved big, rolling rivers like the Missouri, mysterious things that brought water from far away and carried it to unseen oceans.

The fact that the headwater of the Grand River was simply a massive bowl of granite high above the timberline did nothing to diminish the wonder of its mystery. Where did it go? How far to an ocean? What ocean? Isaac doubted that the Utes knew the answers to those questions, and neither did he. He would have to be content with knowing its source. Of one thing he was sure, if the great rivers could tell their stories, a man would never grow tired of listening. Yes, he loved rivers, but the mountains were the womb of the rivers. And mountains, while they might not offer the stories of the rivers, stood alone to touch the first and the very last rays of the sun.

Isaac reined his horse away from the meadow, no doubt turning his back on it forever. He would return to his family but something in the mountains would remain in his soul. They had changed his perception of life and death so very subtly and yet had stamped him with a physical mark that anyone could see. Isaac worried that Catherine and Nathan would scarcely recognize him when he returned to St. Louis. He wore a thick beard, and he looked like a mountain man in the buckskins Chipeta had made to protect him from winter. His eyes had deep crow's feet, the result of struggling for hours through the bright, blinding sun while attending his traplines. His hands were rawhide-tough, ingrained with the smell of beaver, castoreum, and smoke. But I'm not a mountain man, he thought, nor a store clerk nor a farmer either. I'm just a man who came searching for a chance to make something more of himself. And I have, thanks to these mountains.

He shifted the huge pack of prime beaver pelts on his back and the weight, something well over a hundred pounds, felt very good and reassuring. The pelts represented his fortune, the vindication of his resolve to leave his family and seek his place among men. The horses and mule were similarly laden. Isaac was not certain, but he thought he would earn nearly two thousand dollars, more than he had even dared believe possible. Yet, the market for beaver might have died. Things like that had always been his lot in this world and he was prepared for disappointment and even expected disaster. But, pray to God, this time maybe the prices had gone up and his furs were worth even more than he hoped.

As Isaac guided his animals along the river's edge, he wondered if some day he might bring Nathan into the Rocky Mountains and show him where his father had finally changed the fortunes of the Beards, transformed them from poor to prosperous folks in a single season of trapping.

"Come on, Isaac!" Andy shouted, his voice echoing across the meadow and trailing over the mountains.

Isaac turned his face to the east. He was carrying more weight than he should but the three Indian ponies were too wild to be entrusted with his most precious furs, and so he would carry them himself, even if he had to crawl on his hands and knees all the way to St. Louis.

They traveled slowly, glorying in the warm spring weather and the wildflowers. The mountains were lush with the promise of life held somnolent during the long winter. Birds were everywhere and Isaac saw spotted fawns on spindly legs. The men followed the spring-gorged Grand and crossed a million streams and dazzling, snow-fed brooks that gave it power. At the canyon leading off to where the Utes had been last summer, Isaac stopped. He knew the Indians had left but, still, he wished he could thank Chief Kicking Elk for the use of this mountain and the taking of beaver.

"What's the matter with you?" Mack asked. "They're gone and they kicked us out of their village. Remember?"

"I remember," Isaac said, wondering if the bones of Paden Tolbert were scattered where he had fallen. They passed on, climbing steadily toward Spirit Lake and then to the high, treeless ridge where a man could see a million square miles of wide open prairie.

Isaac had forgotten how steeply the river fell upon draining out of the sacred place of the Utes. By the time they had climbed up to the shores of Spirit Lake, their animals were staggering and breathing hard. After the long winter of little food, and even less activity, they were in poor flesh and had no stamina. In contrast, the men, buoyed by their success and superbly conditioned by miles of hiking their traplines, had never felt so vigorous and indomitable.

"We have to stay here a few days and rest them," Isaac said.

Mack objected. "But why? We can just top that treeless ridge and then it's all downhill to the flat plains."

"I know. But remember the climb? How steep and dangerous it was? It will be even more so, descending with such heavy packs. If a horse or mule loses its footing on a trail slick with runoff and breaks a leg, what then? We'd have to leave furs. Leave them to rot. Do you want to take that chance?"

"No," Mack said quietly. "You're right. We need to rest the stock and take it slow. But once on the plains, we can make some time, by gawd!"

"If we don't run into Indians," Andy said, probably remembering how Jim Savage had gotten himself scalped.

"Well, Jesus H. Christ," Mack swore. "If you both ain't a bundle of gloom and doom! We made it this far, we'll make it the rest of the way home."

"Of course, we will," Isaac said, not wishing to upset the man or dispel the feeling of high optimism they shared. "We'll just travel at night on the plains. Take things slow and careful. One extra week won't matter as long as we reach Independence with our hair and these beaver pelts."

Even Peel couldn't argue about that, but it was clear that he was sorely disappointed. "How long do we have to stay right here?"

Isaac looked at the animals that were eating like famished things. Their ribs were strongly outlined against the barrels of their chests. The grass around Spirit Lake was lush and nutritious. "Let's give ourselves two days," he said. "In the meantime, I'll go over the barren ridge and check the trail down to the plains. If it hasn't been washing out this spring, we ought to be on flatland four days from now."

Andy said, "If I never see high mountains again, it'll be too soon."

Mack nodded in vigorous agreement. "Amen to that!"

They both looked at Isaac, knowing he did not share their sentiments. "What about it, Isaac?" Andy said with a grin. "You ever coming back?"

"Probably not."

"But you'd like to see Chipeta again, wouldn't you?"

"No," Isaac said too quickly. "But I'd like to show my son these mountains."

Mack just shook his head in amazement. "It sure does beat me how you can say that after we've lived in a cave like animals all these hard months. Freezin', stinkin', always chilled to the bone. It don't make sense to me how any civilized man could say he'd want to come back."

"The Utes looked to me like they had it pretty good," Isaac said. "I imagine Doug Mellon is thinking so, too."

Mack snorted with derision. "He's probably dead by now. Some Indian got mad at him and cut off his topknot. He was crazy."

Isaac said, "I'll be going over that high ridge in the morning to scout the trail down to the plains."

"Don't wake us up when you leave," Mack said.

Isaac woke up before dawn. He stuffed jerky into his pockets and took up his Hawken rifle. The livestock were still grazing, and the stars, though beginning to fade, were so thick it seemed like a man could not have pitched a rock up through them without hitting one. He pulled on the soft leather moccasins that Chipeta had made for him and left his two slumbering companions. He anticipated that the moment he topped the treeless ridge he would step into daybreak and that the view eastward would be unforgettable.

He climbed the mountains with a surefootedness that now seemed natural. The muscles of his legs were as hard as iron, and his lungs worked like an efficient pair of blacksmith's bellows. Even so, every ten or fifteen minutes, he halted and bent at the waist to draw in deeply of the cold, thin air. He would rest for a few seconds, then move higher. He stepped out of the forest, marking the high timberline, and now he could see glistening snowbanks. Their lower edges were sharp

faced and chiseled by melted water that coursed down the
slopes into Spirit Lake. Isaac kept to the most solid footing and
moved higher and higher. Sunlight refracted through the
virgin snow and each crystal of ice glowed with the colored
intensity of a fine opal.

Don't hurry, he told himself as he pushed on toward the
summit, feeling his heart pound and his lungs burn for oxygen.
But he could not slow down, and when he reached the impasse
of snow he clawed his way through.

With a final burst of strength, Isaac broke through the
deep snow pack and reached the summit where he scrambled
up on an outcropping of rock. He stretched his arms out wide
to greet the rising sun.

He was a towering, bronzed statue standing invincible at
the crest of the world. "Thank you, God the Almighty!" he
roared at the gilded sky. He closed his eyes and swayed on the
balls of his feet, feeling the new day's heat penetrate his skin
and warm the very depths of his soul. "Thank you!"

Stretching out into infinity, the dew-dropped prairies
sparkled like a sea of diamonds, and Isaac was moved to tears
at the beauty he beheld. And when the sheer jubilation he felt
inside could not be contained, he howled and danced with his
voice echoing over mountaintops and sweeping down across
the plains.

"We thought you had gone insane," Andy and Mack said,
alarm evident in their voices after he had descended. "We
could hear your voice and it sounded as if you were shouting
down at the world—like Moses from atop his mountain."

Isaac blushed a little. "A wonderful madness seized me,"
he admitted, taking jerky from his pocket and chewing it with
relish. "I just could not help myself."

Mack and Andy said nothing. With Chipeta gone, they
knew he had changed. Sometimes, he would fall silent for days
at a time. And now this . . . this shouting from the mountaintops. They would have to watch him closely. He was
strong, but sometimes the strongest of men could not bend, so
they snapped. Yes, Isaac would bear watching until he was
safely back with his wife and family in St. Louis. They would
see to that. Ever since Jim Savage had died, just a few miles

beyond the ridge, Isaac had been their leader. But the high mountains and the Ute woman had changed him, changed him in ways that his wife and son would find curious. Isaac talked to himself now, not only when he thought he was alone, as sane men sometimes do, but sometimes even when he knew he was among them.

"What about the trail down to the prairie?" Andy asked. "Is it still there, or has it been washed away by spring runoff?"

Isaac stared blankly at them. In truth, he had been so inspired and awed by the sight from the backbone of the great Rockies that he had completely forgotten his purpose. "I . . . I forgot to study it," he admitted, "but I'm sure we can find a way down."

Andy and Mack exchanged knowing glances. Isaac was under a spell.

The snowcap ran for miles along the top of the ridge, like foam on the crest of a wave. The men had to stomp and beat it down with their feet and even their bodies before a path for the animals could be made over the summit. It was hard, slow, and freezing work that left them shivering and fatigued. They had hoped to reach timberline on the eastern slope of the Rockies before darkness, but the trail was bad and the going treacherous. The horses fell continuously and even the sure-footed mules kept going down. When they hit, they brayed piteously and, if a man was not careful, he could find himself crushed by one of the thrashing animals.

A half mile above the timberline, the trail was entirely washed out by the snowmelt. Isaac expelled a deep breath. "I'll bring up firewood and we'll camp here."

"Here!" Mack shouted, twisting in a full circle. "Why, there's no feed or even a flat place to sleep."

"We have no choice. The light is poor and the trail is gone. We'll need good light to reach the trees. Start making a piece of flat ground," he ordered.

"I'll come with you to gather firewood," Andy said.

"Good. With some hot coffee and food, we'll have a fair camp. We'll just have to hobble the animals or they're liable to go right back over the top of the ridge and back to that grass at Spirit Lake. Can't say as I'd blame them."

They gathered armsful of wood, and it was a tough climb back up to their camp where Mack had cleared a flat place by tearing out rocks and stomping down the mud. He'd even built a small dam to divert the snow runoff from above. The air was growing colder, and a wind came up as they hobbled the stock and then removed the precious furs and stacked them where they'd keep dry.

"I wished I'd shot us a deer yesterday," Mack groused.

Isaac tossed the man a piece of dried jerky and stuffed some into his own mouth, watching Andy build the fire. "Tomorrow, maybe we'll have buffalo hump again," he said wearily.

Mack leaned close over the fire. He chewed the jerky without pleasure and stared into the flames until Isaac spread a deerskin out in the mud, climbed onto it, and fell right to sleep.

They had overslept and morning was full upon them when Isaac awoke, knowing something was very wrong. The horses and mules were too alert, their heads up, their ears pointed down the mountainside. When Isaac followed their gaze, his heart almost climbed up his throat.

"Indians!"

There were at least fifty, and they were armed and riding their tough little ponies as fast as they could up the narrow, slippery trail. They were riding single file and their faces were painted. No one had to tell Isaac that they weren't Utes and they weren't coming to make friends.

"Who are they?" Mack cried.

Isaac grabbed his Hawken rifle and made sure it was ready. "I don't know. They look like the same people that scalped Savage last summer. We got a fight. But not here." Isaac grabbed one of his heavy packs of beaver pelts. "Load up! We're going back to the summit to make our stand!"

Both men lunged for their furs and started trying to haul the massive packs to their stock. But their fear was so real that it communicated itself to Isaac's three Indian ponies. Loosely hobbled and seized with panic, the animals crow hopped up the slopes away from them. The other horses followed, leaving only the mules who were less inclined to panic. Isaac caught his own mule, which began to bray in distress. Dragging their packs of beaver pelts, Mack and Andy were trying unsuccessfully to overtake their frightened horses. "Let them go!" Isaac shouted.

"We ain't leavin' any furs!" Mack shouted. "We got to get those animals back!"

Isaac glanced over his shoulder. Now that they were seen by their enemies, the Indians were whipping their ponies furiously. Had it not been for the slick and steep trail that was largely washed away by spring runoff, they would already have been in striking range.

He threw one of his bundles of furs on his mule and lashed it down but, suddenly, the other two mules broke free and went racing after the horses. Mack and Andy lunged for them but missed. Both men picked themselves out of the mud and screamed with helpless rage.

Isaac cut the hobbles loose from his mule and slapped it across the rump. The animal bolted up the slope with its pack lashed firmly in place. Mack's rifle boomed as he fired at their pursuers but his first shot was wild and far off the mark.

Isaac snubbed down his own blinding fear. The sight of all those Indians chilled his blood but he knew he could not give in to his instinct to run. "Take your time and aim! Shoot low!"

Isaac showed them how. His Hawken crashed fire and smoke. The lead Indian was plucked from the back of his pony. He hit the slope and rolled all the way down to the trees. Andy shot another Indian and they furiously reloaded their rifles. The Indians were insane with the need to exact revenge, and they lashed their ponies harder to get within bow-and-arrow range. But Isaac and his men finished reloading and fired a devastating volley down into them once more. Two Indians died instantly and a third took a bullet in the arm. He dropped his bow and came charging up the mountainside on foot.

Isaac knew he could not reload in time to shoot the man before he was upon them. "Reload!" he shouted. "I'll take him!"

The wounded Indian had courage, and he was as fast and surefooted as a mountain goat. He was also young and strong but the charge up the mountainside had robbed him of his quickness and strength. He was visibly staggering when Isaac grabbed a rock and smashed him in the forehead. The man dropped and rolled down the mountainside in a shower of loose shale.

Andy and Mack fired again and the charge broke. The Indians threw themselves from their mounts and took cover in a screen of rocks. Isaac could hear their wails and sharp yelps of fury.

"Now what?" Mack hissed.

"I don't know," Isaac said. "It depends on whether or not they'll wait until dark to come the rest of the way up this mountainside."

Andy finished reloading. "There's too many," he said. "They'll flank us for certain. Even if we lasted through the night, they'd be all around us come sunrise."

"I know," Isaac said. "That's why we can't stay here. We've got to get away from them."

Mack was trembling. "You got a pack of furs on your mule but we got nothing! We ain't leaving these pelts!"

Isaac looked at the two men. "We'll carry what we can on our backs if they don't slow us down too much. We leave the rest."

"No, damnit!"

Isaac grabbed Mack by the shirtfront and jerked him up so that they were face to face. "They aren't worth your life! Whatever we get out with, we'll split three ways."

"You'd split your furs?"

Isaac pushed the man away. "We either stand together or we fall together."

"All right!" Mack said breathlessly. "So where do we go?"

Isaac watched the Indians fan out across the mountainside. "They won't let us get around them and we can't go through them. That only leaves retreat."

"You mean, back to Spirit Lake and . . . and then where?"

"To find the Utes," Isaac said. "If we can't hide, then we get our horses and find the Utes. They're our only hope."

"If we lead these Indians into their mountains, old Kicking Elk will have us killed if those Indians don't do it first," Mack swore.

"Then you tell me a better idea!"

They glared at each other until Mack's eyes filled with bitterness and terror. "Damnit!" he groaned, fighting tears. "We almost was outa these mountains and here we are all fouled up. Most of our pelts gone. Jesus Christ! Can't a man ever win?"

Isaac's voice softened. "If we have to, we'll come back. We still got the traps up in that cave. We can last another year—but we have to get through this one first."

Mack nodded. He visibly forced himself to raise his head and square his shoulders before he scooted over beside his precious bundle of furs, neatly tied with strips of soft deerskin. Each pack held a hundred prime pelts worth more money than a man could earn in a year, maybe in two years. And they were going to have to leave them.

"Maybe the Indians won't pay any attention to them," Andy said, not fooling any of them.

"I think we'd better try and get back over the top now," Isaac said. "I don't think they're going to wait until dark."

Carrying heavy packs strapped over their backs, they retreated up the mountainside of mud and loose rock but it wasn't pretty. Slipping and sliding, falling and cursing, the only thing that saved them was that the Indians were having just as much trouble. Had they been firing across level ground they would have been within range. It seemed to take them hours to reach the snowbank. The Indians were closing. Three more shots from their Hawkens and Isaac ordered a full-blown retreat down to Spirit Lake where he could see their horses and mules grazing beside the placid waters.

As he ran, Isaac knew full well that, in a very few minutes, the Indians would be on the higher ground and gain the advantage. And they'd remount their ponies once over the crest and come on fast. There were still better than forty of them and Isaac knew they could overrun three men on foot.

They ran like men possessed. The damned Indian ponies bolted and raced into the heavy forest but their own horses, more accustomed to them, snorted warily and held their ground. "Come up on them slow," Isaac warned, even though every survival instinct in his body cried for him to hurry. They caught their saddle horses and the mules. They quickly made rope halters and slashed the loosened hobbles. But the long run down the mountainside had taken the spring out of their legs and, given that they all were toting packs, mounting a spooked and bareback horse proved almost impossible. Andy was lucky. His mount was close to a tree stump and he hopped up on the stump and managed to throw himself on the horse's back before it bolted away in fear. Isaac's fur-laden mule swept past, and Andy made a miraculous grab for its lead rope. The mule almost pulled him off his horse and he nearly dropped his Hawken trying to stay mounted.

Isaac had his own horse by the mane. Because of his long legs he was able to mount his plunging horse despite the weight of his furs.

"Don't leave me!" Mack shouted, his voice high and hysterical. "Help!"

It was all Isaac could do to hang on to his rifle and stay mounted. He could see that Mack was too burdened by his pelts to mount his plunging horse. "Cut the pack!" he screamed over his shoulder.

But Mack would not abandon the remainder of his best furs. Isaac roared at him but it had no effect. The fool kept trying to leap up onto his horse but he hadn't the size or the spring to do it. Arrows began to fill the air and Isaac saw Mack stagger, then finally attempt to cut the pack from his shoulders. But it was too late. The Indians were leaping from their horses. Isaac had one horrible image of Mack's upturned face as the warriors swarmed all over him. Isaac yanked his own Green River knife and slashed at his shoulders. The pack of furs fell away as he raced wildly after Andy with the Indians in pursuit. At least Andy still had the fur-laden pack mule in his grasp. When Isaac finally overtook him, Andy yelled, "Where's Mack?"

"Dead!"

Isaac grabbed the rope from Andy's fist and led the pack horse off into the trees at a run. Darkness would come within the hour and, if they could stay ahead of the Indians, perhaps they could escape or at least gain a few valuable hours of lead time.

But one thing was sure, the Indians would track them to hell and back in order to avenge their dead tribesmen.

"We've got to find the Ute people!" Isaac bellowed. "It's our only hope!"

≈ 7 ≈

As they raced along the shore of Spirit Lake and then followed the Grand River farther into the mountains, Isaac knew their chances of outrunning the Indians were slim and none. Neither he nor Andy was the equal of the Plains Indians on horseback. And the mule laden with furs was slowing them down. Isaac knew that he had to buy some time.

"Keep going!" he shouted as they rounded a curve in the narrow trail and he threw himself out of the saddle. "We've got to have a better lead! Cache the pelts, then turn loose of that pokey mule! I'll try to slow them down."

Andy nodded and pressed on. Isaac reloaded the Hawken and when the first Indian following their trail appeared, he raised his rifle, took aim, and fired. The lead warrior was slammed into the face of the next pony, causing the animal to duck sideways, unhorsing its rider. Isaac remounted, knowing he had created a moment of chaos. The Indians were brave but they had taken enough losses, and he was sure they would be more hesitant, at least until the trail widened again.

When he overtook Andy, the mule and the furs were gone. "Where did you stash them!" he yelled.

"In the bough of a cottonwood tree right beside the river. High enough so the animals won't chew 'em up!"

Isaac was surprised. There had been two packs roped together and they had weighed an even hundred pounds each. Andy must have cut them apart and somehow managed to find the strength to shove them into some overhanging limbs. Isaac hoped he had placed them so high they would not be seen until autumn when the leaves would fall and expose them for anyone to see.

They raced on, following the very canyon they'd passed through only a few days earlier. The water was swift here, the current deep and strong. Isaac studied it carefully, trying to decide whether or not their horses could ford the river. If they could get across, perhaps they could make a stand. If the Indians dared to attack across the river, a lot more of them would die before sundown. But Isaac was unsure if their weary horses could ford such a strong current.

He decided there was no choice. "We've got to reach the opposite shore," he yelled over the sound of the water. "Once across, we can make a stand on the north bank under that canyon wall. The only way they can reach us is to come directly across."

Andy stared at the raging torrent. He shook his head back and forth. "We'll drown for sure!"

Isaac could not argue the point. The river was churning like a caldron and he could see big boulders and sunken trees under the surface. Yet, while the Grand was almost certain death, the Indians would show them no mercy. In their hands, death would be long and horrible.

"Andy," he shouted, "we've got to try! Our horses are almost finished."

Andy could not take his eyes off the river. "Your horse is done, mine ain't! I won't do it!"

Isaac did not know what to do. The thought of leaving Andy was almost inconceivable. And yet, he realized that the odds of finding the Utes and getting help before they were slaughtered were nonexistent. His horse was dead on its feet and the Indians were close behind.

How fickle life was in these mountains! Twenty-four hours ago, they'd been feeling rich as kings. Now . . . they had nothing but their lives and the end seemed very near. "I'm going in!" he shouted.

"Isaac," Andy pleaded. "Don't try it. Stick with me. We can . . ."

"Andy, there's no goddamn choice!"

Isaac lashed his horse. The animal refused to enter the river. He could not blame it, but his time was almost gone. He threw himself to the ground and tied his possibles bag with its powder, flint, and lead balls to the Hawken. He took the big rifle by the barrel and spun it around and around overhead and with all of his considerable strength, he sent the Hawken and possibles bag twisting over the river. Not many men could have done such a thing but he saw the Hawken land in heavy brush and he knew it had not been ruined.

"Dismount and give me your rifle!" he demanded.

Instead of obeying, Andy fired wildly as Indians burst into view. Isaac lunged at him but the young man reined away too quickly and sent his horse galloping downriver. With the screams of the Indians filling his ears, Isaac dove headlong into the water. The river grabbed and twisted him like a corkscrew. It swallowed him and sent him spinning blindly into its depths. He smashed against something solid and screamed as water poured into his mouth and nostrils. His powerful arms and legs churned madly and just when he thought he could hold his breath no more, the current swept him around a bend. He struck a submerged log and was heaved up to the surface. Instinctively, he exhaled and inhaled before he was pulled back under.

He struck another object and momentarily lost consciousness. But again, the river released its hold on him and he came to the surface. For a moment, his body was caught by a set of massive tree roots. He hung flapping in the current until his jacket tore away, and then he went careening over rocks, rolling and being beaten to a pulp. He hit a stretch of clear water and tried to swim, only to discover that he could not kick with his right leg or lift his right shoulder.

Isaac knew he was at the end of his reserves. He had no strength left, no belief in his ability to survive another few hundred yards of the river's pounding. He relaxed and closed his eyes. He felt himself floating, being tossed high and then being slammed into unyielding things that were breaking him apart. With the last feeble will that remained, he kicked and clawed until he struck a fallen tree and was able to pull himself along its length. And finally the current yielded what remained of him. He touched mud and crabbed higher into the cover of thickets. He was more dead than alive, and the Grand had stripped him naked. Isaac's lips were pulp but they moved and, before he lost consciousness, he whispered, "Catherine. Nathan. CHIPETA!"

He awoke once in the night but so much pain enveloped him that he slipped back into unconsciousness. The sun was past its zenith when he awoke again and lay unmoving. With the canyon walls almost directly overhead, there was no sun and the day seemed dark and cold. Isaac was shrouded with pain, especially on his right side. Finally, he tried to lift his arm and it felt like a needle had been thrust into his shoulder joint. Isaac tried his left arm and was satisfied that it was intact. Next, he moved his left foot and bent his leg. But when he tried to do the same with his right, a groan was torn from his mouth.

The right leg was broken. He sat up slowly, afraid of passing out again. He studied the leg and reached for his hunting knife but it was gone. Everything was gone. He was seized by utter despair until he remembered that he had saved his Hawken with his ammunition and flint in his possibles bag. With those things, even with a broken leg, a man could survive. Isaac studied his leg, which had turned purple and was swollen to twice its normal size below the knee. At least, he could not see a bone and that was all important. But what was he to do?

He lay back down, floating on waves of pain, trying to keep his thoughts connected, yet only halfway succeeding. He would need to set the bones of his right leg before doing anything else. But how! He could not even grip and pull the bones, given the state of his dislocated right shoulder. Yet the bones had to be properly set or they would not mend.

Isaac scooted back down to the water. He could think of only one way and that was to wedge his foot and ankle between rocks and then throw his body backward and hope that the bones came together. He easily found two big rocks but he had to maneuver his body almost fully into the river. The water made him shake violently and, when he tried to lift his leg and jam it in between the rocks, he almost lost his senses. It took the last shred of will to wedge his ankle in tightly and then fling himself back toward the shore.

He screamed as the shattered bones grated, tearing both muscles and ligaments. He lunged backward once more, and his face went under the water. The river pulled hungrily at his naked body, and he used his good leg as a lever to raise his bad one. Then he rolled onto his stomach and dragged himself out of the water where he lay gasping until the pain made him vomit. Later, he grabbed a young sapling with his right hand and pulled his shoulder socket back into place. Isaac found a long pole and used it to climb to his feet. Weaving and near collapse, he began to hobble upriver—upriver to where he would find the Hawken and his possibles bag.

He *would* survive! He would find the Utes and they might even help him live to see his wife and children. God willing.

Months later, he had come to believe that it was God and the Hawken that had saved his life and brought him back to his meadow and the cave. He spent the summer mending, watching the afternoon storms and listening to their thunder. Food was everywhere. Isaac shot deer and elk that came almost close enough to touch. Loneliness was his constant companion and during his philosophical moods Isaac often contemplated the reality that he was the sole surviving member of the ill-fated group that had left Independence with such lofty expectations. What fools they had been to think that a band of pilgrims, without an experienced mountain man, could venture into the high mountains and survive! It was a wonder they had even lasted the winter. Their attempt at building a cabin had been disastrous. Its roof had caved in after the first heavy snowfall. Chipeta had saved them by finding the cave and then teaching them how to survive in her Shining Mountains. They had not realized it back then, but it was the truth. Without Chipeta, they would have perished. She had been their steward, their good luck talisman. And when she was gone, they had left the mountains and their blind luck had finally run its course on the eastern slopes.

Isaac knew that his lower right leg had not mended properly. It ached when the nights were cold and he could not put weight on the leg without considerable pain. He would walk with a limp the remainder of his life and, yet, he alone of those who had left Independence still lived. He could not complain. He spent hours lying in the meadow, watching the great cumulous clouds build into towering rain monuments. The summer showers washed his body and cleansed all bitterness from his soul. He walked every day in spite of the pain, and he spent time studying the forest. He delighted in everything living, the birds, the field mice, the deer, and even a huge grizzly bear that rose onto its hind legs and blustered a challenge at him before lumbering away.

Sometimes, Isaac thought he might remain in this place another trapping season, but he knew that was not fair to Catherine or Nathan. He was already overdue. They would be sick with worry. He had to leave before the autumn leaves fell and revealed his two bundles of beaver pelts hidden by Andy in some cottonwood tree.

It was late summer when he felt he could wait no longer. He left his cave and struck out on foot, each step an agony but one that brought him a step nearer to his family. He recited the Lord's Prayer and hobbled on. Two days later, he found beaver pelts resting high up in a cottonwood tree. Isaac used his powerful arms to dislodge them. The heavy bundles fell and, when Isaac picked them up, he marveled at how a young kid like Andy could have found the strength to place such a weight so high. Isaac decided that, when a man's heart was shivering in terror, he could do things that weren't ordinarily possible. Certainly this was an example. Even Isaac, with his height and strength, would have had difficulty. Once more, he blamed himself for Andy's death. He should have torn the boy from his horse and thrown him headlong into the river. At least Andy would have had a chance that way. But he'd let the kid escape and probably die in tortured agony.

Isaac did not even open the bundles of furs to inspect them. He remembered exactly which bundles he had lashed onto his mule and that they were the best he'd trapped. He was so grateful that his eyes stung with tears. If he could carry both bundles, he would be able to repay the debt to his father-in-law and have enough money left over to make a fresh start.

He cut strips of buckskin from his pants and fashioned shoulder straps. When he hoisted the staggering weight onto his back and took his first step, he faltered and his right leg almost buckled. Isaac swayed dizzily for a moment. Too much to take so far.

But he would take it, take it all the way over the barren mountaintop and then down across the vast buffalo grass prairie to Independence and then to St. Louis.

The Utes were camped at Spirit Lake. When Isaac

staggered into their village, Kicking Elk and his people did not even recognize him. He seemed to have aged twenty years. He had lost much weight and it made the bones of his face and large hands jut out so that his flesh seemed like stretched parchment. It was Snow Bird who called his name first and ran to his side. She and another squaw named Woman Who Walks cut the pelts from his shoulders so that they dropped heavily to his feet. Isaac tried to protest but the sudden lack of weight caused him to lose his equilibrium. He staggered forward, his mind so dulled with pain that it could not give him balance.

The two squaws supported him and Kicking Elk, perhaps taking pity, declared that Isaac was welcome and must stay until he was stronger. A medicine man would heal his leg. He would have horses and new clothing. Where did the other white men go?

Isaac told them, his mind working slowly as his bony fingers wove the tale. The old chief nodded. Arapaho! Enemies. How many were killed?

Isaac tried to think. Three or four on the other side of the ridge. One or two near the lake, another at the first bend in the river. He held up seven fingers and shrugged to indicate he could not be certain. The old chief beamed. He was very pleased. Next time, Ute people would help slay the enemy!

Isaac nodded. He allowed himself to be led to a tepee where Snow Bird indicated he should rest until the medicine man came to heal and make him strong again. Isaac wanted his furs. He could not rest until the furs were at his side! Snow Bird seemed angry but she had been the wife of a mountain man and she understood. She left and, several minutes later, she and other squaws brought the furs to Isaac's side.

He thanked them. And he fell asleep before the medicine man arrived.

Three months later, Isaac arrived in St. Louis riding a fast horse he had bought in Independence. There was also a new Green River knife under his leather belt, and he was wearing beaded trousers and a hunting jacket that Snow Bird had made for him. He was not the first mountain man who had eschewed the Missouri River and arrived overland but he was easily the most impressive. His buckskin hunting jacket was beautiful

both in its fit and its design. Snow Bird had given him a
necklace made of silver and the claws of a grizzly bear. The big
Hawken rested easily in the crook of his left arm, and he
gripped the stock just behind the hammer so casually it was
evident it had become a part of him. His powder horn was
polished to a shine, and his moccasins were a thing to behold.
Full bearded, he wore a magnificent coonskin cap with a pair
of eagle feathers sticking out beside where the tail flopped.

Isaac rode with his head held high. He viewed St. Louis
as a stranger, and what he saw did not agree with him in the
least. He saw filth and drunkenness, whores, and all manner of
indolent men seeking wealth without sweat. A powerful smell
assailed his senses and it was of garbage and chimney smoke.
He felt hemmed in by the buildings, nervous about the staring
people, and touchy when he rounded First Street and found it
clogged with too much traffic.

But he also felt a powerful sense of accomplishment. He
had already sold his furs to a buyer in Independence who
swore upon the grave of his mother that he was paying St.
Louis prices. And what prices they were! Six dollars a pound!
Isaac was almost delirious with joy. He had just over eleven
hundred dollars in his saddlebags. Eleven hundred dollars!
Even after paying his skinflint father-in-law—with interest—
he would still have almost nine hundred left for himself and
Catherine. It was unbelievable. Worth the pain in his leg that
even the best Ute medicine man could not dispel entirely.

Isaac passed by the small house in which he and Catherine had lived while he worked for her father. He shuddered to
think that he had once licked Wilke's boots in gratitude to have
such a place. How could one man treat another so poorly,
especially when it also involved his only daughter?

He rode past his father-in-law's dry goods store, feeling
his hackles rise. He could almost sense the old man's presence
inside the building. With luck, maybe Catherine and Nathan
were at Wilke's home and he could spirit them away before the
man returned.

Isaac made the horse trot faster, and its hoofbeats
matched the pounding of his heart. He had come home, and
he had made his stake.

He was shaking in his moccasins when he limped up to

the front door of the Wilke home and banged on it hard. It was midafternoon and he was wishing with all his might that he could just see Catherine and his children and avoid the damned Wilkes altogether. But that wasn't likely. After he knocked on the door, he pulled off his coonskin cap and wrung it in his big hands.

There was a little look-see in the door, and he soon realized he was being stared at by someone inside, who asked, "Sir, who are you!"

Isaac's spirits plunged. It was Mrs. Wilke, and she didn't like him any better than her husband. "It's Isaac." He decided he had better add, "Your son-in-law, Isaac Beard."

He heard the woman gasp just before she slammed the tiny door on the look-see and rushed away.

Isaac was caught in a moment of indecision. He'd expected to catch hell from the Wilkes, but had not been prepared for the possibility that they would not even let him inside to see his family.

He doubled up his fists, and his face grew red and angry. "Open up!" he shouted. "I want my family."

When no one answered, he pounded on the door so hard it shook and, when that didn't do any good, he reared back on his bad leg and kicked it in with his good one. "Catherine!" he shouted. "Nathan!"

He heard a baby cry, and then Mr. Wilke rushed out into the dim hallway with a pistol in his fist. "Raise your hands and don't take another step, Isaac! You're trespassing and you're under arrest!"

Isaac planted his feet and tried to keep from lunging at the only man on Earth that he hated. "Is that my baby I hear?"

"It is! But you'll never hold him!"

Isaac could contain his anger no longer. He threw himself forward in a rage. The pistol belched smoke and fire. Isaac felt a searing brand across his cheek and knew that the ball had opened up the side of his face. He didn't give a damn. He grabbed Wilke by the throat and slammed his head against the wall twice before he hurled the unconscious man away. Mrs. Wilke screamed, and Isaac heard the back door slam. He bulled past Wilke and, when he entered the room, he stopped in his tracks.

"Nathan, my son!"

The boy was standing by a crib, and his eyes were round and staring. He flattened himself protectively before his infant brother and shouted, "You aren't my father! Go away!"

"Yes, I am," he said quietly. "Ask your mother."

"She's dead. My daddy's dead, too!"

Isaac leaned back against the wall. "Catherine is . . . is dead?"

Nathan dipped his chin. "Who are you? Why did you hurt my granddaddy?"

"When did your mother die?"

"Christmas. Now go away. You hurt my granddaddy and you're making my brother cry."

Isaac took a faltering step forward. "How did your mother die?"

The boy stood his ground but he looked scared. "She just did. She got sick and the angels took her to heaven."

Isaac walked over to the crib. The baby looked up at Isaac's bloody face and screamed even louder.

When he could speak, he reached down and lifted the baby in his huge hands and studied it as best he could through the tears. "What's his name?"

"Matthew. Matthew Wilke."

"No!" Isaac shouted, losing his self-control and causing his infant son to scream louder and wave his arms about in a frenzy. Isaac raised him to eye level. "You can be called Matthew, if that's what you're used to. But, by gawd, your last name is *Beard*. Matthew Beard!"

"Put him down!" Nathan cried. "Put my brother down!"

Numb with shock, Isaac laid the boy down and said, "I'm your pa, Nathan, and I loved your mother. I'd never have hurt her for anything in this world. I loved her and I love you. Nathan, get your things, we're leavin' St. Louis. I'm taking you and your brother to somewhere far away. In the mountains, where you can both grow up big and . . ."

"Grandpa!" Nathan cried. "Grandma, help!"

Isaac heard the front door slam again. He whirled around, knowing that there was trouble coming down the hallway. His new hunting knife came easily to his hand, and he held the screaming infant to his chest and waited.

Two lawmen appeared in the doorway with leveled revolvers. "You're under arrest!" one shouted. "Put that kid down!"

Isaac shook his head. The knife came a little forward. "These are my sons. I'm takin' them away."

"No, you aren't," the older of the pair said. "I'm the sheriff of this town and if you got any decency and/or sense left in you at all, you'll put the baby and the big knife down and come along peaceful. Otherwise, that baby might get hurt."

Isaac thought about that for a moment and he agreed. Matthew's life was more important to him than that of anyone else on Earth, except for Nathan. He looked to his older boy. "I *am* your father and I loved your mother. You always remember that. No matter what, you remember that much. Hear me!"

The boy nodded involuntarily.

Isaac put his infant son back in the crib. He turned on the men and stepped sideways until he figured there was no chance of a bullet hitting his baby boy. "I won't go to jail," he told them in a quiet but very firm voice. "I won't do it, not for trying to get my family back."

"Drop the knife! You're under arrest for thievery, horse stealing, and maybe murder if you killed Mr. Wilke. Drop it!"

Isaac could finally see the way of things. Thanks to Wilke, he wasn't just going to jail, they were going to send him to prison. He had never seen a prison, but he'd heard stories about them. They'd lock him up in a prison cell, and they'd throw away the key until he died clawing at the walls.

Isaac closed his eyes and tried to think of the mountains. His huge body began to tremble. A primal roar welled up from deep in his chest and he lunged forward with the knife, crying, "No!"

The young deputy jumped forward and cocked back the hammer of his gun and then started to pull the trigger. Isaac's wrist flicked forward in a snapping motion and his knife made two complete revolutions in midair before its blade sank in the man's chest. The deputy fell backward into the sheriff and, before the older lawman could get a clear shot, Isaac smashed him across the face, then went racing down the hallway. He managed to reach his horse. Swinging into the saddle, he turned the animal west and let it run flat out as gunshots filled the street.

If he was overtaken, he'd be shot or hanged on the spot for killing the deputy. There was no turning back now, not ever. He would never know his sons, never tell them of the mountains and the Ute people, never give them presents, support them when they were sick or hurt, love and protect them until they were stronger than himself. "Oh, sweet Jesus," he sobbed brokenly. "What have I done?"

He rode hard and the animal between his legs was the fastest that could be bought when he'd purchased it in Independence. Isaac outdistanced whatever pursuit was mounted. By the time he reached Independence, the shock of killing a quick-triggered lawman had worn off, and he was thinking clearly again. Gone were his dreams of owning a farm and raising his sons. That was ashes now. But he was not by nature a man who could live alone or without a dream so he set his mind on the future. If he was banished from the cities and his two beloved children, he would live with the Utes in the mountains of Colorado. He had come to love the mountains, maybe he could find peace with Chipeta.

Guilt assailed him. Shouldn't he mourn Catherine's death for a time before thinking of another woman? Yes. But he could not help feeling the way he did, and there was no sense trying to deny the fact that he was not the same man who had left his family in St. Louis more than a year before. What was done was done. He would not lose himself in yesterdays. Instead, he was determined to build a new life, a life that he could not have imagined during the awful years he had worked in his father-in-law's general store. A life of freedom.

Isaac raised his chin and galloped into Independence, resolved to rebuild and renew himself. Maybe someday he could reclaim his sons. Certainly, he would send them letters whenever he could, though he doubted they would ever receive them.

In Independence, he bought a string of eight pack and saddle horses, along with four hundred dollars' worth of beads, cloth, knives, and other trade goods. He also bought three new Hawken rifles and enough ammunition for a year. Isaac declined buying any beaver traps or whiskey.

"What kind of mountain man are you that isn't interested in drinking whiskey and trapping beaver?" the store clerk asked with a smile.

"No mountain man at all," he said quietly.

He loaded the eight horses and rode west toward the Shining Mountains of Colorado. The tracks he followed across the sweeping prairie were his own, and he saw nothing for weeks except millions of buffalo and prairie dogs, along with a few hawks and antelope. With unerring direction, he went straight over the ridge to Spirit Lake, and then followed the Grand River until he found the Ute village where he had traded Chipeta.

His arrival created a sensation. The Utes were renowned for their horse-stealing ability, but for a single man to have so many loaded with trade goods was impressive. In sign language, he said, "Where is Running Wolf?"

The warrior emerged from his tepee. Isaac dismounted and, in swift movements, he told the warrior that he had come to trade for Chipeta.

Running Wolf must have been surprised, though his face revealed no emotion. His eyes passed over the heavily laden string of horses. He said that he was very pleased with Chipeta. She was a good woman.

"Five horses," Isaac said, making the sign for horses and not caring that he was rash with his desire for the Ute girl and willing to pay anything for her. Indians liked to dicker, Isaac did not. "Running Wolf, you gave me only three horses for the woman."

Running Wolf shook his head, and his hands moved quickly. "Now, I want eight horses."

Isaac said no. He went to his pack and brought out a handful of beads and one of the new Hawken rifles. He signed, "Five horses and the rifle, beads, and ammunition. With such a rifle, Running Wolf will become rich and a great chief for slaying all his Arapaho enemies."

The warrior could not contain his joy. He grabbed the rifle and studied it lovingly. His chest swelled, and his eyes

shone with pride as he surveyed the horses and the trade
goods and beads. With a slashing motion, he said, "Done!"

Isaac clapped Running Wolf on the shoulder. He showed
him how to load the rifle, and then he demonstrated how it was
to be aimed and fired. The new Hawken was a thing of power
and beauty. Isaac pulled the trigger and a pine cone hanging off
a limb forty yards away exploded. The village children
screeched and ran to examine what was left of the shattered
cone.

Out of the corner of his eye, Isaac saw Chipeta standing in
front of Running Wolf's tepee. He felt his mouth go dry with
the desire to hold her and gaze into her face, to hear her
laughter again and her singing. As he handed the rifle and new
powder horn to Running Wolf and watched the warrior as he
reloaded, Isaac could barely keep his wits about himself.

"Now aim and squeeze the trigger slowly," he said.

Running Wolf also aimed at a pine cone. When the big
Hawken banged out fire and smoke, Running Wolf was kicked
halfway around. His bullet smashed off a limb that fell to the
ground, and the village cried out with surprise and admiration.

Running Wolf's shoulder must have hurt something terrible, but he was grinning from ear to ear.

Isaac walked over to the Ute woman. He did not trust his
voice to speak but he said, "You're a wild woman, Chipeta.
Wild and beautiful. I'm taking you away."

She understood and, though she was trained not to show
emotion, he could see tears of happiness fill her eyes. They
would leave at once, find Kicking Elk's village, and live one
day and one season at a time. With Chipeta, it would be
enough.

≈ **BOOK TWO** ≈

≈ NATHAN ≈

Fourteen years had passed since Nathan had followed a procession of black-clad mourners through the streets of St. Louis. Imprinted in his young mind like a daguerreotype was the image of the deputy's widow—grief stricken, accusing, filled with sorrow but also of hatred for Isaac, and even for his two small sons. Nathan and Matthew had grown up in St. Louis cursed with a stigma that nothing could erase. They were the sons of a murderer. Sons of a man who had deserted his wife.

"I hate our father!" Matthew had confessed one day after a crowd of schoolboys had taunted, then provoked him into a fight he could not win.

Nathan had kept his own feelings to himself for they were confused and troubling. It would have been very easy to also hate Isaac except for one thing—he alone had seen the deputy start to pull the trigger that would have ended Isaac's life. The deputy had been a fool. But still . . . Nathan could not bury the memory of how his father had driven the huge knife into the young lawman's belly so hard it had lifted him off his feet. Just the image of the deputy's face at his moment of death sometimes caused Nathan to awaken in the night bathed in a cold sweat.

The frightening image of that moment had never changed, but the city had. St. Louis was now busting at the seams of its breeches and there was little time to dwell on the past. Their general store was expanding to meet the needs of a growing population. And the mountain men, instead of floating their plews down the Missouri River in bull-boats, now traded furs for supplies at the annual rendezvous, so there were fewer of them on the streets of St. Louis. Yet, whenever Nathan saw an especially tall, broad-shouldered trapper dressed in buckskins and carrying a Hawken, he felt his heart beat faster until he was sure it was not his father. There were times when he wanted to see his father and ask him so many questions about the mountains and the Indians, about trapping, and what it was like to live your life in the wilderness. But Isaac had, it seemed, forgotten his sons.

Matthew had not forgotten the father he had never known. From his earliest years, his grandparents had fostered a hatred for Isaac Beard that bordered on an obsession. When Matthew was thirteen, he'd declared he would kill his father if Isaac were ever crazy enough to return to St. Louis. But Nathan was sure that would never happen. Isaac Beard was a bad memory, almost a nightmare. He would not return.

But in a way, he did. On a quiet spring morning, Matthew approached his older brother on the street and handed him a letter.

"What's this?"

"Open it and see," Matthew said. At sixteen, he was already taller than Nathan and ox-strong, with heavy brows, powerful arms, and a massive, pugnacious jaw. His nose was bent and he looked ten years older than he was because of his intimidating size and battle scars. "There've been others like it. Some I threw away, some Grandpa tore up before I saw 'em. You know who they're from."

"No, I don't."

"It's from him," Matthew spat. "Just open and read the damned thing and tell me what you think."

Nathan stared at the soiled, crumpled envelope. "Him" could only mean his father, yet, after all these years . . . "Why didn't you tell me about them before?"

"'Cause I figured the sonofabitch would stop sending 'em after a while. But he didn't. I just got tired of keeping it a secret."

Nathan removed and then unfolded the letter and began to read aloud, not caring that the paper shook in his grasp.

Dear sons,

    Once more I send greetings without daring to hope you will receive this message or care if I am dead or alive. But I am alive and content living in the

Rocky Mountains with my adopted people, the Ute Indians. I told you before about how I bought Chipeta back and she became my woman. I guess you can call me a squaw man and think bad of me, but maybe someday you will come west to see us and know better. It is spring and trappers are at work along the rivers and the ponds. Someday, the beaver will be all gone and then the trappers will go, too. I will be glad.

Well, that is all I can say now. I will explore the Grand River again this summer. Maybe find me an ocean or even gold. I will write this fall and send the letter if someone comes through to deliver it to St. Louis. Grow strong and wise. I still remember your beautiful mother.

Isaac Beard

When he finished reading the letter, Nathan looked up to see his brother's face contorted with rage. "He remembers my mother! Does he remember he deserted her to die! They say he's a giant. Bigger'n me. Well, he's old now. And if I ever get my hands on him, I'll tear him apart."

"If you do that, Grandma and Grandpa will remember that you're just like your father. Somehow, you've managed to hide your black moods and anger from them."

Matthew expelled a deep breath. "It tears you up inside that I'm the favored one, doesn't it? You, with your quiet ways and perfect manners. You who are always under control, never shouting or saying anything in anger. You're the one that's always curried their favor. Working all the time in that damned general store. It won't make any difference. I am favored."

Nathan managed to say, "I want to see any more letters that come for us."

"Why?"

"Because he's my father!"

"What about Mother!"

Nathan was shaking with anger. He no longer cared if Matthew could whip him or not. "I WANT those letters."

During the next few years, more letters came from Isaac, and Nathan kept and treasured them all. The letters did not vary much in their content. They were always about the mountains, the animals and the forest, the trees, and Isaac's adopted Ute people. Little by little, Nathan learned of the Ute customs. For instance, he learned that the Utes loved to sing and dance. There were important dances for almost every occasion, even for the tribe's arrival at a new campsite. They would dance before leaving on one of the very dangerous, but vital, buffalo hunts they made in enemy territory down on the Great Plains. They would also dance to build courage before battle and after a battle, either in victory or defeat. Dances were held for every season and, in springtime, the most important spiritual dance of all, *"mamaqui mowats,"* the Bear Dance, was held. In a very long letter, Isaac told his sons that the "Bear Dance" originated centuries ago when a Ute brave dreamed he had come upon a great hibernating bear late one spring day. Knowing that the bear should have awakened weeks ago and might die of starvation if it continued to sleep, and having too much respect for the bear to kill it while it slumbered, the Ute hunter risked his life to gently awaken the bear. As a reward for his bravery and respect, the Spirit Bear took the warrior to a spiritual place where every bear in the world was dancing to celebrate the end of a hard winter. In his honor, the bears taught the Ute warrior their special dance and told him to teach it to the Ute people for it would bring them good fortune. Ever since, the Ute people had celebrated the springtime regeneration of life with a Bear Dance.

Through the letters, Nathan came to understand that his father's mind was simple and direct, like the man himself, and Nathan came to feel he could almost see Isaac, though he had no picture, and the image of the giant man in buckskins was a murky fantasy. Sometimes the letters came with drawings. Lots of them. They were always unsigned, but of rare artistic quality. As detailed and as vivid as anything Nathan had seen published from the Lewis and Clark or Fremont expeditions, they showed scenes of Indian camps, Indian clothing, and the dances that his father so loved to be a part of. Some were of wild animals, and Nathan learned what a live beaver looked like after seeing thousands of their pelts.

When Nathan was twenty-two, his grandfather died but only his grandmother shed real tears. Everett T. Wilke had not been a likable man, only a very successful one. The funeral was brief, and the guests who came calling were few. A few days later, when Grandma recovered enough to speak, she said, "It was your grandfather's wish that you and Matthew inherit the general store when I am gone to join him. Serve me well, and his will shall be done. Someday, you will be rich young men. And you can thank your dear Grandpa."

"Will I run the store?" Nathan asked.

"Oh no," Mrs. Wilke said. "You are still too inexperienced. Besides, I'm afraid there's too much of your father in you for that much responsibility. Mr. Beard could have had everything, and he threw it all away. I can't take the chance you'll do the same. Your Uncle William will be coming from Baltimore to oversee the store."

Nathan bit back angry words. He had met Uncle William once and still harbored an intense dislike for the bloated, opinionated man.

"We don't need him," Matthew said.

Grandmother waved her hand in dismissal. "I now make the decisions."

Nathan worked for his uncle because he had no trade, nor had he ever thought about anything but being in a general store. But it was hard. Their uncle was a pompous man in his fifties who made no effort to hide the fact that he deeply resented that the store would one day pass to his nephews instead of himself. He did everything possible to make Nathan look like a fool.

"You're as worthless as your father was in here," William would complain. "You ain't as big or as clumsy, but you're just as slow to get the work done."

It was at the end of a particularly trying day when a mountain man sauntered through the door just as the store was closing. He was of medium height and had probably been considered handsome in his youth. His buckskin hunting jacket and breeches fit tightly, as if he'd made a squaw take great care to fit them so they accentuated his wide shoulders and slim waist, his powerful arms and muscular thighs. Few mountain men gave a damn how they looked but this one was an exception. The beadwork on his jacket was extraordinary and his hair was even cut so that you could see his ears. He wore a seashell ring on one finger and a big silver bracelet inlaid with turquoise and jade around one wrist that must have weighed two pounds. It was a magnificent piece of Indian jewelry that Nathan would have paid plenty to own.

But the man's youth was fading. There were streaks of gray in his hair and anyone could see that he was a good ten years past his prime and that the sun and wind already had etched deep wrinkles in his face. Still, he was such an unusual sort that Nathan had watched him walk up the street, noting how he seemed to lean way forward as if he could not get anywhere fast enough. His eyes were deepset, and they flicked around the interior of the store as if he could examine every one of the thousands of items in a single glance and dismiss all but a precious few as beneath his interest. His mustache and beard were thin and scraggly, not at all becoming. He radiated vitality and looked ferret-quick.

"May I help you, sir?" Nathan asked.

But William pushed forward and said, "Sir, I'm afraid we've just closed shop. You can come back tomorrow."

The mountain man leaned back and seemed to sniff the air as if for some unseen danger. Finding none, he snorted, "You ain't closed. Why, I just walked through your front door, didn't I? Besides, I ain't here to buy nothin' today. I come to see Nathan and Matthew Beard."

"I'm Nathan Beard."

William wasn't pleased. "You know your grandma don't like you talking to strangers."

The mountain man ignored the remark and stuck out his hand, which was as rough as the bark of a tree. "I'm Julius Aubrey and I got a letter from your pa but it's over at the Buffalo Gal Saloon along with my saddlebags and rifle. You or your brother want it?"

Nathan looked at his uncle. If he said yes, he'd catch hell from his grandmother. "Yes!"

"Good!" Aubrey grinned and gestured toward the apron that Nathan wore. "When you get rid of that damn thing, come join me over at the saloon for a drink. That is, if you drink."

Aubrey was toying with him and it infuriated Nathan. The reference to the apron had been uncalled for. "I'll be there," he said, aware that his uncle was glowering his disapproval.

When Aubrey slammed the door on his way out, his uncle wasted no time in giving him hell, "Nathan, you know better than to associate with the likes of him! He stinks. They all do. And even worse, he's a friend of your father."

Nathan untied the apron. "What my father is or isn't doesn't concern you."

William's lips curled with contempt. "You're a Beard, all right. Both you and your brother are cut from the same dirty bolt of cloth. You're . . ."

Nathan hit him. His fist connected on the point of his uncle's jaw and sent him crashing backward into a shelf of canned goods. The entire shelf collapsed and William was buried by tinned goods. He waved his arms feebly but could not find the strength to push the cans away and get back on his feet. Instead, he hissed, "Just wait until I tell your grandmother. Just wait! All along we knew you were no good—and you've just proved you're violent and dangerous."

Nathan ripped the apron from his waist, balled it up, and hurled it to the floor. "You may deprive me of all this, but you won't ever get it away from Matt. Try to discredit or dishonor my brother and he'll beat you to death with his bare hands."

Nathan tore his starched white collar from his throat and headed for the Buffalo Gal Saloon. For years, he had endured his grandfather's disapproval and slurs. It had seemed like a godsend when the intolerant old man had finally died. Now, Uncle William had driven him out of the store and probably even his share of the inheritance. Grandmother would not tolerate violence, and she'd always believed that he was a violent man. For some reason, she had chosen to overlook Matthew's dark and dangerous moods. Oh, the hell with it all!

He pushed into the saloon and spotted Aubrey at the far end. The man was sitting alone, loose-like, with his chair tipped back against the wall. His big buffalo rifle was lying across his lap and a pair of saddlebags were on the table along with an empty glass.

Nathan felt angry and reckless. He bought whiskey and took two dirty glasses back to Aubrey. Filling the glasses to the brim while the mountain man watched, he grabbed the bottle and drank from it straight. "I'll have my father's letter."

While Aubrey dug it out of his saddlebags, Nathan drank

both glasses full of whiskey and, almost immediately, he felt a whole lot better.

"Sit down and rest your legs," Aubrey said, sliding the letter across the scarred barroom table and watching the younger man. "You seem techy. But then, any man who'd have to work all day in a store *would* be techy. How come you stayed all these years in this stinkhole town instead of comin' to the Rockies to live with your father?"

Nathan took the letter and jammed it into his pocket. "My father deserted my mother, and I never even knew he was alive until just a few years ago."

"Do you remember anything about him?"

Nathan shook his head. "Is he a good man?"

"The best. He's known as Tall Horse among the Utes, and he's killed plenty of their enemies. He could be a chief if he wanted and have a bunch of squaws. But he sticks with Chipeta. Your pa loves that woman. He says he ain't no mountain man, and maybe, since he don't trap much except to get some things for the tribe, maybe he really ain't no mountain man. But he'll do. Your pa will do any way you care to measure man against man."

Aubrey took a long pull on the whiskey bottle. He wiped his black beard with the back of his sleeve. His eyes had already begun to shine with the glow of his drinking. "One thing I'll have to admit, city whiskey is a hell of a lot better'n what Ashley and his boys bring to the rendezvous for tradin'."

Nathan had heard of the famous gatherings of the mountain men called the rendezvous where mountain men traded their furs for whiskey, supplies, and the favors of Indian women. It was said that the rendezvous were orgies the likes of which had not been had since Roman times. Every young man in St. Louis would have given his right arm to attend one, and Nathan was no exception. "I'd like to go to one of those," he said.

"They be something, all right. Waugh!" Aubrey barked, the sound not unlike that of a circus bear Nathan once had seen who wrestled men for two bits. "They be mountain men that are livin' legends. Indian women plenty damn willin' to hop into the willows with a mountain man for a few beads or some pretty-dads or jingos."

"My pa wrote once and said he never went to a rendez-vous."

Aubrey's wide grin melted. "Your pa, he's sorta a queer fella. He just don't want a whole lot to do with white people. Oh, he'll be sociable enough to a man who don't try to trap all the beaver outa his territory or take too much of the Utes' game. But except for crazy old Mellon and . . ."

"Who's Mellon?"

"The artist! The one that married Snow Bird and travels around writin' and sketchin' things. He's mighty good. Cost you plenty to have him do your picture, but he'll do it." Aubrey winked. "You want to see mine?"

"Sure."

Aubrey reached into his beautiful hunting jacket, which seemed to have lots of pockets sewn inside. "Feast your eyes on this!"

Nathan watched the man unfold the sketch and smooth it out on the rough wooden table. It was done in pencil and it was very flattering and exceedingly good. Nathan recognized the style. "My pa has sent some of his drawings to Matthew and me. I saved them."

"Well, you oughta! Everyone keeps telling crazy Mellon he could be rich if he brung his drawings to St. Louie. But he don't care about money any more'n your pa. They say they don't want nothing you could buy with money." Aubrey shook his head. "I tell you, both of 'em strike me as being teched."

Nathan handed the sketch back to the mountain man. "I whacked my Uncle William after you left," he said, deciding he didn't need to fool with a glass either.

"Good! I'd a done it myself, except that the law would probably want to come put me in jail, and then I'd have to kill one or two like your pa did years ago."

"It was self-defense. I was there. I saw the whole thing."

"Sometimes lawmen need killin' most of all. I generally have no good use for a man with a badge. They figure they can do about what they please with a man—could be that is the way it's done in the city. But no one will ever lock a mountain man up for long. He'll either die fightin', or he'll die behind bars. Mountain man, he gotta be free! Always free! It's in our blood."

He squinted and poked a forefinger at Nathan. "Could be, it's in your blood, too, and you don't even know it!"

"Maybe." Nathan drank more whiskey. "Mr. Aubrey," he said, "I want to see my father and the Rocky Mountains."

"You sure?"

"Yeah. I'm finished here. I could tuck my tail between my legs and beg forgiveness but it'd half kill me and lately, I've already been feeling half dead."

"Then I'll take you! It'd make your pa most happy. And we'll take your little brother, too!"

"Uh-uh," Nathan said. "In the first place, he ain't so little. He's a couple inches taller than me and a damn sight stronger. And in the second place, he hates Isaac's guts. He'd as soon shoot him as cuss his name."

Aubrey's face clouded. "That's mighty wrong," he said gravely. "A man should never hate his father or his mother. And if he kills 'em . . . well, that'd be about the worstus sin I could ever think of. For a fact, it'd be."

"Matthew blames his father for everything. You see, after the deputy was stabbed to death, it was mighty hard on us for a long time. And Matthew, he looks like his father. They say he's almost as big. Right now, he's only eighteen but he's fully grown. He backs down from no man."

Aubrey had another drink on that. He pulled at his scraggly mustache and looked troubled. "When you want to leave town?"

"How about now?"

Aubrey smiled. "You're sudden, boy. But sudden or not, you're still going to need supplies. A horse and a Hawken rifle."

"I got a horse and the rest of it I got coming from the store," Nathan said. "I've outfitted enough men like you to know what I need and don't need."

"Then do it," Aubrey said. "And when you're ready, you just let out a holler or fire your Hawken. I'll know the sound and come runnin'."

Nathan stood up and was surprised he felt a little dizzy. But even if his mind was clouded by drink, his purpose was clear as he headed for the door.

Late that evening, Nathan slipped into the big house

where he and Matthew lived with their grandmother. A pale shaft of moonlight guided his way through the back door, across the kitchen, and down a narrow hallway, past the old German grandfather clock. But he had to tiptoe in darkness up the stairs to his brother's room. Out under the apple tree where he'd left it tied, his big sorrel gelding stood, saddled and carrying his new Hawken rifle and a few provisions. He did not have a pack animal, so he'd be living off the country.

Clearheaded again, his mind was awhirl with excitement, and he could barely keep himself from racing up the stairs and shouting the news of his new adventure. The grandfather clock struck one and Nathan opened the door to his brother's room.

"Matt?" He was praying that his brother was not carousing somewhere down by the waterfront as was his nature.

"What do you want?"

The sudden wakefulness of his brother's voice caught Nathan by surprise and he stammered, "I came to say good-bye."

"Where you going?"

"To see the mountains. And Pa."

"Jesus Christ!" Matthew swore. "You been drinking too much whiskey or what?"

"I'm serious."

"Then you're a fool. If you run out now, it's finished. You won't get anything. Not a cent."

Nathan bristled. "The store has brought me no happiness. It won't bring you any either. And if you'd try to forgive Pa for . . ."

"Enough!" Matthew rasped. "I don't want to hear your craziness. There's never been a Beard that's had anything of his own. I thought you and me would change all that."

"I hit Uncle William."

"So I heard. I'll take care of him if that's what this is all about."

"No. It's more than that. I'm finished here. St. Louis is no good for me."

"How can you say that! We were born and raised here. You don't know anything *but* this town. Use your head, Nate! If you walk out now, there's no coming back, and you're going to regret this for the rest of your life."

"I said it's finished."

"You stupid . . . aw, Christ, get out of here! You disgust me. You'll wind up old and broken, with nothing but rags on your back and a fat, ugly old squaw to sit in the dirt and pinch fleas with."

Nathan looked out the second-story window and saw the pale moon shining down on the apple tree and his horse. "I've never been so happy as I am now," he whispered. "I should have gone long ago."

"Then you and I are finished. It's done between us. I won't have people saying that my brother wasn't worth anything more than my pa. If you go, then you stay gone!"

"I'll stay."

He was in such a hurry to leave that he missed a step and almost tumbled down the stairs. But he caught himself on the railing, and he heard his grandmother calling out his name. She'd want to berate him for striking Uncle William. Well, he thought, she could count sheep until hell froze over before he'd crawl and grovel under her thumb one more minute.

Outside, the air seemed sharp and sweet. He mounted his horse and gazed up at Matthew's window. His brother filled the opening. Nathan waved but Matthew turned away, leaving the window vacant.

Nathan galloped into town, and when he reached the Buffalo Gal Saloon, he remembered that Aubrey had told him to signal with his Hawken. Hell, he'd never even fired one before but this was as good a time and place as any—or was it? The street was lined with horses tied to the hitching rail, and the thought passed through Nathan's mind that firing a fifty-caliber buffalo rifle in downtown St. Louis might not be the best idea in the world. But the hell with it! He was going west to be a mountain man, wasn't he? And mountain men obeyed their own rules.

Nathan raised his new Hawken to his shoulder and pulled the trigger. The explosion astonished him. The roar filled his ears, the smoke his nostrils, and the kick of the rifle knocked him sideways in his saddle. His horse reacted no less dramatically as it bolted, sending him crashing into the dirt. Horses all along the street reared back and broke their reins and, a minute later, men plunged out of the saloons. Cursing and yelling, they went racing after their horses. A knot of men from the Buffalo Gal, whose horses had been stampeded by the tremendous blast, gathered around Nathan. One of them, a burly man in a red-checkered wool shirt, said, "You dumb sonofabitch! You ran off my horse and I'm gonna take yours!"

Nathan sprang to his feet. "The hell you are!"

The man swung, and his fist exploded against Nathan's jaw. For the second time in as many minutes, Nathan found himself sprawled on the ground. He had trouble getting to his feet. Groggy and weaving, he tried to defend himself, but the big man waded in and sent him back to the ground once more. Nathan tasted blood in his mouth. With considerable difficulty, he managed to get to his knees and, as he was pushing himself to his feet, the man kicked out with his boot. The boot was directed at Nathan's exposed throat. It would have broken his windpipe or his neck but the boot never connected. Julius Aubrey's Hawken slashed downward and cracked the man's shinbone. He bellowed in pain and began to hop around on one foot.

Aubrey grabbed Nathan by the collar and helped him to stand. Blood was running from his mouth and his eyes were glassy, but there was nothing wrong with his hearing, and he distinctly heard Aubrey say, "Soon as I teach you how to ride and shoot, I'm going to show you how to fight. I sure can't let your father see such a helpless son."

Nathan nodded woodenly and allowed himself to be helped onto his horse. Aubrey's mount was the only one still tied at the hitching rack. It knew the sound of a Hawken, too.

They rode out of St. Louis with a lot of angry men cussing at them. This sure wasn't the way Nathan had intended to leave. As a mountain man would have said, "It ain't got no shine to it at all!"

Yet, it seemed to Nathan somehow fitting that—like his father—he had set his course in life and there was no turning back.

Nathan Beard was fully aware that buffalo were huge beasts.
He'd heard many a story about how hard they were to kill.
He'd also seen thousands of buffalo hides stacked by the
Missouri River waterfront, the hides often so green that they
stank mightily and drew swarms of flies. They were never
cleanly scraped—except those handled by squaws—and pieces
of meat and fat would give off a stench that could be detected
for miles. Because of the stench and the flies, one did not
venture too near the hide yards, but the piles of huge hides
could still be seen, even from a distance. So Nathan had every
reason to believe that he was prepared for his first glimpse of
a bull buffalo. Yet he was not.

Like his father before him, Nathan was astonished at their
size. The bulls stood six feet at the shoulders, and some
weighed nearly a ton. A fully matured male was a magnificent
creature, often buff colored in the forefront then darker back
toward the tail. Since it was late summer, the ones he saw
were out of coat, and great patches of hair dangled from their
bodies.

Julius Aubrey said, "Them buffalo are the best eatin'
critters on the face of the Earth. Better'n venison or beef.
Better'n elk or even beaver tails roasted over the fire."

"Are we going to hunt some?" Nathan asked.

Aubrey raised his Hawken. "Yep. We'll carve out the best
parts. It'll be our present to the Utes when we arrive."

Nathan had often heard buffalo hunters tell how the herd
would make a stand, and they would kill as many as ten or
fifteen of the great beasts before they stampeded. He asked
Aubrey if that was how they were going to hunt these buffalo.
"Hell, no! That kind of killin' is way too tame for me," he
barked. "No sport in it a'tall. What we'll do is chase 'em down,

shoot a couple of young cows, and butcher 'em. Check your rifle, Nate."

Nathan checked his rifle. He watched Aubrey put an extra ball into his mouth. It made a lump in the outline of his cheek but it did not impair his speech. "An Indian or a good hunter can creep up slow and get within a hundred yards of 'em before they'll notice. I seen Indians wearin' the skins of wolves, or else holding brush up in front of them, get close enough to kill a buffalo with an arrow. But that crawlin' stuff is not to my likin'. Most likely, they'll spot us horseback within a quarter mile and start runnin'. If your sorrel is as fast as it looks, you'll catch 'em quick enough. Then you gotta make your first shot count."

"Where do I shoot? Behind the ear?"

"Aim right behind the shoulders. Hit the lungs or the heart but don't expect the animal to fall. I've shot a ball right through the center of their heart and they still ran for a couple more miles. I saw a Comanche drive his lance clear through a bull's lungs and he kept runnin'. They're tough to bring down."

"I'm not a good shot," Nathan confessed.

"Well," the mountain man said, "as you can see, there's plenty more buffalo to shoot than you got bullets or powder. With practice, you'll get better. If you miss or take a bad shot, just reload on the run. Pound the butt plate of that Hawken to seat the bullet after you've set the powder charge. It'll work. Best check your cinch. I once seen a man's cinch come apart during a chase and we couldn't find any pieces of him after the dust finally cleared."

Nathan dismounted and checked his cinch. He could feel his heart starting to pound with anticipation. He put a ball into his mouth and tongued it around to rest against the inside of his cheek. His nervousness infected his horse, and the animal began to dance. Nathan knew that they were in for a long chase, and his horse was already sweating. He remounted with no small amount of difficulty.

"Them buffalo will try to find rough ground," Aubrey said in a low voice as they closed in on the herd. "The rougher the country, the better their chances for escape. They seem to know that a man on horseback doesn't like to risk his neck.

They kin run across a prairie dog town at full tilt and never put
their hooves in a single hole. But a man on a racing horse . . .
just don't go down under 'em."

"I've no intention of doing that," Nathan replied. They
were within a half mile of the herd now. Several of the bulls
lifted their heads and sniffed the breeze. They began to walk
nervously back and forth.

"Do they see us?"

Aubrey nodded. "Kit Carson says they got weak eyes, but
I don't believe that none. They see us all right or else they
caught our scent, even though we're coming from downwind.
They'll be stampeding in a minute or two."

Nathan held his breath. He could not believe he was
hundreds of miles west of St. Louis and on a buffalo hunt.
Nothing he had ever done had even approached this kind of
excitement. "There they go!" he cried.

Aubrey had anticipated the herd's sudden movement, and
he got out to a twenty-yard head start over Nathan. But the
sorrel was fast and caught, then raced past, the mountain man.
All at once, Nathan was enveloped in the huge cloud of dust
that billowed up behind the fleeing herd. Missouri River fog
had never been thicker than this, and he had no choice but to
give his horse free rein as it plunged after the buffalo herd. His
eyes teared badly, and he felt as if he could not breathe. With
the Hawken gripped in one hand and his reins in the other,
Nathan tried to lift his bandanna over his nose, but failed. He
tasted grit in his mouth and prayed his gelding would see any
obstacles or holes in its path.

On and on they ran, with dirt and gravel stinging his
cheeks. All at once, he seemed to be running right up the
backs of the cows and calves. Nathan spotted a cow that looked
as if she had no calf. He reined his horse too close. The cow
reached back and hooked at Nathan. Her horns caught his
stirrups and, for a terror-filled instant, he thought he was
going to be ripped from his horse and sent tumbling under the
buffalo he had already overtaken.

But his stirrup pulled free, and Nathan leaned forward,
the barrel of his rifle extending to within three feet of the
running cow's side. He could see the animal's left eye. It was
blue-black and flecked with blood. The cow tried to hook him

again with her short horns, but now both horse and rider were prepared and stayed just out of reach. Nathan was drunk with exhilaration. Forgotten was the dust and the very real danger of hidden prairie dog and badger holes. All he could see or think about was the cow just a yard from his right knee. He could hear her tortured breathing and see her nostrils dilated with fear, smell her sweat and the sweet, grassy taste of her breath.

Nathan leaned sideways and shoved the big Hawken out from his body until its muzzle was only a hand span from the cow's side. With a primal yell in his throat, he pulled the trigger and the big rifle belched fire and smoke. Its recoil almost sent him flying. The cow staggered and ran on. Nathan gaped with astonishment, for he could see the round hole in her side where blood began to pump from the chest cavity. It was bright red, and he knew that he had shot the cow through the lungs and maybe even the heart.

"Fall, damn you!" he shouted as he pulled in the Hawken and reached for his powder horn. But the cow kept running. Slower, yes, until the rest of the herd passed them by and they were alone. Nathan spilled powder all over himself trying to get some poured down the barrel. When he thought he could waste no more, he tongued the ball into the barrel, then set it by slamming the gun butt up and down on his saddlehorn. He lost three percussion caps before he got one set firmly onto the nipple and thumbed back the hammer.

The cow was crazed with agony as she staggered after the vanishing herd. She bellowed pathetically, as if calling for help. Her cry sickened Nathan. Eager to dispatch the cow from her misery, he pressed in close and pulled the trigger. The Hawken roared again. Its muzzle blast struck the buffalo cow behind the shoulder, and the beast catapulted into Nathan's path. His horse was unable to dodge the tumbling cow and fell. Nathan kicked loose from his stirrups and was launched into the air. He struck the ground and had the wind slammed from his chest. For a second, he lay stunned, then staggered to his feet, but so did the mortally wounded cow. His gelding stayed down, head thrashing against the earth, foreleg broken.

With its last breath, the cow lunged at the fallen horse.

Her little horns caught the helpless sorrel in the neck. Nathan drew his big hunting knife and rushed the cow, wishing he had never seen a buffalo. He wrapped his arms around her shaggy head and drove the blade of his knife into her throat. Warm blood poured down his sleeve and bathed his torso. The cow moaned, then collapsed and died.

Nathan recoiled from the animal. His horse was still thrashing on the ground, and he swore in helpless fury as he went for his Hawken. His hands were slick with blood and shaking so badly he spilled several ounces of powder before he had a full charge. He found another ball and nipple and reloaded once again before walking unsteadily to his horse. He knelt beside the animal and spoke to it softly and when it quieted for a moment, Nathan shot it behind the ear.

He stood up and surveyed the prairie. He recognized the dark humps of three more buffalo stretched out across the horizon. Two of Julius Aubrey's buffalo were still twitching. Long minutes passed, and the prairie was incredibly empty. Silence expanded the distances, and Nathan felt himself shrink against the huge land. He had never felt so alone, just the sky, the grass, and the dead buffalo. He waited impatiently and when it felt as if hours had passed, he saw Aubrey on the northern horizon, just a dark speck against the tabletop of grassland, then a figure, and then a man and a horse. Aubrey dismounted at the most distant kill. Nathan saw his knife glint in the sun as it was drawn from its sheath to be plunged into the buffalo.

Nathan reloaded his Hawken, for Julius Aubrey had already impressed upon him that it was the first rule of survival. Always. He took his saddle blankets, bedroll, and provisions from the dead sorrel, feeling very low and vulnerable on foot. It grieved him to leave his saddle and to lose such a fine horse, but he was a man learning not to dwell on his mistakes so he started walking. He would have to do a lot of walking before he reached the Rocky Mountains. It was said that a man afoot was doomed on the Great Plains. Nathan pulled off his shirt and scrubbed the blood from his arms and torso. He felt sick about the way this whole episode had turned out, but maybe he was lucky to be alive. And now that his heart was starting to beat normally again, he had to admit that the hunt had been the greatest thrill of his young life.

I will learn to butcher buffalo, he resolved, and then I will feast like a mountain man.

"All right, Pilgrim," Aubrey said, disgusted about the loss of a good horse, "the way to butcher a buffalo is to roll her over on her belly and pull out the legs so she'll stay right side up. So grab a leg and give me a hand."

Nathan did as he was told. The cow looked ridiculous, lying on her stomach with her legs pointed out in all four directions, her massive jaws resting on the grass, and her tongue lolling out of the side of her mouth.

"First, you cut out the tongue."

Nathan quailed. "I don't think I'd like tongue."

Aubrey grabbed the tongue and pulled it far out of the mouth before sawing it off with his Green River knife. He pitched the tongue aside, made an incision along the spine, and then quickly cut down both sides so that two squares of hide lay flat on the ground. "I favor the 'boss'," he said, slicing off a small hump on the back of the neck, "and then the hump itself."

Nathan watched in morbid fascination as the mountain man went at the dead cow. After the boss and the hump, Aubrey took the "hump ribs," which appeared to Nathan to be the meat along the upper vertebrae. Next, he took what he called the "fleece," which was the meat between the spine and the ribs. Finally, he sliced off the "side ribs" and cut himself a generous slab of "belly fat."

"You like liver?" Aubrey asked, eating the belly fat raw so that globs of it stuck to his thin mustache and beard.

"No."

"Damned greenhorn," Aubrey muttered, burying his knife into the cow and quickly pulling out big chunks of liver. "Before you leave the Shining Mountains, there'll be winter days when you'll like moccasin leather."

Nathan started to feel a little queasy when Aubrey again jammed his fists into the abdominal cavity and tore out a five-foot length of intestine that bulged with partially digested feed.

"These are called 'boudins'," the man growled, "and you can't be a mountain man lest you eat 'em raw!"

To demonstrate, he held up the quivering white entrails and threw back his head. Then, before Nathan's horrified eyes, he fed the entire length of intestine into his mouth, his throat and jaws working like those of a big snake when it devours its prey.

Nathan turned around and vomited.

Ten days later, Nathan stood on the snowy crest of the Continental Divide. It was fall, and down in the gulleys and ravines, carved and fed by spring runoff, the aspen were ablaze with autumn colors. As Nathan gazed back at the Great Plains, he marveled that he had survived, even enjoyed, the long walk across the plains and then the climb up the eastern slope of the Rockies. Every ounce of fat he'd carried out of St. Louis had been expended and now he was long-limbed and angular. His face was dark brown, as were the backs of his neck and hands. He already carried his rifle like a man who considered it a part of himself, and his eyes had taken on the farsighted appearance of one who was accustomed to vast, empty distances. To the east and south, dark thunderclouds blanketed the plains, and Nathan could see bolts of lightning dart out to strike the Earth. Wisps of thunderclouds steaked down to the prairie where heavy rain fell. The chain of peaks he saw reaching to the north butted up against an overhang of dark thunderheads, and a fresh, cold wind blew a veil of snow off their crowns. But directly overhead, the sky was a soft, lazy blue, and the sun was shining. Nathan turned his face to the sun and even though he was sweating heavily and his legs were shaking from the long climb, he felt good. Hell, straddling the top of the world, he felt like a god!

"Is that Spirit Lake down there?" he yelled into a stiff wind.

"Yep."

Nathan greedily sucked in the thin mountain air, and his eyes tracked beyond the lake to catch glimpses of a river. It was silver in the sunlight and wound south rather than west as he had supposed it would. When he asked Aubrey about it, the man said, "It turns southwest and flows into the Mormon's desert. Nobody knows where she runs after that. Isaac has seen as much of it as any man."

Nathan straightened and eased the makeshift pack straps that bit into his broad shoulders. When he'd lost his horse, he'd been forced to abandon everything except what he could carry or talk Aubrey into shifting to his pack animal. He'd saved some traps and a few trinkets, as well as his father's letters. "Do you think Pa will mind me trapping beaver in this country?"

"I'm doing it, ain't I? Hell, Nate, I consider Isaac my friend and he'd be the first to say the beaver don't belong to him. Maybe they don't even belong to the Utes. I say they's free to take by any man."

"I'd want his permission," Nathan said. "And if it wasn't freely given, I'd keep on going until I passed out of these mountains and found new streams."

Aubrey barked a laugh. "You're a regular Jim Bridger, ain't you?"

"No," Nathan said, "but the more I see of this country, the more I want to see."

Aubrey nodded with approval. "You just give yourself a little time to learn the lay of the land, Pilgrim. Learn how to live off it and how to avoid gettin' your scalp raised."

"I'll stay with Pa awhile," Nathan said, "but I won't burden him."

"Let's push on down," Aubrey said. "They's a storm comin' our way and I want to be in the trees when she hits. It'll be cold after sundown."

Nathan followed the man, and he had not walked more than a few miles down into the forest when the sun seemed to vanish and the first heavy raindrops of a summer storm wet his eyelashes. Aubrey rode faster now and as the storm drew down upon them, it became intense. Huge bolts of lightning crashed, and the skies seemed to open up, leaving Nathan drenched and chilled.

"It ain't the rain I mind," Aubrey shouted, "it's the damned lightning! You don't want to be up above the timberline when it's stormin' like this!"

As if to punctuate the message, a massive lightning bolt struck a tree near the summit, and Nathan saw it smoke and flame. He hurried on, squeezing rainwater from his eyes and trying not to slip on wet pine needles. Up above, the trees were moaning as strong, gusty winds whipped their boughs into a frenzy.

"This is as good as there is to be found," Aubrey yelled, pulling in under a thick canopy of trees and dismounting. He hobbled and unsaddled his horse before he dragged his gear under an overhang of rocks and ducked under them himself for cover. "Gonna be a real pisser, this one," he said, looking up at the rain sheeting through the trees. "Might as well hole up for the rest of the day."

Nathan was not sorry to rest. Like the horse, he was hot and steamy from his run, and the air temperature was plummeting. "How about a fire?"

"If it suits you, go ahead."

"Well," Nathan said with irritation, "you're going to want to share it with me, aren't you?"

"I reckon I will," the mountain man replied. He laced his fingers behind his head and squinted upward. "But that don't mean I'm gonna help you build it."

Nathan caught a head and chest cold that wet, miserable night. In the morning, his throat was sore, and his nose ran continuously. He felt lethargic and fevered.

"I guess you better ride and I'll walk," Aubrey grumped. "I can't be bringing Isaac his son half dead."

Nathan thought he should protest but just when he tried he was seized by a chill that left him weak and shivering. It took all his strength to climb into Aubrey's saddle and hang on to the saddle horn. It was drizzling rain, and Nathan yearned for a warm bed.

"There's a little cabin off yonder," Aubrey said. "It belongs to that crazy Mellon fella I told you about, the artist with the squaw and the prettiest little half-breed girl you ever laid eyes on. You want to pay 'em a visit?"

"Yes," he whispered.

"I thought you'd say that," Aubrey grumbled. "I generally stay wide of that man but you look damn peeky to me. I guess there's no choice but to hole up until you're feeling better."

Doug Mellon had watched Julius Aubrey and a tall young

man coming down from the divide for more than an hour. He knew Aubrey and did not care much about him, one way or the other. Aubrey, like all mountain men, was as tough and as merciless as the country and the Indians they fought for their survival. It was Mellon's theory that Julius Aubrey and his kind never gave, only took. They slaughtered the beaver, the bear, and any redmen who got in their way. They sought nothing of a moral, spiritual, or scientific value in the mountains and would not even have come to them had it not been for the prospect of wealth—wealth through the plundering of beaver, or gold and silver.

Mountain men were coarse and cunning. They could not be trusted and had few loyalties except to the almighty dollar. They were barbarians, throwbacks to a bygone era. They were also survivors, men whose senses were often keener than the Indians they emulated in dress and manner. As Mellon watched, he noticed the tall young rider and wondered if he were another would-be mountain man. If so, he was already a failure because it was clear he was sick, weak, and possibly dying.

Snow Bird and sixteen-year-old Justina Mellon also watched the two men approach, one afoot and leading the other on horseback. To Justina, the arrival of strangers was a welcome sight, for it meant conversation and laughter and maybe even some presents. As soon as she recognized Julius Aubrey, she was even more pleased and shouted, "It's Mr. Aubrey. His friend looks ready to fall off that horse. Father?"

"We'll help them," Mellon said. "Prepare food."

"Hello the cabin!" Aubrey shouted. "Sick man a'horse-back. Can we take shelter and food?"

Man and daughter stepped out into the cold rain. "You may. Bring your friend inside."

Justina hurried out to take the reins of the horse. She looked at the sick man and noted that he was quite big and very young. She saw her father and Aubrey help him down from the horse, and she led the animal under the lean-to, where their own horses were kept, and then unsaddled it. She pitched the animal some dry meadow grass and hurried back inside, feeling the air grow colder. Tonight the rain would turn to sleet and hail.

That evening, they ate elk steaks, wild onions, and wild plums for dessert. Justina was as surprised and delighted as her father when the young man, roused by food and warmth, told them he was the elder son of Isaac Beard.

"I know Isaac well! He and I first came to these mountains sixteen, no, I guess it was eighteen years ago. He was our leader, and a good man he was, the only one besides myself to survive this long."

Mellon filled a pipe with tobacco and lit it before continuing. "I guess I know more about you than you could imagine. Nathan, your father loved your mother very much. He mourned when he learned she'd died and he's been talking about you and Matthew for years. Does he know you've come?"

Nathan shook his head.

"What about your brother?"

"He wanted to stay in St. Louis." Nathan did not elaborate.

Mellon just nodded. "That's too bad. You know, maybe me and my family will tag along with you to rejoin the Utes. I'd like to see your father's face when you finally meet after all these years. It'll be something to remember. We'll leave as soon as you are fit to ride."

"I'll be fit tomorrow," Nathan promised.

"We'll wait and see about that. You might be better, but you could be worse."

Nathan said, "My father told me a good deal about you. He said you were . . . different."

Mellon seemed pleased by the description. "I take that as a compliment. I *am* different. Both Isaac and I know what it means to lose our wives. I also lost a son. But that's history. At the time I met your father, I was still half blind with pain. I was searching for redemption in the eyes of a scientific community that I once overvalued."

"Scientific community?" Nathan did not understand.

"Yes. I'm a scientist, an observer of the plan of nature."

"I see," Nathan said, not seeing at all.

Mellon tamped his pipe. "Men like Mr. Aubrey will tell you that the mountains are killers."

"Amen to that!" Aubrey muttered.

"But they're not," Mellon argued. "These mountains are healers of the mind's sickness and once you learn their secrets and appreciate their beauty, they'll give you something worth far more than money."

Aubrey shifted on his buffalo robe. "Pure hogwash!"

"Yes, sir," Nathan said in a distracted tone of voice, for he was unable to keep his mind off the girl. The firelight bathed Justina's skin, giving it a most wonderful glow, and made her black hair shine. It was obvious that she was a half-breed, yet her features were a delicious blend of the Indian and white races. She'd been blessed with her father's lithe build and her mother's large, intelligent eyes, eyes that sparked in the firelight and seemed warm when they touched his face. No doubt about it, Nathan thought, Aubrey had not exaggerated when he said that this girl was beautiful. Nathan looked at the many sketches that were tacked to the cabin walls, remarkable sketches and paintings that included the girl and her mother. "You are a fine artist, Mr. Mellon."

"But I'm not an artist! I remain a scientist. I've been trained in science, like my father. Except for the sketches of my wife and daughter, everything I draw was to be included in my scientific journals. I developed a rudimentary drawing ability to illustrate my articles."

"Beg your pardon," Nathan said, determined to make his point, "but your skills are far more than rudimentary. Have you ever tried to sell any drawings?"

It was the wrong question. "In Chicago, I was offered money for my drawings while my scientific findings were dismissed as if they were of no importance. The members of the Biologic and Anthropologic Society branded me a heretic when I tried to explain that Indians live a way of life far better than most whites."

"My father wrote, stating exactly the same feelings."

"Believe him!" Mellon said with heat in his voice. "It took only one trip back East to remind me how cruel a civilization can become. Ten years ago, I made the mistake—the tragic mistake—of taking Snow Bird and Justina to the city. We dressed in buckskins and beadwork, like Sam Houston when he made the error of wearing Cherokee trappings to impress upon Congress the grim plight of the so-called Five Civilized

Tribes. I also thought . . ." Mellon shook his head as if he might ward off the memory of his return to society, ". . . I thought that by being in tribal dress, we could better be understood. But, like Houston, I was scorned and made a mockery."

Nathan looked to Snow Bird and her daughter. They would not meet his eyes and he suspected they too had been humiliated. "I'm sorry you weren't accepted as a scientist."

Mellon's eyes grew distant. "Someone told me that I could sell my pictures, but could never buy credibility in the scientific community. Not in America. Not in Europe."

"Did you sell your sketches?"

"No."

The mountain man was growing impatient. "Well, why the hell not! Money's money."

Mellon came to his feet. The cabin was small, the roof barely high enough for him to stand upright. "I do not deny there is genius in art," he said, choosing his words with great care, "but art has little purpose save to entertain. It is science and science alone that can elevate the plight of mankind, lead it to a better understanding of the world and the rich diversity of its people. I have no interest at all in art for art's sake. When I sketch or draw, it is but a comic attempt to mimic nature and all her glory. No artist who ever lived could equal nature's brushstrokes. No artist can even approach the beauty of nature or achieve her grandeur."

Nathan did not begin to understand this strange man or the complex workings of his mind. Maybe old Julius was right and Doug Mellon was a little crazy. But to Nathan's way of thinking, he was also a gifted artist.

"Do you understand what I am trying to tell you?" Mellon asked, his voice almost pleading.

"*I* sure as hell don't," Aubrey growled. "I think you were crazy not to sell your pictures."

Mellon threw up his hands in a gesture of exasperation. "Aubrey," he said, "that is exactly what I expected you to say. But there's no going back. I burned my notes and sketches just before leaving Chicago. And that was when I knew I would never return to the corruption and chaos of the cities, their perversions and politics. I started writing again. I came to understand that only the quest for knowledge is important. Now, I am content to write and sketch for my own enjoyment and the enjoyment of my family, who also try to tell me I have some small talent."

Julius Aubrey looked at Mellon and shook his head. "You are crazy as a coot to have burned good pictures worth cash money. Next time you do a fool thing like that, I hope I'm around to shoot you."

Mellon's eyebrows lifted, and then he began to laugh.

≈ 10 ≈

The storm lasted three days and left the high country blanketed with an early snow. Nathan struggled with chills and a raging fever. His lungs were filled with phlegm, and sometimes, when he awoke, he found himself drenched in his own sweat and coughing so hard that lights exploded behind his eyeballs. He knew that Julius Aubrey had gone away. The man simply had not felt comfortable around Doug Mellon. Nathan was too sick to care. He slept and lost track of time.

"Nathan, wake up!" an urgent voice called to him.

He opened his eyes to see Doug Mellon, Justina, Snow Bird, and another Indian standing around the bed. Justina was wearing a stricken look that made Nathan realize something was very wrong.

"This is Walks Long," Mellon said, nodding toward the gaunt young Indian at his shoulder. "He's from another clan of Utes. They've just been attacked by a huge party of northern Cheyenne warriors. We've got to help. Snow Bird's brother, Speckled Snake, has been killed and many squaws and children were taken as slaves."

Nathan was fully awake now. "What can I . . ."

"Nothing," Mellon said quickly. "You and Justina are to stay here until we return."

"But . . ."

Mellon knelt close. "You can do nothing," he repeated very firmly, "except protect my daughter with your life. Justina has been told to keep you here until you are fit to travel. Unless the Cheyenne get past us. In that event, you and Justina had better get out of this country. If we're not back within two weeks, then find your father. He'll know what to do. Do you understand?"

"Yes."

Mellon relaxed just a little. "Justina is wise in the ways of the mountains. Trust her judgment. She has also been taught how to shoot."

Nathan's mind was reeling. "Two weeks, you say?"

"Yes. We must go now."

Nathan watched as Justina embraced her parents, then followed them outside. He heard their hurried farewells and then the sound of hoofbeats. A moment ago, he had been half confused and in a daze. With the door of the cabin standing open and the sound of the hoofbeats receding, Nathan pushed himself up and swung his feet to the floor. Almost at once, his head began to spin, and then he was coughing so hard that he thought his ribs would break.

The door of the cabin slammed shut, and the girl's voice cut at him. "What are you doing?"

He could not speak until his coughing fit subsided, and when it did, it left him so weak he lay back down. Justina covered him with a blanket, and her voice was angry. "I heard my father say you are to guard me with your life. What life will you have if you cough yourself to death or die in bed? You must obey me or you will not be fit to ride in two weeks!"

She was upset and he knew she had every right to be angry. "I'm sorry your uncle is dead," he told her.

"I am sure he fought well and killed many of our enemies. Speckled Snake died in battle, I am happy for him. That is what all warriors hope for. A man who grows old . . ." She left the sentence unfinished.

"I don't understand that at all."

"How can you? You are a white man. Even my father cannot understand such Indian things."

"But you're half white."

She stood up and walked slowly over to his bed. "I am Indian," she told him. "I love and honor my father, but I think and feel as an Indian."

Nathan did not buy that, not completely. "I've seen you reading the classics from your father's library. Your mother doesn't read, but you do and you *are* different because of your father's blood. You use big words and even speak like your father. You're more a part of him than you realize."

Justina said nothing. She turned and left the cabin.

Outside, there was a cold wind blowing, and the pines were whipping the sky. Her mother and father had left two horses, and it was her responsibility to keep them close so that, should the Cheyenne appear, she and the young man inside would at least have some hope of escape. But if the Cheyenne came, it would mean that they had killed her mother and father. Justina would rather fight to the death than run . . . only she did not have the luxury of that choice. Nathan Beard was her responsibility, and she had pledged to her parents that she would do as they wished.

Standing in the yard with the hard wind cutting at her face, Justina knew that she resented the white man and his sickness. If not for him, she would have gone with her mother and father instead of having to wait.

She went back into the cabin. It was not his fault. He was not the enemy. The Cheyenne were the ones to blame. "I am sorry I was angry with you," she told him.

"You're upset. So am I and I didn't even know those people. I don't understand why Indian tribes fight each other."

"And your people don't?" she asked, looking him right in the eye.

"You know that they do. Listen," he said, "I realize that you didn't want to stay here with me. I don't know if there is any way that I can make it up, but if there is, I'll try."

Justina knew that they must get along and try to pass the time. His words about her being more a part of her father than she might care to admit were troubling. Her mother was full-blooded Ute, and her father had discarded the white man's ways, as had Isaac Beard. To Justina's way of thinking, that meant that the white ways were bad. Besides, after having seen the nightmare that was the white man's crowded cities, she could not imagine why any of them would stay in such places. Maybe that was the reason more and more of them were coming west. Still, except for the trappers, few whites had entered their mountain strongholds. Justina had heard that the Plains Indians were fighting the whites, who were already spilling across their hunting grounds. Her father had told the Ute people exactly the same things that Isaac Beard had told them. They could not hope to defeat the white people. They must somehow keep their mountains through treaty. They must understand the whites and learn how to live with them in peace. All right then, she would try to understand this white man.

"I would like you to tell me about your cities."

"But you've been to Chicago."

"I was just a child. Everything was unreal. We rode so many trains. I saw people everywhere, and they stared at us. Some laughed or made faces at our clothes and said unkind things. I was frightened and even Mother was afraid. Father said it was a mistake. All a mistake. We ran from the city. I never want to go back." Justina frowned. "But sometimes . . ."

"Sometimes what?"

She tried to put into words her feelings, but it was difficult. "Sometimes, I wonder if it was as awful as I remember. I understand now what they did to my father. At the time, I understood nothing. And maybe I did not understand the city, either. Maybe it was not so bad. And if it was, are they all like that one called Chicago?"

"To be honest, I haven't seen that many. Just St. Louis and Independence. And they're so different you couldn't even compare them."

"Do you like cities?"

"I guess. I don't know. You like what you grow up with, I suppose. Maybe it's because that's all you know so you either learn to like it, or you're always unhappy."

"My father grew up in a city but would never go back. Maybe you'll never go back either—like your father."

"Yeah," he said, thinking of Matthew and their troubled parting. When Nathan thought about the way things had gone between him and his brother, it left an empty feeling in the pit of his stomach. And if he thought about Matthew too much, what he'd said and how he'd said it, the hollowness inside brought a sharp ache. It felt like a wound that would never heal.

"You have beaver traps in your pack," she said, unable to hide her disapproval. "Do you want to be like Julius Aubrey? A trapper?"

"Why not? Besides, I had the impression you liked him."

"I do. But my people believe that it is wrong to kill things for money. The Great Spirit did not put animals in this world that their skins should be sold for money. Indians believe all men should live in harmony with nature. They should have deep respect for the earth, the sky, water, animals, and even plants."

"The earth is here for us to live off," Nathan said.

"No," Justina said forcibly. "All living things possess a spirit. If a thing must be killed, then it should be for food or clothing. For example, when a Ute warrior kills a deer or rabbit, if he is a spiritual man, he will say, 'Excuse me, deer, for taking your life, but my people are hungry.' In this way, he does not anger the spirit world."

Nathan shook his head. "I never heard of such a thing. How many gods do your people have?"

"Many. We believe that there are gods for almost everything. There are animal gods, war gods, the gods of thunder and lightning. We pray and speak to them all. It is too bad you have only one god. He must be very lonely."

"One is enough to answer to. He doesn't like false gods, either."

Justina reminded herself to be tolerant. This young man was her father's guest. She must excuse his ignorance. Her mother would never insult or argue with a guest. She must exercise the same good manners. "I must look after the horses."

"Is there a horse god?" he asked. "If there is, why not ask him to do it?"

"That would be stupid," she said. "Do not say stupid things, Nathan."

"Wait," he said. "I apologize. What I said was stupid. Stay and talk to me awhile. You said you were interested in the white man's cities. Why?"

"My father says it is good to understand how bad such places are."

"St. Louis wasn't a bad place to grow up in. There was good fishing in the river, frogs to catch, lots of things to see and do."

"Were you happy?"

He wanted to say yes, but said no. "My brother and I lived with my grandmother and grandfather. They hated my father and blamed him for the death of their daughter. They blamed me, too."

"Why?"

"I don't know. Grandpa was always upset. Always critical. He and I never got along. My father didn't like him either. But for some reason, my grandparents liked Matthew better. They seemed to think that the Lord took Mother's life and gave back Matthew in return. You'd think they'd hate Matthew for that, but a preacher in St. Louis said it's God's way of doing things. The Lord giveth and the Lord taketh away. All I know is, they liked Matthew. He could do no wrong; I could do no right."

"Do you like him?"

"My brother? Of course I do!"

"You spoke of him when you were very ill. You said bad things about your brother."

Nathan swallowed. He was temporarily at a loss for words. He clenched his hands together and said, "Matt and I are very different. We always were. I never understood him and he never wanted to understand me. As we grew into manhood, I found, if anything, that I feared him." Nathan met her eyes. "I never admitted that before, not even to myself."

She touched his forehead, and her fingers were cool and soft. "It is the fever," she told him. "I am sure of it."

Nathan closed his eyes. He knew better. The fever had nothing to do with the way he felt about Matthew. He did love his brother, but he also feared him. Was that possible? Nathan decided it was.

"I have to go see to the horses now," she said, leaving him to his dark and troubled thoughts. "You rest."

"Yes," he mumbled, "I need rest. I'm not sure I'm thinking very well anymore."

At the door, Justina turned to watch the man lie back down on his cot. He had lost weight and his color was very pale but she could tell by the sound of his breathing that his lungs were clearing. A few more days, she thought, in a few more days, he will be well enough to ride.

The days passed slowly. Each afternoon Justina would go to a high place and wait for her parents until sunset, then hurry down in the failing light. Each day, Nathan could see that she was more concerned about her father and mother. By the end of the week, she had lost interest in food and conversation. She seemed lost in worry, and at night he awoke to find her sitting awake.

Nathan no longer thought about his own health, but only of the girl's. He was weak, but able to stand, walk, and go outside to feed the horses. He could breathe deeply without pain. But Justina was visibly failing.

"Let's ride north," he told her one afternoon as she stood at the edge of a meadow and looked in that direction. "Let's go find your mother and father."

She turned suddenly, her expression intent, questioning. "You do not understand the danger."

"I realize that," he said, "but I do understand that you have to find out about your parents. I think you might die if you don't learn their fate before winter. You're wilting like a flower. I can't bear to watch it anymore!"

Justina blinked rapidly, trying to fight back tears.

Nathan stretched out his arms. "Come here," he told her. And to his surprise, Justina flew into his embrace. He held her and felt her tremble. She whispered in his ear, "You see right through me. I have been dying every day in worry. I *must* know!"

"Then I'll catch the horses and saddle them," he told her. "You gather whatever we can carry, food, warm coats and blankets, our weapons and ammunition."

That very morning, they rode north into a strong and biting wind, one stiff enough to make the pine needles sing and to unfurl a thin banner of snow off the peaks. They both knew that they might be caught in a blizzard but that possibility seemed nothing compared to what they feared they might find in the remains of a Ute camp to the north.

Not a moment passed that they did not hope to see Justina's mother and father come galloping over a mountain to say that everything was fine, that the Ute people had rallied to defeat the Cheyenne and reclaim their captive friends.

They found the village six days later, found the ashes and the wailing old squaws and the dead. Speckled Snake was among them but Mellon and Snow Bird were not.

Nathan had never seen such devastation. Every tepee in the village had been burned to the ground. The Utes had been camped in a huge meadow, and the Cheyenne had surrounded and attacked from the trees just as daylight was breaking over the mountains. A few squaws had managed to escape and hide, thus avoiding death or slavery. But afterward, they'd disfigured themselves with knives so that they were terrible to behold. Few had had the time to gather blankets or buffalo robes before making their desperate escape, and now they were huddled around small fires, too numb with grief to do much except rock back and forth on their knees and wail and weep.

As for the Cheyenne, so great had been their numbers that the battle had lasted less than fifteen minutes. Ute warriors, caught half asleep and ill-prepared to defend the village, nevertheless had fought like men possessed, but they were overrun.

They learned that Justina's parents had gathered a few wounded warriors and followed the victorious Cheyenne north in the desperate hope of overtaking them and freeing the Ute slaves.

"I am going after them, too," Justina said, her voice as dead as the corpses strewn around the remains of the Ute village.

Nathan said nothing as he remounted his horse. His bones felt as if they were filled with ice instead of marrow and he knew that he was not at full strength. But he also knew that he would never be able to live with himself if he remained in this place and allowed Justina to ride to almost certain death.

"What about these people?"

"I have told them that they must go south for help. They understand."

"But some of them are very old and . . ."

Justina turned her back on him and kicked her horse into a gallop. Swearing, Nathan went after her.

The great Cheyenne party that rode north was confident. The warriors were in high spirits. Not only had they taken many scalps and killed their ancient enemies, the Utes, but they had done so in the Shining Mountains, something that

was never easy. Their prize was beyond even their highest
expectations. Because the Ute counted their wealth in horses
and had many of them, the Cheyenne had taken over four
hundred of the animals. They had also taken many slaves,
along with buffalo robes, wampum, and arrowheads. Most
prized of all were the white man's rifles, cooking utensils, and
steel knives.

Every mile the Cheyenne rode took them deeper into
their own territory. They followed the Medicine Bow River
down into the high plateau country, which was broken by
stunted mountain ranges and fed by dozens of cold, clear
rivers. They camped along the western base of the Laramie
Mountains and hunted buffalo for weeks while they enjoyed
the newfound pleasures of their Ute squaws and made them
jerk winter meat and work buffalo hides into fine robes.

One stormy night, not long after their arrival on the
Medicine Bow River, they'd been attacked by four Ute
warriors, a squaw, and a white man. The warriors had been
killed quickly and the others taken prisoner. The white man
had been stripped naked, tied to a tree and used for target
practice. Unfortunately, he had died too soon because Goes to
River pierced his heart with almost the first arrow. The Ute
woman's screams had filled the air. After much debate, she was
given to the huge warrior, Bear Claw, a man who had many
Ute scalps and many squaws already and who, with his size and
strength, could tame a panther. As war chief, he had claimed
the beautiful Ute woman. But on the first night with her, she
had tried to kill him. In anger, Bear Claw had used one mighty
blow to silence her forever.

Thinking the death of the brave Ute woman to be bad
medicine, the war party had broken camp and galloped north.
Very soon, they would be among their own people and they
would be looked upon with much respect. Next year, they
would raid again, only deeper into the mountains. They would
take more slaves, more Ute ponies, more wampum, scalps,
and weapons.

Justina's shriek caused Nathan's head to snap erect. She
threw back her head and cried again, and then she lashed her

horse forward toward the tree where her father hung with arrows protruding from his chest, stomach, and groin.

Nathan raced after the girl, wanting to stop her but knowing he could not. He watched helplessly as Justina flew from her horse, then staggered toward the corpse of Doug Mellon.

Nathan felt sick. He turned away and when he saw Snow Bird lying stiff and battered near a pile of rocks, an involuntary groan escaped his lips. He rushed forward, tearing off his coat, and laid it over the Ute woman's battered face.

"It would be better if . . ."

"No," Justina cried. "Just leave me alone!"

She ripped the coat away. She screamed once more and fell upon her mother. Nathan didn't even try to pull her away. He clenched his fists and raised them to the sky in helpless anger. Doug Mellon had said these mountains were a *healing* place. Nathan didn't believe that. In the mountains, death came quickly and all too often.

Nathan buried Doug Mellon but made no cross for his grave because the white man had replaced Christianity with the Indian's religion. They bound Snow Bird up in one of the two precious buffalo robes they had with them and placed her high in the bough of a tree, according to Indian custom. Justina poured ashes over her hair and clothes. She ground them into her face and smeared them over her arms and legs. She collapsed under the tree where her mother lay high above, and she rocked back and forth and chanted things that Nathan believed he would never understand.

That evening, he went hunting and killed a pair of nice sage hens, but neither he nor Justina had any appetite. The fire held no warmth, and the north wind had the taste of winter but the girl did not seem to feel its chill. Nathan waited two days before he lifted Justina in his arms and placed her on one of the horses. "Come," he said quietly, "we have Ute women and children to save."

She nodded, her eyes dull with pain.

A storm followed them south as Nathan and Justina led the surviving Utes through the mountains. The squaws could not be hurried, but walked with heads down. Every so often, wails of sorrow were torn from their lips. It was the younger women and the children who would survive this long trek south. They started out with almost forty women and children, but by the time they reached the Grand River, the old women were gone. They did not fall on the trail, but slipped quietly away to die alone, like wounded or weak animals falling behind a migrating herd.

Each night, the women and children built a great fire and sat crosslegged around it without speaking. Nathan supposed that all the women would be taken in by other members of the Ute clans. That was the Indian way. A squaw whose husband had died would usually be taken by the husband's brother or some other relative. She would be treated the same as the other wives but, if food became very scarce and a warrior's first wives or his children were hungry, then the widowed squaw was expected to leave and go off alone.

There was no joy in Nathan at the prospect of meeting his father after all these years. He felt empty except when he looked at Justina. He fed her, held her, blanketed her, and kept her warm through the long nights. She had also refused to ride her horse, giving it instead to someone weaker than her. Nathan watched her constantly. He was afraid that she might . . . what? Break? That was ridiculous. The half-breed girl was too strong. She would survive. She would smile and laugh again as she had the first time he'd met her.

Nathan was glad that he had known Mellon. The white man had been strange, moody, bitter, and confused, but he had loved the Utes and had devoted the final part of his life to capturing on paper their customs and culture. His scribbled scientific notes made little sense to Nathan, and he knew that they, like Mellon's sketches and paintings, would never be published. At first, that seemed a pity, and then Nathan remembered that was exactly the way Doug Mellon had wanted it. When they had passed by his cabin, Nathan had gone inside and taken everything. Mellon's food and blankets saved a number of the Indian children, and Nathan took some comfort in that knowledge.

"Just around the bend in the river," Justina said quietly, "we will find the Ute village your father and his wife have taken as their home."

Nathan took a deep breath. He felt no elation at this

long-awaited reunion. After all the stories he had heard about
Isaac Beard, the giant, the killer of Ute enemies, Nathan felt
nothing. His thoughts were totally absorbed by the Ute girl at
his side. "You are alone now," he said. "Who will you go to?"

She shrugged. "Perhaps your father. He was my father's
best friend."

But Nathan shook his head. "No. If you will have me, I
will take you to wife."

She looked up into his eyes. "I am a woman with no joy."

"Then I will return your joy."

"And you will stay here among the people?"

"Yes," he said. "Like my father."

She took his hand. "Then I will live with you always."

Nathan wanted to hold her. But when he looked at the
survivors he was leading, his own happiness withered. So he
just took the Ute girl's hand in his own and walked around
the bend of the river. To meet Isaac Beard. To find a new home
for himself and Justina.

Nathan and Isaac Beard paddled their canoe to shore and disembarked. They walked up to a high point where they could see the country and the path of the Grand River for no less than a hundred miles.

"See," Isaac said, pointing southwest. "It cuts through those towering bluffs and flows into the high desert country the mountain men call Utah."

Nathan shielded his eyes from the bright sun. He could feel the heat rising from the vast desert below. Ahead, he could see how the big river had carved a canyon through wind-sculpted pillars of red and yellow rock to the north and south. To the east, pinion, juniper, and sage had replaced aspen, birch, and sugar pine. "I'll miss the smell of pines and the taste of the high mountain country."

"So will I," Isaac said, "but I've been this far and I'd like to go on down where they say the Grand meets the Green River."

Nathan glanced up at the sun. "We've still got a few more hours of daylight left. Let's use 'em."

"What about Justina? You promised we'd be gone only one month. We've already used up half of that and our return will be slower, climbing back up into the mountains."

Nathan deflected the question back to his father. "What about Chipeta? You made her the same foolish promise."

"I'll make it up to her," Isaac said with a slow grin. "And I guess you'll do the same."

"I will," Nathan said with a wink as he started back down the bluff toward their canoe.

They'd explored more than a hundred miles of the Grand River, and after looking out on the Utah badlands, Nathan wasn't so sure he wanted to see any more. He had never faced desert country but he'd heard stories from those who had.

They'd agreed it was damned hot, with little water and slim pickings to eat. Also, there were some mighty unfriendly Indians out there, but Nathan guessed he and his father would be all right as long as they stayed in their canoe. Isaac had made sure that his son quickly became a marksman. They had plenty of ammunition, and the river ran faster over a distance than any Indian pony.

They pushed the canoe back into the river and paddled into the center of the current. They considered themselves an experienced team. Nathan knelt in the bow and was on constant lookout for rocks and any other obstacles, while his father supplied the raw power, if and when it was needed, to change course in a hurry. Though in his fifties, Isaac was still immensely powerful and as lean as a cougar. His long hair and beard had turned gray, his bushy eyebrows, too. But he was a man who could still portage a canoe for miles and hike up and down mountains until younger men begged for rest.

Nathan had found his father a little more puritanical and old-fashioned than he would have supposed after living in the wilderness for so many years. Isaac had adopted almost all the Ute ways. When he had first seen Nathan's beaver traps, he'd said nothing, but it was easy to see that he was troubled. Because of that, Nathan had never taken up trapping. There were mountain men who did who passed through on their way to or from the rendezvous. They spoke of the high old times they had swapping furs for squaws and whiskey, supplies, and doodads for their Indian friends. But, privately, the trappers were worried. Most of the country had already been trapped out of beaver, and the take was getting leaner every year. But when they were all together, bragging and carrying on, it sounded as if the beaver would last forever. Isaac would listen, and he'd never offer criticism, but Nathan could tell that his father had no use for that kind of goings on.

After two years, Nathan had pretty much come to respect the same things his father and the Utes respected: honor, their families and traditions and, perhaps most of all, nature and the mountains. There were times when he wished he could return to St. Louis. He often wondered about Matthew and the general store. Had his brother inherited it yet? He must have or he'd have come west, too. One thing was sure, his brother would not let Uncle William remain long in charge. Matthew just would not put up with such a man.

In regard to Matthew, Isaac had not been able to accept the fact that a son of his would insist on total ownership of the general store—and actually intend to operate it for the rest of his days. Sometimes, right out of the clear blue sky, Isaac would surprise Nathan by muttering, "I can't believe Matt'd do that. I had better journey back to St. Louis and see if I can straighten him out."

Nathan would say, "I think you'd best leave him be. You don't know Matt like I do. He's bullheaded, and once he fixes his mind on something he doesn't change it, not for anyone."

"Well, he's your brother and he's my son. I owe him a chance. I just hate to see anyone spend his life behind a dry goods counter when he could be living like this."

Nathan did not tell his father that Matthew hated him. It would have hurt too much. And he meant to do everything in his power to keep Isaac from returning to St. Louis. That was one reason that Nathan had been eager to satisfy the man's itch to explore the Grand River.

At night, they camped right on the beach and listened to coyotes howl. Once they reached the desert, afternoons were brutally hot, though the nights cooled down nicely. By setting out fishing lines before they went to sleep, they caught catfish to supplement their diet of jerked venison and elk. As they traveled on, the river lost its clarity and became silty but they drank from it anyway. To keep himself cool, Nathan spent hours in the water, swimming beside the drifting canoe. He was ready to go back to the Shining Mountains but Isaac kept pushing on, always looking for the junction of the Grand and the Green rivers.

But one morning, they awoke to an absolute silence. Usually, there were plenty of sounds in the brush, a rabbit or a fox, a sage hen or at least a wren sharpening its beak. But this particular morning, nothing.

Isaac sat up and turned to study the brush. He took his rifle and slowly raised himself fully upright. Nathan did the same.

Suddenly, there was a soft whirring sound that they both recognized as the flight of an arrow. An instant later, the sky was filled with them.

"Where the hell are they?" Nathan cried, hitting the bank and rolling toward the canoe.

"I don't know," Isaac said. "But let's get out of here!"

They shoved the canoe off the beach, tossing in their camping gear. They could both hear the Indians howling off in the brush and moving closer. "Let's go!" Isaac shouted. "Get in!"

"You first," Nathan said, "I'll cover until you're in the current and then swim for it."

But Isaac just grabbed Nathan by his buckskin jacket and threw him headlong into the canoe. A moment later, he also was in and they were both paddling furiously as the Indians charged out of the brush and unleashed more arrows.

"Duck and stay low!" Isaac bellowed.

When an arrow plucked his sleeve, Nathan twisted around in the bow of the canoe and fired his Hawken. An Indian toppled headlong into the river.

"What the hell did you do that for?" Isaac shouted.

"Because they're trying to kill us!"

"Well, damnit, they didn't get it done and now you've split their blood and they'll stay after us like a swarm of hornets!"

Nathan was stung by the anger in his father's voice, yet supposed it was his due. "I'm sorry, but I'm not used to having Indians trying to kill me!"

"Paddle faster," Isaac growled.

They quickly outdistanced the Indians, and when they rounded a bend in the river, they sat up straight and, lungs pumping, caught their breath. "Now what are we supposed to do?" Nathan asked. "We're going deeper into their land and farther away from ours."

"I noticed," Isaac said. "Best thing we can do is keep paddling for another day or two and then send the canoe on down to the Green River while we double back on foot. That's what we was afixin' to do anyway, isn't it?"

"Yeah. I just didn't expect we'd have to navigate our way through a bunch of hostile Indians."

"Well," Isaac said. "If you hadn't shot one, maybe we could have talked our way out of a fix. Now, if they catch us, we're cooked rabbit."

With that assessment on his mind, Nathan spent a somber two days as they paddled deeper into the Utah country. He had never seen such a desolate land. There were no beaver here. Hell, even the rabbits and coyotes he saw coming to drink looked half starved. And, come to think of it, those Indians had looked pretty hungry, too.

"You know what tribe they were?" he asked.

"Can't be sure. It happened too fast to get a good look at 'em. But I'd say they were either Paiutes or maybe some desert Ute or Arapaho."

Nathan was stunned. "How could they be Ute? *We're* Ute."

"No, we're not," Isaac said gravely. "That could be a fatal mistake in your head. We're married to Ute and live with them and even follow most of their customs, but we are white people and that's all that matters to unfriendly Indians. Those kind wouldn't have believed us to be friends."

"But I still can't believe they were Utes. Why, those people were thin and dressed like beggars in rabbit furs and coyote hides. They looked awful."

"It's a tough country out here. These people are real poor. Snow Bird said that one of the seven clans of Ute are from this part of the country and though they speak the Ute language, they're altogether different, a lower kind of people who have few horses and who eat bugs and lizards and live in mud wickiups. The other mountain Utes stay shy of their desert cousins. Now, I ain't sayin' that's who they were, but it's possible. Important thing for you to remember in order to keep your hair is that all Indians—except them you know personally—might be enemies. Never shoot first, but be prepared for a fight."

"Well, that's what I did!"

"You shot a little quick to my way of thinking."

Nathan paddled on a ways before he said, "I think we've gone far enough. Every mile we float down this river is going to be one hard mile to walk back."

"All right," Isaac said. "Come dark, we'll send the canoe down the river and strike out across the desert. Stay maybe two, three miles just easy of the Grand and that way we're less likely to run into trouble."

They floated on until sunset, and then they rowed over to the east bank. Since they'd known all along that they'd be ditching the canoe and coming back upriver on foot, they'd traveled light, just a few blankets, some food, their Hawkens, possibles bags with flint, ammunition and lead balls, fishing line and hooks, and a couple of other odds and ends.

"Three weeks," Isaac said. "That's how long it'll take before we sleep with our women again."

Nathan wiped the sweat from his brow and then plunged into the brush after his father, who had angled northeast. The Rocky Mountains were just a blue haze in the distance, and even after they got to them, it would be a hell of a climb.

"Pa?"

"Yeah?"

"If you're still dead set on going to St. Louis next summer, then we'll go. Can't be worse than this."

Isaac twisted around. A sheen of sweat covered his broad forehead. "I'm going this fall, Nate, after I get meat for the winter. I'm going to get my other son and bring him out West. But you gotta stay and take care of our families."

Nathan clamped his mouth shut. There was no use telling Isaac again that Matthew wouldn't come west, not if he owned the most profitable general store in St. Louis. And not if he hated his father.

Their return to the mountains did take them nearly three weeks, but at least they did not see any more unfriendly Indians. And true to his word, that fall, when the nights began to chill and the leaves turned bright colors, Isaac Beard left his wife and headed for St. Louis. Nathan wanted to go but Justina was with child and his father expected him to take care of both families. Still, Nathan could not help but feel a deep sense of foreboding. His father was a mountain man. Once on the plains, all his mountain skills would not help him a whit against the Sioux or the Cheyenne. And even assuming Isaac did reach St. Louis safely, how could he be sure that someone would not remember he was wanted for murdering a lawman? It had not been so many years since he'd killed the deputy. People who saw Isaac Beard never forgot him. He stood head and shoulders above a crowd, and he would not be able to hide behind the silver beard he now wore.

There was something else that worried Nathan. What would Matthew do and say when they finally met? Matthew had a dangerous temper and was quick to explode in violence. Nathan had tried to warn his father that Matthew held things against him but Isaac hadn't believed a word of it.

"He's my son, same as you, Nathan! We just need to talk it out."

But Nathan knew better. They might both be Isaac's sons, but that was all he and Matt had in common. And as for the likelihood that Matthew might do his unsuspecting father real harm, that worried Nathan so much he had trouble sleeping at night.

As owner and sole proprietor of the biggest general store in St. Louis, Matthew was a man of wealth and influence. He seemed much older and far more worldly than his years and most people thought him to be in his mid-thirties. On the day his rich grandmother had died, Matthew Beard had driven his terrified Uncle William away with a buggy whip. That same day he had had the name of the general store changed, as well as the locks. His grandmother had willed almost all of her estate to Matthew and what she left to Uncle William, Matthew claimed for himself.

Like his father, Matthew wore a beard, but he wore it cropped close and it was thick and black instead of long and silver. Matthew's suit was tailor-made and of the finest quality. His mustache was waxed, and there was a large gold ring on his left little finger. He was said to be the most eligible bachelor in town but he had no use for marriage and favored the sporting ladies. On Friday and Saturday nights, he liked to hang out at Delmonico's Dinner House and Sports Club where he played faro and sometimes roulette. There were a couple of young ladies who worked there and they both knew Matthew Beard to be a generous and a passionate lover.

Matthew knew that he had the drive, the ability, and the determination to do whatever he wanted to do in life. Being St. Louis's biggest retail merchandiser, he was the first to suspect that beaver hats were beginning to lose their popularity. He had heard rumors that in Paris tall felt and silk hats were becoming fashionable. Matthew knew that Americans followed the French fashion trends slavishly. If felt and silk were the rage in France, it would not be long before every man would be setting aside yesterday's beaver hat in favor of a new felt one. No man of any stature could afford to be seen in yesterday's fashion.

Matthew also realized that the ramifications of change in hat styles was of no small importance to the entire Western frontier. It had been furs that had led the first white man into the wilderness. With the Frenchies in the vanguard, they'd found beaver in the Great Lakes regions, and when the region had been trapped out, they had pushed southwest. They had discovered the rivers, fought the Indians, climbed and named the mountains, and eventually laid a claim for the United States to territories that might otherwise have been kept by Spain, France, England, and Russia.

Matthew knew this better than most, for he and his grandparents had long profited from the fur traders. Now, he wondered about the mountain men, especially about his father and his brother. What would they do? How would they—or any of their kind—survive? Every mountain man that Matthew had ever seen was fiercely independent, scornful of the cities, and totally unemployable. They were dinosaurs of a dying age.

Sometimes, Matthew had a dream of going to the far mountains and riding up to see Isaac and Nathan. He would be mounted on a blooded horse, riding a custom-made saddle, and sporting the finest hunting rifle in the world. And then he would look down at the two of them in their stinking buckskins and say, "I wanted you to know that at least one Beard finally made something of himself."

It was a cruel, cruel dream. Matthew supposed it was one that he would never actually realize, but whenever he saw a mountain man, the prideful dream materialized and he would swell out his great chest and study his manicured fingernails and know that he had succeeded beyond even his own lofty expectations. But if the demand for furs was going to decline, Matthew knew that his own business would suffer because many of the fur companies were regular customers. If they were to go out of business due to a lack of demand for beaver, then Matthew knew that he would see his own profits fall. To avoid that, he decided that it would be wise to diversify into something of the future—like steam. Steam engines were

already starting to propel the railroads west. Steamships were
rapidly displacing the old sailing ships.

Yes, he thought, *steam* was the future. Believing that the
fur trade was soon to end, Matthew was thinking of selling his
general store and investing in a steamboat, perhaps one in
New Orleans or New York or—God help him—out West in
San Francisco where it was said that steamers were reaping
enormous profits from a budding Oriental trade. And if . . .

"Hello, son," a deep voice said, "I've come to ask you to
go with me to Colorado."

Matthew's bones seemed to harden so that he could not
move. He stood frozen behind his store counter, knowing with
dead certainty that he was looking at his father, the man whose
notorious reputation he had tried to overcome all his life. Isaac
was huge. Even a Hawken looked like a child's toy as it rested
in the crook of his arm.

A clerk who had been waiting at the cash register looked up
at the two grim giants. Like everyone else in town, he had heard
all the legends of Isaac. His gulp sounded unnaturally loud and he
said, "Excuse me, Mr. Beard, if you don't mind, I'll. . . . "

"Stay where you are," Matthew rasped. His eyes bored
into those of his father and then he jabbed a thick forefinger in
Isaac's chest. "You come with me."

Matthew's thoughts were a jumble. He wanted to grab his
father by the throat and kill him, but he knew that would be
crazy. From childhood, he had fantasized about the day he and
Isaac Beard would meet. And, in almost every fantasy, he had
struck his father to the ground and scorned him for abandoning
his wife and sons, for leaving them nothing but a sordid name
to live down.

Matthew's fists were clenched as he stomped into his
office, then whirled to face a man as large as himself, as large
and as thick, but one whose face was deeply lined and who
looked as old as Methuselah, one who has long since left his
prime. Matthew's office was plush, with deep carpets, rich
mahogany furniture, brass, pewter, and silver. Isaac smelled of
horse, grease, smoke, and sweat, like an animal or like a
damned savage Indian.

Matthew watched his father as the man studied the
expensive desk, the high-backed leather chair, the gold pen-

and-ink set, and the framed citations on his walls in appreciation of charities he had benefited. "Why did you come here?"

Isaac shifted in his moccasins. "They always said you and I were copies, but they forgot to tell me you're a lot better looking."

"*Don't*," Matthew growled. "Don't try to flatter me, damn you! It doesn't fit your reputation."

Isaac leaned on his Hawken. He suddenly felt very old. His son's eyes were hot and unforgiving, and he remembered Nathan's warning. "This is nicer than any banker's office. Nicer'n anything I ever seen. When I worked for your grandfather, I used to stack boxes I unloaded right here. I'm glad you've done well."

"What do you want? Money? Provisions? What?"

"I want you to come live with us in the Shining Mountains."

Matthew's lips twisted with scorn. "Are you insane? Have the mountains made you crazy? Look at me! Look around you. Everything in this place is mine!"

Isaac actually turned his head to look back into the store through the doorway. Then he said, "I used to dream I'd own all this some day. But now . . . now, I'm glad I've got no part of it. Wouldn't trade my tepee for the whole works."

"Damn you!" Matthew balled his fists and swung with all his might, not caring if he killed this ignorant sonofabitch. When his fist connected, he felt a jolt of pain drive all the way up to his shoulder. Isaac staggered, his smashed lips flowed redly. "Was that for your mother?"

Matthew threw himself at his father and drove a tremendous uppercut into Isaac's stomach. He saw the man's eyes bulge with pain, and then he stepped back and smashed Isaac to his knees with a vicious left that opened the man's cheek to the bone.

"Get up and fight!"

Isaac shook his head as he stared at the floor. He felt paralyzed and sick. "You gonna kick me a few times so you'll feel even better?"

Matthew wanted to. He ached to drive his boot up under his father's jaw and break his windpipe and leave him to strangle to death. But he couldn't do that. Instead, he unclenched his great fists and collapsed in his leather chair. He reached into his drawer and brought out a glass and a decanter of imported brandy. His hands were shaking as he poured one for himself and drank it neat.

He poured another. "You drink or smoke? I heard you didn't."

Isaac managed to shake his head. He picked up his rifle and crawled to his feet. "You hit hard," he said, "as hard as I ever did."

"You're bleeding on my carpet," Matthew said, yanking a silk handkerchief from his coat pocket and tossing it at his father. "Get the hell out of my store! We've nothing to say to each other. Not after all these years."

Isaac had to grab the big desk to pull himself upright. "Don't you even want to know about your brother?"

When Matthew just clenched his jaw and said nothing, Issac said, "He sends his regards. He's married and his wife is expecting a baby."

"Why didn't he come instead of you?"

"He wanted to be near his wife when she had their child."

Matthew lit a cigar and saw that the knuckles of his hand were bleeding. He glared at the man before him. "Do you have any idea what it was like growing up the son of a murderer? People always said we looked too much alike not to be cut from the same cloth. Respectable families kept their daughters away from Nathan and me. I never even blamed them. I blamed you."

Isaac wiped his busted lips with the back of his leather sleeve. "I'll take the blame but you're big enough to know it shouldn't have mattered what people said."

"That's *all* that matters to a boy!" He struggled to gain his composure and said, "What do you really want?"

Isaac suddenly knew that anything he said would sound foolish. But he had to try. "I want . . . I want to teach you . . . things."

"What things, goddamn you! Things like how to trap beaver? Well, the beaver trade is dying! How to live like a dirty savage? Shoot a goddamn bow and arrow or cut up a buffalo? No, thank you!"

Isaac shifted on the balls of his feet. The Hawken rested straight up and down in front of him, and he leaned slightly on its barrel as if it were a badly needed support. He was beaten.

This was not his son, and he guessed he'd been a fool ever to suppose he would be. "Nathan said I'd be wasting my time."

Matthew threw down his brandy and jammed his cigar into a silver ashtray. He came around his desk and stood with his face close to Isaac's. "You're damn right, you are! Now get out of here before I grab you by that stinking buffalo robe of yours and . . ."

"My wife Chipeta made it," Isaac said in a very still voice. "And I'll thank you not to lay your hands on me again."

Matthew grabbed his father, and that's when Isaac slammed the Hawken's muzzle straight up under Matthew's chin. His head snapped back and before he could recover, his father had him by the hair and was propelling him forward into the wall. When he struck the heavy paneling, it splintered and he collapsed on the floor. Before he could recover, Isaac placed a moccasined foot on the back of his neck and said, "I'll be going now. I'm glad to see a Beard took over this store. It was my dream, too, once. Before I knew any better."

The words were soft and with no anger in them at all. Matthew had intended to get up and attempt to beat his father to death, but the tone of the man's voice just took the fight out of him. He raised his head and watched Isaac fill the aisle on his way to the front door. Isaac was old and he limped, but even Matthew could see there was something magnificent in the way his father moved and carried himself.

"Wait!"

Isaac ignored the order and walked past the front counter and then closed the door behind him.

Two flustered clerks stared at Matthew, unsure of what to do. "Get back to work!" he yelled, scrambling to his feet.

Outside, Isaac was untying his horse when five lawmen surrounded him with drawn guns. "Drop the rifle, Mr. Beard," one said. "Drop it or I'll blow a hole in you where you stand."

Isaac wanted to turn and fire but found that, just now, he didn't have the heart either to kill or to be killed. He dropped the Hawken, jarred by the sudden discovery that old men valued life more than young ones. Twenty years ago, he'd have killed one or two and been killed himself rather than be locked up in a jail or prison. But not anymore. Not with Chipeta and the Ute people needing him in Colorado. Isaac's wrists were manacled. One of the lawmen knocked his coonskin cap to the dirt and stepped on it.

"He's the one all right, Sheriff!" An old man cried. "I told you it was him. Couldn't be no other."

"Shut up," the sheriff growled. "Of course, he's the one. And you'll have your reward all right. I still got Beard's wanted poster on the wall. It's yellowed and fly-specked, but it's him."

"That young deputy, he tried to kill me first," Isaac said. "He left me no choice."

Matthew pushed through a gathering crowd. "Sheriff."

"Matt, we got your pa. You always said he'd come back some day. You were right. What'd he want? Money?"

Matthew looked at the excited faces and then at his father standing with his head down, staring at his coonskin cap. Matthew picked it up, slapped it against his pants to dust it off, then handed it back to Isaac. "You're just a huge fool," he said with a sad shake of his head. "I finally see the way of it. A fool is all you've ever been, isn't it?"

Matthew didn't expect to get an answer and he didn't receive one. So he just turned on his heel and went back into his store.

≈ BOOK THREE ≈

≈ MATTHEW ≈

Matthew could not sleep that night, or the next or the next. He tried both liquor and women until his senses were dulled and his mind and body were numb but still awake. Whenever he closed his eyes, Isaac's face appeared, that old, weather-beaten face the color of brown shoe leather.

The question that was driving Matthew insane was, WHY? Why had Isaac returned to St. Louis at the risk of his life? To appease his guilt? To try to make amends for abandoning his sons? No doubt, the man did harbor much guilt. But perhaps he really believed that living in some wretched Indian village and sleeping on a buffalo robe somehow was better than living like a civilized man. Matthew had seen enough trappers to know they were warped and often hostile toward their own people. They were voluntary outcasts who shunned their families and turned their backs on their civilization. They had regressed to the level of the Indian and reveled in ignorance and squalor. To Matthew's way of thinking, they were living like Stone Age cavemen.

But Matthew knew the real question concerned his own feelings. He knew he had to ask himself what kind of a son could allow his own father—even one who'd lived his life as a well-intentioned fool—to be hung from a rope for defending his own life? Nathan alone had seen the killing and it had left such an indelible impression on him that he had remembered every detail. But even if Nathan were here now, who besides himself would believe a witness who had been only four years old at the time? No one. And because of that, Isaac would hang or at least go to prison for the rest of his life.

Matthew stared up at the ceiling of his bedroom. A pretty dance hall girl slept at his right side and at his left was a half empty bottle of whiskey. He had reached for both too many times this week, and neither had brought relief. Matthew stood up and stretched his powerful body, then shuffled to the window. Dawn was just coming up and from his upstairs bedroom window he had a magnificent view of both the Missouri and Mississippi rivers. The sun was just beginning to put a veil of gold on the rippling waters. The cottonwood trees were bare, and it was cold outside.

Matthew knew that deputy Art Logman was on duty this night as he would be every night this week. Logman was the sheriff's brother-in-law but he had no loyalty to the man responsible for his job. He was jealous of his brother-in-law and never missed an opportunity to disparage his reputation. Logman would enjoy embarrassing his brother-in-law and Matthew knew the man took bribes and would do almost anything for money, even allow an accused murderer to escape.

"Honey?" She was heavy-lidded with sleep and her voice was drowsy. "It's so early. Come back to bed."

Matthew turned to look at the woman. She was slender and attractive but she was a whore, and he felt little affection for her. "Go to sleep," he said. "You'll have to earn your money tonight."

The woman pouted but closed her eyes again as she said, "I earn my money *every* night, Matt, especially in your bed."

He smiled, pulled on his boots, and closed the door behind him on his way out. She wouldn't dare steal in his absence. Besides, this would be a quick visit. He'd be back in time to wake her up again before he finally got some sleep.

Ten minutes later, he was knocking softly at the sheriff's office. "Logman, it's me, Matthew Beard. Unlock the door."

He heard a groan and pounded a little louder. The streets were still empty, and he wanted to be in and out before they got busy with the early risers. "Open up, damnit!"

Art Logman was in his long johns, and his hair was mussed. Tall and skinny, he had a little potbelly and a sunken chest. "What do you want, Mr. Beard? I can't . . ."

Matthew pushed the man aside and entered the office. He closed the door behind him and glanced at the rear door leading to the cell where his father was being held for trial.

Logman was trying to sound angry, but barefooted, in

long johns and half asleep, he was a pathetic specimen of manhood. "I can't let you see your father at this hour."

Matthew sat down on the sheriff's desk. "You want to earn some big money or get your head busted?"

"Huh?"

"You heard me. Money or pain?"

Logman was awake now. His eyes narrowed over his overly large nose. He licked his lips and stumbled over to his cot along the east wall. "Say it plain, Mr. Beard."

Matthew knew he was taking a risk, but what action could be taken against him merely for offering a bribe to a deputy? It was just Logman's word against his, and the deputy was not respected in St. Louis. "I'll pay you four hundred dollars to let my father escape tomorrow night."

Logman's jaw dropped. Four hundred dollars was more than he'd make in a year. It was enough to set a man up in some kind of business of his own. "Are you serious?"

"Very."

Logman swallowed and scratched his jaw. "I'd need more than that," he said, managing to sound doubtful. "If Sheriff Moss found out, I'd be in deep trouble. I'd get fired . . . maybe worse."

Matthew had anticipated the man's objections and easily countered them. "Why should he find out? Maybe *he'll* get fired. Or maybe you could use the money to run against him in the next election. You're well liked in St. Louis. Everyone knows your worth."

"Think so?" Logman asked, his eyes warming to even a hint of praise.

"I'm sure of it. Look, I'll give you five hundred dollars in cash. Half this afternoon and the other half when my father is safely out of town. That's the best I'll do."

The eyes narrowed to slits. "Mr. Beard, I need a thousand."

"I won't pay it."

"Seven hundred and fifty, then. I'll do it for seven-fifty."

Matthew did not have time to dicker. He did not want to be seen leaving the sheriff's office at this hour of the morning. "All right, but my father will want his own horse and saddle tied in the back alley," he said. "You stop by my store late this afternoon and I'll pay you half."

Logman rubbed his hands together nervously. "Sheriff Moss will go crazy when he learns that his prisoner escaped. He'll threaten to fire my ass, but I'll just up and quit."

"You better take your money and leave town," Matthew said. "If he finds out you have all that money, he'll get suspicious."

"I'll tell him I won it playing poker. I'm good at cards, Mr. Beard. I win my share and then some."

That was not the story Matthew heard. Everyone in town knew Logman was a terrible gambler who was continually in debt. But what the deputy did with his money was his own business.

Matthew eased off the desk and walked to the door. "This afternoon. You better not mess this up, Deputy."

"No, sir!" Logman almost came to attention. "You can depend on me."

Matthew wished there was someone more trustworthy, but Logman would have to do. He stepped outside and walked quickly toward the Mint Cafe. He knew he looked disreputable for he had not yet shaved, and his eyes were bloodshot from too much whiskey and too little sleep. To hell with it. He'd have a fine breakfast and then he'd return to the woman and his feather bed and let his employees earn their money this day.

At two o'clock the following morning, Isaac was awakened by the deputy. "Time to go back to Colorado," the man said, holding a candle up over his face.

Isaac blinked. "What are you talking about?"

"Your son paid me to turn you loose. You got a horse out in the alley and your Hawken and stuff is tied to the saddle-horn. You better get up and just skedaddle, mister."

Isaac came to his feet, and the deputy stepped back, his hand gripping the butt of his holstered revolver. "Just you stay back from me," he warned. "You killed one deputy already."

Isaac was wary. "How do I know this isn't some excuse to gun me down?"

The deputy had an answer. "Step up to the door. Your son

is sitting in that second-story hotel room window just one door to the north and across the street. You can see his face where the curtain is parted."

Isaac moved out of his cell. He hurried to the front door and eased it open. He peered in the direction the deputy said, and sure enough, he saw the face of his son in the window. Relief flooded through his limbs. "Is he coming?"

"Naw," the deputy said. "The deal is that you go, and you go alone. Besides, how would it look if he disappeared the same night as you? Everybody'd know he had a hand in letting you free. I'd be in real trouble."

Isaac glanced over at the rifle rack, then impatience got the better of him, and he pushed out the front door. He rounded the office and ducked into the alley. There was no city man alive who could ambush him by surprise in the darkness. The alley was just ahead, and when he came to it, he froze against the wall and listened. All he could hear was his horse stomping impatiently. That, and the damn city noises. Shouting, laughter, an out-of-tune piano banging somewhere. An argument and a cry of pain.

Isaac cussed the city and all the men who loved it. He took a deep breath and moved toward his horse. Now that he was out from between the buildings, there was moon and starlight.

A dog began to bark just down the alley, and as he neared his horse, the barking became louder. Isaac touched the muzzle of the horse and untied the reins. True to the deputy's word, the big Hawken, along with all his other supplies, was tied to his saddle. He'd misjudged Matthew. Matthew was his son and maybe he'd come along in a day or two. Isaac decided he would clear out of this part of the country and wait on the plains, just in case. He quickly checked his cinch and put one foot in the stirrup with the sound of the barking dog filling his ears.

"Going west, mountain man?" The sheriff held a huge dog on a leash.

Isaac froze at the familiar sound of the sheriff's voice. "Just leaving," he said.

"Escaping is what it is. Now that you're escaped, that

means *I'm* the one that will get the reward. Turn around, Beard."

With his foot still in his stirrup, Isaac turned to face the sheriff's gun. "I'm sorry it had to be this way," Moss said.

Isaac knew he was a dead man. He lunged at the sheriff but his moccasin twisted in the stirrup, and with the roar of the gun blanketing the space between them, he felt the jolt and the burning tear of bullets striking his chest. His horse bolted, and just as Isaac was reaching for Moss's throat, the horse jerked him off balance and dragged him at its side. Isaac dimly felt the animal's hooves striking his face and head. With the last of his strength, he tried to reach for his Green River knife to cut himself loose. But then he remembered the sheriff had taken his knife away. He momentarily lost consciousness and relaxed. His foot broke free of the stirrup, and he went rolling into some garbage where he lay unable to move, feeling his heart slow to almost nothing and hearing the dog and the sound of the sheriff running away. I am a dead man, he thought as tears filled his eyes. I'll never see Chipeta again, or the Shining Mountains, or Nathan. Worst of all, Matthew has betrayed me.   .

Matthew had seen the door to the sheriff's office open a crack. He'd pulled back the curtains and lit a cigar. He'd held the match longer than was necessary, and his father had looked up and had seen his face for an instant. The old mountain man hesitated and then headed around the corner of the sheriff's office to the alley where his horse had been waiting.

Now blowing cigar smoke out into the chill night air, Matthew said aloud, "I'll come some day and show both you and Nathan that I did the family proud."

He was about to rise from his chair when the sound of three gunshots bracketed the street. The cigar fell from his lips. An instant later, he saw his father's horse come racing out between the sheriff's office and the gunsmith's shop. The horse was riderless, and Isaac's empty stirrup leathers flapped like broken wings.

Matthew swore as he raced out of the room and down the stairs past a startled night clerk, who yelled, "You better stay out of harm's way!"

Matthew leaped off the boardwalk and charged across the street with a sick feeling of dread. He almost collided with the sheriff and the deputy.

"Evening, Mr. Beard," Sheriff Moss said, with his dog on a leash and his voice betraying nothing except a hint of regret. "I'm afraid your pa is dead. Best leave it be."

Art Logman came running up, but when he saw Matthew he froze and took a step back. "Art," the sheriff said almost conversationally. "Go find the undertaker. Tell him he's got some business in the alley."

People were starting to gather. Moss leaned forward and said, "My deputy lost a pile of money early this evening at a poker game. I wondered where it came from, and we had a little talk. I believe you and I also need to have a little private conversation before morning."

Matthew nodded, his big hands clenched at his sides. The dog, a fierce-looking mongrel, growled and bared its teeth.

"He's a vicious animal," Moss conceded, "but a loyal one. About your father, I think I understand how you feel. Isaac was your father, but you never even knew him and he left you nothing but troubles. Meet me down by the levee in about an hour, Mr. Beard. I'm afraid I have some more bad news for you."

Matthew shoved past the lawman and headed for the alley on the run. It was as dark as a tomb between the buildings, but when he reached the spot there was enough moonlight to see his father stretched out on the ground with three bullets in his chest, side and back. It had been target practice. It had been a setup. Isaac's face was pulverized, and Matthew wanted to vomit. He started to cover his mouth, and then he heard the rattle of his father's throat.

"Matt?" A whisper. No more.

He placed his face to the man's ear, even though it was torn half away. "It's me!" he groaned. "We were betrayed! I'm so goddamn sorry, Pa!"

Isaac felt as if he were falling toward the center of the Earth. His body was separate from his mind. The body was dead, the mind clawed at the hole through which it dropped. He willed his mouth to say, "It's . . . all right!"

He wanted to say more. Much, much more. But it was

enough, and the mind, knowing it was enough, spun into eternal darkness.

"I'll kill him for this," Matthew said in a voice ragged with fury. "I'll kill them both!"

Matthew held his father for a long time until the warmth left the old man's body, and then Matthew realized that he and his father were not alone. Men with lanterns had invaded the alley, gawking and whispering. Matthew shouted, "Get the hell out of here, goddamn you!"

The lights dimmed as the spectators retreated farther into the shadows. But they didn't go away. Instead, they stood and watched and waited.

Matthew had to struggle to pick his father out of the garbage. He carried him out of the alley while the undertaker hurried ahead to make his preparations. And when Isaac was laid out under the pale light of a kerosene lamp, Matthew really saw what terrible damage had been done to the old mountain man.

"I can't . . ." The undertaker threw up his little arms in a helpless gesture. "Mr. Beard, what do you want me to do?"

"I want you to bury him in a pine box, no fancy casket. I want him up on the hill over the river, where he'll face west toward the sky and the prairie."

"But . . ."

Something horrible in Matthew Beard's face made the undertaker grow very still and quiet. And then Matthew went to see the sheriff.

He and the sheriff met beside the river. The mongrel strained at its leash, a deep rumbling growl in its throat. The sheriff held a gun in his fist.

Matthew was thinking now. "The gun isn't necessary, Sheriff."

Moss kept the gun aimed and cocked. "I guess I've learned to be on the cautious side after all these years. I'll hang on to the gun, since you haven't heard me out yet."

Matthew glanced at the dog. He shifted onto the balls of his feet and weighed his chances of killing this man with a single blow to the neck. The odds, complicated by the dog, were not good. He forced himself to relax. "I think I can guess.

You intend to blackmail me. You figure that your word, and that of your deputy, are enough to put me behind bars for helping a prisoner escape."

Moss wanted to be reasonable. "Matt, there's no need to sully your fine reputation. All I want from you is a hundred dollars a week."

"That's a lot of money."

"You'll hardly miss it," the sheriff said. "Besides, I promised Art a cut. Neither of us will ever be as rich as you but it's nice to spread the wealth around, don't you think?"

Matthew stared at the sheriff until he grew uneasy, and the dog lunged at him and had to be held under control. "He don't like you."

"The feeling is mutual," Matthew said.

"You don't have to pay me until next week."

Keeping his eyes on the dog, Matt said, "Where?"

"Right here is fine. Same time."

Matthew turned and started to walk away.

"Why'd you do it?" Moss blurted. "Isaac was nothing to you but a name. The man was a complete stranger and yet you put yourself into this position. I always took you for a very intelligent man, one who never made the dumb mistakes. What happened?"

Matthew turned. For a moment, he almost went for the sheriff, but he knew the dog would stop him long enough for Moss to use his gun. "To begin with, my father was innocent of the charge of murder. He killed a foolish young deputy in self-defense."

"Is that all?"

"No. Isaac thought enough of me to risk his life coming back to this town."

'He was a fool."

"That's right," Matthew said, "but he didn't deserve to be shot down in an alley, did he? All the man wanted was to get back to his damned mountains, his squaw, and his adopted Indian people. Doesn't seem like he should have died for that."

"Take it from me. A lot of good men have died for a whole lot less. And though you won't believe this, I'm sorry it was your father. It's just that the stakes were too damn high to play it any other way. You see, when your pa stepped back out on the streets tonight, he was free again and that means I'm the one who gets paid the reward money, not Sipple. I'm forty-three years old, Matt. That's pushing a lawman's luck. You're twenty years younger and already rich. You can understand why I had to use the opportunity, can't you?"

Matthew knew better than to answer.

A month later, St. Louis was hit by a fierce winter storm. There was broken ice along the edge of the river, and the wind was driving snow slantwise when Matthew approached the sheriff to make his weekly blackmail payment. The man had not brought his dog and Matt was not particularly surprised. The huge mongrel was a short-haired breed. It would have frozen outdoors on a night like this. Even bundled up in a sheepskin-lined overcoat, Moss was shivering, with his hands deep in his pockets. Matt took it for granted that anyone as smart and experienced as the sheriff would be holding a gun in his right fist.

"You're late!" Moss yelled into the howling wind. "I'm freezing my ass out here and you're late!"

Matthew's lips pulled back across his teeth in a rigid grin, and he made no reply. He extended a wad of cash, hoping that the sheriff would take his right hand out of his pocket, but Moss reached for the money with his left, confirming Matt's suspicion that he had a gun in his hidden fist.

Gun or not, Matthew knew that this was the night he had been waiting for. The dog had been the sheriff's edge until this moment. So, when their hands met, Matthew drove his left fist into Moss's right side. The gun exploded in the sheepskin-lined pocket and the wool lining caught fire. Moss screamed and yanked his hand out of the pocket, but by then his fingers had already been seared by the muzzle's fire. He was in Matthew's grasp.

"Your coat is on fire," Matthew shouted into the sheriff's face. "Too cold to take it off, so I guess you better go for a swim."

"No!"

Moss dropped the money onto the icy levee. He struggled like a rabbit caught in a noose as Matthew backed him to the river's edge. "Please," he cried. "I swear I won't . . ."

Matthew didn't want to hear any more. Instead of Sheriff Moss's mask of terror, he saw Isaac's face, battered almost beyond recognition. With all his strength, Matthew hurled the sheriff off the levee. Moss hit the water and had time to cry for help only once as the swift current saturated his heavy overcoat and pulled him under.

Matthew watched the sheriff's head disappear in the dark water. He retrieved the wad of greenbacks, and then he started back to pay a visit to Deputy Logman. If anything, the blizzard was intensifying when he reached the sheriff's office and banged on the door.

"Open up!"

Logman opened the door and before he realized his danger, Matt's fist smashed his throat. The deputy collapsed and began to writhe on the floor, clutching his crushed windpipe. His face turned purple and his eyes bugged out of his face. He stared up at Matt, pleading in silence.

"Sorry it worked out this way, Art," Matthew hissed. "But you made a deal and then you double-crossed me and let my father pay the price. Now, it's your turn, only it's going to take a few minutes, as it did for Isaac."

Logman's hands lifted in supplication, then began to flutter, the fingers working spastically. Matthew forced himself to look at the dying man. "I've sold everything I own in St. Louis, so I won't be around to see your funeral. I'm heading west."

Matthew stepped out of the office and the deputy clawed at his legs, dragging his body along until Matthew slammed the door shut and leaned back against it to hold the knob tightly. Even over the moaning wind, he thought he could hear Art Logman's fingernails scratching against the door. Matthew took a deep, shuddering breath and closed his eyes for a minute, then opened them. This was all such a nightmare, a goddamn tragedy that was like a runaway train. Once started, it had to go on until it was finished. Now, it was finished.

The streets of St. Louis were empty, and when the scratching died, Matthew turned the knob and threw his shoulder to the door to push it and the deputy's body aside. He stared at Logman and watched the swirling snow enter the warm office and melt. In an hour, the room would be freezing, and the snow would cover the floor, the desk, and the body.

California was supposed to have a lot of sunshine and damn little snow. Now that he had balanced the scales of justice against the betrayers who'd killed his father, he could write Nathan a letter of explanation. The slate was clean. It was time to look to the future. To steam navigation. In the morning, he'd withdraw all his money and take a Mississippi riverboat to New Orleans and then another to San Francisco.

He could hardly wait.

≈ 13 ≈

Matthew Beard stood at the wheel of his stately four-decker steamship, the *St. Louis*. It was September, blazing hot in the Central Valley, and the worst time of year to navigate the shallow Sacramento River. From the wheelhouse, Matthew could see dozens of vessels carrying passengers and cargo back and forth between the great port of San Francisco and the inland terminal of Sacramento. The *J. D. Miller*, a sixty-ton passenger steamship, emerged around a wide bend and Matthew skillfully eased his vessel up a deep channel that would bring him closer to the eastern bank of the river. He blasted his whistle in greeting and the *J. D. Miller* responded, just as she had been doing for the past seven years.

Matthew wore a navy-blue captain's jacket with gold piping. Gold braid decorated his cap's brim. The *St. Louis* was the finest passenger steamship on the West Coast and Matthew was proud to say he had designed and watched its construction every step of the way. It was 160 feet long, 38 feet across the beam, and could transport 220 passengers and over 50 tons of cargo and ballast without drafting more than 40 inches. Pretty as a tiered wedding cake, it boasted teakwood rails and polished brass fixtures from stem to stern. In the staterooms, galleries, ballroom, and two saloons, the floors were resplendent with floral carpets, as rich as anything in San Francisco. Oriental tapestries decorated the most desirable cabins, and European artwork graced every bulkhead. In the main dining room, the first-class passengers ate five-course dinners accompanied by orchestra music.

But there were passengers who crowded the lower decks who never saw the fine staterooms and saloons of the *St. Louis*. For these gold-fevered argonauts, Matthew offered third-class rates that were far less than what he charged for first-class passage. In foul weather, these people slept in the hold of his steamship, and when it was fair, they slept right on the lower deck under the stars. There was no great profit in argonauts, and a few first-class passengers resented them, but Matthew refused to drop the service. He enjoyed the gold seekers and admired both their courage and their enthusiasm for the adventure that lay ahead. They came from all over the world in hope of striking it rich. Most were desperately poor, half starved, ill-clothed, and inadequately provisioned for the rigors they would soon encounter. Others seemed better prepared. Some of the Mexicans, Welsh, and South Americans were experienced miners who knew exactly what they faced in the Sierra Nevadas.

On every voyage up the Sacramento, a few women would be among the argonauts. Often, they were prostitutes. Occasionally, there were also married women with their children, either traveling with their husbands or journeying alone to rejoin their men, some of whom had been in California for years dashing frantically from one rumored new strike to another while their families back East waited and prayed for them to return. But they rarely did, and when waiting became unbearable, the women and their children would sometimes find the means to come west in search of their lost husbands and fathers.

Matthew gave these women and their children every consideration. This trip, he had a tall, handsome Irish woman with a charming little girl of about seven. Like her mother, the child had large green eyes and strawberry blonde hair. Her mother was probably in her late twenties and attractive enough so that Matthew had studied the passenger list and learned her name was Mrs. John O'Day. Matthew wondered at the courage of such a woman who would travel halfway around the continent in search of a fool.

He turned to his first mate and said, "No fog, so they ought to be getting their first glimpse of the Sierras when we round that bend and have a clear view to the mountains."

"Yes, sir." First Mate Ben Edgerton shook his head as he followed Matthew's gaze down to the crowded lower deck. There were no less than a hundred people jammed up near the bow with their eyes fixed toward the Sierras. "They look like they expect to walk streets paved with gold," he said.

"Maybe they do expect to see gold in the streets. You know, the Chinese call the Sierras 'Gum San.' It means 'The Mountain of Gold,' or something like that."

"I don't like the Chinamen," Edgerton said. "They're too damned clannish and think they're superior to all other races. Why, all they want to do is find gold and take it back to China."

Matthew said, "But they're sober and industrious and I like 'em a hell of a lot better than Indians."

"Not many of them left," Edgerton said. "Forty-niners have about wiped 'em out. Modocs were the last in California to put up any kind of a fuss."

Matthew saw Mrs. O'Day jostled by a dirty, rough-looking fellow in a leather coat. "Take the wheel," he said, stepping to the rail. But it was not necessary for him to intervene, because several other young men were already demanding and receiving an apology from the ruffian, who stalked away. It amused Matthew that the young argonauts were falling all over themselves to impress the woman even though it was obvious she was married.

The argonauts sometimes made Matthew feel old, old and wise. How many of these stalwart adventurers would find anything but defeat in the icy rivers of the Sierras? But at least they had a dream and enough optimism to believe that working twelve to fifteen hours a day in an icy stream qualified as high adventure.

The little O'Day girl happened to look up and catch his eye. She smiled and Matthew waved in greeting. The girl laughed and the sound of it lifted his spirits. Rose was her name and he almost wished he'd fathered one like that for himself. "He *was* getting old!

As if reading his thoughts, the first mate said, "Captain, do you think that woman will find her husband?"

"Nope. He's either dead or crazy. Otherwise, he'd have gone home by now."

"More and more are bringing their families, though," the first mate said. "They're settling down in the San Joaquin Valley. They say it's the best soil in the world for growin' wheat, corn, fruit, or hay."

There were crops and farms as far as he could see. The soil was dark and loamy and the California growing season was truly remarkable. "I suspect that soil is California's real gold. But if the farmers keep draining the river for irrigation, we'll soon be out of the steamship business."

"Are you still considering a sea-going vessel for the Los Angeles and the San Diego trade?"

"I am," Matthew said. "I've mastered this river. I know every sandbar and snag all the way north to Red Bluff and a hundred miles south into the San Joaquin. But it's changing too fast. Besides the farmers draining off so much water, hydraulic mining and dredging is killing the fish and sludging up the deeper channels so navigation is getting damn near impossible by late summer. It won't be but a year or two before you won't be able to get up and down this river with anything bigger than a rowboat."

"You're one of the few men who can do it now with a ship this size."

Matthew was going to say something, but just as he opened his mouth, the *St. Louis* struck a hidden sandbar, and everyone was thrown violently forward. The bow railing broke, and Matthew caught a glimpse of people tumbling overboard into the river.

He hollered into the speaker's tube down to the engine room. "Reverse engines!"

It seemed like an eternity before his order was relayed and the paddles slowed, stopped, and then were finally reversed. He could feel the entire ship tremble as the powerful engine struggled to pull the huge sternwheeler off its sandy berth.

"Sir!" a member of the crew shouted up from the lower deck. "Port side, Mrs. O'Day and her daughter are being carried back toward the sternwheel! They got past us!"

Matthew bellowed into his speaking tube. "Stop engines! Stop engines!"

Not waiting for a response from below, Matthew raced over to the edge of his ship and looked off the port side. He was horrified to see the woman and her little girl being swept alongside the ship's hull toward the great paddlewheel. Matthew knew it would take at least twenty seconds for the paddles to stop their ponderous rotation completely. By then, it would be too late. The huge paddles were churning crazily at the river, driving water and tons of sand upward, then twisting it into an angry whirlpool that would almost certainly swallow the woman and girl in a single gulp.

Matthew ripped off his blue cap and coat, then threw himself off the upper deck of the ship. It was a good fifty feet to the river and when he hit, Matthew went far underwater but immediately clawed his way up to the surface and began to swim powerfully toward Mrs. O'Day and her daughter, who were already being spun around in a slow but deadly circle toward the vortex.

Matthew entered the whirlpool, trod water, and let the current spin the woman and child to him. He grabbed them and shouted, "Hang on!"

Matthew could feel the undertow lessening and, all at once, the whirlpool filled, like sand sliding into a hole. Moments later, they were bobbing in the muddy Sacramento River a good mile from his grounded steamship.

"Let's swim for shore," he said, feeling the muscles of his arms already growing heavy. "Rose, stay on my back. Mrs. O'Day, can you make it that far?"

"Yes, I think so." But her brave words could not hide the fact that she was not a good swimmer and that her heavy dress and undergarments were dragging her under. Matthew gauged the distance to shore. More than a hundred yards. The woman would never make it. Heavy clothing was dragging her down and acting like a sea anchor.

"Take them off!" he shouted.

"What!"

She could barely keep her head above water. "Don't die for modesty, take off that dress!"

"No!"

He ripped the dress off with his bare hands and was none too gentle about it. She tried to fight him but was too weary, and once the dress was gone and she was covered only by a light chemise, even through her anger she could see that the move had a dramatic result.

"I'm sorry," he gasped, "but it was necessary."

"I . . . know," she panted. "I think I can make it now. Just don't let go of Rose."

"I won't," he said, staying close to the woman as she paddled toward shore. "But don't give up! We'll make it."

She stopped for a moment, and he thought she was going to go under but instead she said, "Of course, I'll make it!"

They swam for what seemed like hours until Matthew's fingers touched the muddy bottom of the river, and he knew they had made it to safety. He stood up, and the water was still up to his waist as he carried Rose nearer to shore, then rushed back and helped her mother into shallow water.

She was totally exhausted, and it was several minutes before she could even speak. Brushing mud and water from her eyes, she said, "Sir, you saved our lives."

"How could I do less? I'm the captain. It's my fault that you and your daughter were hurled into the water."

She blinked. "Yes," she said, "I guess it is at that. But . . . well, you've certainly redeemed yourself, Captain . . ."

"Beard," he said. "Matthew Beard. I want to buy you and your daughter new dresses."

At the mention of her dress, the woman suddenly looked down at herself. The thin chemise was very revealing, and she let out a little cry of alarm and covered her breasts and crossed her legs, then scooted deeper into the water where he could not see her body clearly.

"Damnit!" she cried. "I not only lost my dress, but the last of our funds."

"I'll replace those, too," he said, "every penny. And I'll do whatever else I can to help you find your husband."

"Not only do you know our names, you know our mission! How?"

"Your situation is not uncommon, I'm afraid. Where are you going?"

"Columbia. Is it far from Sacramento?"

"Couple of hundred miles."

The woman frowned with disappointment. "I was hoping it was close. But then, after coming from Boston around Cape Horn, I guess two hundred more miles isn't such a trial."

"Is that where your husband is?"

"I can't be sure. But the last letter we received from him had that postmark."

"It's a hard country," he said. "A lot of men go into the gold camps and never come out."

"John is alive," she insisted. "I can feel it, though I don't expect you to believe in that sort of thing."

"If he's alive, then why hasn't he written recently?" Matthew regretted the question. "I'm sorry, that's none of my business. I shouldn't have asked."

"Captain, I believe in God and Satan. If my husband is alive, the only reason he would have forsaken us is if he has lost his soul to the devil. And if that is the case, then it's up to me and Rose to save him."

"That's admirable," Matthew said. "But in the gold fields, you'll find little of God. And I don't know if there's a Satan or not, but those camps are wild and they're full of the devil. It's no place for a woman on her own and a little girl."

"We have to go, Captain . . ." A sudden change of pitch in the *St. Louis*'s engines brought Matthew's head around and caused the woman to say, "What's wrong?"

A loud bang that carried across the water was followed by a tower of steam from the vessel. "Damn," Matthew swore, "I think she blew her boiler!"

"That sounds very serious."

"It is. She'll be out of service for at least a month. I'll probably have to have a boiler shipped across the Isthmus of Panama, if I can't find one in California. I'm out of business for a while, Mrs. O'Day."

"Helen," she said. "I won't stand on etiquette with a man who has just saved my life. And I'm sorry. Very sorry."

Matthew expelled a deep sigh. "Oh, well. I haven't had a break for seven years. Maybe the boiler was due to go and it was a sign I need to get away for a bit. Tell me, how would you and your daughter like it if I took you to Columbia?"

"It would not be proper."

"Mother!"

She looked down at the girl, who obviously disagreed. "I'm sorry, Rose, but it wouldn't."

Matthew saw a rowboat being lowered from the *St. Louis*. Two men with two oars would bring the boat swiftly downriver to them. "Listen," he said. "I don't want to alarm you, but there are highwaymen on the road to Columbia. And murderers, too. It's dangerous, and there are no stages running. I could offer you both safety. Is it really worth appearances to risk your life, and that of this lovely girl?" He patted Rose on the head.

Helen O'Day's expression changed. She said, "Captain, you are a very conniving man."

"I am," he admitted. "But that doesn't mean you should remain obstinate in the face of reason."

"I won't stand for any foolishness. I'm a married woman. All I want is my husband and this child's father."

"Fair enough."

"May I have your sworn word that you're entirely honorable?"

"I'm not honorable at all," he said with a straight face. "But I swear that I'll behave. Rose, do you believe me?"

"Yes."

"See!"

Helen O'Day had little choice but to accept. "All right then. But this rowboat of yours that is coming, unless they have brought me a dress to wear, I will not get out of this water."

"It's not likely they have."

"Then send them back for one," she said.

Matthew thought that she might be kidding until he looked deep into her green eyes and saw that she was not. "They won't be happy about this."

"Well," she said, sinking a little deeper into the muddy water, "I'm not very happy either."

He looked at Rose, and she just shrugged her little shoulders and smiled. It was a sign that told him Helen O'Day could be a very stubborn woman. "Very well," Matthew said, unable to hide his disappointment at not seeing the woman stand up, "I'll send them back for the damned dress."

Hangtown, Drytown, Fiddletown, Tuttletown. Mokelumne Hill, Chili Gulch, Sutter Creek, Carson Hill.

On their way to Columbia, Matthew had seen them all and been surprised at how much those towns had grown. Tall brick buildings had replaced the tent cities he'd seen when last he visited the gold country. Sure, there were a lot of boom-towns that had just disappeared and were forgotten already, but now there was an air of permanence in the Sierra foothills. Agriculture, timber, and finance had become a part of the economic structure of most of the communities that had survived the first wild years of boom and bust. Helen and Rose were impressed with the lovely foothill country with its rich red soil, heavy green forests, and great wild rivers.

Matthew had rented a carriage, and now, as they ap-proached the town of Columbia, he was keenly aware of the woman at his side. There was such a tension in her that it screamed for relief. He wondered if she was more afraid of learning that her husband was dead than of the possibility of finding him living in mortal sin. If John O'Day were dead, then he could be mourned. But if he were alive and had taken up with another woman or succumbed to drink and debauchery, what then? Their brief ride down through the Sierra gold strike country had left no doubt that gambling, whoring, and drinking were the three primary occupations of the forty-niners.

"Matthew?"

"Yes?"

She studiously avoided looking at him. "Matthew, forgive me for asking, but what do you expect to get out of this?"

For a moment, he said nothing. Then, stalling for time, he asked, "What do you mean?"

"I mean that we can't give you anything in return for this kindness. I don't want you hurt or disappointed."

He forced a bad laugh. "What the deuce are you talking about! I needed a vacation from the river and this was my excuse. That's all."

"Good!" She said, touching his arm. "I'm so relieved. You'll have to forgive my question . . . and my foolish conceit. I thought perhaps . . ."

"What did you think?"

"Nothing," she replied.

He thought she had been about to say she was worried that he might have become attracted to her, worried because, no matter what, she'd never give her heart to him. He was too big. Too coarse . . . perhaps even too ugly. There was a gentleness, a refinement and, most of all, a shining spiritually about Helen that would be repelled by a godless giant such as himself. A closet murderer.

Matthew's spirits fell and a darkness closed over his mind, for he was certain that she had divined the blackness of his soul. Her next words did nothing to dispel that notion.

"Matthew," she said, "I want you to understand that our welfare is not your concern."

When he could not speak, she added, "Will you please understand that?"

"You might need help." It was all he could say.

"The Lord is our strength. His is even greater than your own."

"But the Lord can't . . ." Her eyes touched his and protest withered on his lips. How could anyone question another's faith? There was no logic, nothing to refute. Faith like Helen's was unassailable with words. Matthew just clamped his mouth shut and drove into Columbia.

The town had been leveled twice by fire, so its residents had reconstructed from the ground up, using red bricks and adobe. They'd planted shade trees all along Main Street, and the result was that Columbia had become one of the prettiest communities along the western slope of the Sierras. It had a prosperous air and, unlike some of the wilder towns, here they saw women and children strolling unmolested along the boardwalk, shopping and visiting. They passed St. Ann's

Catholic Church and the Fallon House Theater, then the
two-storied Wells Fargo office with its signature dark-green
iron shutters and fancy grillwork. Jut a few doors away,
Matthew spotted the newspaper office.

"Helen," he said, "I suggest that we start asking about
your husband at the local newspaper. People are what make
the news and the editor would be the one most likely to know
if your husband is still in these parts."

"All right," she said as he pulled up in front of the office,
"I would not have thought of that. Rose, wait here with Matt.
I won't be long."

"I think I'd better accompany you," he said, climbing
down and offering her his hand. "Rose can wait right here on
this bench by the door. We'll be just inside."

Helen was too preoccupied with her emotions to argue,
and they went in. The *Columbia Gazette*, cluttered and
chaotic, looked like every other newspaper office Matthew had
seen in California. There were trays of lead type, stacks of
newsprint, and right in the center of the confusion sat a big
Washington Printing Press where the editor stood with an ink
roller in his hand.

"Good afternoon!" he called, pushing back a green eye-
shade to reveal prematurely gray hair and a receding hairline
that somehow made him look very intelligent. "Did you come
to place some advertising?"

"Afraid not," Matthew said.

"Then to buy a paper? Only two bits and . . ."

It was Helen, with her nerves stretched to the limit, who
uncharacteristically interrupted him. "Sir, I am Mrs. O'Day. I've
come to Columbia in search of my husband. Can you help me?"

The editor's pleasant smile melted. "You're John O'Day's
wife, come from Boston?"

"Then you do know him!"

The editor's glance flicked to Matthew, then back to the
woman. "Ah . . . Mrs. O'Day," he said, "I'm afraid I have
some very bad news about your husband."

Helen blinked, then lifted her chin. In a small voice, she
said, "Is he dead?"

"No." The editor wiped his ink-stained hands on the dirty

apron he wore. "Listen," he said, "I think it would be better if
you talked to the sheriff."

"No!" Matthew said.

The editor swallowed and walked over to a counter where
stacks of papers were resting on a table. "Let me see," he
began as he thumbed through the pages. "Yes, here it is. Take
this paper free of charge, Mrs. O'Day. It will tell you about
your husband far better, and in greater detail, than I could
relate under these circumstances."

Matthew started to protest but Helen took the newspaper
and started for the door. He let her go, and when the door
closed, he turned on the editor and said, "All right. You tell me
to my face. What did O'Day do?"

"He's a murderer," the editor said. "A callous, cold-
blooded murderer who is certain to hang. Now, if you'll excuse
me, I have a paper to get out."

Matthew moved around the counter and continued, "I
want to hear what happened firsthand. Who did her husband
kill and why?"

The editor walked over to his type and began to sling lead
onto the tray as he talked. "I didn't want to tell that lovely lady
the truth, but John O'Day is as good as a dead man, and I say
good riddance. He started prospecting, made a strike, and
bought himself a saloon and gambling hall. Before we knew it,
he had hired bullies to collect gambling debts won on his
crooked card tables. He took claims worth thousands for debts
that amounted to hundreds. He brought prostitution into
Columbia and controlled it by hiring murderers. Perhaps most
unforgivable of all, he and his madam, a creature named Irma
St. Clair, flaunted the morality of our lovely town by attending
church every Sunday with their stable of ladies."

"Even whores need religion," Matthew said. "Who did he
kill?"

"His lover, Miss St. Clair. He tried to strangle her with
her own stockings, and when that failed, he shot her twice
through the heart up in their room. And after she was dead,
the heartless bastard threw her out the second-story window of
the Shasta Hotel. Of course, Irma was as rotten as he was, and
the whole town was glad to get rid of her, but it was still
murder."

"I'm surprised he didn't get lynched on the spot."

"There was a tense confrontation that almost resulted in wholesale slaughter. Fortunately, reason prevailed and O'Day's henchmen left town. We have a dedicated sheriff who took it upon himself to see that O'Day was whisked off to Sacramento where he'd live long enough to stand trial. 'Course, he'll hang there as certain as he would here. And there are many of us who will go to Sacramento to watch and cheer."

Matthew rubbed his temples in thought. "Did you express that sentiment in the newspaper you gave her?"

The editor's hands stopped flying over his typesetting tray, and he bristled with anger. "Of course not! I print the facts, sir. Honestly, Besides, I couldn't tell her the ghastly details and watch her crumble at my feet, now could I?"

"No," Matthew said. "You couldn't. Thanks."

Somewhat mollified, the editor stepped over to his front window and pulled the shade aside to look out at Helen and Rose. "Damn shame that handsome, decent woman and her child had to learn the truth. It's impossible to figure why a man would desert his wife and daughter when he could have taken his money and gone home. I knew John O'Day right from the start. He was a good man when he arrived in Columbia. Money *does* corrupt. After John made his strike and hooked up with Irma, well . . . he just changed. He bragged he was going to be the richest man on the Mother Lode. And you can quote that."

"What about his saloon and properties?"

The editor's eyes widened with understanding. "Well, of course! If he's hanged, they're likely to go to his legal widow and his children. That means that Mrs. O'Day and that pretty little girl would inherit quite a lot of money."

Matthew nodded and headed for the door. He had just learned all that was really important.

Their trip back to Sacramento was grim and silent. They had not talked about John O'Day at all, and Matthew had read the newspaper himself and the details were as the Columbia editor had described them, only in kinder terms. Matthew felt badly for Helen and Rose, though it was clear that the child did not know or love her father. He wished that the citizens of

Columbia had strung up O'Day and then all this business
would be over. Maybe, he thought, as he drove the carriage
through bustling Hangtown and then turned west down the
slopes of the Sierra foothills, the man has already been
sentenced and hanged. Frontier justice was swift, and it was a
fair possibility.

There was one other article in the *Columbia Gazette* that
caught his attention. The United States Army was sending a
Lieutenant Joseph C. Ives to the Gulf of California with orders
to explore the Colorado River from its mouth to its headwaters
to determine if the river was navigable up to the Utah
Territory. Apparently, the Army was interest in finding out if
military troops and supplies could be moved upriver from Fort
Yuma, Arizona Territory, in order to quell an outbreak of
hostilities between the Mormons and the United States government. The expedition was forming in San Francisco and
would be leaving that port on a schooner called the *Monterey*,
with supplies and the expedition's small, disassembled steamship, the *Explorer*, which had just arrived from Philadelphia.
The newspaper ended the account by describing the Ives
expedition as "daring and bold."

Matthew could not put this piece of news from his mind.
He was already a rich man but he yearned for adventure. And
he recalled that the Colorado River had been a constant source
of fascination to Isaac. What if he offered his well-seasoned
river navigational skills to the United States Army? What if
he—rather than his father—was among the chosen few to map
and explore the Colorado, or Grand River, as the old-timers
still called it.

Now that was a delicious thought. Not only could he show
up Nathan, who had thought him avaricious and timid for
remaining in St. Louis, but he would also snatch a piece of
history for himself and prove that he was every bit as much of
a frontier explorer as his father.

Helen touched his hand. She had been very withdrawn
since leaving Columbia. "Matthew?"

He pulled himself back to the present. "Yes?"

"If my husband is still alive, will you help him?"

He knew how difficult it must have been for her to make

the request, so he responded with care. "I'm not sure there's anything I can do."

"But you must be acquainted with many influential people in Sacramento."

"I know a few, but . . ."

"Please help. For me and Rose, if not for John."

"I'll do what's best," he hedged. "I don't want you to worry."

She actually leaned her head against his shoulder. "I've never had a man for a friend. And . . . I hope you won't take this wrong . . . but I'd never have picked one like you."

"Why not?"

"Because . . . well . . . because, on the surface, you look and act so . . . so hard. Then after I got to know you, I realized it was just your size that's so intimidating. Inside, you have a wonderful heart. There are not many men who would do this for a stranger. I shall never forget you, Matthew. And neither will Rose."

Matthew could not speak in reply. He was frozen with the realization of what he would soon be losing. He cursed himself silently for falling in love with a married woman—with a faithful Catholic married woman who'd never be his as long as her husband lived, a husband who had gone rotten, murdered a whore, and thrown her body out of a second-story window. Anger and hatred for the man threatened to choke Matthew, and he had no choice but to shout, "I hope he's already dead, Helen. Forgive me, but I do!"

She recoiled and, as he drove along, he watched her cover her face and cry.

"Damnation!" Matthew cursed under his breath as he stepped out of the sheriff's office and headed for the carriage. "Damnation!"

Helen O'Day stood a half block away with Rose at her side as Matthew strode down to tell them that their husband and father had been sentenced to a long prison term instead of the gallows.

"He's alive, isn't he? I can tell by your expression."

"Yeah."

She sighed with relief. "Where can I see him?"

"You can't," Matthew snapped. "Not until visiting day next Sunday. Helen, the sheriff said your husband hired the best lawyer money could buy and, even so, he'll be in prison a minimum of twenty-five years."

"He's my husband," she said. "I'm a Roman Catholic and you must know we don't believe in divorce. I've no choice but to wait."

Matthew's voice hardened. "For a quarter of a century? Helen, come to your senses! Rose will be grown and have children of her own by then! And how are you supposed to live?"

"Stop it! Please don't say another word!" she cried. "No matter what he has done, there is always room for forgiveness."

Matthew groaned and balled his fists. "You don't know what you're saying, and I can't sit by idly and watch you martyr yourself and Rose, just throw twenty-five years of your life away on someone who abandoned you."

"It's my life. My choice!"

"Please," he said, knowing he was losing and there was nothing he could say or do to change her mind, but also knowing he had to try. "I admire you so much. You're good, and strong, beautiful and kind, but in twenty-five years you'll have sacrificed too much. You'll have given the best part of your life to loneliness and poverty and you'll be a tragic old lady. For what? For a man like John O'Day! Helen, he's not worth the sacrifice. It's wrong!"

She did something totally unexpected. She reached up on her toes and kissed his mouth to silence him. "You've tears in your eyes, Matthew. I . . . I'm sorry it ended this way. I really am. Goodbye."

"Helen, *please!*"

But she left him, and he knew there was nothing he could do about it. Helen O'Day was one of the few things in life he had ever wanted with all his heart and been unable to buy. "I won't let this happen," he whispered, "not to her, nor to little Rose, not even to me."

Matthew headed for the Sacramento docks where the hardest men in town hung out. Murderers and thieves, ex-convicts, too. Helen had left him no choice. If he could reach O'Day himself, he would kill the sonofabitch with his bare hands and then face the consequences, no matter what. But that, of course, was impossible. So he'd have O'Day murdered, and if Helen was right and there really was a God in heaven, maybe he'd spend yet another million years in hell for killing again. Either way, Matthew no longer gave a damn and John O'Day was already as good as dead. It was just a matter of finding the right people who could smuggle a knife and money into prison for the assassination.

John O'Day stood off by himself in the prison exercise yard. He huddled close to the stone wall, out of a cold wind, and his eyes were dark and haunted with fear. Something was wrong, terribly wrong. He was being avoided by the other inmates, and he was not sure why. Maybe it was because he had paid a man to beat up a weasel named Smitty Waters. Was it his fault that Smitty had died from the beating? The man was not supposed to have been killed, only warned that all gambling and protection debts were meant to be paid. Must be paid. Only now, someone was out for revenge.

O'Day racked his brain to think of who might want his blood. Smitty had no close friends. Hell, did any man have real friends in prison, friends he'd associate with outside? So, who was it? Who was the man keeping everyone away from him?

O'Day studied the other inmates like pieces of a puzzle. None seemed a likely candidate.

He dreamed of escape, and he had someone on the outside who was working on a plan. If an inmate had money, he could find ways to escape.

A guard stepped into the exercise yard. He put a whistle to his lips and blew two shrill blasts, the signal that it was time to return to the inside. O'Day was glad. Inside, he would be locked up alone in a cell where he would be safe until tomorrow at this time.

"All right, everyone inside," the guard yelled. "Single file!"

One hundred and fifty-seven inmates started to gather in a line, and John felt his heart quicken as he noticed that no one wanted to be in front or in back of him. Annoyed, he hurried forward but, suddenly, he felt a sharp pain in his lower back.

He staggered and a veil of bright red dropped across his eyes.
Two more steps and his legs went numb. He heard shouts and
the shrill whistles of the guards. He felt very alone, and he
slowly turned in a full circle. The other prisoners stepped back
from him, and when he reached around to the painful place, he
was not really surprised to touch the handle of a knife
protruding just under his rib cage. He felt dizzy, and a warm
wetness covered his hand as he tried to pull the offending knife
from his back. "Guard," he choked as the world began to spin.

He was down. On his face. The red veil had been bright,
now it grew dark, and he knew absolute terror. He could still
hear voices, smell the hard-packed clay prison yard, but he
could feel nothing. And that was most terrifying of all. You
could live if you could feel, couldn't you? But a corpse didn't
feel, and he could not abide the idea of being a corpse.

"Don't pull it out!" someone shouted. "Everyone get back!"
A whistle began to shriek in his ears.

"He's dying," a voice said close to his ear. "Pull the
damned knife out and roll him over!"

John's body arched as the knife was torn from his flesh.
His mouth opened and closed but he could not speak or even
breathe. A single question flooded across his mind. WHY!

"Poor bastard. He's dead."

In a sleazy waterfront bar, a giant they knew to be
Matthew Beard sat drunk and alone. Sometimes, he lurched to
his feet and stared at the rough men who shared the stinking
barroom, stared and swayed and clenched his fists, daring
anyone to say anything. Rumors were he had sold the *St. Louis*
for half its value while it was still in dry dock. Rumor had it that
Beard had fallen in love with a God-fearing woman who had
jilted him for his unworthiness.

When the giant swore at them, all conversation died.
Men looked to their drinks and finished them and waited for a
sign that the giant was leaving. Only he didn't leave. He might
urinate in the sawdust or shout for another bottle of whiskey,
but he stayed until a man came to see him.

Those in the barroom who dared sneak a glance at the
giant saw him pass money to the visitor and then smash him to

the sawdust and drive him out of the barroom on his hands and knees.

"Mr. Beard," the bartender said, reaching under the bar for a gun in case he was forced to save his own life. "You should go away."

"Where!" he cried. "Where can a man run from his pain?"

The bartender felt sweat burst from every pore as the giant advanced, his face terrible to see. "To the Barbary Coast, sir. That is where a man should run. And if that is not enough, then maybe to the sea."

Matthew halted, his mind swirling like bilge in a bottle, and a sea of guilt almost drowned him in its wash. But the bartender's desperate words reminded him of something. Concentrating hard, he blinked and wiped his face and, finally, he remembered the Ives expedition.

With slow, deliberate determination, he nodded and unclenched his fists. "Thank you," he rasped. "I will do that."

He reeled about and crashed through the door into the night. And the hard men behind him expelled a long sigh of relief.

≈ 15 ≈

Still drunk and murderous, he had booked passage on the *J. D. Miller* to San Francisco, where he deposited his sale money with the Wells Fargo office on Market Street. Knowing he would not have any chance of signing on with Lieutenant Ives in his present condition, he forced himself to stop drinking, to bathe, and to buy new clothes. For a week, he swam every afternoon in the treacherous waters of the bay, but if it were a cleansing of the spirit he sought, it did not come. Yet, sober, he could face the could truth that he had lost the only woman he would ever love and a child he had somehow grown to think of as his own. He had run from them, knowing that his eyes would have betrayed his vile deed. They would only have had to take one look at his face, and then they would have known.

But at least Helen could grieve and be done with John O'Day. Someone would find and marry her, make a father for Rose, realize his treasure and thank the Lord for Helen, some decent man without the stain of blood on his hands and soul. Matthew went back to his Barbary Coast whores but he shunned liquor and readied himself to leave California.

He knew his sanity depended upon new faces, new country, a new challenge, one different and dangerous enough to take his mind off his foolish fantasies about Helen and his little strawberry-blonde angel. He would accompany Lieutenant Ives even if he had to pay his own way and sign on as a common deckhand.

He found the lieutenant busily overseeing the loading of a steamer called the *Monterey*, which would carry the expedition's supplies and the disassembled *Explorer*. The little steamer had been shipped by railroad across the Isthmus of Panama and then had been brought up to San Francisco by coastal packet.

"Excuse me, Lieutenant," Matthew said, "but I'd like to have a word with you."

The lieutenant seemed too young to be in command of such an important mission. He had sandy hair, blue eyes, and dimples in his cheeks. He looked very innocent and inexperienced and Matthew was not sure he wanted to take orders from a boy when he had been accustomed to giving them to men.

Ives stopped for a moment and looked up at the huge man. "I'm pretty busy. What can I do for you?"

"It's I who am here to help you," Matthew said. "My name is Matthew Beard, and I'm an experienced steamship captain. There's probably none better on the Sacramento, and I want to be the captain of your Colorado steamer, which I am told is to be christened the *Explorer*."

"You're correct about the ship's name, but I'm surprised you haven't heard that I've already commissioned a captain for the expedition. The *Monterey* is under the command of Captain Walsh, who will deliver us to the mouth of the Colorado and then return to this port. The *Explorer* is to be under the command of Mr. Harold Antwerp."

"Antwerp," Matthew groaned. "The man is totally incompetent! He's a rum pot and a . . ."

"Mr. Beard, please! I will not have my ship's officer maligned."

"But Harry Antewerp has grounded vessels on every sandbar between the bay and Red Bluff. I've ten times his riverboat and navigational experience. I have—until only two days ago—been the owner and captain of the *St. Louis*, she being the largest steamer on the Sacramento."

Ives frowned and it was clear he did not believe Matthew. "Listen," he said, in a placating tone of voice, "I appreciate your offer but I have already made my decision. Besides, the Sacramento has nothing in common with the Colorado and Mr. Antwerp has navigated supply ships up to Fort Yuma."

"But anyone could do that during the early months of the year. You're planning a low-water expedition between now and spring, the lowest water of the entire year. A good navigator can tell by the ripples in the water where the channels are to be found. I could save you and your ship, sir."

"I'm sorry," Ives said, turning to leave.

Matthew knew when he was beaten, but only for the time being. Antwerp would knuckle under the first pressure, and he could take the fool's place then. In the meantime, he must first ensure himself a place on the expedition. "Then I'll sign on as a sailor."

"I have all the sailors I need."

Matthew swallowed the very last of his pride. "Very well, Lieutenant, then I'll work for free as a common deckhand."

"Why? Are you running from the law?"

"Hell, no! Ask around town about Matthew Beard."

"I don't have time."

Matthew scowled. He turned full circle, spotted some sailors, and whistled loudly. When he had their attention, he motioned them over. They were a rough-looking group, and he said, "Explain to Lieutenant Ives that I am the best captain on the Sacramento River."

"Matthew Beard is the best captain on the Sacramento River," a tall, cadaverous-looking man repeated. His companions nodded in agreement.

"See?" Matthew said, irritated that he would have to call on anyone to corroborate his achievements.

The lieutenant studied the motley collection. "All right, Mr. Beard, you are invited to accompany my expedition. If some misfortune should befall Captain Antwerp, I'll need a replacement."

"What about us?" the tall sailor asked.

Matthew shook his head. "You boys wouldn't be interested in steaming up the Colorado River and fighting off Indians for free, now would you?"

They shook their heads and walked away.

Ives said, "We sail on the *Monterey* tomorrow morning at high tide. The schooner is already stowed, with everything on board except a few charts and the navigational instruments I'll be taking on the expedition."

Matthew didn't understand. "What do you need 'navigational instruments' on a river for? We'll just follow the damned thing and see where it leads, right?"

"It's not that simple, Mr. Beard. This is an exploration party. We will map both the headwaters of the Colorado and the country surrounding it. That means I must enter a log and take celestial readings and measurements and I don't know how that is to be done any way except by the use of instruments. We'll also be joined by Dr. Newberry, a scientist who will collect geological and botanical specimens."

"I see. The account I read led me to believe the purpose of this expedition was solely military."

"Nothing could be further from the truth," Ives said. "We sail early tomorrow morning at high tide. Please arrive early."

Matthew knew that the tide would go out at 6:45 A.M. and that there was no time to lose. Still, it had been a riotous night on San Francisco's Barbary Coast, and he had enjoyed a farewell worthy of any man. Now, as he and the tall mulatto woman weaved their way down to the harbor, he could see the *Monterey* with her sails being unfurled. A brisk ocean breeze and a favorable tide would soon carry them safely out onto the Pacific, and he might never return to this fair city.

"Zena," he said, kissing his companion and then taking a swig of rye whiskey. "I'm late. I must run or I'll miss my ship!"

But the mulatto clung to him. She was exotic, with high cheekbones and full lips. Her eyes were large and her lashes wet with the fog. She threw her head back, tossing her full mane of black hair, and said, "I will go with you!"

"Uh-uh," he said, kissing her throat.

She shivered with delight and kicked off her shoes. "If we must run, then we should do it, eh! So come on!"

His heart was filled with admiration. Helen O'Day could never have drunk, sung, and danced all night the way this woman had. No sir! And now, she was pulling him down the steep hill toward the waterfront still almost a mile below. The cobblestones were as slick as ice, and they both kept losing their footing and tumbling. Whenever that happened, Matthew would bounce up to his feet, yank her erect, share a long pull on the rye, and then start running faster and faster until they fell again. They were out of rye whiskey before they reached the *Monterey*. Wet, dirtied from the street, and completely out of breath, they were too exhausted to run or laugh anymore.

Matthew looked up at the deck of the ship and saw the

rum pot, Harry Antwerp, and a small, sensitive-looking man with gold braid on his cap who must have been Captain Walsh. "Request your permission to come aboard!" Matthew shouted, mocking the customary protocol expected of a new man coming aboard ship. The sailors on deck and up in the yardarms gaped at him and the statuesque mulatto, whose heaving breasts strained at her thin silk blouse.

"Permission refused!" Antwerp cried before Captain Walsh could respond in the affirmative. "Cast the lines!"

Matthew kissed the woman and someone whistled. He reached into his coat pocket, pulled out a thick roll of greenbacks, then shoved them down the front of her blouse. The sailors began to make catcalls. "You take care of yourself. Invest in something and don't let any man take it from you."

The woman nodded, her expression turning serious. "You come back to me, Matt," she crooned, rubbing her long, supple body against his. "I make you forget anything."

Matthew laughed and finished the rye. As the sailors cast off the lines and the *Monterey*'s sails chattered with a filling wind, he leapt on deck, as wild and as savage looking as a pirate of the Caribbean. "Captain Walsh, may I acquaint you with the fact that Lieutenant Ives and I have an agreement!"

"Ives is below deck and you must remove yourself from this ship!" Antwerp yelled.

Matthew looked over the railing of the vessel and down to the black waters. "Too late."

Antwerp was a heavyset man in his fifties. He grabbed a belaying pin and charged forward. "Matthew Beard," he screamed, "I ordered you to remove yourself from this ship!"

Matthew was sober enough to duck. He buried his right fist in a place just under the captain's heart. Antwerp doubled up in pain, yet managed to cry for help, and the sailors came running to swarm all over Matthew. Their blows rained on his face and cleared the whiskey haze from this mind. He put his back to the chart house and sent lesser men reeling backward in pain. When the sailors backed off for an instant, and the way was clear, Matthew jumped forward. In two steps, he was on Antwerp and heaving the man over the ship's railing. Antwerp hit the water with a tremendous splash but came to the surface.

"Come back again and I'll keelhaul you!" Matthew roared.

Antwerp must have believed him because he took off swimming for the pier. Matthew laughed at the man and was turning when a belaying pin crashed against the side of his face and brought him to both knees. Sensing victory, the sailors piled onto him, but he was not yet beaten. Rolling, punching, and gouging, he fought with a cold joy, but the crew's blood also was up. They were hard, tough fighters and their sheer weight kept Matthew down. He managed to get two sailors in a headlock. He bashed their skulls together twice and they went limp. Suddenly, Ives was firing his gun almost in their faces and the crew was scrambling away.

Lieutenant Ives was furious. "Captain Walsh, what is going on here!"

The *Monterey*'s captain had been decked by a stray punch and was out cold.

Ives spun on his heel and barked, "Where's Captain Antwerp?"

"In the bay, sir. That's him swimming back to the pier."

Ives went to the railing and saw his captain thrashing toward shore. "This . . . this is outrageous! Mr. Beard, are you responsible for this carnage!"

"I was attacked." Matthew spat blood and managed to pull himself erect. "All I did was report for duty as we agreed. Antwerp went insane."

"And you took it upon yourself to throw him overboard and then batter my entire crew?"

"I was only defending myself, Lieutenant." One of Matthew's eyes was swollen shut, and its brow was badly torn. Matthew glared at the sailors and took satisfaction in the fact that two were still unconscious and the rest looked as if they'd tried to clear out every saloon on the Barbary Coast waterfront. "I'm sure these boys and I will learn to settle our differences peaceably."

Matthew grinned at them and his teeth were crimson.

Ives swore to himself and looked back at the pier. He slammed his fist down on the railing and said, "Bosun, see that Captain Walsh is taken to his quarters at once. The rest of you, back to your duties."

The sailors jumped to the order, leaving Ives and Matthew alone.

"What kind of a man are you?" Ives demanded.

Matthew wiped his face with the back of his torn sleeve. He could not think of an answer just now, for his ears were ringing something awful.

Ives expelled a deep breath. "I'll tell you what kind of a man you are, because I've taken your advice and asked around about you. By everyone's account, you are a madman."

"But a fine riverman!" Matthew said hoarsely. "I'm the best there is!"

"Yes," Ives conceded. "That's what I've been told more than once. So I'll take you as my navigator—not my captain—but my navigator. Is that understood?"

"But why?"

"Because I can't trust you," Ives said. "It's navigator or nothing."

"Navigator then," Matthew said.

Their eyes locked and then Ives expelled a deep breath. "Captain Walsh is out cold. I need your services."

"As captain of the *Monterey*?" Matthew asked, attempting a smile that was painful.

"Yes, damnit! But only until we are safely out to sea and then, if Captain Walsh is still incapacitated, I'll sail this vessel myself."

"I understand, sir."

"Good. Now get us out of this bay and headed south, Mr. Beard."

"Aye, aye!" he said, making a mockery of his salute.

His ears were still ringing when he gripped the wheel and steered them a course past the great Army Presidio of San Francisco. And in spite of the beating he'd just taken, he could feel the strong pull of the tide and the full driving force of the wind clear out his pain like the sun when it burned off the sea fog.

Out on the foredeck, Lieutenant Joseph Christmas Ives stared at the bloodied, shirtless giant. Matthew Beard was half crazy. Everyone he'd spoken to had agreed to that. But every one of his vocal critics had also sworn that Beard possessed an indomitable spirit. The man simply refused to be beaten. And that was why Ives had employed Matthew Beard instead of having him locked in irons and taken to the Presidio under military guard.

The *Monterey* made a fine run down the coast of upper and lower California, and on the evening of the seventh day, it sailed past Cape St. Lucas, the southernmost point of the Baja peninsula. But the wind died that night, and for the next seven days they were caught in the doldrums. It was miserable. The burning tropical sun baked them, and there was no cooling at nighttime. Tempers flared, and at every whiff of a breeze the entire rigging was unfurled so that their schooner might beat a few miles up the Gulf of California. On the fifteenth day, a fair north wind sprang up and sent the *Monterey* racing up the gulf. They passed Ship Rock on the starboard bow and approached the mouth of the Colorado River to drop anchor at five fathoms.

Early the next morning, with a fortuitous headwind, and on a high tide, they entered the mouth of the Colorado and sailed upriver. It was dangerous, tricky navigation, and Matthew stationed himself on the bow with a sounding pole while the other crewmen watched for sunken trees and other debris that could rip the hull of the *Monterey* as if it had been made of wet paper. At midday, the tide turned and their ship was within a half mile of Montague Island.

"Look for a trough or a gully of sorts to beach this vessel!" Ives called.

With the tide rapidly falling, they at last found a trough, and Captain Walsh, who was a good seaman but no riverman, gratefully sailed the *Monterey* into it with her hull scraping the bottom. Two hours later, and with the tide and the river at its lowest, the schooner was beached in wet mud between two shelves of land.

"God help us if we can't get her off," Walsh moaned. "The owners of this schooner will have me imprisoned."

Ives tried to calm the *Monterey*'s captain. "We might have to wait until the next high tide, but we'll get her back into the river for you. After that, you can sail or float back to the gulf and you'll be back in home port before the end of the year."

"I hope so. I've never done anything like this and I'll never do it again. Give me Cape Horn anytime."

Ives ordered his crew to work. They would have to dig another trench wide and long enough for the *Explorer* to be assembled, then floated back onto the river, probably on the same high tide that would free the *Monterey*. There was little time to spare.

The crew and members of the expedition set right to work unloading the boiler and the unassembled parts of the *Explorer*. Next, they scoured the bottomlands for driftwood logs, and when they had twenty of them, they began to dig a trough for the *Explorer* sixty feet long and fourteen feet wide at a depth of five feet. It was hot, difficult work. The decaying logs they had picked up in the muddy river bottom proved to be nearly worthless for shoring, and every shovelful of mud they dug clung to their shovels and had to be scraped off. The country all around them was desolate. Because the river flooded and then ebbed, there was no vegetation, just sun-cracked mud flats and swarms of seagulls and other water fowl.

Two filthy Indians showed up dressed in skins and the lieutenant endeavored to send them on to Fort Yuma with a message. But the Indians refused and made it clear that, should they go that far upriver, they would be killed by Yuma Indians. They were pathetic creatures and Matthew ignored them. It seemed obvious to everyone but him that the ignorant savages were interested in nothing but seeing how much of the expedition's food they could eat. The pair were always ravenous and showed no inclination to work for their keep. Matthew could not understand why Ives should bother with them at all instead of just running them out of camp. He wondered if the Ute Indians, whom his father had praised so highly, exhibited any of the same pathetic and disgusting characteristics as these fellows.

At last, the *Explorer* was bolted and riveted together. The tide again came in and both vessels began to float. The *Explorer*'s boiler was filled with water and everyone held his breath when the steam engine was fired up. A signal was given and the sternwheeler's paddles were gently set into motion. To everyone's delight, they began to churn at the muddy trough of water and both the *Monterey* and the *Explorer* floated out onto the Colorado.

Ives shouted, "Let's get out of here!"

No one on either vessel needed urging. The thought of going to so much work only to realize they might never be lifted by the tide had preyed on everyone's mind for too long. The *Monterey* headed downriver; her sails were unfurled and began to snap in the wind. It was a beautiful sight as the big schooner, under the power of both a favorable wind and the river's tide, moved smartly toward the gulf.

But no one on the *Explorer* had time to watch the ship disappear. They were too busy guiding their little steamer upriver toward Yuma. Matthew took his place as navigator on the bow and sat down with his feet dangling over the side. He had a big grin on his face.

Now, he thought, the real fun begins.

16

Matthew spent all his time at the bow of the little steamer with a sounding pole gripped in his big fists. The river was muddy, treacherous, and low, far lower than he'd expected. Even worse, in some places, the bars of sand and mud seemed to shift before his eyes. He had to keep shouting over the roar of the steam engine to Ives and his assistant. "Hard to port, now to starboard. Stop engines! Reverse engines, slow forward."

He knew that he could read a river as well as any navigator, but he'd never been challenged this way by the Sacramento. The Colorado would be nine or ten feet deep one moment, two feet or less the next. And despite his great skill, they were continuously hanging up on the bars. Whenever that happened, the men would have to unload the cargo and pile it all on the bank so that the *Explorer* could rise a few precious inches and perhaps slide over the bar. But when lightening the load did not help, anchors were attached to rope and the men would carry them upriver to a place where the bottom was solid. Then would begin the backbreaking toil of cranking the huge windlass and actually dragging the fifty-foot-long *Explorer* along the riverbed. If the bed was sand, it wasn't so difficult, but if it was gravel or rock, they would be forced to listen to the terrible screech of protesting steel and wood. Sometimes the hull would snag on something and a swimmer would go underneath the *Explorer* to determine if it could be pulled forward without risk. It was difficult, dangerous work, and Matthew was often the one who volunteered. The way he figured, if he erred by navigating onto the bar, it was his job to get the vessel off that bar.

At the windlass, he was awesome to behold. No two men could match his strength and endurance, and once Ives had called, "My god, man! Give someone else a chance. You can't do it alone, and you'll kill yourself in this heat."

It was hot even though it was winter, not as hot as it was in the summer, but hot all the same and the reflection from the river blinded a man and burned his skin until it was black.

The curious Indians of the Cocopas tribe followed them along the riverbanks and, at night when the *Explorer* pulled into shore to make camp, the Indians would cluster all around. Matthew found them disgusting. "Why the hell do their women wear that damned blue mud packed over their heads?"

"I have no idea," Ives said. "But when the sun sets tonight, I figure I had better run them off or, when we awake in the morning, half our supplies will be gone."

Matthew sat down along the riverbank. He was tired and irritable. "I hear 'em mimicking me all day. I don't like it."

"It's mostly just the children."

"They're all children!"

Ives looked at a particularly attractive young woman dressed in nothing but a short skirt made of reeds. "I'm afraid I have to differ with you on that."

Matthew scowled and slapped at the mosquitos that plagued the expedition. "Even worse than the mimickin' is the way they laugh every time we get hung up on a bar. There we are, working ourselves like draft animals, and they sit up on the bluffs and laugh. I tell you, Lieutenant, it's enough to make a man lose his good humor."

Ives smiled wryly. "Since when did you have a 'good humor'? You strike me as a man who was born angry."

"Maybe I got reason to be."

"I don't think so. You're blessed with size and enormous strength. You have at least ten thousand dollars to your name, which is about ten times more than I'm worth, and you're a man of considerable talents. Seems to me you ought to feel blessed."

Matthew snorted with derision. "Lieutenant, I know all about you. You're a graduate of Yale and West Point. Furthermore, the reason you got this command is because you were smart or lucky enough to marry Secretary of War John Floyd's daughter. Isn't that true?"

Ives stiffened. "I was born of a poor family in New York City. I've earned everything I have."

"Well, so have I," Matthew said. "So don't give me any more bullshit about how I ought to feel blessed. What I got I fought for."

Ives bristled and turned to leave. "I don't know why you're so foul-tempered or why you came along on this expedition. But I'll tell you this, if you start any fights or make any move whatsoever against the Indians we encounter along this river, I'll have you bound in chains and sent to the guardhouse at Fort Yuma. Do you understand me?"

"I understand this—you need my skill, Lieutenant. Without me, you won't make it ten miles beyond Fort Yuma."

"Don't put me to the test," Ives warned as he stalked away. "That would not be wise."

They reached Fort Yuma and it was the usual stockade that the Army erected out West to try to protect the overland emigrant and supply trains that passed between Sante Fe and San Diego. Matthew watched the soldiers being drilled on a dusty parade ground. He ate corn and beans at the mess hall while Ives ate with the officers. It rankled him the way the enlisted men were treated as if they were a race of lesser human beings.

"A man gets used to it," a big, leather-faced sergeant named Dan Rupp told him as they stood watching the sun color the river gold and then fade into the low, western hills. "Twenty years ago when I was a green recruit, it didn't matter because I didn't expect anything better."

"That was your first big mistake," Matthew said.

Rupp had a potbelly that he was fond of scratching. With his grizzled gray hair and red nose lined with purple veins, he looked like a man who had been around and seen a lot of frontier and saloons. He snapped his suspenders and said, "Maybe it's easy for you to talk. But for some men, they never had nothing and never will have nothing. At least I got the Army and that means a place to sleep and food to eat. Government ain't never going to tame these damn Indians anyway. Especially the Apache. Hell, even the Mojave and the Yuma Indians we run across are shifty enough to strike a column of soldiers, then vanish into the creosote brush and be gone before we can return a shot."

"You ought to desert the Army."

"And you and that damned steamboat ought to go back down the river! It'll never reach the Mormons of Utah."

"What makes you so sure? How far have you been up the Colorado?"

Rupp shrugged. "Not more'n fifty miles or so," he admitted. "Not past Mojave Canyon. But I heard there's some mighty unfriendly Indians and they'll know you're coming."

"Who told 'em?"

"Nobody told 'em—yet. But there's Indians all along this river. They may fight and kill each other, but when it comes to white men going into their lands, they stick together. Probably won't trade trinkets for food either."

Matthew scowled. "You're a real encouraging fella, Sergeant. How come you're so down on this expedition?"

"'Cause the captain volunteered me to go," he said, "and because I hear tell from the Indians that there's this great big canyon somewheres up the river that's gonna swallow up that damned little steamer like it had floated off the edge of the world."

"Lieutenant says we leave in the morning, Sergeant. It sure is going to be a pleasure to have you and the soldier boys tagging along to protect us."

"Go to hell," Rupp muttered.

"I'll be doin' that first thing in the morning," Matthew said.

It was midmorning by the time they had everything loaded and lashed down. A fresh supply of wood was stacked along both sides of the boiler, and the *Explorer*'s whistle blasted its shrill farewell as it began to thrash its way upriver. Matthew took his usual position with the sounding pole but they had not gone two miles, and were still in sight of the fort, when they were caught dead in the water by a sandbar. It was galling and Ives was furious because he knew that everyone at Fort Yuma was watching and probably laughing their heads off.

Rupp and his soldiers doffed their boots and jackets and went into the water with the biggest anchor on board, but they quickly discovered that the bar was composed of quicksand.

Barely escaping with their lives, the men fought their way back to solid footing.

"What do we do now, Lieutenant?" Rupp asked, standing in water up to his chest and looking as if he was the miserablest man in the Army.

Ives's answer was decisive. He was young and inexperienced, but West Point had taught him that a good officer never vacillated or showed indecision. "We do the only thing we can do—unload the vessel and try to build up enough steam to drive us over the top."

"You mean both them piles of firewood? Why, there must be . . ."

"You have your orders!"

Rupp turned beet red. He jerked his big hand out of the river and to Matthew's delight he gave the lieutenant a watery salute. The situation was so ridiculous that it was all Matthew could do just to keep from doubling up with laughter. But after four hours of hard labor, when they finally got the *Explorer* over the bar of quicksand, Matthew was no longer laughing. That evening, they steamed upriver long after dark and Matthew figured it was because Ives wanted to at least get out of sight of Fort Yuma.

In the days that followed, they were to find themselves stuck on many bars, in spite of all that Matthew could do. On some days, they made little more than ten miles. Thank heaven there was plenty of wood along the river, but there were also plenty of Indians, first the Cocopas, now the Yuma, and next the Mojave.

The Yuma were not as friendly as the tribes farther south, who were accustomed to seeing an occasional steam packet carry mail and provisions up to Fort Yuma from the Gulf of California. The Yumas could not understand why anyone would be stupid enough to go to so much trouble, trying to navigate a big ship in a shallow river. Over and over, they would shout and race along the banks, or else jump in their canoes and paddle furiously, as if to demonstrate how easy it was to travel if the white men would only abandon the *Explorer*.

"Can you blame them for laughing at us?" Rupp growled

as he and his men worked side by side with the others of the expedition to drag the *Explorer* over yet another bar.

Matthew was down in the river. Shirtless, muscles tight with fatigue, and sweat stinging his eyes, he blamed the damned Indians plenty. "They need to be taught a lesson in manners," he said, casting a glance at the steamer's little four-pound howitzer, which sat squatting on the bow.

"If you're thinking of usin' that damned thing," Rupp warned, "you better think again. You start a war up here, we might not get out alive."

Matthew said nothing but his eyes smoldered with anger as Yuma Indians paddled a canoe out to watch and to laugh. And when they closed in, he reached down to the riverbed and felt along the bottom until he located a rock the size of a goose egg. With malicious satisfaction, he hoisted the rock and whispered to Sergeant Rupp, "See the one standing up and waving his arms?"

"Don't do it!" Rupp said, almost pleading.

"I just want to put the fear of God in him," Matt said.

"With a rock that size, you'd kill him if he gets it in the head."

"Then I'll aim considerably lower," Matt growled as he reared his arm back and hurled the rock.

His throw was hard and flat and perfect. The rock struck the Indian in the groin, and the man's laughter jumped several octaves as he screamed, grabbed his privates, and tumbled into the river, capsizing the canoe.

"I hope all them bastards drown," Matt said as the outraged Indians swam furiously toward shore. The laughter, both on the water and along the bank, died. The big Indian who'd been hit with the rock was being carried back to shore and anyone could see he was in agony.

Matthew could not contain himself. For days, the Indians had been mimicking and making sport of him in particular, for he was the most vocal man, calling out the depths and the navigation. So now, as the big Indian was being dragged through the mud to writhe on the shore, Matthew began to jump up and down on the bow of the steamboat and jeer at the natives. "Ha! Ha!" he crowed. "Do you think that's so funny? Huh?"

The big Yuma Indian roused himself enough to roll over in the mud and grab a rock. He threw it in the general direction of the *Explorer* and the rock fell short. But his action triggered a barrage of rock throwing. Hundreds of Indians picked up rocks and began to hurl them at the vessel.

"Full steam ahead!" Ives shouted. "Head for the middle of the river!"

Soldiers who had been hauling on the rope now swam or waded furiously as they were pelted by a hail of stones that struck the boiler and dented it badly. Rocks also bounced off the paddles as they churned with fury, and the *Explorer*'s hull screeched in protest.

Matthew and the sergeant pulled themselves on board. There was no place to hide on the *Explorer* and Matthew took a rock in the back, and then another one numbed the side of his face.

"Damn you!" he roared, jumping to the howitzer that was kept primed and loaded. He swung the little cannon around, slammed its barrel down, and lit the fuse, not knowing or caring if he hit anyone.

"No!" both the sergeant and Ives yelled.

But it was too late. The cannon boomed and jumped a foot off the deck. Fire and smoke belched out of its muzzle and Matthew stared in amazement as the ball smashed through the trunk of a young cottonwood tree, knocking off the top twenty feet.

The Indians dove for cover, and then scattered like quail as a huge cloud of black smoke rolled across the water. The echo reverberated over the desolate hills for a hundred miles in all directions.

"Sergeant!"

Rupp looked around to see Ives livid with rage. "Sergeant, arrest Mr. Beard and clap him in irons!"

Matthew's amused expression was replaced by one of disbelief. "What the hell for?"

"For firing this company's artillery without permission. For assaulting an Indian. For taking unauthorized action to incite a riot and for jeopardizing this entire goddamn expedition!"

"The hell you say!"

"Sergeant! I've given you a direct order!"

Rupp called for the manacles, and when they were placed in his hand he stepped forward. It was clear by the expression on his face that he was worried but determined to carry out his orders. "I got twenty years in the Army and I mean to make it twenty-five and retire with a pension. So you'll stick them big arms or yours out and let me put these on or I'll have one of my men put a bullet in your thick skull."

"But, Sergeant, you saw what they were doing out there! And you know I didn't aim to hurt any of 'em!"

His argument was wasted on the man. Rupp shook his head and growled, "All I got to say is that it's a damn good thing you can't shoot a howitzer like you can throw a rock. Now stick your wrists out and don't give me any trouble."

Matthew knew he was beaten. The soldiers all around him would shoot to kill if he tried to resist arrest. Maybe he could knock the sergeant down and dive over the side to escape. But then he'd be at the mercy of the damned Indians, and they'd probably roast him slowly. There was no place to run and no place to hide.

"All right."

He saw the relief in Rupp's face, and the old soldier put the manacles and the chains on gentle-like.

"Now chain him to the boiler apparatus," Ives snapped.

"Aw, come on!" Matthew shouted. "Hell, as if it weren't hot enough out here without being tied right next to a can of boiling water. And who's going to navigate for you?"

"Sergeant Rupp, you take the sounding pole!"

"But I don't know anything . . ."

"I've given you another order! And if you don't stop questioning me, I'll bust you down to private!"

"Yes, sir!"

Looking for all the world like an old riled-up bear, Rupp hauled Matthew over to the boiler pipes and chained him in place. "You asked for this," he muttered as he took the sounding pole and went up to the bow of the ship. He eased himself down so that his legs were hanging over the sides, and then he jammed the pole into the muddy water. It did not touch the bottom, and he almost toppled over the side. "Damn deep, sir!" he called.

Ives scowled. The *Explorer* churned on upriver and th
angry Yuma Indians returned to the shore to examine th
splintered white wood of the beheaded cottonwood tree wit
cries of amazement.

Without Matthew stationed at the bow to call out th
dangers hidden below the Colorado River's surface, the *Ex
plorer* spent more time grounded on one impossible sandba
or shoal after another than she did plowing her way upriver
Matthew stood manacled to the boiler for three days and wa
unshackled only at mealtime or when he needed to reliev
himself. The boiler radiated waves of heat, and he had to drinl
gallons of water to avoid heat prostration. He knew tha
Lieutenant Ives could not long do without his eye and hi
sense of river navigation. The lieutenant replaced Rupp th
first day and had tried nearly every soldier under his com
mand, but no one had a feel for the channels or the way of a bi
river. The Colorado was as fickle as a canyon wind.

"All right," Ives said, on the fourth day. "Are you ready t
follow orders?"

Matthew was too hot and weary to crow about his ow
indispensability. He nodded his head and said, "But I'm no
sorry for what I did back there."

"You don't have to be sorry. Just give me your word you
won't do it again."

"You've my word."

Ives did not even try to hide his relief. "Take your place
at the bow and get us up this damned river. According to my
information, we're entering Mojave land. And they're not
known for their friendliness."

"So you may have to use that howitzer again."

"That's always a possibility in hostile country. But it's a last
resort. If we incite the natives, we cannot hope to win from the
deck of this vessel. We're just too vulnerable."

"How can they oppose our rifles?"

Ives shook his head. "I guess you've never seen an Indian
use a bow and arrow before. They can drill a soldier at fifty
yards without any difficulty. As you've noticed, the banks are
lined with brush. They'd fire from hiding and pick us off one by
one. It would be like shooting fish in a barrel."

Matthew had not been aware that the Indians could fire

that accurately or that far. And the lieutenant was right when he pointed out that there was no place to take cover in the middle of the river. "I'll keep my head about me," he said, "but maybe my blowing that tree in two was a blessing. The word will get upriver and give us a measure of respect."

"Respect? We'll see. We'll just wait and see."

In the days that followed the confrontation, the Indians left them alone. They were seen following along the banks, but no longer did they come out in the open, and their mimicking voices were stilled. In a strange way, the monotonous thump-thump of the steam engine and the thrashing of water under the paddles seemed a little unnerving. The river grew deeper: the bluffs around them steepened.

One afternoon, they passed through a low purple gateway of rocks and entered a red canyon that was magnificent. The cliffs bordering the river became almost perpendicular from the water's edge. High above them, their turrets, spires, and jagged peaks and pinnacles stood like sentinels against a corridor of blue sky. The water grew very deep and the *Explorer* plowed uncontested up the river until the rocks fell away and the expedition moved between a series of low foothills.

"We've reached the Mojave Indians' country," Sergeant Rupp said. "Sometimes they're friendly, sometimes not. We'd better keep soldiers posted at all hours, Lieutenant."

That night, Ives took his astronomical readings and announced to everyone," We've navigated 224 nautical miles north from the Gulf of California. Two days ago, we passed the previous northernmost point of exploration on the Colorado River. We are charting waters and seeing country whose geography has never been recorded or mapped. Again I want to remind you of the importance the United States places on being able to navigate this river as far north as the Mormon territory."

Matthew looked at Rupp and the other soldiers who nodded their heads. He said, "I beg your pardon, Lieutenant, but it seems to me we've proven that any vessel drafting more than about three feet of water wouldn't stand a chance of getting up this river. How could the Army hope to mount a military campaign from this river?"

Ives did not looked pleased. "It rises and falls with the seasons, Mr. Beard. This is the lowest time of year, which is precisely why we are making the attempt now. If we can navigate north in January and February, it ought to be far easier in the spring and summer."

"Maybe, maybe not. That canyon we just passed through would be very powerful if the water was up five or ten feet and I doubt this vessel would have the steampower to fight the current."

"Your point is well taken and will be included in my written report. However, it is for the Army to decide, not you."

Matthew, stung by the curt rebuke, moved away to be by himself. He stood on the bow of the ship and felt the hot air on his cheeks. He thought of his father and his brother and he wondered if this expedition would follow this great river right to their Shining Mountains. Matthew hoped so. He wanted to show Nathan that, though he'd been out West a shorter time, it was he who was making history.

The Mojaves they encountered the very next day were wary people. They came to the shores of the river and watched the *Explorer* but, unlike the Yumas, they said nothing. The men carried bows and arrows but, because their squaws and children were among them, they created no real anxiety on the part of the expedition.

"Look!" a soldier called one evening, just after they had beached the *Explorer* for the night and started making preparations for supper. "That must be their chief on the opposite bank, and he acts like he wants us to come and visit him."

"That's exactly what it looks like," Ives said, "but we've just released the steam and the fire is almost dead. It'll take an hour or more to rebuild enough pressure in our boilers to cross this swift river."

They all tried to make sign language to the band of Mojaves but it was clear they did not understand.

"I could swim over there," Matthew offered.

"And what would that accomplish?" Ives shook his head. "No, the only one who could do us any good is Sergeant Rupp, and I don't think he'd make it."

"Damn right I wouldn't," the old potbellied sergeant barked. "I'd sink about halfway across and drown."

"Then we'll just have to build up steam and hope the chief doesn't feel insulted," Ives said. "Fire the boilers!"

But before the order could be carried out, the Mojave chief had a better idea. He ordered a raft and placed a stool in the center of it while four of his strongest young warriors took the corners and towed the raft out into the current. When the water reached their chests, they used strips of leather to tie the raft to their waists and began to swim.

"Would you look at that!" Matthew said with grudging admiration. "Did ever a man have a more regal method of crossing a river than what we're seeing?"

The four young Indians were powerful swimmers. The Mojave chief assumed a pose of boredom as he crossed the Colorado, looking for all the world as if he did this every day. Ives and the others went to greet him. He spoke English but it was gibberish, for although he had memorized a great many English words, he was ignorant of their meaning.

"Money Sunday no good!" he cried out in greeting as he stood to face Ives. "Gun goddamn river. Okay? Bird tomorrow? Horse captain boat!"

Ives could only nod his head up and down as if he understood perfectly.

"Mojave. Go. Whiskey hoot hoot."

"Yes, yes," Ives said. Then, turning to Rupp, he whispered, "Speak to the man in sign language, Sergeant! This is getting us nowhere."

Rupp quickly made sign and the chief, whose name they learned was Cairnook, seemed almost reluctant to bother with sign language. He wanted to impress his four young warriors and so all during the time he and Rupp were signing he kept up a constant chatter of nonsense.

"Beans yes gone! Letter are dog. Okay? Am horse hungry loose pants. Fire shirt bye bye beads."

And each time that Ives or even Rupp nodded his head, trying not to offend Cairnook, he took that as a sign that he was doing very well. He would cast his warriors a very superior look and talk even faster. "Fish corn Yuma. Mountains meat, okay?"

"What is he saying?" Ives cried with exasperation.

Rupp said, "He says you are welcome, except that the Mormons have told him and his tribe that you come to take their land. He is afraid you will shoot them with the great iron boom-boom that killed the tree."

"Tell him that is untrue!" Ives tried to catch Cairnook's eye but the chief was talking and gesturing so fast that it was impossible. Rupp had the look of a man who was about to scream. But somehow, he managed to convey the message that the expedition had come in peace. Once this was understood, the chief turned to his warriors and spoke rapidly in their language. A moment later, the warriors were at the river's edge and motioning the rest of their tribe to cross the river.

"I guess he believed you," Matthew said. "Look at them come!"

It was quite a sight. An armada of reed canoes and small rafts pulled by swimmers or poled by their passengers carried the women and children over. Dozens more just jumped into the current and swam across a good half mile of swift water.

Matthew had always prided himself on his own swimming ability but he had to admit that these people were more than his match. Even seven-year-old children swam like little brown otters.

The Mojaves were fascinated by the *Explorer's* steam paddlewheel, which was painted red, their favorite color. And despite all Sergeant Rupp could do, he was not able to explain to their satisfaction how the great paddles could go around and around without anyone touching them. The chief said it was a sign that the white men had big magic.

The tribe came to spend the night and that worried Ives. The Mojave women were attractive with their shy, sweet smiles, even though all of the young ones were either pregnant or carrying at least one child on their hips. The children got into everything and though Matthew had no use at all for Indians, he enjoyed the Mojave children who seemed attracted to him because of his great size. Trading was brisk and Ives seemed pleased to exchange beads for bushels of corn and beans. The Mojaves were obviously good farmers and offered to take the expedition to their village and their fields.

"Tell them thank you for their gracious offer of hospitality," Ives said to his sergeant, "but we must decline. Ask them about the river. How far can we go north?"

Rupp asked and Chief Cairnook made sign language for a long time. His gestures were swift and even a little theatrical.

"Well?" Ives asked, his impatience showing.

"Many days to the north there is a great canyon. Bigger than the Earth."

"That's impossible."

"I know that, sir," Rupp said, "but you asked me to interpret what he said, and that's what I'm doing."

"Yes. Yes."

"The chief says the walls of the world rise up higher than an eagle can fly, higher even than the world beyond. He says we cannot go through the canyon."

Ives frowned. "Ask him if the canyon is even bigger than the one we passed through a few days ago."

"Cairnook says *much* bigger. He says it is the father of all canyons. Again, he says we cannot pass through and to try would be to die."

"Tell him thank you for his advice but we will go on," Ives said wearily. "Tell him good night. We must sleep now."

Cairnook listened and nodded solemnly. He stood up and turned to his people and spoke to them. Immediately, they stopped chattering and lay down in silence.

"What are they doing?"

"Lieutenant, they are going to sleep."

"They can't sleep here with the men. Some of those young women are . . . well, they just can't."

Rupp shrugged his shoulders. The firelight betrayed a hint of a grin. "I'm afraid we can't ask them to leave their own land. That would be an insult and they'd not take it well, sir. But if you insist . . ."

"No, no, damnit! But I want you to post a double watch." Ives raised his voice so that everyone on the expedition could hear him. "And if any man forgets that he is a soldier and tries to inflict himself on one of these girls, I'll personally have him court-martialed and shot, if these Indians don't kill him first. Is that well understood?"

The party nodded. They obviously liked what they saw in

the girls, but the Indian men of the tribe were dangerous looking. There would be no funny business this night.

The next morning, a runner arrived from Fort Yuma with news that the Paiute Indians had been told by the Mormons that the expedition was bent on conquest. According to the runner, the Paiutes were expecting trouble.

"It's exactly what I feared," Ives said as they bid farewell to Chief Cairnook and his tribe. "Keep a sharp lookout, men!"

No one had to be told twice to keep a lookout and also to keep guns and powder dry and ready. Despite the friendliness of the Mojaves, Matthew sensed the atmosphere on board the *Explorer* was tense. Ahead, they faced a canyon said to be impossible and a tribe of Indians who had been made to believe that they were coming to invade Paiute lands. Up to now, the expedition had been hard, but without great danger. It seemed that was about to change.

Matthew grinned. Good. He was primed for excitement and he'd do his damndest to take care of whatever trouble came their way.

17

They thrashed upriver, the great paddles straining to propel the *Explorer* forward against a swifter current. Along both shores, black mountains towered, and that afternoon they hit their first major series of rapids.

"Full steam ahead!" Ives shouted as his men grabbed whatever they could hang on to to keep from being thrown into the current.

Matthew grasped the railing and stood firm on the bow of the steamer. The roar of the white water filled his ears. The *Explorer*'s bow rose and crashed over and over as the paddles churned under full power. Inch by inch, the steamer mounted the river.

The rapids were six miles long, and it took nearly four hours to reach a short stretch of calm water again. "We're out of wood!" Ives shouted. "We'll head for shore and make camp."

Within a mile, they found a calm inlet and steered the *Explorer* into a safe harbor. The men were shaken. The steamer itself had taken such a pounding that they were all worried that her rivets would start popping. And, just ahead, the mountains seemed to lean over the river, and the water became white again. It probably meant that they were about to enter the great canyon that the Indians had foretold, the one whose sides reached to heaven.

Ives said, "We'll leave the *Explorer* here and take a small survey party out of this canyon. Up on top, we can see better. Sergeant, you and . . ."

Rupp began to shake his head. Even in the shadowed canyon, he was sweating heavily and it was obvious to anyone but Ives that he was unfit to hike up to the bluffs. "Lieutenant," he began, "I hope you'll understand that I'm not shirkin' my duty, sir. But hiking isn't exactly the thing that I do best. We've some eager young soldiers here who'd do much better than me at that sort of thing. Besides, I think that if we're worried about attack from the Paiutes, I'd better stay right here with a few soldiers to protect this vessel."

Ives was caught off guard. "Are you refusing to obey my order, Sergeant?"

"No, sir!"

The lieutenant wisely relented. "In that case, I agree that your services are better needed here. I'll take four men and go on up to scout the river. If the rapids get progressively worse, we can't risk taking the *Explorer* any farther north."

"I'd like to come along," Matthew volunteered.

"No. You've proven you can't be trusted."

Matthew flushed with anger. "Here," he said, handing the Army officer his revolver. "How much damage can I cause if I'm unarmed?"

"You're dangerous with no more than a rock in your hand."

"That won't happen again. I promise," he said, again shoving his revolver, butt first, at the officer. "I *want* you to take it."

Ives took the weapon. He unloaded it and handed it back to Matthew. "All right," he said, "but if you disobey my orders or act on your own in a way to endanger our party, I'll not wait to return you to Fort Yuma. I'll shoot you on the spot. If the Mormons have already stirred up the Paiutes, things will be difficult enough for us without having to worry about your temper."

"Fair enough," Matthew said.

"Sergeant, keep two sentries posted at all times. We're in Paiute country and we don't want to be caught by surprise. Have the rest of the men try to catch some fish. But no hunting. I don't want the Indians or the Mormons to hear us, and in these canyons, a shot would echo for miles."

Rupp detailed the men, then said, "Lieutenant, we're getting down to the last of our corn and beans. I sure hope we can catch some fish. Either that or we might have to start eatin' lizards and horned toads."

"We'll eat whatever we have to in order to stay alive and

carry out our orders. Me and my men will take a two-day supply of food."

"How come just two days?" Matthew asked quietly. "I thought we were going to follow this river all the way to the Mormon territory. Maybe even to Colorado."

"If the river proves completely impassable, then we'll split the expedition. Half will return on the *Explorer* to Fort Yuma and I'll take the others on to search for Fort Defiance, which is at least three hundred miles east of us, almost to New Mexico Territory."

Matthew shook his head. "A long walk."

"And right through the heart of Indian country. If it's adventure and danger you crave, you'll have your fill of it before you reach Fort Defiance. That is, if you don't get shot, drown, or die of thirst or starvation when we cross the Great Basin deserts."

Matthew wasn't worried. He was sure the secretary of war would never send his son-in-law on an expedition that had little chance of success. "I figure I'll survive just fine. And so will Sarge here. Why, he's got belly enough to live off of for a couple of months."

Ruff bristled. "You've a mean sense of humor and a sick sense of adventure if you think trying to blaze a trail to Fort Defiance is going to be any fun. Me, I'd rather take the *Explorer* back to Fort Yuma, if it's all the same to you, Lieutenant."

"It's not all the same to me," Ives said. "While you may not be the man I'd choose to climb rocks, you're reported by your superiors to be the best tracker, interpreter, and Indian fighter at Fort Yuma. So rest up during the next few days, Sergeant Rupp. You'll see a lot of new country before you sleep in an Army barracks again."

The sergeant's doleful expression almost caused Matthew to feel pity for the man. Almost, but not quite. When a man chose security over personal freedom, he pretty much got what he deserved.

They left at once, and before darkness fell they managed to hike almost ten miles upriver, where they spotted a campfire. Matthew squinted into the failing light. "Unless I miss my guess, that fella down there is a white man."

They moved closer. "You're right," Ives said. "But what would a white man be doing here unless . . ."

"Unless what?"

The lieutenant pulled out his map. "The Mormon Road is supposed to be only twenty or thirty miles north of us. Maybe that's where he came from. Could be he's an emigrant who got separated from his wagon train or even survived an attack."

"Let's find out," Matthew said.

They stood up and walked into the camp, calling out a warning. The man, a tall, cadaverous fellow in his mid-thirties, was dressed in a black suit. His clothes were badly rumpled and soiled. He wore a flat-brimmed hat, and his eyes were close set and betrayed his excitement. "Thanks be to God, you've arrived! I've been praying for a miracle and here you are."

"Who are you?" Ives demanded.

"My name is Jacob White," he said. "There are Paiutes on the warpath along the Mormon Road. You're going right into the jaws of death."

Ives frowned. "Where did you say you were heading?"

"To Los Angeles, but the Indians were waiting on the Mormon Road. I tried to reason with our guide to detour around them and thus save our lives. But he was an obstinate man. I fear they have all been slaughtered by the Paiutes, just as you and your men most certainly will be if you continue up the Grand River."

Matthew pushed his way forward. "Mister, the only people who call this river the Grand anymore are the ones in Colorado or else the Mormons of Utah. I say you belong to the latter group and that you're a liar!"

The man shrank back.

"Mr. Beard," Ives shouted. "You have no right to voice such an accusation!"

"I'm sure he's one of those Mormons, sent by Brigham Young to try to turn us back!"

"Why, no sir!" White cried, his face a mask of denial. "I have no idea what you're talking about!"

Matthew ached to grab the man by the throat and shake the truth out of him. "Lieutenant, you know he's lying and so do I. No man just wanders around in this kind of country unless he's crazy. This one isn't crazy, but then again, he isn't very smart either. His story stinks!"

"Mr. Beard! That's enough! If you say another word, I'll have you bound and gagged and placed under arrest." Ives turned to the man, who had been badly intimidated by Matthew. "I apologize. He's not a soldier and I should never have brought him along."

The man nodded, his eyes wary and distrustful. "Can I accompany you on your steamer? I fear for my life out here."

"Of course. But we're going upriver again tomorrow."

"But Lieutenant, the Paiutes!"

"I'm afraid we'll have to take our chances."

The man began to shake his head. "I . . . I won't go. I'll stay right here and wait for your return. I won't go back into the jaws of death."

Ives said he understood, and then he ordered the men to make camp and post the watch. "We'll push on at first light," he said to them all. "Mr. White, we'll be happy to take you back to the *Explorer*."

Matthew motioned the lieutenant down to the riverside where the sound of the water would drown out their voices. "Did you catch it?"

"Catch what?"

"Besides calling this river the Grand, he knew we'd come on a steamer! No one had said a word about it and yet . . . he knew!"

Ives looked closely at him. "Yes," he said. "The man *did* know, but . . ."

"It's like I told you, he's a Mormon spy. What other explanation can there be?"

"None," Ives said. "None at all. But as a United States Army officer, I cannot force him to confess."

"I can."

"Uh-uh. You'd either kill or hurt him. I want neither."

"Then what if I just scare a confession out of him?"

"Can I trust you?"

"With your life . . . and his."

"Very well. What do you propose?"

"If he's a spy, he'll shadow your party. When I catch him doing that, I'll wring a confession out of him."

"Your choice of the word 'wring' makes me nervous."

Matthew smiled his most disarming smile. "A mere slip of the tongue, Lieutenant. Nothing more."

"Very well. You have my permission."

Matthew was pleased. That night, he slept well, and at daybreak he left with Ives and the soldiers who climbed straight up the bluffs and out of the narrow canyon. A mile farther on, he doubled back and found a hiding place. The sun came up stronger, and away from the river the temperatures would be far hotter.

Matthew huddled behind his rock and waited. Ives and his men had already vanished into the maze of rocks and brush. The sky was a washed-out blue without any clouds. Overhead, a pair of buzzards glided in lazy circles a mile above the Colorado River, whose muted roar could be heard far below.

Matthew watched the buzzards, and his eyes kept turning toward the distant canyons that could be seen to the northeast. As the sun rose higher, the land took on more color and no longer seemed so drab. Red and yellow dominated the hills and mountains, and at their peaks he could see the faint outline of pine trees. It was awesome and beautiful.

The scrape of a rock warned him that he was not alone. Matthew did not know if the Mormon was armed or not but it seemed prudent to take no chances. He reached for his revolver, and only then did he remember that it was empty.

The spy appeared, winded and puffing from his strenuous climb up from the river. He shielded his eyes with one hand and then he started forward. Matthew waited until the man was close, and then he stepped out from cover with the empty gun in his fist. If the man was armed, he would quite naturally assume that Matthew was as well. "That's far enough, Mr. White, or whatever your name really is."

White turned, and when he saw Matthew, he jumped back over the side of the bluff and disappeared.

"Damn!" Matthew bellowed, taking off after the man. "Hey, I just want to talk!"

But the man didn't believe him. He had a good twenty-five-yard head start, and by the time Matthew reached the edge of the bluff and started down, the fellow was moving with surprising speed and agility. Matthew went after him. The trail was not fit for a mountain goat. It was narrow and slippery from mist rising off the river. Worse yet, every time Matthew glanced down, he could see that the man was gaining ground on him. By the time he reached the river, White was a hundred yards ahead of him. He had thrown himself into the river and was swimming furiously, making a strong bid to increase his lead.

Matthew took a second to kick off his boots before he jumped into the water. The current was powerful but he swam like a man possessed. Each time he raised his head and took a lungful of air, he saw that he was gaining on his quarry. White had tired badly, and halfway across the water he looked to be in danger of drowning.

"Help!" he screamed. "Help! Cramps in my legs! Help!"

Matthew saw the thin man disappear under the water, then pop up about fifteen yards downriver. His face was the color of a fish's belly. Matthew went after him and grabbed his collar just as he was going down for perhaps the last time. They struck a boulder and Matt felt a sharp pain in his side as they were twisted through a narrow gap where the river roared.

"Grab for that tree trunk!" Matthew yelled over the sound of the river. "It's your only chance!"

The man understood, and they just managed to grip the mossy trunk of the half-submerged tree. They hung on for a moment with the river whipping the lower part of their bodies as if it were alive and unwilling to let them go.

Matthew finally was able to drag himself out of the river, and with a strong heave, he pulled the thin man up to temporary safety. They were both exhausted and out of breath and it was a long time before either spoke.

"What do you want from me?" the man wailed.

"I want the truth. You're a Mormon spy sent to turn us back. Admit it!"

"No!"

"Suit yourself," Matthew said, "but as soon as I catch my wind, I'm swimming out of here and leaving you. You'll never make it to shore without me."

The man clung feebly to the tree and his eyes were wide with fright. "I doubt even you could save me!"

"I'm your only hope, mister. Now tell me the truth."

"All right, I *am* a spy. But our people are only trying to protect ourselves. Do you really believe we'd have any chance against the United States Army?"

"It doesn't seem possible," Matthew admitted. "Are you the one who has been telling the Paiutes that we're coming to take their land?"

"No!"

Matthew didn't believe him. "Good luck," he said as he prepared to abandon the shivering and frightened Mormon. "In a few weeks, maybe someone will see what's left of your skinny carcass as it floats past Fort Yuma."

"Wait, I beg of you! All right, I'm the one. But we never told the Indians to attack you."

"But you didn't tell them the truth, either. You will now or I'll leave you right smack in the middle of this river. Do you understand that?"

Beaten and without any choice, the man nodded.

Matthew stood up and carefully studied the river just below them. "We'll swim for that big, flat rock."

"I'll never make it," the man said.

"Sure you will."

The man balked. "There's got to be a safer . . ."

Matthew picked him up and jumped. The water caught them and whirled them around, then bounced them over some submerged rocks. They hit a clear stretch of water and swam with the last of their reserves until they were washed up on the rock.

"I'd never do that again!" the man cried.

"Me neither," Matthew said. "Now let's go find that Paiute village and straighten out any misunderstandings."

The Mormon nodded and had to be helped to his feet. He looked like a drowned rat, and he was so cold that his teeth chattered. Matthew wondered why such a skinny little fellow would volunteer to be a spy. He must have been trying to work his way into Brigham Young's good graces.

The Paiute village was less than a mile away from the river, though hidden from view and impossible to find without a guide. Like the Yumas, these Indians lived in crude reed and stick huts. Their camp was poor and the chief was the only one who had more than a thin wool blanket for protection on cold desert nights. The women and children were hollow-cheeked and fearful. Matthew saw five Indians waiting to devour a single jackrabbit that he alone could have consumed. It was about what he had expected of savages, a people too weak and stupid to leave the desert and find a better homeland.

However, his opinion of the Paiutes was elevated somewhat when the chief of the tribe welcomed them with respect, despite their bedraggled appearance. Matthew listened very carefully as the Mormon explained to the chief that the Ives expedition was no longer interested in conquest, that it wanted no land and no slaves.

The chief grinned from ear to ear. He took them into a huge reed and mud hut with a firehole in its roof. Not wishing to offend their host, Matthew tried roasted insects mixed with pine nuts. Actually, they tasted pretty good, though not very filling. Afterward, when they were left alone, Matthew said, "You did well. We'll be leaving at daylight."

"But for where? I prefer to remain in this village," the Mormon said.

"Not on my life," Matthew told the man. "You asked the lieutenant if you could ride the *Explorer* down to Fort Yuma. That's exactly what you'll do. I think the United States Army might have some questions for you to answer."

The man looked bleak, and as far as Matthew was concerned he had every reason to be. He was also out of sorts now that he'd failed his mission.

"Mister," he said. "I don't understand why the United States would wage war on our people in Deseret. Haven't we been persecuted enough?"

"It's like I said before," Matthew sighed, "I don't know anything about the troubles Brigham Young and your leaders are having with the government."

"At least you and I both know they'll never invade our lands by coming up the Colorado," the man said with grim satisfaction. "There is no way you'll get through the great canyons."

"I'm sure that's true."

"Then why don't you turn back?"

"Can't."

"But why not?"

Matthew thought on that for a few minutes before he said, "You ever hear kids sing the little ditty about the bear that went over the mountain?"

The man's expression was puzzled. "You mean about the one who went over just to see what he could see?"

"Yeah. Well," Matthew continued, "I'm just like that bear. I want to see what I can see. I want to follow this river to its headwaters in the Shining Mountains. Ives is pretty much the same."

"You're crazy!"

Matthew laughed outright. "Maybe I am, but I'm not crazy enough to leave you here to tell that chief you changed your mind about our expedition and we really do plan to attack his tribe. Now, *that* would be crazy."

The next morning, they left the Indian camp and returned to the river to discover Lieutenant Ives bubbling with excitement. An Indian runner had just informed him that a long-awaited pack train had crossed the desert with fresh provisions and mules so that they could push eastward toward Fort Defiance.

"What about him?" Ives said, gesturing toward the Mormon.

"There will be no more Indian trouble, at least not from the Paiutes," Matthew said. "We straightened everything out."

"Good! Then we'll return to the *Explorer* and divide the forces. Mr. Beard," Ives said, almost gushing, "just wait until you see the size of the canyon just north of us!"

"Big?"

"It's . . ." Ives grinned and spread his arms wide. ". . . It's like the Mojaves promised—bigger than anything you could imagine. We didn't even enter it, but I swear it is the most awesome sight you will ever see in your entire life. It must be the grandest canyon in the world!"

"I wouldn't miss it for anything," Matthew said, already tingling with anticipation.

Ives started making preparations to return to the *Explorer*. But he stopped and then came over to Matthew. "By the way, I want to tell you that getting Mr. White to assure the

Indians we mean them no harm was a job well done. We'll be
traveling in hostile country all the way to Fort Defiance, and
we'll have enough provisions to supply only twenty soldiers.
That's not a great deal of protection. I've sent for a couple of
Yumas to guide us into the Hualapais Indian lands. One of
them is named Ireteba. He's supposed to be a good man. At
any rate, we're going to have to make friends or we'll never
reach the fort alive."

"I understand."

Ives visibly relaxed. "I was sure that you would."

The preparations for their overland trek were finished at
last. The maps of the Arizona Territory that they would have to
cross, though sadly incomplete, were carefully wrapped in
oilskins. Report and log books, food, ammunition, and survey
instruments also were packed on the mules. The men shook
hands all around and then those who considered themselves
most fortunate boarded the valiant little *Explorer*. With a shrill
blast of the steam whistle, they turned the vessel downriver
and steamed rapidly toward Fort Yuma.

"I wish I was going with them!" Sergeant Rupp whispered. "Lucky bastards. After twenty years of brave and
honest service, you'd think that the lieutenant would give an
old sergeant a rest."

Matthew chuckled. "Nonsense. Ives is smart enough to
realize that we need your experience. Besides, all the walking
we'll be doing will slim you right down to the size you were at
fifteen."

"I was a fat kid," Rupp said, mopping his face with a red
bandanna. "And even then, I hated to walk. That's why I
joined the cavalry. They never said nothing about me ever
having to be a foot soldier."

Matthew clapped the burly soldier on the back. "Cheer
up! The lieutenant says we're going to see one of the greatest
natural wonders in the world."

"What does he know?"

"He knows a grand-sized canyon when he sees one."

"Big deal."

Matthew gave up on the sergeant. Rupp was so awash in
self-pity that, if there were a hundred naked desert nymphs

waiting for them over the next hill, he would still have been griping.

The *Explorer* gave one last blast of her steam whistle just as she rounded a bend in the river and disappeared. The whistle's song flowed up and down the Colorado River and then fed into the little side canyons and tributaries. It was a high and a lonesome sound but it did not bother Matthew at all.

18

The country grew wilder as they traveled parallel to the Colorado River, and Matthew marveled at the incredible vistas. As far as the eye could see, there were endless plateaus leading like giant stepping-stones up and down, through great valleys and over steep mountains. It was a hard journey, and with their mules braying for water and the heat almost suffocating them, they finally reached a single huge tabletop that rose gently to the north. Unlike anything before it, this plateau was covered with a cedar forest. The mules seemed to know that there was also the promise of water. With their long ears stretched forward, their pace quickened.

"It must be just beyond," Ives said. "The canyon *has* to be just beyond."

Rupp was suffering terribly. Sometimes, he would ride their biggest mule but, with little feed and even less water, the animals, though weak, were also becoming vicious and rebellious.

By evening, they still had not crossed the tabletop, which they had at first estimated to be no more than ten miles wide. The air was so clear that distances expanded and ten miles became fifteen or even twenty. That evening, again without water, the party made one more dry camp. The mules had begun to bray in distress but, an hour later, the braying brought into view a pair of Haulapais Indians.

"Speak to them," Ives ordered their Yumas. "We must find water!"

Ireteba and his companion set off after the Haulapais, and at about midnight, the two Indians finally were persuaded to come into the camp. They were the most wretched-looking specimens of manhood that Matthew had ever seen. Neither Indian stood much over five feet tall and they were both filthy, half starved, and naked except for a few rabbit skins tied loosely around their scrawny waists.

Ireteba had made it plain that he and his companion, being Yumas and a long way from their own lands, were in mortal danger from the Haulapais or any other tribe they might find. The Yuma guides wanted to turn back and Ives had reluctantly agreed to pay them and let them do so when they had found themselves new Indian guides. So now, Ireteba and his companion were speaking earnestly to the sorry little Haulapais in a sincere attempt to recruit their own replacements.

"What do they say?" Ives asked his sergeant impatiently after the conversation had gone on for at least fifteen minutes with all four Indians chattering and no one seeming to listen to the other. "What do they say?"

Rupp pushed his weight in between the Indians. He was twice their size and his scowl brought their conversation to a halt as he began to make sign language to Ireteba, who in turn translated the information given by the Haulapais. "They say they were out hunting and got lost."

"That's impossible!" Ives snapped. "They're lying."

He swung around and yelled for one of the soldiers to bring an ammunition box they had filled with beads and other trade goods. When the box was opened, Ives pulled out several strings of pretty beads. The two little Haulapais grew animated and tried to snatch the beads and run but Ives pulled them out of reach. He dangled them in the last rays of sunlight so that they shone as brilliantly as rubies and emeralds. There was no doubt in anyone's mind the Haulapais had never seen anything so beautiful and would give anything to possess such treasures.

Ives took a deep, confident breath and said, "Sergeant, tell Ireteba to inform the Haulapais that we reward our guides with these fine beads. Tell them that, if they help guide us down into the great canyon and also find us good campsites with grass and clear water, we will give them each a string of beads."

Again, the conversation, with its wild gesturings and excited language, went on and on.

"What are they saying, Sergeant!"

Rupp had to grab their Yuma guide by the shoulder and pull him aside. A moment later, he said, "The Haulapais want *two* strings of beads each, sir."

"Well then, agree and let's be done with this haggling!"

Rupp looked grieved. "You don't understand. They insist on getting their beads *before* they guide us."

"Absolutely not!"

"What about one string each now, one later?"

Ives considered it and was about to nod his head when Matthew interjected a piece of advice. "You do that, Lieutenant, they'll be gone in a day or two. I've sold hundreds of those cheap strings of beads to trappers. They'll break apart and spill all over the place and then you'll have angry Indians who won't give a damn about shiny beads. Besides, if you give them one string, they'll figure they're already rich enough and leave us stranded."

Ives considered that. "For a man who never even saw an Indian before this expedition, you seem mighty free with Indian advice."

Matthew did not get ruffled, but said, "Indians are like children. They'll die for something until they have it and then, next day, they just want something else. It's human nature. Nothing more, nothing less. Indians and children. They act the same."

"I'm inclined to agree with him," Sergeant Rupp said. "Only difference is, these children can kill us."

"All right then," Ives said. "Tell Ireteba to keep bargaining."

When this information was relayed to Ireteba, it was clear the Yuma and his companion were greatly annoyed. They could not understand the white man's reasoning. So the bargaining went on. Every time the Haulapais started to walk away, Ives would be obliged to dangle the beads over the firelight. Finally, the Haulapais gave in and agreed to the bargain, but they were not happy. Instead, they seemed nervous and in a hurry, which was fine with everyone except the mules and Sergeant Rupp. Even so, the Haulapais proved their worth the next morning by leading the expedition to a hidden spring. Afterward, they made rapid progress across the tableland, where they saw many antelope and deer feeding.

They could sense the great chasm before them, but it was not until they broke through a thick stand of cedar and gazed suddenly downward that they beheld the magnificent canyon.

"I'd never have believed anything like this could exist," Matthew said reverently. "Look at the size and the colors!"

Even the Haulapais, who must have seen the grand canyon every day of their lives, were impressed enough to stand and look in obvious appreciation. The canyon was inspiring in its terrible broken beauty. Thousand-foot spires of red, yellow, and gold rock stretched upward like crooked fingers reaching to the sun. The colors were ever changing and they reflected the sky and the clouds above. When the men peered into the great chasm, the Colorado River so far below was no more than a thin silver ribbon. They marveled at gnarled trees that jutted out from crumbling cliffs and at small game trails in terrain that seemed accessible only to eagles.

The expedition's geologist, Dr. Newberry, could not contain his excitement. "No one in the world has *ever* had such an opportunity to study the formation of the Earth's crust!" he cried. "Just look at it, a virtual map of geological time, every sedimentary layer as clear to read as the words on a page."

Matthew was as awed by the sight as anyone, but nothing except the air was clear. "What do you mean?"

"Every layer of sediment tells us a story about the geological formation of this entire continent," Newberry proclaimed, his voice loud enough to echo over the great abyss. "Using the principles of geology, I can determine whether or not there were plants and animals in each geological era. There may be fossils of the great dinosaurs that roamed the Earth thousands of years ago."

"I don't see any bones sticking out of the rocks," Matthew said with a mischievous grin.

"Don't even attempt to be impudent with me, Mr. Beard. A sight like this is the closest thing to heaven for a geologist."

Matthew let the man alone. They rested for an hour, and then the Haulapais began to lead a descent into the canyon. The mules balked. They had to be pushed onto a thin, winding trail, then whipped each time they came to a sharp switchback. They'd brace their hooves in the dirt and almost have to be lifted up and carried around the narrow bend. Matthew considered himself a brave man. He had risked his life on the Colorado River many times as he'd inspected the hull of the *Explorer*. But this . . . this standing only inches from the edge of a thousand-foot drop . . . this chilled his blood and made him giddy.

Ives himself worked as hard as any of the men to keep the mules moving. He didn't play it safe either, but took risks equal to any of them, and that shamed some of the terrified soldiers enough to get the job done.

Sergeant Rupp was pale and almost as wide as the ledge itself in some of the worst places. "I swear if I ever get to the bottom of this sonofabitch, you'll have to shoot me before I'll come back up this trail."

"If you want to live down there in a mud hut and lose your retirement and rocking chair, that's up to you," Matthew said, hugging the cliff walls and willing himself not to look over the side.

It seemed to take forever to reach the bottom, and when they did, the mules could not be held and stampeded for the turbulent Colorado River. Once on flat, solid ground, the men collapsed with relief. They lay on their backs staring up at the walls that seemed to lean over them until a tightness built up in their chests and they had to close their eyes.

It was hotter in the depths of the canyon. Grass grew in thick clumps and the plants were of a different kind than what they had found on the south rim. Ives and Dr. Newberry, each of whom had some expertise in botany, were fascinated by the entirely new spectrum of botanical life. While they eagerly collected specimens, the soldiers were given time to rest. They might have gone swimming because the air was so warm, but due to the swiftness of the river, no one dared. Down in the bottom of the great knife slice of rainbow rock, the river churned redly, and anyone could see how, over the centuries, the water had carved this magnificent creation.

Ives and the expedition rested only a few days while the mules, which had been half starved from their long desert crossing out of San Diego and Los Angeles, regained some of their strength. The Haulapais village to which their guides led them was small, the people not much better off than the two nearly emaciated guides who had led the Ives expedition down

into the canyon. In the ascent of the canyon walls, the same
two guides led them up a different trail, one far longer but not
quite so narrow. Yet it was an extremely difficult climb.
Matthew fell behind with Sergeant Rupp, who was struggling
with every ounce of his will and body to keep climbing. The
man was pale, even his red nose had lost its color. He was also
gasping, and his clothes were drenched with sweat. Rupp had
to stop every twenty or thirty yards, and then he'd lean up
against the cliff and close his eyes, trying to catch his breath.

Matthew did not quite know what to say to the man. In a
saloon brawl or under an Indian attack, he had no doubt that
Rupp would be the best man in the company to stand beside.
But under these bad circumstances, he was the worst. "Maybe
you ought to give me your watch and any money you might be
carrying, and then jump," Matthew offered, trying to flag the
soldier on by pricking at his considerable pride.

One bloodshot eye glared at him. "I should do the
lieutenant a favor and grab hold of you, and then we'll both go
over. You're the meanest, most heartless bastard I ever been
on a campaign with! It just beats the hell out of me how Ives
ever decided to let you come along."

"He must have seen I was good with Indians," Matthew
deadpanned.

His comment brought a low chuckle from the distressed
sergeant, and then Rupp staggered on up the trail.

They joined the rest of the expedition that night and the
sergeant was so exhausted he could barely speak. His condition shocked and upset the lieutenant. "I should have known
better than to insist he come, but I had no idea the canyon
would be so deep."

Matthew glanced over at the sleeping sergeant. "He'll be
better in the morning. Order him to ride that big black mule
for a few days. It's strong enough now."

"It cuts at his pride."

Matthew said, "Pride has nothing to do with it anymore.
When the sergeant gets rested, he'll be himself again and
before this expedition is over he'll prove his value. But if he
doesn't rest, he's not going to recover and he'll die out here."

"Maybe his commanding officer at Fort Yuma should give
him a medical discharge," Ives said.

"No!" Matthew lowered his voice. "He wants to make twenty-five years. He deserves that much."

But Ives shook his head. "Looking at him right now, I wouldn't bet on him lasting through the next twenty-five days."

As they traveled northeast, the country became more arid and Ives's barometer showed them to be at an altitude of six thousand feet. There was no grass, and the mules suffered badly. Matthew watched them stagger onward, day after day, and he saw how Ives worried.

On the first day of February, they were struck by a sudden and violent snowstorm that sent them fleeing into a small canyon where they huddled and shivered for almost thirty-six hours. The Fort Yuma soldiers were not outfitted for cold weather, and everyone stayed close to the fires. All night long the mules brayed weakly, and Matthew fully expected the poor beasts to be either dead of starvation or frozen by morning.

But they were not. Remarkably, they were all alive, though wobbly and weak. "We *have* to find grass and water," Ives said, leading off.

But as they continued on, the country showed little promise of either grass or water. To Matthew's way of thinking, it was the most desolate and yet one of the most beautiful places on Earth. They passed through more cedar forests and range after range of mountains, always searching for a spring and the small patches of grass that would surround it.

At the end of February, they faced another hardship besides the constant shortage of water and feed. They entered a great high-desert basin that stretched at least seventy miles and whose floor was lava rock. Almost at once, the mules, now unshod after being away from civilization so long, began to go lame. Their feet were extremely hard, but even obsidian would have been chipped away or ground down to nothing if exposed to the volcanic lava bed.

"Keep them moving!" Rupp would yell to his soldiers. "Don't let them stop."

Matthew and the soldiers beat the mules onward. It was one of the most unpleasant tasks he had ever been forced to perform. The mules, already terribly thin and struggling to carry even hundred-pound loads, did not have the strength to go much farther, and with their lameness, each step seemed as if it would be their very last. Their brays changed to something akin to a cry, something that cut into the hearts of the men.

At last, the lava bed was crossed, and they came upon the great valley that cradled the Little Colorado River where they found an abundance of grass and water. After the arid, desolate plateaus and the valley of lava rock, it seemed like a paradise. Ives ordered a two-day rest, more for the benefit of the starving mules than for the men.

Two days later, after leaving the river, they found themselves lost in a painted desert. Mesas and eroding bluffs stood proudly against the sky, their colors blending into one another like an artist's palette. The temperature grew hotter and their thoughts again were consumed by the need for grass and water. Despite the brilliant colors, the expedition was seized with melancholy, for the country in which they traveled was one of utter desolation. Not a tree or even a shrub could be seen, and the flaming red-and-gold sand mirrored the sun's glare so ferociously that they were half blinded.

Ives ordered the expedition to cut muslin veils, and that brought some comfort to their swollen and weeping eyes. But the mules were almost finished, and with the rainbow panorama and shimmering heat waves laid out before them, it was clear that it would be disastrous to proceed any farther.

"We have no choice," Ives said to them all in a voice that reflected great weariness but also determination. "If we go another day without finding water, we will all die of thirst. I won't take that risk. Sergeant, order the men to turn the mules and we'll try to reach the Little Colorado again. It's our only hope."

Rupp nodded, his throat was too parched and swollen to speak without pain. The column of soldiers and their mules turned and began to retrace their steps through the red sand.

It was almost a death march, and by the time they reached water, they had been without it for fifty-two hours. The mules again broke loose from the soldiers when they were still a mile east of the river. No one blamed or tried to halt their mad charge. Sergeant Rupp fell twice, so Matthew and the biggest

soldier in the company pulled the sergeant to his feet and half
carried, half dragged him to the river.

For two days, while the ravenous mules ate and the men
rested, Ives paced without stopping. He sent scouts downriver
and they found a well-traveled path that led due north
between a pair of huge mesas.

"There are supposed to be Hopi villages just to the north
of us," Ives said. "I'll bet anything it leads to them. I've wanted
to visit the Hopi and the neighboring Navajo right from the
start."

"Why the hell do we want to see any more desert
Indians?" Matthew asked. "Haven't we disturbed enough of
the poor wretches?"

Ives, lips cracked and crusted with blood, looked up and
said, "It is my understanding that the Hopi and Navajo are
among the most civilized Indians in the world. It would be
valuable for you to see them, Mr. Beard. I think you might
learn something."

"Civilized, you say?" Matthew shook his head. "Do they
ride around in carriages or wagons? Have factories, farms, or
advanced irrigation systems? *Those* are a few of the standards
by which civilizations are measured. And my own observation
of the Cocopas, the Yuma, the Mojave, and those poor devils
we saw down in the big canyon, the Haulapais, has confirmed
my long-held belief that all Indians are backward savages."

Sergeant Rupp overheard this and said, "You obviously
have never seen the Plains Indians. Have you even heard of
the Cherokees?"

"Of course!" Matthew retorted, knowing that the Cherokee were very advanced and had even developed their own
alphabet. "All right then, I'll admit I haven't had your frontier
experience, but as for what I've seen, the Indians of the
Southwest are a collection of dismal societies tottering on the
brink of starvation."

Ives looked away, his expression one of exasperation.
"Your opinion of Indians is of no concern to me or to the
United States Army, as long as you do not antagonize the Hopi
or Navajo. In fact, I've decided that the men and the mules are
too exhausted to go much farther. Dr. Newberry and I, along

with a few volunteer soldiers, will detach ourselves and go
north to find the Hopi and express our country's message of
peace. You, Mr. Beard, are quite welcome to remain with
Sergeant Rupp, who will lead the main expedition directly to
Fort Defiance."

"Suits me."

"I figured that it would. Given your low opinion of all
Indians, why should you risk learning the truth about an entire
civilization?"

Matthew's cheeks burned at the insult, and the sergeant
grinned, but was wise enough not to say anything.

Matthew stalked away, angry and troubled. That night, as
he lay on the bank of the Little Colorado and traced the stars
high above, he knew that he would have to go to the Hopi
villages for no other reason than to show both himself and Ives
that he was fair and open-minded. No man liked to be branded
a bigot, and if he ever met up with his brother, he wanted to
be able to state his opinions with conviction and the full
knowledge that he spoke the truth.

Early the next morning, when Matthew made it clear he
was going with the lieutenant, the old sergeant laughed out
loud. "You're not as smart as I thought you were," Rupp said.
"The lieutenant threw out the bait and you snapped it up like
a big, dumb fish."

Matthew shrugged. "And you're not as tough as I thought
you'd be, Sergeant. You've been a weak sister on this expedition ever since we left the *Explorer*. You're too old for
soldiering and too dumb to know it."

Rupp's grin slipped a little but he stuck out his hand. "I
like a man who doesn't try to pull his punches. I consider
myself one of the few honest men in the Army and I consider
you one of the few honest men in civilian life. But I never liked
you much."

"Goes both ways," Matthew said, taking the sergeant's
rough hand. "I still think you ought to be a deserter."

"Uh-uh. Five more years."

"If an Indian doesn't scalp you, that old heart of yours will
quit first."

The sergeant chuckled. "That's another thing I always
appreciated about you, Matt. You're such a callous bastard.

Take care of the lieutenant for me. He's one of the few good officers we got."

"I'll do it."

Matthew never looked back. They took a couple of the strongest mules and followed the well-marked Indian trail north for almost twenty miles until they came to a tall bluff. At first, it seemed as if they were blocked from going any farther, but closer inspection showed them a narrow crevasse, which they entered with the sides of the mules almost brushing rock. The crevasse led them through the bluff, and when they emerged on the north side, it was to see a line of blue peaks on the horizon. The path was clearly marked again, and they camped at sunset without water.

The next day was windy and overcast. By midmorning, pellets of cold rain were falling, and both men and mules turned their faces to the sky and licked their parched lips, hoping the drops would slake their thirst. Soon, the sky opened up to release a torrential downpour. It became so heavy that they could not see. The hard, red rock upon which they stood began to run like wet paint, and soon every gully and low place was filled with red water. There was no place to seek cover so they just stood on a table of rock and watched the storm crash and rage all around them. The earth was rocked by thunder and lightning that was almost deafening. After two hours, the rain suddenly ended, the sun broke through the black, roiling canopy of clouds, and the red earth began to steam.

Matthew squeezed the rain from his beard and removed his soggy coat and shirt. Like the others, during the hardest moments of the rain, he had cupped his hand in front of his mouth and drunk his fill. Now, the grateful mules were sucking up the red water. By late afternoon the following day, they had found some grass for the starving animals, and by using his spyglass Ives could see a big Hopi village resting on a high mesa eight or ten miles away. Matthew and the others eagerly shared turns with the glass. Matthew had seen pictures of European castles enclosed by high stone walls, and this Hopi village reminded him very much of them. It had towers, battlements, and many tiers of buildings. And later, after darkness fell, they could see the winking eyes of fires,

maybe a hundred of them, on the levels just above the great
Hopi walls.

"I told you they'd be different," Ives said. "What we are
about to see is a very advanced civilization."

Matthew just nodded. He had seen enough to know that
the lieutenant was right.

Early the next morning, they broke camp and headed
straight for the distant mesa. The land was open, and before
they had gone five miles they saw a horse carrying two Indians
approach them from the still distant Hopi village. As they
drew closer, Matthew saw that the front rider, who was
handling the reins, was a far different breed of Indian from
those he had seen up to now. Because the air was cool, the
rider wore a blue woolen jacket, cotton pants, a sun-bleached
flat-brimmed black hat with an eagle feather in a rattlesnake
hatband, a belt of ornate brass plates, and a magnificent
turquoise necklace. The horse, a small, thin bay, was also
brightly bedecked with ribbons in its bridle and a shiny silver
Spanish bit.

"Do you think he's their chief?" Matthew asked.

"No," Ives said, "I would imagine he and his companion
are no more than the tribe's official reception committee."

This proved to be the case. Proving less facile than
Sergeant Rupp but still effective, Lieutenant Ives used the
universal sign language to indicate that he and his men had
come in peace and sought only food, water, and grass for their
starving animals.

The two Hopi informed them that they had come to the
great village of Oraibi and they made it clear that all would be
provided. They wore broad smiles and waved toward their
village, whereupon hundreds of people came out from behind
the walls to greet the expedition. And to Matthew's amazement, each Indian . . . men, women, and even the older
children . . . insisted on shaking the hand of every white
man. Matthew had never seen such happy and clean people.
They looked well fed, and when their huge fields of corn and
beans were pointed out, Matthew saw that the Hopi had
developed a sophisticated system of irrigation. They had
constructed many reservoirs and water ditches, all lined with

masonry. There were even tile aqueducts and pipes to carry the water to the most distant of their fields.

"Amazing, don't you think, Mr. Beard?" Ives asked.

"Amazing is right."

Ives looked very pleased with himself as they passed through the gate walls and beheld the pueblos themselves. They were laid out in a perfect square, and they crowded the surrounding fortress walls, which were at least fifteen feet high and wide enough to form a landing along the top from which their warriors could defend themselves and the city from attack. Flights of stone steps led from the walled landings down to the doors of the pueblos, and all the living quarters were connected by architecturally correct causeways, tunnels, and archways. There were also large, round subterranean chambers big enough for fifty or more Indians. The Hopi called them *kivas*, and indicated that they were ceremonial meeting places. Matthew noticed there was no litter at all and even the floors of the passageways were swept clean by corn brooms. They climbed a ladder and had to duck to enter a low apartment with smooth adobe walls, a hard-clay floor, a fireplace, and a chimney. They could see many other rooms that were adjoining, and though the light was poor, one was obviously a storage place for corn, another a sleeping compartment, and yet another seemed to be a kitchen from which mouth-watering aromas wafted. A few minutes later, the Hopi chief was led into their presence.

He was stooped but dignified, a very ancient man who smiled without teeth and then indicated they should recline on some animal skins. The chief's wife brought a beautiful pottery vase of cool water and a tray filled with what looked like thin blue wrapping paper rolled up into bundles. Using sign, the chief explained that the food was made from cornmeal, ground very fine, made into a paste, then baked. When properly cooked, it assumed a texture not unlike paper, and the sheets were folded or rolled together to form the staple item of food used by his people. He called it *piki*. The Hopi had been blessed by rain this past year and they had many melons and, to Matthew's delight, even fresh peaches from the little trees that were grown from peach pits brought in centuries earlier by the first Spanish conquistadores.

Matthew was famished. He could hardly wait to eat, and when the chief motioned for him to do so, he devoured the little rolls and more were provided until his hunger finally was satisfied.

A peace pipe was lit and exchanged between the chief and every member of the expedition. Its tobacco tasted like a burning weed, but Ives and his men were careful not to cough or make an unpleasant face.

The chief was very curious about white men coming to his village from the west. He had seen white soldiers and others come from Fort Defiance to the southeast, but never had whites visited him from the Little Colorado. Ives explained that they had come from far beyond the Little Colorado on a ship plying a river he called the Big Colorado. The chief was greatly impressed. He invited the whites to remain for a few days in his village and Ives accepted. They would trade the last of the expedition's beads and trinkets for corn and a few sheep that could be butchered on the way to Fort Defiance.

It was nearly sunset when the talking and the trading ended. The chief and his wife took them outside where they climbed a series of ladders that led up to the highest rooftop in the village. Here, the view at sunset was spectacular and the chief proudly explained that no enemies could ever strike without being seen while still many, many miles distant. He also pointed in many directions, like the spokes of a wheel, to indicate that there were seven Hopi villages altogether, the others being Shungopavi, Michongnovi, Walpi, Shupaulovi, Hano, and Sichumovi. Each village had its own chief and the Hopi rarely visited each other. Each village was self-sufficient and expected to make its own defense against the dreaded Apache and even the Navajos who sometimes tried to steal their sheep and their corn from the fields.

The following morning, they were greeted by the heralding of the town crier while he stood with arms and legs widely spaced before the bright orb of the rising sun. In a clear soprano voice that rose and fell like the vespers of European monks, he invited all the Hopi people to come join him in prayers as they stood on the crown of their fortress walls. What an impressive and moving sight they were! Women, children, old venerated men wrinkled by ten thousand desert suns.

They all carried handsful of cornmeal over which they breathed their morning prayers for a good life and for gentle rains for their precious crops. When the prayers were over, they tossed their cornmeal from their lofty perch in a tribute to the morning sun. Then, they solemnly conducted their daily ritual of washing their hands and faces, then cleansing their long black hair and braiding it in the fashion of their people.

Ives was ready to push on. He finished his trading and was given a sack of dried peaches as a special present from the chief, along with several beautiful blankets and a few pieces of lovely painted pottery. Matthew traded his own Green River knife for three of these blankets. He could always buy a knife, but the blankets were priceless, and he'd never seen such fine weaving or intricate designs.

They left the Hopi and started toward Fort Defiance. On the way, they would pass through the Navajo lands. Ives said that the Navajo were at least as advanced as the Hopi. This time, Matthew kept his mouth shut. And as the Hopi lined the high rock walls of their fortress and waved goodbye, he waved back. He'd been a complete fool. If he could be this wrong about the Hopi, he had no doubt that he was also wrong about the Navajo and perhaps even his father's people, the Utes of the Shining Mountains.

19

Matthew flexed his cramped legs in the Concord coach and stared at the Colorado River just north of Fort Yuma. It was springtime, almost five months to the day since the *Explorer* had steamed up this stretch of water. It seemed more like five years when he remembered all the things he had seen and done on the Ives expedition. At Fort Defiance, all the soldiers and other members of the party had been happy to learn they'd been ordered to new Army posts in the East. Fort Yuma was considered the worst Army post on the entire Western frontier.

Sitting in the stagecoach across from Matthew, Lieutenant Ives was trying to write a hurried report but the road to Fort Yuma was so potholed and washboarded that correspondence was all but impossible. Still, Ives was giving it his best effort. Frowning with irritation, he gripped his ink pen as if trying to strangle it.

"The driver said we'll be in Fort Yuma within two hours," Matthew said. "Why don't you just wait and get your paperwork done then?"

Ives glanced up with a look of distraction. He had aged considerably during the expedition. The sun had burned his youthful face, and there were faint beginnings of squint lines radiating from the corners of his blue eyes. "I won't be staying at Fort Yuma but an hour, and then I'll take this stage on to San Diego."

"What needs to be done in Yuma?"

"I'm going to attend to a few odds and ends. I left some things there when we went upriver and I need to instruct the post commander as to the disposition of the *Explorer*. After that, I return to Washington, D.C."

"For a hero's welcome and assignment to another Western expedition, I presume."

Ives smiled. "Hardly. I've a wife and she thinks I'm more suited to engineering than to being another John C. Fremont. I'll leave the pathfinding to the pathfinders."

As usual, Ives was being overly modest and Matthew told him so. "You did a pretty fair job on the Colorado. After that, Washington will seem drab. Besides, what's to do there that is so important?"

Ives folded his notebook. "I've been trained as an engineer, Matt. I also enjoy architecture. It seems that strings have been pulled and I've been given a position as a project engineer on something called the Washington Monument. It's to be rather important, I'm told."

Matthew was not impressed. "Sounds pretty tame to me."

Ives chuckled. Now that the expedition was over, he was much more at ease. "I'm ready for something tame. What about you? Back to the Sacramento River trade?"

"I don't know." In truth, the Sacramento River had lost its allure for Matthew. It was no longer a challenge. "I might find another river."

"Why?" Ives leaned forward. "Stay to ply the Colorado. Fort Yuma is growing and the Army needs a private steamship pilot to haul supplies and mail up from the Gulf of California. I'm afraid there's going to be trouble with the Mojaves."

"Why? I thought we'd cemented good relations."

"So did I," Ives said, "but there've been some problems with emigrants and freighters coming across from Santa Fe. Fouled water holes and such. As more and more people use the Overland Trail, it's just bound to create difficulties. My information is that Chief Cairnook is really on the prod."

Matthew remembered the little old chief who'd sat so proudly while being towed by his warriors across the Colorado River. Thinking back to that day still brought a smile to his lips. Cairnook was the first Indian he'd ever thought of as an individual with the same feelings of pride, amusement, and irritation as himself. He had *liked* Cairnook. "It just doesn't seem possible that Cairnook would start raisin' hell."

"From what I've heard, I'm afraid he is," Ives said. "But the main thing for you to understand is that, if there is Indian trouble, it will take a daring man to be the first to work the river. I think the task would suit you perfectly."

"But I'm fresh out of steamboats, Lieutenant."

"What about the *Explorer*? You know the vessel is perfect for the job. Provided she returned in good shape, I might suggest you purchase her from the government and bid a freight and mail contract."

Matthew raised his brows in mock surprise. "Why, Lieutenant! I remember you once told me that I was completely unworthy of trust. A madman, in fact. Are you now saying that you would recommend me for a vital supply contract?"

"Of course! As long as you give me your word of honor that you'd not throw rocks or shoot that four-pound howitzer at any more Yuma Indians."

"Agreed," Matthew said, "providing you don't try to skin me on the price of the *Explorer*. After the pounding it took going up that river, I'm not sure it can be considered a sound vessel."

"Nonsense!" Ives exclaimed. "There is none better for this river and you know it. If it eases your mind, I'd suggest you inspect the hull."

Matthew remembered all the times he'd gone into the muddy waters and blindly inspected the vessel after it had hit a submerged rock or tree. "I know how to do that. What about money? My funds are deposited in San Francisco."

"That's no problem," Ives assured him. "You can give me a letter of credit and I'll take it to your bank and have the funds withdrawn and deposited on account for the United States Army. What do you say?"

Matthew looked out the window of the Concord stage and considered the proposition carefully. He had been thinking of Helen O'Day lately and that was bad. He wondered what had happened to her after he'd disappeared, leaving only a letter of goodbye telling her that he'd gone to San Francisco to join the Ives expedition.

"This is a hellish country," he mused, watching a thousand-foot-high whirlwind of dust funnel and dance across the sage and creosote brush. "It's no place for a woman."

"No," Ives said, "it's not. But as you know, there are women at Fort Yuma, both the wives of officers and enlisted men. They organize social events and seem to have adapted very well."

"This sun, heat, and dust could dry out a woman in just a few years, make her old long before her time."

Ives studied him closely. "What . . . what are you thinking? That you might want to marry down here?"

"Hell no! I've no use for any man who'd drag a woman to Fort Yuma, Fort Defiance, or any other damn Army fort where the temperatures reach 120 degrees in summer and there's nothing but cactus and rock, tarantulas and scorpions. Lieutenant, this is as near to being in hell as it gets on Earth."

"I know that, but I'm the one who's leaving for Washington. If you feel that way, then you ought to return to Sacramento. That's fine country."

"The river is being ruined," Matthew said. "A couple more years and it won't even be navigable. I know how to run a general store, but that's not for me anymore."

"Then buy the *Explorer* and you'll have more than your share of adventures."

Matthew looked the young officer right in the eye and pushed the foolish thought of seeing Helen O'Day and her daughter out of his mind. "I will," he decided out loud. "Damnit, I will!"

Matthew bought the *Explorer* that very afternoon and signed a long-term contract to supply Fort Yuma with hay, provisions, and mail. The price and the terms had been most reasonable.

As for the *Explorer* herself, she'd suffered no damage on the return trip to Yuma and Matthew knew she was worth every penny of her purchase price. His St. Louis store and the sale of his luxurious Sacramento River steamer had left him a wealthy man. Funny, but his goals had changed during the months he'd been with Ives. No longer was he preoccupied with accumulating money. Instead, he wanted to be a part of building something permanent. And though it probably sounded crazy, he thought he'd live to see the day when new and thriving communities sprang up along the Colorado River. The post commander had all but promised that the Army would soon be establishing another post, called Fort Mojave,

up the river about where Ives had chained him to the fiery
boiler. As soon as the fort was built, Matthew was sure he'd
have to employ the famous Reaney, Neafie & Company of
Philadelphia to build a copy of the *Explorer* and then hire a
captain and a crew of hardy men to operate her. Business
would double overnight.

"Congratulations," Ives said when the papers were signed
and his stagecoach was ready to leave. "Matt, you're back in
the steamship business."

"Yeah, this time I'm plying a river running through hell,"
he replied. "By the way, what about that Mormon uprising
that was supposed to be the reason for everything we did?"

Ives shook hands with several officers and swung up into
the stage. He closed the door and said, "Nothing ever came of
it. Confidentially, I think it was all just a ruse by the Army
brass in Washington. It was a good excuse to explore the
Colorado—as if we needed one."

"But we only saw the lower part of it. No one knows about
the rest."

"They will, one of these days," Ives assured him. "You can
bet the Army has it down as one of its future expeditions."

"I hope you'll be the man to lead the party. If you
are . . ."

"No," Ives said quickly. "Washington Monument, remember?"

"Yeah, that's right." Matthew hid his disappointment.
Exploring got into a man's blood all too quickly. He was ready
to go again and, maybe . . .

"By the way," Ives said, folding Matthew's draft for
deposit on his San Francisco account, "I forgot to say that you
have a letter waiting in the postmaster's shack."

Matthew was rudely jerked back to the present. "How
could that be? No one knows I'm here."

"Someone must. Feminine hand from the looks of it and
postmarked from Sacramento."

His first and only thought was of Helen and Rose, even
though he told himself not to dare hope. But if she had
written . . . "Why didn't you tell me when we first arrived?"

Ives waved up at the driver to depart. He yelled back, "I'll
leave you to figure that one out for yourself."

"You sly bastard!" Matthew hissed as he walked swiftly toward the postmaster's shack. "And all the while I thought he was an *honorable* man."

The letter was postmarked almost two months earlier and Matthew tore it open and read it quickly.

Dear Matthew:

I do not understand why you left us so suddenly and with no warning. I don't know if you even heard that my husband, John, was savagely murdered while in prison. Words cannot describe my feelings, for they are too deep for me to understand. I have learned that my husband left extensive and valuable property in Columbia for myself and my child, so, thankfully, we are well taken care of financially. I miss you, even though I suppose it is shameful for so recent a widow to make such an admission. So does Rose. She asks about you every day.

I am not sure what I will do now. I cannot go back to Boston and face the questions or the old memories that would haunt me to my grave. Thank you for everything. I pray you remain in good health.
Sincerely, Helen O'Day

Matthew read and reread the letter until he knew it by heart, and then he wadded it up in his fist and walked over to a soldier who was smoking. "Got a match?"

"Why, sure."

Matthew took the match and touched it to the letter. He held it until his fingers burned and then he dropped it and ground it under his heel.

"Must have been a real bad piece of news, huh, Mr. Beard?"

"Yeah," Matthew said quietly. "Real bad. Where can a man buy a bottle of whiskey around this goddamn place?"

"In these parts, ten dollars will buy you a bottle of tequila or a willing Mojave girl," he said with a wink.

"Deliver 'em both to the *Explorer*."

The soldier stuck out his hand and Matthew started to give him the money, then changed his mind. "Forget the

Indian girl," he said in anger. "Just get me two bottles of
tequila."

"*Two* bottles? Man, you don't know how strong that
Mexican cactus juice can be! Two bottles would kill a horse."

"Just do as I ask, soldier," Matthew growled. "And don't
crowd me with any of your advice."

The soldier's grin slipped badly. "Yes, sir, Mr. Beard. I'll
have two bottles delivered within the hour."

Matthew stalked out to his new vessel. He should have
felt good being the owner of the faithful and historic little
steamboat, but instead he felt rotten. Helen had ruined things
for him, ruined 'em even as she'd tried to make them better.
She sounded as if she wanted to see him again. She'd not come
right out and said it, but if a man knew that woman even a
little, he'd understand what she'd written between the lines.

Goddamnit! How could he even see a woman like that
again, knowing he'd had her husband—the father of her
daughter—murdered in a prison yard?

The answer was that he could not. When he'd paid to have
John O'Day stabbed to death, he'd burned his bridges with
Helen and the girl. He'd not be able to look Helen or Rose in
the eye, much less ask them to share his wicked and deceitful
life.

Matthew boarded the *Explorer* and began loading the
firebox with wood. He'd wait long enough to get the tequila
and then he was going to get drunk and run this goddamn dirty
river all the way to the gulf. Maybe he'd sink the vessel and be
done with everything once and for all.

It was the middle of August and the temperature had
soared to 116 degrees in the shade when Matthew steamed
toward Fort Yuma with eight tons of alfalfa hay for the cavalry's
horses and one ton of food supplies for the officers, soldiers,
and military dependents. He had learned the Colorado River
well enough to know that he would never really be able to
avoid every sand and gravel bar between the Gulf of California
and Fort Yuma. Still, he was getting better every trip. Like the
three men he hired to work the fifty-foot steamer, he wore no
shirt and his pants were cut off at the knees. The sun had
burned his skin until he was darker than most Indians, and

he'd let his black hair and beard grow down to his shoulders, wild and unruly. With his great size, he was an unforgettable figure as he stood at the wheel of the *Explorer* and guided her swiftly up the hidden channels.

As he neared Fort Yuma, he gave three shrill blasts on the steam whistle to tell the soldiers and officers that he had arrived with mail and provisions. He knew that it would touch off a celebration. Receiving mail and packages from their hometowns was the highlight of the month for the soldiers. Matthew had become friends with almost all of them. At the sound of the *Explorer*'s steam whistle, practically the entire fort came hurrying down to the dock where the hay and supplies would be unloaded. First came the children, and there were more every time Matthew arrived, and then the soldiers and finally the wives.

In spite of the intense heat and still, oppressive air, it was a happy crowd who awaited him as Matthew expertly navigated the steamship into the dock where his men tied it securely. The children came rushing onto the vessel, and for a moment, there was laughter, shouting, and great confusion. But when the officers arrived, they ordered the children back to shore and formed a work detail. A line of Army wagons came down from the fort and the unloading began in earnest.

Captain Harold Lawson was a spare, serious-looking commander who rarely smiled and yet had an excellent sense of humor, if you liked it very dry. "Good to see you on time as usual, Mr. Beard," he said, not offering to extend his hand in greeting because he was a little put off by anyone who paraded around half naked.

"Thank you, Captain! The river is falling now and in a couple of months it'll be slower."

Captain Lawson was not interested in the river. Ives had demonstrated that the Colorado had no military usefulness and, therefore, it did not greatly concern Lawson one way or the other. He allowed his soldiers to fish and swim in its muddy waters. He also allowed them to plant cottonwood trees along the riverbank below the fort so that they could picnic on Sundays. And finally, he allowed the women and children to build small irrigation canals to their vegetable gardens. No one was more amazed than he when the desert soil proved highly fertile.

"You have a visitor . . . rather, two visitors," the captain said without revealing that he was astounded that any woman in her right mind would come to this summertime hell to see a wild man like Matthew Beard. "They're up there waiting."

Matthew threw back his head and looked up at the fort and saw Helen O'Day and Rose waving at him.

He was struck dumb with surprise. His emotions were momentarily out of control, and he could only shake his head and ask, "Why?"

"How should I know? But you really should wear something decent," Captain Lawson said with exasperation.

Matthew was pulled back to his surroundings. He absently touched the sweat-matted hair on his chest. "Yeah," he said, "I guess I should. My seabag is stowed by the wheel. Besides a shirt, I'll get long pants on, too."

"And shoes, Mr. Beard. You need to wear shoes."

"Yeah. I still have shoes." He hurried to change into decent clothes. But first he dove into the cool water and scrubbed the sweat and the salt from his body using fistfuls of coarse sand. "Throw me my pants!" he bellowed, pulling off his short ones and standing entirely naked, but up to his chest in water.

One of the sailors followed orders and tossed him the required garment. Matthew guessed it was going to look funny, him standing in front of Helen soaking wet from the chest down, but there was no choice. It was certain that he was not going to get everyone from the fort to turn their heads while he changed on board the *Explorer*.

When he had his pants buttoned, he clambered on board and found an old towel he used to wrap steam pipes when they ruptured or sprang a leak. He dried himself in a hurry and pulled on a rumpled white shirt, then a pair of shoes, cursing because he could not find his socks.

Running his fingers through his long, wet hair and plastering it to his skull, he stood before the captain, almost as if at attention and ready for a military inspection. "Better now?"

"Hardly," the officer said. "But I suppose that's as good as it gets, eh, Mr. Beard?"

"Damn right it is," Matthew grunted, hopping onto the pier and starting up the road to the fort.,

Helen and Rose met him halfway. At least, Rose did. The girl broke away from her mother and came flying down the road to throw herself into his arms.

Matthew lifted the child as he might a wiggling puppy. He let her bury her face against his shoulder and tickle his thick beard. He was already sweating and still river wet, and he hoped that would hide his tears.

Helen came right up to him. She studied his face, his unkempt hair and beard, and his dark, guilt-stricken eyes. "Why didn't you ever come to see us?" she asked him softly.

He held on to Rose. "I wanted to come."

She reached out and placed her hands on his shoulders. "I know you did. I felt it every day and, finally, I just grew exasperated with waiting. I came for you, Matthew. We both did."

He set Rose down. "She's growing so fast. I didn't realize she'd grow like that."

"Matthew, I . . ."

His eyes lifted to view the searing desert that encircled Fort Yuma. He could see the heat waves punishing the land. "This is no place for a girl, Helen. Nor for a woman like yourself. You should go back."

"No."

Her voice was calm and assured, and he felt caught between his own desires and his guilt. "Helen, look around you!"

"We've been doing little else but look for the past two weeks. This desert country has its own beauty."

He tried to argue but she touched his lips, and he remained silent. "Matthew, this country is much like you. It's rugged and hard on the surface. But if one looks deeper, then it becomes very special."

"But it'll steal the softness from your cheeks! It'll put wrinkles in the corners of your lovely eyes. You'll grow to hate it, and me as well."

Her chin lifted. "There are other women and children

here who would say it's not so bad. They fish, garden, swim, socialize. We're staying—with your permission or without it."

"You're not staying here!" he roared, loud enough to be heard down at the water.

For an instant, she shrank from him but then stood her ground. "You don't have to shout and I won't be ordered about."

Matthew shook his head. "What about the money from Columbia?"

"I sold the saloon but not the hotel. It is beautiful . . . perhaps we could, someday, I mean."

"Helen, you must go back!"

Suddenly, her eyes filled with tears. "Matthew, what on Earth is wrong?" she cried. "You love me! You love my Rose. I can see it burning in your eyes! *What is the matter?*"

He stiffened and pushed her away. He wanted to tell her what was wrong, that he'd had her murdering husband killed just to free her of her marriage bonds. But he didn't say anything, not a word. For the first time in his life, he was deathly afraid. Afraid of what he'd see in her eyes. Revulsion. Shock, then hatred.

He turned from her and felt her hands slip away. In a voice that did not sound like his own, he said, "You and Rose are taking the first stagecoach out of Fort Yuma."

She pushed around in front of him and her face was pale, her lips quivering with hurt and anger. "We are *not* leaving! You can't force us to go! I don't understand what is wrong with you, but I swear I will find out!"

"It's another woman!" he shouted. "Is that what you need to hear?"

She grabbed his collar and studied his eyes. "I don't believe that—not today, not tomorrow, not as long as I live. You do love me. Now tell me so!"

Matthew shoved past her and hurried back down the road to the *Explorer*. He would drive the soldiers to unload his steamer and then *he'd* be the one who was leaving!

20

Nathan Beard stood on a high bluff overlooking Green River City and marveled at the great ribbons of steel that marked the route of the Transcontinental Railroad, which had been completed less than two weeks earlier at Promontory Point, Utah Territory. He shook his head in amazement, for he had never believed the West would ever be spanned, the buffalo herds decimated by hunters, and the beaver all but eliminated. And yet, it had happened, and nothing in the West symbolized progress so much as those iron rails stretching east and west farther than the eye could see.

Where had the frontier gone? he asked himself as he searched the rugged Wyoming tableland. Nathan felt as if he were a hundred years old, when in fact he was only half that age. But he had seen much tragedy in his life . . . and also much joy, joy in his knowledge that before Justina died, they had raised four children, all of them now strong and moral. There was also joy in the knowledge that he had played a small but perhaps crucial role in gaining for the Utes at least a decent chance of survival in this modern age. Along with the great Chief Ouray, they'd negotiated the most favorable treaty possible, some sixteen million acres of land in western Colorado for their permanent homeland. True, Spirit Lake and the headwaters of the mighty Colorado River were lost, along with millions of acres of forest and wilderness that had belonged to the Ute people for centuries, but Nathan realized that they could not have hoped for better terms.

They had lost their Shining Mountains forever and it had all happened so quickly. First the whites had come for beaver, then gold and silver. Especially gold and silver. The first big gold strike had been at a place called Cherry Creek, in what was now being called Denver Town, and when that strike was over, thousands of gold-fevered whites had streamed up the eastern slopes of the Rockies to claim Spirit Lake and the headwaters of the Colorado River. Nathan had pleaded with the Indian leaders not to start a war that could never be won, so the Ute Indians had fought the invasion with words instead of ammunition. But each year, the people of the Shining Mountains had retreated deeper and deeper into the wilderness.

And still the whites had come, from Pike's Peak, Silver City, Cripple Creek, always taking the land from the Indians, always driving them toward the deserts of the Great Basin. Nathan expelled a deep sigh. He was glad that Isaac had not lived to see the sad changes. Very glad.

But now, he had been asked by the government to offer his services to a Major John Wesley Powell on an expedition down the Colorado River. Nathan smiled with self-deprecation. It was his own damn fault. He was the one who, after his father died, had felt it somehow necessary to keep exploring the great river, always going farther and farther. And look what it had done for him.

Nathan no longer carried a Hawken rifle with powder, wadding, lead balls, and percussion caps. There were few buffalo to hunt and even the mighty grizzly bears were almost gone, slaughtered like everything else that opposed the whites. He carried a fine new forty-four-caliber Henry repeating rifle. It was lever action so that in a single motion a man could shoot and the new metallic cartridges would eject themselves and another round was ready to fire. The Henry could deliver thirty shots a minute and he especially liked its polished brass breech and the fact that the weapon weighed only nine and a half pounds. Yep, the Henry might not have the wallop of his old Hawken, but it would sure deliver the firepower a sight quicker.

When Nathan entered Green River City, it was about what he had expected. A filthy, riotous tent city populated in the main with whores, gamblers, and thieves. The gambling men wore white shirts and black vests. They smoked cigars and they had a pale, sinister look that came with too much living indoors. The whores had the same color skin, waxy, unhealthy looking. When they spotted big Nathan, they called

him "Mountain Man" and said things to him that made his ears
turn red. One, a redheaded woman with a dress that showed
half of her teats and who smelled so strongly of cheap French
perfume that it gagged Nathan, brazenly tried to grab his arm
and pull him inside her tent, but he jumped clean away from
her and ran as if chased by an evil spirit. It made the other
whores laugh and whoop and it made Nathan feel awful. When
he saw such women, he saw nothing but wickedness and a
sickness in their dead eyes. Nathan remembered Doug Mellon
once telling him long, long ago that he'd had the same feeling.
It hadn't made much sense then, but it did now.

Dressed in his beaded buckskins and moccasins, with his
hair long and cut straight across the back at the level of his
shoulders, Indian style, Nathan attracted plenty of attention at
each street corner. But despite the gray in his hair, no one
except the whores dared challenge or insult him, for he stood
six feet one and had inherited Isaac's great rack of shoulders
and muscular build.

"Can you tell me where I can find Major John Wesley
Powell and his river expedition?" he asked a pair of old-timers
sitting with their feet propped up on an empty chair. Nathan
did not look directly into their eyes, for he was more Indian
than white, and it was the way of the Indian to look sideways
and listen respectfully. But what he heard was not given with
respect.

"Down to the damn Green River, o'course! Say, you an
Injun lover, or what? Look me square in the eyes, mister. I
know you can't be a mountain man, they're all dead by now!
What the hell are you, a damned escapee from a Wild West
show?" The pair laughed outright, amused at their humor.

"I'm a white Indian," Nathan said, striding away, for he
did not wish to associate with such men. When it came to
Indian hating and baiting, the old men were far worse than the
young, probably because they'd suffered during the taming of
the frontier and perhaps lost kinfolk and friends.

Nathan strode toward the river, his walk and manner that
of an Indian, his eyes missing nothing and disapproving of
almost everything. He had once been a part of the white man's
world. Now, it seemed rotted and decadent. He hoped Powell
lived up to the billing that he'd been given a few months

earlier. According to the Army officer who had recruited Nathan, Powell was a man of rare insight and wisdom, a self-taught naturalist, geologist, and topographer who had learned a deep appreciation of nature from years of solitary meanderings along the Mississippi and Missouri rivers. He was married and had fought bravely in the Civil War, which Nathan had heard was about slavery and states' rights. Powell had fought on the Union side and had lost his right arm at the battle called Shiloh. Fortunately, his bride of only one month had been an Army nurse and saved her husband's life. After the terrible war, Powell had become a professor of geology and had organized the first chapter of the Illinois State Natural History Society, an outfit dedicated to teaching people about the natural wonders of their country. Powell and his wife had also traveled extensively in the West and, two years ago, she had been the first woman ever to climb Pikes Peak.

Nathan had liked everything he'd heard about Powell, and that's why he'd agreed to join the party here at its jumping-off place on the Green River, which joined the mighty Colorado River several hundred miles to the south. Powell was still a relatively young man and it was said that he had designed special riverboats that could withstand the rapids and falls to be found in what was being called by a man named Ives and his expedition as the Grand Canyon of the Colorado.

"I'm almost fifty years old," Nathan had told the officer who had arrived at the Ute reservation to urge him to join the expedition. "A river like the Colorado is for young men like yourself."

"I'd give my own arm to do it," the lieutenant had said, "but everyone says you're the only white man who has been all the way to the north end of the Grand Canyon and seen it from the top. Without you, the Powell expedition might go right over a falls before they realized they were in trouble. Ain't no boat ever made that can stand up to a waterfall."

Actually, Nathan had not seen the entire length of the Grand Canyon. He'd seen it from about eighty miles away the year Isaac had gone to St. Louis and never returned. And after Justina's death from an epidemic of the pox, Nathan had spent a great deal of time exploring new country, maybe hoping beyond hope that he could find an unclaimed and unspoiled mountain range for his people. It had been a fool's dream. The whites had taken it all. They'd claimed the Sierra Nevadas twenty years earlier during a gold rush, and they swarmed over the other mountains, too.

Nathan found the expedition and was directed to Powell, a vigorous-looking man of average height with an intelligent face and an empty sleeve where his right arm should have been. "Good to meet you!" Powell said, extending his left hand. "You're the last piece in my puzzle. We'll be leaving soon. I'll introduce you to the other eight men and show you the boats."

It took very little time to see that the major had left nothing to chance. He was quick to acknowledge that everyone who had ever tried to run the river through the Grand Canyon had disappeared forever. "But what I have, they didn't have," he said with a wink. "Just look at our boats. Did you ever see anything built so well or so adapted to river use?"

Nathan had not. There were four boats that had been build by a shipyard in Chicago according to Powell's own design and exacting standards, then delivered here by the Union Pacific Railroad. Three of them were twenty-one feet long, built of oak with double ribbing and strongly reinforced at the stem and stern posts. The fourth boat had been christened the *Emma Dean* after Powell's wife. It was only sixteen feet long, lighter, and built for fast rowing. It was the boat that Powell intended to use as a vanguard. All four of them were sleek and highly waxed, with covered bows and sterns under which were water tight pockets for the storage of food and scientific instruments.

"Didn't cost us a dime to ship 'em," Powell boasted. "It's free publicity for the Union Pacific and they made the most of it. There's supposed to be a huge farewell celebration when we go, speeches and all that. But hell, unless you want glory and headlines, me and the boys are just going to slip away without all the fanfare. The last thing I need or want is a bunch of nosey reporters asking stupid questions like, 'Major Powell, aren't you afraid of drowning? What if you go over a hundred-foot waterfall?'"

"Suits me fine, Major. I'm still trying to find out why you wanted me along."

"Besides the fact that everyone tells me you might be the only man who's ever peeked down into what we call the Flaming Gorge and the northern end of the Grand Canyon, I once ran into a man named Ives. He built the Washington Monument. I guess you know all about him."

"Can't say as I do," Nathan said.

Powell did not try to hide his surprise. "Why, he's the one that took a steamboat two hundred miles up the Colorado and then led an expedition across Arizona Territory to Fort Defiance! But even more interesting was the fact that one of his top men was your brother, Matthew Beard."

Nathan's jaw dropped. "Are you sure?"

"I wasn't until I saw the size of you. Hell, it *had* to be your brother. He's a riverboat man on the lower Colorado. Runs a steamship line up and down to Fort Yuma and Fort Mojave. Big, big fella. Originally from St. Louis, by way of Sacramento."

"I'm also from St. Louis."

"Beard isn't a common name and you boys aren't common-sized men. It's your brother, all right. And when this river run of ours is over, we'll float into Fort Yuma and you can have a big reunion. I can guess how fine it'll be after all these years. That's my own brother, Walter, over there. He wouldn't let me do this without him."

Nathan glanced at Walter. He did not resemble his brother at all, but from the tone of John's voice it was clear that they were close. Nathan felt a pang of regret and even jealousy. He did not have the heart to tell the major that he and Matthew had neither spoken nor heard from one another in almost thirty years. As far as Nathan knew, Matthew might even have killed their father in a rage and been forced to flee St. Louis. Matthew was capable of doing something like that.

For the rest of the day, Nathan helped load supplies and many strange instruments called barometers, chronometers, and sextants. They were obviously very important to Powell, for he stored them in the special water tight compartments. When the loading was done, Powell gathered his nine-man crew together.

"We'll push off at first light, without saying a word to anyone. I guess I can't say anything you don't already know.

This journey will be very dangerous. I'll try to minimize the risks by staying out front but that's no guarantee we won't be carried over a waterfall and drown or be bashed to smithereens. You were each chosen for good reasons and not the least of them was that you've all demonstrated that you are men who enjoy adventure and challenge. Well, this will be a historic challenge. That is all, good luck . . . and good night."

With that, and without any sign of a meal coming that evening, Powell climbed into his bedroll and instantly fell asleep.

They left at dawn and found that the Green River was both swift and deep. It caught the four heavily loaded boats and sent them flying downriver. Because of his own size, strength, and river experience, Nathan was assigned as steersman on the most heavily laden boat, whose full name was *Maid of the Canyon* but which everyone called the *Old Maid*. Along with him was a man named G.Y. Bradley who had served courageously in the Civil War with Powell and who had a quiet dignity that Nathan appreciated. The third member of the crew was W. R. Hawkins, who manned the oars and would be their cook. During the first morning, they busted one oar and lost two others but managed to retrieve them before the fast current took them out of reach.

Powell, to everyone's great surprise, broke out in song. He had a fine voice, and after a short while all the men joined in, even Nathan, who had already decided he was going to enjoy this adventure fully.

By evening, they were dog-tired and no longer interested in singing. Nathan steered the *Old Maid* into a quiet cove where they made camp. They had come a tremendous distance in just one day but, now, they were deep in the wilderness. If they should get hurt or undergo some calamity, there was no help available. None at all. They were on their own.

The second day, a storm drenched them with a cold and heavy rain. That night, they built a roaring bonfire close under a cliff. The morning broke with sunshine and blue skies, and for the next week they floated along at a good rate. Whenever the river widened and they hit calm stretches of water, they relaxed and let the current do their work. They leaned their heads back and gazed at the intriguing side canyons and small waterfalls that poured into the Green River, feeding its strength.

They reached Henry's Fork and plunged into the treacherous but fantastic Flaming Gorge. All at once, they were shooting between towering red cliffs a thousand feet high. The boats were caught in a maelstrom, and as they raced over long series of rapids, they were bucked and twisted like leaves in a freshet. It was almost impossible to steer but Nathan rooted his feet on the deck of the *Old Maid* and used every ounce of his strength as Bradley shouted warnings of rocks ahead. Even so, the *Old Maid* often crashed into mossy boulders and once even landed on a rock that caused them to teeter-totter back and forth for a heart-stopping moment before they tore free and surged on. The white water crashed over the bow, sending spray high overhead, and before they finally reached another stretch of calm, the *Old Maid* was carrying four inches of sloshing river water. They paddled into an inlet and immediately set to work unloading supplies and instruments, checking and drying everything, and inspecting the hulls of the boats.

By nightfall, they were tired but satisfied. "We had our first test," the major told them. "We passed with flying colors. But as Nathan can tell you, this is just the beginning. The worst is yet to come."

At ten o'clock the next morning, Powell heard the ominous roar of their first waterfall, and they paddled crazily to reach shore as the river poured over a twenty-foot drop. It would be necessary to carry out a "let down," as Powell called it, in which everything was unloaded and laboriously hauled around the falls. The boats were lowered by ropes and then reloaded. It was hard, dangerous work and a misstep on the slippery rocks would have been disastrous. Each man knew that to fall in the river would mean drowning. That same day, the expedition "let down" over three more waterfalls, and by nighttime they had gone only eight miles, all of it dangerous white-water rapids.

"You can tell by the composition of the rocks how much white water we're going to have up ahead," Powell said.

The men looked questioningly at him, and he smiled and

explained. "My friends, these canyons were obviously carved
by the river. But if you'll notice, in some places the rock is soft,
made of lime or sandstone and easily chipped or scrubbed
away. Where this occurs the canyons will be wider, the water
slower. But when we come to granite or rocks of an igneous or
volcanic nature, then you will see that the river has not been
nearly so successful in cutting its gap. The walls will be just as
deep, for the water must run downward, but they will be close
together and filled with angry water."

Nathan was impressed, but like all the others, quite
apprehensive about what lay immediately ahead. "What do
you see in the rocks now?" he asked.

Powell removed his knife and noisily scratched the rock
under his feet. "Solid granite."

The men exchanged knowing glances. Tomorrow and the
days just ahead would be bad, very bad.

The river's roaring was so loud that they had to shout to
hear each other. Nathan was drenched with perspiration and
spray. The Green was wild and undulating like a tortured
snake. They were pitching up and down so violently that it was
almost impossible to stay seated and Hawkins had broken one
oar. Nearly half a mile ahead of them, the *Emma Dean* could
be seen only in glimpses as she rose and fell and then
disappeared in the crashing waves. Nathan was worried. For
the first time on this expedition, he felt that Powell had really
erred in not portaging around this terrible stretch of water.
With one oar, they were nearly helpless, and behind them the
other boats were lost entirely. Maybe sunk.

"Hang on!" Bradley yelled from the bow.

Suddenly, Nathan felt the entire front end of the *Old
Maid* lift high into the air. He saw Bradley falling. Their boat
seemed to rear back on its stern for an instant and then it went
over. Nathan was not prepared for the power of the river.
Powell had instructed them that their only hope was to hang
on to the boat. Almost miraculously, both Bradley and Hawkins surfaced. "Grab on!" Nathan bellowed.

They clung to the overturned boat, and whenever a rock
loomed up ahead to rip away their legs, they shouted in
warning and somehow managed to throw themselves up on the

hull. Sometimes the *Old Maid* slammed into the rocks and flung them from her back, and then there was a period of sheer terror as they strove to reach her again.

"Ride it out!" Nathan yelled. "We can ride it out!"

Hawkins and Bradley didn't seem to hear him. They were pale and little more than their heads were above the churning white water. Nathan's fingernails dug into the smooth hull, and he hugged the *Old Maid*, knowing he would not last five minutes alone in the current. He'd be hurled against a boulder and when the current swept him on, every bone in his body would be smashed.

It seemed like hours before they began to feel the river slow down. Maybe it was only ten minutes, but when they finally sailed through the last narrow canyon and the river widened again, they were so weak that they could scarcely pull the *Old Maid* onto the beach.

"Where are the other boats?" Powell shouted.

"I don't know," Nathan wheezed, spitting up muddy water and lying in the shallows, too weak to stand. "Behind us somewhere."

"There!" Powell cried, pointing. "They're still afloat!"

Nathan twisted around in the water and saw the other two vessels, *Kitty Clyde's Sister* and *No Name*, come shooting out of the rapids. A few minutes later, they were all together on the warm sand. Nathan looked over at their leader. "What do the damn rocks say now?"

Powell walked over to a massive boulder and studied it. Then, with a hint of the dramatic, he scratched POWELL, 6-20-69. It explained better than words that the rocks ahead were soft now and that the explorers were in for at least a brief period of calmer water. The rock also told Powell that they had probably reached the southwest corner of Wyoming and were about to cross into Utah Territory where he knew the great Flaming Gorge canyons would soon begin. But how far until the Green joined the Colorado? That was still the question that no one could answer with any precision.

For the next few weeks, the Green was gentle, and sometimes they even had to use the oars to hasten their progress. The surrounding country was high desert with little greenery except for the cottonwood trees that drank the river water and crowded the riverbanks. Powell named this area Desolation Canyon, and because the water was slow and it was easy to disembark, he stopped frequently to make barometrical calculations that he said could tell him the altitude above sea level and thus, if taken frequently, the river's rate of fall, a valuable piece of information to include in the topographical maps on which he constantly worked each evening.

One man, a quiet, obviously nervous fellow named Frank Goodman, accompanied Powell on an outing along the bluffs, and when they found a small Mormon settlement, Goodman decided he'd had his fill of adventure and asked for permission to leave the expedition. Powell reluctantly bade him farewell and returned alone. Nathan did not care, their food was running low and Goodman had become increasingly morose and discouraged. As far as he was concerned, it was good riddance. They were down to nine men, but it was still a constant difficulty to get enough food and clear water to drink. Each evening, he and Hawkins, who had proved himself an excellent hunter as well as a cook, would hike into the side canyons in search of game. Sometimes they shot a rabbit or a rattlesnake, which tasted much like chicken, or even a sage hen, but, very often, they subsisted on fish, the already moldy salt pork, coffee, and dried beans that were so wet they were beginning to sprout.

Two days later, they were back in the canyons again, larger than ever, and the water began to churn. But at least they had a full complement of oars this time. Nathan and the men had chopped off the largest and straightest limbs of cottonwood trees they could find and then carved new oars. But cottonwood was soft and the oars splintered easily against barely submerged rocks.

Nathan never tired of looking up the canyon sides. Sometimes, they saw big-horned sheep and even bears on small trails etched into the rock cliffs. Major Powell amazed them with his knowledge of geology. He could read the layers of rocks and explain how they were formed, using such scientific terms as anticlines and synclines, until the members of his party possessed the working vocabulary of trained geologists.

Early in July, they stopped at the mouth of the San Rafael River where they made camp.

"Look here!" Powell shouted, reaching down and picking up flint chips and broken arrowheads. He turned and surveyed the brilliant orange-colored sandstone cliffs. "See up there," he said pointing. "An Indian trail, probably leading to some village. Mr. Beard?"

Nathan stood up, holding some of the flints.

"How far do you think we are from the Colorado River?"

"I don't know. When I found the junction, all I had was a Hawken rifle. No sextant, no barometer, just an old rifle."

Powell grinned, for he enjoyed demonstrating that applied science and modern technology would soon chart the entire wilderness. "Well, Mr. Beard, you may not have had the instruments or the knowledge to chart your position by the land and by the stars, but you possess the keen eye of an experienced frontiersman. Please hazard a guess."

Nathan had been thinking about the junction of the Colorado and Green for the past week. He remembered certain mesas and bluffs that stood out on the harsh Utah plateau as landmarks, and though the Powell expedition was approaching them from a different direction, he thought that several now in plain view were familiar. This country was also very similar in its rock formations and vegetation to that he recalled near the grand junction of the two mighty rivers. Geology and plant life were things of which he was more keenly aware since being with Powell. "I would guess that we are within fifty miles of the Colorado River," he said. "Certainly no more than one hundred."

"And the condition of the Green between us and the Colorado?"

"Thanks to your lessons in rock strata and geology, that's easy, Major. Anyone in this party will tell you that we are crossing desert with sandstone cliffs so, for the distance just south, this river will flow wide and easy."

Powell fairly beamed. "For a white Indian, you are very astute, Mr. Beard."

Nathan bowed modestly as the others in the party hooted with good-natured laughter.

Two days later, they heard a roar and assumed they were

coming to another canyon, but this time it was Nathan who shouted to the other members of the party. "It's the Colorado River!"

The men in the battered and leaking river coats cheered. They had already made history. No one had ever come down the river so far, and no one but Indians and perhaps some lost Spaniards had ever seen what lay ahead, except Nathan, and then only from the vantage of a distant peak.

"There's nothing but more canyon up ahead. Bigger, deeper, more dangerous than any we've yet seen," he told Powell privately that very evening.

"I know that and I suspect the men do as well. It's what we've come this far to see and to test."

"The boats are leaking pretty badly," Nathan said. "Maybe I should hike up on the mesa and find some pine trees. We could bring back pitch to seal the seams."

Powell wholeheartedly agreed. "Good idea! We'll stay here an extra day so that the men can relax while we hike up to the pines."

Nathan stared up at the cliffs. They were almost straight up and down. He could see the outlines of small pines hugging the rim. It would be a hard, hard climb. "Maybe you ought to let me do it," he said.

Powell chuckled. "You may be the mountain man among us, Beard, but you're also the longest in the tooth. I'll hike the tail off you before we reach that summit."

Nathan's eyebrows rose. He loved a good challenge. "All right!" he shouted. "We'll just see!"

They stood on what seemed like the rim of the world. They had finally gathered their precious store of pitch, and now, as they prepared to descend, neither man could quite bring himself to leave this high, wonderful vista. A pine-scented wind blew warm and fair. Ahead of them stretched a great slash in the Earth that went as far south as the eye could see. Was this the fabled valley of the Grand Canyon?

Powell said it was not. He had the longitude and latitude of that canyon, thanks to the Ives expedition that Matthew had been on. How ironic, Nathan thought, that my brother should have been a part of something that is now so important to me.

Who would have believed they would each play such a role in the story of this great river?

Without a word, Powell started down the impossibly narrow trail. Nathan waited a moment, then went, too. Somewhere to the south was Fort Yuma and on these very waters, Matthew.

Had he changed? Had anything changed and, most important of all, when they met, would he kill his brother for murdering their father in St. Louis long, long ago? Only time would tell. Only time and this great river.

21

The Colorado and the Green slammed together like two
onrushing trains. Their violent union created towering waves
that almost swamped the expedition and cast its puny boats
downriver like small twigs, bobbing and jumping on a flash
flood's tide. Nathan was afraid, really afraid, and he knew that
everyone in the party, including Powell, felt the same. With
two rivers joined, the Colorado's power was multiplied five
times. The water boomed off the sides of the sheer canyon
walls, and the only good thing that could be said was that the
river was so deep that there was no danger of having the hulls
torn out of their vessels. Water chutes, whirlpools, and angry,
treacherous waves became commonplace as each man strove
mightily to do his share. Very quickly, it became apparent that
the men could not hope to out-muscle the currents with their
oars but had to trust to God and to providence for their safety.
The canyon kept deepening. Powell judged the walls to be
fifteen-hundred feet high, then two thousand, but the current
was too swift to risk unnecessary landings and measurements.
The canyon seemed to drop into the Earth itself, until the men
felt like small insects contemplating the overhanging trees of a
mighty forest.

Shivering threads of spray cut mistily across thin, pene-
trating shafts of glossy sunlight to create spectacular rainbows.
Nathan and the others dared to throw their heads back and
watch streams gush forth from the world above to filter like
silent rain into the canyon and be lost in the mighty torrent.
Up there, Nathan understood the world was calm, the sun and
the land warm in late July. Perhaps there were even grassy
meadows, dry and quiet, with deer browsing placidly and
birds flitting across the azure bowl of sky. But down in the
canyon, the guttural, ceaseless roar of the Colorado was
omnipotent.

At the end of the day, Powell signaled his men into one of the few places of calm water they had seen for many miles. Muscles cramping, bones aching with cold and fatigue, the men pulled their craft in for the night. There was no warm sandy beach to sleep upon, no dry driftwood fit to burn and brew coffee. There was only wetness and shadow. The men huddled closely together on the damp, slippery rocks and watched the night blot away their strip of sunlight.

The next day was little better. And the next and the next. The salt pork and the flour got wet and half ruined. The coffee stayed dry but their salt cans were broken open, and what was saved tasted like sea water. There was no time to strain and dry it pure. Yet, they were rewarded by the sight of a band of six white mountain sheep that skipped acrobatically from rock to rock hundreds of feet overhead. The sheep seemed to adhere to the vertical rocks as if they were magnets tight against steel.

"Pull in and take a shot!" Powell shouted to his exhausted, hungry men as they paddled furiously toward shore.

Nathan, his heart in his throat, chose a place in the rocks and brought the *Old Maid* crashing into boulders. A desperate grab was made for the safety of rocks as the boat was torn from the current. Powell, in his *Emma Dean*, and the others were less fortunate and went spinning away, fighting to avoid being capsized.

Nathan leapt toward a flat rock. It was covered with moss, and he slipped and almost toppled into the river. Somehow, he pulled himself back up to safety. "Toss me my rifle!" he shouted.

A Winchester was hurled to his outstretched hands. He levered a shell into the breech and raised the barrel, spray clouding his eyes so badly that he had to wipe his face with the back of his soggy sleeve. He took aim again. The sheep had never seen a hunter. They froze against the face of the sandstone cliffs, looking like nothing so much as one of John Audubon's cherished wildlife paintings.

Nathan's rifle sounded puny against the river's thundering reverberation. But the men in the boats saw one of the sheep leap out into space and come spinning down into the river.

"Another!"

Nathan seemed hardly to take aim. There was no time to

aim, because the sheep were bouncing from rock to rock, higher and higher, toward the sky. Nathan fired, missed, and fired again. The leader of the flock stiffened in midstride and then peeled off the wall and plummeted like a stone into the churning water far below.

Nathan jumped for the boat, and the men paddled furiously after the floating carcasses, already a hundred yards downriver. Powell and the others dug in their paddles and slowed until the sheep came bobbing down to them where they were grabbed and tied to the boats. Off-weighted, the men struggled to keep from overturning. They became even more desperate, yet no one considered cutting the sheep free. Hours and miles farther south, the canyon widened and the men cheered to spy a patch of sunlit grass and cottonwoods. Starved, exhilarated, and whooping in celebration, they dragged the hairy carcasses up onto the sand and fell upon them with knives while a fire was made.

"Goddamnedest shooting I ever saw in my life!" Bradley cried, pounding Nathan's shoulder blades. "Amazing!"

Nathan finished his butchering. He wiped his Green River knife on the fine white sand and replaced it in his sheath. Taking a bloody haunch in both hands, he carried it to the fire where Hawkins, their cook, skewered it on a green branch of cottonwood and hung it over the fire, saying, "That second shot didn't seem hardly human."

Nathan blushed. "It was human, all right. With a Hawken in his hand, any decent mountain man could have brought down another before they made the rim and disappeared."

Powell heard that. "I think not," he said, "but the fact of the matter is that you made the shots that counted. We were in serious difficulty with our ruined food. There's just no telling when we'll see more sheep or deer. Nice work, Mr. Beard."

Nathan dipped his chin and watched the meat sizzle. To get such a compliment from a man like Powell was almost as good as the meal he was about to enjoy. No moldy bread, soggy beans, or dried apples tonight. No sir! It would be strong coffee and all the mutton a man could hold.

Early the next morning, Nathan and Major Powell climbed the canyon walls to reach a vista from which they could follow the canyon's progression for miles. The country around them was a harsh region of naked, multicolored rock with cliffs and broken buttes stretching as far as the eye could see.

"When God made this country," Powell said, "he intended it for nothing more than snakes and scorpions, lizards, and other crawlers. It sure isn't fit for man, white or red. Outside of the river, there's no sign of water, and yet we've seen ten thousand waterfalls at least. It's a hard and terribly beautiful land, Nathan."

"It is that," he said. "The canyons will be even deeper as we go south."

Powell followed his gaze. "I'm afraid the worst is still to come. I'm also afraid that the Howland brothers and Bill Dunn are looking for a way to escape these canyons and our expedition."

Nathan was caught by surprise. "I've heard nothing of it."

"Well, I have," Powell said. "And even if I hadn't, I'd have seen it in their faces and the way they are acting. All three are close to breaking. I'm surprised they haven't tried to recruit you to lead them out of here."

"To where?"

Powell shrugged. He scratched the stump of his arm, which often seemed to itch. "Anywhere, as long as it's off the river. You know Dunn claims he's a pretty fair hunter."

Nathan knew that Dunn had been a mule-packer around Denver. He dressed in buckskins and had long black hair that hung far down his back. He was quiet almost to the point of being taciturn. Nathan had not taken a liking to him and thought the man overrated his abilities. Maybe he had hunted and done a little trapping and packing, but that was in Colorado and this was altogether new territory, a thousand miles from the nearest settlement or help. Despite Powell's pronouncement only moments ago that this land was not habitable, Nathan suspected there were probably Indians within a few miles of the river, Indians who might not be friendly.

"Dunn doesn't surprise me with his plan to desert, but the Howland brothers don't seem to be the type."

"Yeah," Powell said. "I know. Maybe I can talk some sense

into all three before they make a mistake or even convince some of the others to go along with their crazy idea of hiking out of this wilderness. It would help if the canyon got easier."

"But it won't," Nathan said. "We can see that now."

Powell nodded. He started down, and from the look on his face, Nathan knew that the man was deeply troubled. It wasn't that they could not go on without the three if they chose to desert, but Powell simply felt a responsibility for everyone's safety and well-being. And Seneca Howland was a young, pensive, and courteous man who was everyone's favorite. His older brother, O.G., was a printer by trade, an editor, and a self-taught outdoorsman. He had the habit of taking off his hat whenever he was worried and then wringing it like a dishrag. More and more, O.G. had wrung his hat for hours beside the river after dark. With his long, wispy beard and hair flying around his face in the wind, he had a wild, haunted look, like a sorcerer whose last spell had somehow gone wrong.

In the days that followed, Nathan watched the Howland brothers and Bill Dunn separate from the others. They just pulled away by themselves and twice he saw them speaking with other members of the party, hoping to increase their numbers and thus their chances in the wilderness escape they planned. Powell entreated them to remain with his expedition, but they did not listen. All they seemed to hear was the din of the mighty river, and they swore that everyone was going to be lost in some waterfall just up ahead.

It was hard to argue with them on that point. They were "letting down" two and three times a day when it was possible, and sometimes they had no choice but to trust to good fortune and run the rapids, taking their scary chances.

They came to the junction of the Little Colorado, and their worst fear was to round a corner of the canyon and discover, too late, that they would be thrown over a waterfall. Because of the power of the current and because they had to pick their way through the deepest chutes of water to avoid being capsized, there was no hope that they could be prepared for a sudden waterfall. The constant roaring of the Colorado deafened them to all other sounds, even that of falling water. The specter of them going over a cliff and plunging to their watery graves was one that gave them sleepless nights.

Whenever they came to a bend in the corridors of stone, their
hearts beat a little faster. And yet, who could deny that this last
great canyon was the grandest in the world? Was this not a
sight that would please even a pagan's god?

The pinnacles, towers, dizzying spires, and craggy multicolored monuments of rock were so breathtaking that they
never grew tired of seeing the panorama unfold. Marble, lava,
sandstone, and iron cliffs soared to the heavens all around
them.

"This is the one being called the Grand Canyon," Powell
told them one evening after he had made his readings and
consulted his precious maps wrapped in oilskin pouches. "This
is the canyon seen from its south rim by Ives and his men years
ago."

Nathan almost added aloud, "The one my brother looked
down upon," but caught himself just in time. Still, the idea
that he and Matthew, like John and Walter Powell, were
among the first white men to see this majestic canyon country
struck him as being somehow prophetic. If Matthew had seen
this, then it could not help but have changed him inwardly.
Why had he come to the West? And why, of all things, had he
joined a famous expeditionary party when he had a St. Louis
dry goods store handed to him on a platter? The thought that
Matthew had somehow lost his inheritance or had it snatched
from his grasp never occurred to Nathan. Matthew gave
nothing away that he did not want to. So, why? Had he indeed
killed their father as he'd so often sworn? Soon, Nathan told
himself, you will have all the answers. If they could survive
this, the last and the greatest of the canyons.

The walls of the canyon pinched in ever more sharply
and, even worse, turned to granite. Everyone knew that the
water ahead would be worse then anything they had faced yet.
The waves played ball with them, batting and pitching the
boats back and forth with the men clinging to their oars, always
half in, half out of the turbulent waters. In the worst stretches,
they attempted to grab driftwood sticks wedged between rocks
and then toss them far up ahead so that they might better see
how the currents ran and how to steer. In such rapids, there
was no steady flow. The river wheeled or rolled crazily back

and forth and sometimes even upriver a few yards as it boiled over the rocks and surged from one canyon wall to the other. There was no order of procession. Powell realized that it was every man and every boat for itself, and each crew labored in terror for its own survival. And when the rapids were run, each crew would immediately bail out its vessel in preparation for another onrushing stretch of the angry white water before daring to waste a moment to look fore and aft to see if they were the only survivors.

To make matters worse, it rained for two days, cold, drenching rain, that further muddied the angry water and made it impossible for them to start a cooking fire. Dark rain clouds breached the rim of the canyon, making it seem as if they were entering a long, watery tunnel. The cliffs were black, the water was brown or white with foam, and the underbellies of the cloud ceiling were gray. The overall effect was enough to cause the stoutest of men to tremble. Nathan had never seen such downpours, not even in the Rockies. Huge bolts of jagged lightning speared into the narrow canyons and the thunder clapped so loudly that it hurt their ears and drove them half insane. Sometimes the lightning seemed to stab the river itself and turn it red and shimmery, other times the bolts hit the soaring rock walls like cannon shot and sent rocks hurtling down on them.

"We're leaving!" O.G. Howland said that night. "To go on is madness. Major, give this up before you all are lost. You are doomed in this canyon!"

Powell stood his ground. "It is you who will face death if you abandon us," he shouted over the elements. "I *beg* you to stay."

But Dunn shook his head. He was big and dangerous and never more determined. "Major, if we stay any longer, we'll be trapped in this canyon with no way out. I saw a trail up the north rim. We can take it—all of us. We can find the Overland Trail and reach help. Major, it's finished. You tried, but it is done!"

Powell shook his head. "We'll push on in the morning, and as soon as the clouds disappear, I'll use my sextant and give you our location. It will . . . "

"No sir!" Dunn said. "We can see the river up ahead. We're not going back into the boats."

Powell gave it one last try. "Listen," he pleaded, "by my best guess, based on the maps and our last readings, we're only about forty-five miles above the mouth of the Rio Virgen River. This canyon will peter out in a few days and we'll float right down to Fort Yuma. We can make it!"

Dunn toed the wet sand. He listened to the thunder and felt it rock the walls. Glancing at the Howland brothers, he saw them look in fear to the north rim. "I'm sorry," he said in a low, discouraged voice. "We'll be leaving at first light."

Powell's mouth crimped and his shoulders slumped with defeat. Nathan could see how badly this hurt his pride. He was responsible and now . . . now for these three at least, that responsibility was over. "I wish you Godspeed," he whispered before turning away to huddle near the river in the rain.

In the morning, they said their farewells. Dunn and the Howland brothers refused to take any food but did accept two rifles and a shotgun. They would find plenty of game to eat on the north rim.

"Take my watch and give it to my wife if we do not make it," a man named Sumner told them, handing it over to Seneca.

Others, including the major, had written hasty letters to their families and given them to the three. "Just in case you're right and we drown." Powell also gave them notes of the expedition to deliver to the proper authorities if the worst should happen and the expedition was lost.

The three climbed the north rim and Nathan wanted as badly as any to leave the river and join them. But he stuck with Powell, and when the trio finally breached the high rim, they waved for a long time before they disappeared, probably never to be seen again.

"All right," Powell said to his remaining five men, "we don't have enough men left to take but two boats the rest of the way through the canyon."

Everyone expected one of those boats to be Powell's beloved *Emma Dean*, but he showed his character when he said, "My craft is in the worst shape of the lot, we'll take *Old Maid* and *Kitty Clyde's Sister* on down. Anything that we don't absolutely need must be left here. We'll never make it through what lies ahead if we're overloaded."

To prove his point, Powell abandoned his prized fossil and mineral collections along with one of his water-damaged barometers. "Let's go," he said, turning his back on the *Emma Dean* and joining Nathan in the *Old Maid*. "Let's give this river hell!"

Nathan grabbed the tiller and the two boats shot out into the current and, almost at once, they began a dizzying ride into the deepest part of the canyon. It was a ride that Nathan could never have described to anyone. He felt as if he were sledding into hell on a water chute. The other boat was running ahead when it shot over a twenty-foot drop and vanished. In desperation, Nathan and his crew tried to reach the banks but they were caught in the jaws of the river and thrown over the waterfall. In midair, the *Old Maid* twisted out from under them and Nathan grabbed his Winchester as he was driven into the river harder than a nail into wood. He momentarily lost consciousness, and when he awoke the rifle was gone and he was spinning around and around in a huge whirlpool at the base of the falls. To his utter amazement, so were the others and their boats and supplies.

Somehow, they got the men and the boats together and went on because there was no longer any choice. The walls dropped vertically into the river and there remained no chance of portaging back over the falls. So it was onward or nothing. Before darkness, they capsized twice more. The hulls of both vessels were badly torn and they lost their oars. The next morning, they pushed off using sticks and thinking of themselves as dead men. Helplessly, they felt the current grab them and send them careening downriver.

Food gone. Strength gone. Only will survived until they felt the river's heartbeat slow, and when they dared to look up, they saw the clouds were gone and the canyon walls were changing to sandstone and widening.

Powell bowed his head and said, to no one in particular, "We've made it! Almighty God has delivered us from the Grand Canyon!"

With his face wet with spray, Nathan, along with the others, bowed their heads and wept with gratitude.

22

Major Powell and his five weary expeditioners had found
Mormons fishing with nets at the confluence of the Rio Virgen
River. Half starved, the expedition had feasted well on fish,
squash, and melons. The next day was one of farewell, for John
Wesley Powell and his brother were to accompany the friendly
Mormons to their settlement of St. Thomas, just a few miles to
the north. From there, the Powell brothers would be escorted
by the Mormons north to Salt Lake City. After a few days of
Mormon hospitality and a well-deserved rest, they would
board the newly completed Transcontinental Railroad for a
triumphant return to Washington, D.C., to receive a hero's
welcome.

Powell was not interested in glory, but was extremely
eager to be reunited with his wife and family. His scientific
journals would tell Americans the story of the upper Colorado
River, which no one had ever succeeded in running. Before
their farewell, the one-armed major had expressed keen
interest in reassembling his party and making another, even
more scientific exploration of the Colorado the following year.
Not surprisingly, Nathan and the others had been less than
enthusiastic, although every one of them promised to send
Powell his new address and would not rule out the possibility
of another river voyage.

But now, the three men with Nathan were intent on
reaching California while he was more concerned with locating
Matthew. The thought of finding his brother created
both anticipation and anxiety. They had never been close, and
if Matthew had indeed killed Isaac in St. Louis . . . Nathan
pushed the thought out of his mind, refusing to consider that
grim possibility.

"There she is," Bradley shouted, "Fort Yuma!"

Nathan searched for Matthew's steamboat and seeing no vessels whatsoever, he relaxed. It would have been too much to expect Matthew to be in Fort Yuma on this very day. In spite of the intense heat, Nathan was surprised at how much had been done to make this isolated fort hospitable. The soldiers had planted many trees along the water and there were picnic tables and even grass that someone obviously was watering. In truth, it was a desolate place, a small, sun-blasted Army post, but after three months of seeing nothing but river and canyon walls, right now Fort Yuma seemed as big and as beautiful as St. Louis. Nathan watched the American flag wave in a gentle afternoon breeze and it filled his chest with pride to know he had played a small part in his country's history. Just like Matthew and Isaac.

Back in St. Louis, during all the difficult and unhappy years of Nathan's childhood, when he had neither a real father nor mother, people had said the Beards were of bad blood, rootless, godless boys to be avoided by respectable children. They'd keep bringing up the fact that, years earlier, the sweet and lovely Catherine Wilke had, despite everyone's pleas, insisted on marrying Isaac Beard. With great reluctance, her father had given the giant a chance, a real chance at making something of himself, but look what he'd done! He'd deserted his wife for the mountains and left her to die in a fever, calling his name. Then he'd returned, years later, for his sons and murdered a deputy and run away again. The man *did* have bad blood, and so did his accursed sons.

Nathan gripped the tiller and steered the *Old Maid* into the beach near the picnic tables as people came down from the fort to greet them. He guessed the Beard name would never be redeemed in St. Louis. Maybe Isaac had known that long ago and that's why he'd run to his Shining Mountains with an old mountain man. It didn't matter anymore. Nathan was sure that he and Matthew had made their contribution and the West was a new beginning for both of them.

While the soldiers stood by, waving and looking hot in their heavy blue uniforms, the young boys jumped into the muddy river and swam out to help pull the *Old Maid* onto the beach. There was great shouting and laughter.

"Which one of you is Major Powell!" a lieutenant yelled.

"None of us!" Hawkins, their cook, hollered back. "We're just a bunch of starving civilians. The major and his brother went north up the Los Virgines River to St. Thomas with the Mormons."

"Too bad!" a sergeant crowed. "They ain't got any whiskey like we do!"

The young lieutenant shot a reprimanding look at his veteran sergeant that was completely ignored. Everyone was staring at the leaking, crippled river boats that Powell had designed. Their water tight compartments had long since lost their value and the sleek vessels were so battered and beaten that they looked best suited for firewood. Oh, Nathan thought, but if wood could speak, the stories those hulls could tell.

"Is Matthew Beard here? I'm his brother."

"No," the lieutenant said. "He left about ten days ago. Be the end of the month before he's due back with mail and supplies."

"What day is it?"

The lieutenant smiled. He had a nice laugh. "It's September 7, 1869."

Nathan looked at his sun-blackened companions. "We've been gone over three months."

"Seems like three years," Hawkins said. "If I never see another river again, it'll be too soon."

"I don't believe that. By now, we've got river water in our veins instead of blood. If and when the major sends for us to go down the Colorado again, we'll be ready."

Hawkins said nothing and neither did the others because, right now, with everyone laughing and people congratulating them, it was easy to see that they'd done something very special.

"Since there appears to be no one in charge," the lieutenant said, "I guess that Captain Pope will want you all to dine with him and the officers tonight."

Nathan touched his ragged shirt and pants. After months of sun, rain, sand, and river, his clothing was rotting away and was little more than rags. He rubbed his beard. "I'm afraid we're not presentable at anyone's table, Lieutenant."

"You'll have new clothes, a bath, a shave if you want. Everything will be provided."

"Thank you."

"Excuse me!"

Nathan turned to face a remarkable looking woman with strawberry blonde hair and stunning green eyes. She was tall, and when she looked at him, he felt uplifted. Her smile had more radiance than the hot, blazing sun.

"I heard you ask for Matthew Beard, and when you said you were his brother . . . well, I should have known. There is some resemblance. Not much, but some."

Nathan was acutely aware that he looked more disreputable than a street beggar. He straightened and bowed a little in greeting. "And you are . . . "

"Mrs. Helen O'Day, a very dear friend of his," she told him. "And this is my daughter, Rose."

Nathan bent down and looked at the girl who curtsied and had a sweet but slightly impish smile. "You're going to be as pretty as your mother."

"Prettier by far," Helen said. "Did Matthew know you were coming?"

"I think not."

"Well, then, we have much in common, Mr. Beard. He didn't know I was coming either, and when he saw me, he ran."

Nathan was taken aback. He could see that she was not jesting and that there was a hint of pain in her voice. "I find that impossible to understand," he told her, "unless my brother has gone mad or blind."

"Neither. He has just gone away. Can we talk in private, Mr. Beard?"

"Of course!" Nathan felt self-conscious as he took the woman's arm and guided her away from the others. When they were alone, he said, "Can I help you in some way?"

"I'm not sure," she told him. Her green eyes had a faraway look. "I was just hoping that . . . perhaps if we became friends while we both wait for Matthew, that I might better understand him. He's so . . . "

Helen struggled for the words she wanted to describe Matthew. Finally, in exasperation, she said, "He is just so mysterious! I can't understand him at all. I thought he loved me and Rose, and yet when we arrived, he treated us as if we had leprosy."

Nathan raised his hands and dropped them loosely to his sides in a gesture of helplessness. "I can only say that Matthew and I were never close and I never understood him either. Not in St. Louis, and certainly I have no idea of what to expect now. Tell me. Did he ever speak of his father?"

"Yes, quite often. And of you, though much less frequently."

Nathan pressed toward the question he did not want to ask. "My father left his adopted Ute people. He was going to St. Louis and he never returned. Did he find my brother?"

Helen nodded and the lights in her eyes dimmed. "Then I guess you don't know that your father was shot to death by the sheriff. Matthew tried to help him escape but was betrayed. Matthew . . ." she took a deep breath, then blurted, ". . . Matthew admitted that he killed both the sheriff and his deputy in revenge."

Nathan did not quite trust himself to speak, so great was his relief that Matthew had not killed his father as he had vowed all those boyhood years.

Seeing this, the woman took his arm. "I will walk you up the hill to the fort and make you something to drink, perhaps some cool tea. Yes, with a little desert mint for flavoring. Would you like that?"

He managed to nod his head.

"Good! We have much to talk about while I work at my laundry. Very much indeed."

Nathan held the wash basket and watched Helen O'Day hang washing on the line. It was ten o'clock in the morning and already the temperature was in the nineties. It would top 110 by two o'clock. Children were already swimming down in the river and there wasn't a cloud in the vast blue sky. As far as the eye could see, there was nothing but broken hills and sagebrush . . . and the life-giving river. Nathan still thought of it as the Grand, and now he wondered at how it had come so far, from the Utes' legendary Spirit Lake high in the snow-capped Rockies. Thanks to Lieutenant Ives and Major Powell, only now could its long, dramatic course be mapped

entirely and its vast importance understood. To Nathan's way
of thinking, it was indeed a "grand" river, the most magnificent
American waterway west of the Mississippi.

"I try to get all the ironing done before nine," she was
saying as her hands moved swiftly to apply the clothespins,
"and my washing by noon. Of course, since Friday is inspection, I never meet that schedule on Thursday. There's just too
much to do."

Nathan only half listened as Helen went on. He was more
absorbed in watching her than anything else. He liked to see
her beautiful arms and fingers move and he marveled at the
way she could hold ten pounds of clothes over her left forearm
and a dozen clothespins in her left hand and still somehow
hang everything with a speed that defied explanation. Her
face, her arms, and her throat were tanned and he knew she
worried about her complexion. Yet, she seemed happy enough
to be kept busy and was obviously everyone's favorite. There
was a steady procession of young officers who brought her
washing.

But Helen paid little attention to the officers, and it was
clear that she wanted to marry Matthew. "He's a diamond in
the rough," she said more than once, "and I told him as much.
He just needs to smooth off the edges. There are a lot of them,
but heaven knows, I'm no saint. If my late husband were alive,
he'd tell you as much."

"What happened to him?"

Helen stilled and her face grew pensive. "He was killed,"
she said. "He was killed in prison."

"I'm sorry."

"I don't know what to feel, Nathan. I loved him. He was
Rose's father but, by the time he died, we had not been
husband and wife for such a long time. And he lost his religion
and Christian morals in the California gold fields. He left me
a hotel in a beautiful town called Columbia. It's much nicer
than any other of the gold towns. I would live there if it weren't
for Matthew. You know, I could run the hotel and do very
nicely."

"But there is Matthew and this river."

She smiled and finished hanging the line. "Yes. He saved
Rose and me. He's wonderfully generous, your brother, but

strangely troubled." Helen frowned and looked right at
Nathan. "Is there some dark secret he possesses? I know about
his killing the sheriff and his deputy. For a long time, I could
not live with that knowledge. It's breaking the Lord's com-
mandment, you know. I prayed and prayed for understanding,
and it came."

He smiled and snapped his fingers. "Just like that?"

"Not quite." She reached into the wicker laundry basket
that he held and laid another batch of washing over her left
forearm. He followed her to an empty line. "It never
comes . . ." she snapped her fingers before grabbing a bunch
of clothespins, ". . . just like that. The Lord answers us
slowly. He asks for our patience in return for His own. But the
answer did come. Matthew was to be forgiven. And I told him
so. But there is still something wrong, something hidden deep
inside." She shrugged. "I had hoped you could tell me what
that something might be."

"I can't," he said. "I doubt if Matthew and I know each
other very well anymore. We parted long ago and not on the
best of terms. He's made a new life and I did, too."

"As an Indian?"

"Yes, as a white Indian, a member of the Ute tribe."
Nathan told her about the Utes and about his family. He was
just beginning to tell her how much he loved the mountains
when, suddenly, a messenger came galloping into the fort. He
came so swiftly that he raised a cloud of dust, and Helen had
a fit to see her wash grayed.

Thirty minutes later, an Army patrol was formed on the
parade ground and they were fully armed. There was Indian
trouble. Old, old Chief Cairnook of the Mojave had led his
warriors in attacking an emigrant wagon train to the north.
Some of the whites had been slaughtered.

The next few days were tense at Fort Yuma. Wives and
children waited nervously, afraid that their husbands and
fathers were fighting for their lives someplace out on the
searing desert. But on the third day, a column of dust on the
northern horizon signaled the company's return. Cairnook and
several of the Mojave's tribal leaders had surrendered, know-

ing that it was the only way to avoid having their tribe annihilated by the superior Army force.

Nathan and the others in the fort watched the proud old chief, hands and feet manacled together, shuffle off to the guardhouse along with his fellows.

"They're old men!" Nathan said in anger. "Why, Cairnook must be in his eighties. I don't understand why he has to be shackled hand and foot. The others are nearly as old."

Helen just shook her head and held onto her daughter. "I don't know either. I'm just glad that he surrendered. The Mojave often come here to trade, and they seem like gentle, harmless people, though I'm sure they can be dangerous if wronged."

Nathan was tight-lipped. That afternoon, he learned that the emigrants had fouled one of the few good water holes left in the desert this late in the year. When reprimanded, they'd grown belligerent and a fight had broken out. The emigrants had buried their dead and hurried on across the terrible desert, but not without first swearing that they had been viciously attacked without provocation.

"What do you think will become of Cairnook?" Nathan asked one of the officers.

"He'll probably hang. The commander can't let them loose without setting an example."

"But what if he's innocent and it happened exactly as he states?"

"Are you going to take the word of a redskin over a white man?"

Nathan turned away. Damn right, he would! He'd spent the last twenty years living with the Ute Indians of Colorado. And if the Mojaves were anything like them, they did not lie. They might steal horses and they'd fight to the death if pressed by enemies, but they did not lie.

"I want to see the Mojave," Nathan said.

"They're under heavy guard. You'll have to take that up with the captain."

"I'll do that."

Captain Roscoe Pope was a short, balding man, all spit and polish, rules and regulations. Displeased by Nathan's request, he said, "I intend to bring the chief before a military

court right here. We'll try and sentence them fairly. I know
Cairnook. He's responsible for his tribe. There is no good that
can come of your request, and I must forbid you to visit him in
the guardhouse."

"But why?"

Pope's eyes narrowed. "Because, sir, you fancy yourself
more Indian than white. I don't understand or condone that
and I'll not have you meddling in Army affairs."

"But . . ."

"This discussion is over," Pope said, sitting down behind
his desk. "Corporal?"

"Yes sir!"

"Show Mr. Beard outside."

Nathan was seething as he went back to Helen. "I don't
understand men like that," he said. "I wasn't going to create
any trouble. I thought I might be able to find out exactly what
happened and plead the Mojaves' case."

Helen nodded. "When Matthew arrives, there will be
terrible trouble. He thinks a great deal of that old chief. He
and Ives first met Chief Cairnook when they came upriver on
the same *Explorer* he now owns."

Nathan looked out at the river. "He's due in tomorrow."

"I know," she said. "That's all I've been thinking about
since he ordered Rose and me to leave Fort Yuma. And now
this thing with Cairnook. No good can come of it, Nathan. We
must talk to Matthew before he does something that he will be
very sorry for."

Nathan took a deep breath and expelled it slowly. Like
Helen, he was worried.

Matthew blasted his steam whistle three times and
watched the children come running for the river. He raised his
hand and shielded his eyes from the merciless sun and
wondered if Helen and Rose were gone. He had decided that
he'd been right to order them to leave Fort Yuma. Not that he
could order anyone to do such a thing, but at least Helen
would understand that they had no future together. If he
hadn't paid to have John O'Day murdered in prison . . . but
hell, if he hadn't done that, Helen would have forfeited any
chance at happiness while waiting years for her worthless

husband's release. No regrets on that score, he told himself. I
did what I had to do. I've always done what I had to do. Killing
is necessary sometimes. It was necessary in St. Louis as it was
in Sacramento and it might be again. Helen would never
understand that. It had nearly torn her apart to forgive him for
killing the deputy and the sheriff in a fit of revenge. She would
never be able to forgive him for having her husband murdered.

"Stand by to unload," he growled to his crew of three men
when they neared the fort. "I want . . ."

He forgot what he wanted the moment he saw Helen,
Rose, and his brother. It had to be Nathan, though he was
much, much changed, far thicker in the chest and broader in
the shoulders. He stood out from the others, and his face was
the color of mahogany.

Matthew grinned so broadly that his lips split and bled
but he did not notice. As the *Explorer* neared the beach, he
surprised the entire fort by leaping off the bow of his steamship
into chest-high water and bulling his way up to shore. "You
Ute Indian sonofabitch!" he bellowed, grabbing Nathan
around the waist and lifting him off the ground. "Damn, it's
good to see you again, brother!"

Nathan could not describe the relief he felt to hug his
brother. Matthew *had* changed. He was gray-haired and
grizzled and immense, bigger now, it seemed, than even Isaac
had been.

Matthew dropped him and stepped back. He looked first
at Nathan and then at Helen and, when he did, his smile died.
"You should have gone away," he said to the woman. "There's
no future for us. None at all."

Helen's green eyes misted. "There could be, if you'd let
it. There could be so much for us, Matthew."

He turned away from her and grabbed Nathan and
clapped him on the shoulder. "Let's get drunk and swap lies
about the last twenty years."

Nathan wanted to say something to Helen, but there was
no chance. Later, but not now. After all these years, he was not
going to risk destroying this long-sought reunion.

"Hey, Matt," a sweaty little Army private called as he

rushed up to the Beard brothers. "Did you hear about old Chief Cairnook!"

Matthew slowed his stride because he was worried about the little old man. The last time they'd drunk a little mescal and gotten funny together, Cairnook had seemed very frail and in poor health. The man would not live many more seasons. "What about Cairnook? Is something wrong?"

"He's in the stockade." The private was obviously delighted that he was the first to inform Matthew of the important news. "Him and some of his friends. They killed some whites and, most likely, they'll hang."

Matthew swung around and grabbed the soldier by the throat and jerked him right off the ground. "Who says?"

The man had not expected this and his eyes bugged with shock and fear. Realizing his terrible mistake, he somehow managed to choke, "I . . . I didn't mean . . ."

Matthew hurled the soldier aside and, just as he was about to whirl and march up to the guardhouse, there was a cry and shots were fired.

"They're trying to escape!" a sergeant yelled.

The soldiers took off running, and then Nathan looked up and saw Cairnook and six of his warriors, who had timed their escape to coincide exactly with the arrival of the *Explorer* and their time in the open exercise yard. Old Chief Cairnook had grabbed a guard and was trying to keep him from opening fire on his fleeing warriors. The guard was young and strong and, even as Matthew began to run and shout, the guard knocked the chief to the earth and when Cairnook tired to grab his ankles and trip him, the guard's bayonet glinted in the sun and then buried itself in Chief Cairnook's shrunken little chest.

"No!" Matthew screamed, yanking a pistol out of his waistband and firing at the guard. "Goddamn you, no!"

Everything went to pieces as Nathan jumped and ran after his brother. He saw the guard fall wounded from Matthew's bullet, and then two other guards opened fire on the riverboat giant. Matthew seemed to lose his footing as he struggled forward toward Cairnook. The smoking six-gun slipped from his hand, and he staggered as a full volley was fired. He went down and so did three of the Mojaves as the rest dove into the Colorado and vanished in the swift current.

Soldiers raced to the water and tried to find the Indians but they had swam this river since childhood, and they knew how to stay under the dark, roiling water until they were carried beyond the next bend in the river.

Nathan dropped beside Matthew. With great difficulty, he rolled his brother over onto his back and hugged him with all his might as wracking sobs were torn from his throat.

Matthew was riddled with bullets and he'd died on his feet. Overcome with grief, Nathan could not help but remember that it had always been Matthew who had despised anything Indian and now . . . to die like this. To give his life for an Indian. At least, Nathan thought, I have that to remember.

Three days later, Nathan helped Helen and Rose onto the *Explorer*, and they waved farewell to Fort Yuma.

"Can you operate this?" she asked as the little steamship drifted out into the current.

"We'll make it," Nathan vowed, tearing his eyes away from the fresh mound where he and the Mojave people had buried his brother. "I talked to one of the sailors. He told me everything I need to know. Down the river to the Gulf of California, then around Cape San Lucas, then up the coast to Baja to San Diego, Monterey, San Francisco, Sacramento. And, if you want, we'll go from there to the Sierra Nevada Mountains I've always wanted to see."

"We could have taken a stage."

He took the wheel of the *Explorer*. "I asked you if you wanted to go by stage. You said no."

"Because I knew that you didn't. Why not? Is it because this ship is so much a part of him?"

"I guess that's it," Nathan said as he threw the lever that started the paddlewheels turning. "It's part of history. Just as he was."

"And you, Nathan. You, too."

Helen O'Day stood beside him, and she did not ask about any tomorrows and she tried not to think about any yesterdays. She had loved Matthew, but somehow feared him, too. She would never know what had stood between them, and maybe that was just as well.

Helen stroked her daughter's hair and bent down to whisper, "Don't cry about leaving, my dear, for there are wonderful things ahead for us all. I promise you."

"I'll make that same promise," Nathan said. "No matter what, we're all going to make out just fine."

He kept his eyes straight ahead to gauge the mood of his mighty river, born of Spirit Lake, home of the Ute people. Nathan remembered that his father had always wondered where his Grand River had at last melded with the sea. Now, with the sound of the paddlewheels thrashing in his ears and the hot sun sparkling off the roiling water, Nathan Beard, son of Isaac, brother of Matthew, would complete the river's full journey . . . and he would know.

If you enjoyed Gary McCarthy's epic tale THE COLORADO, be sure to look for the next installment in the RIVERS WEST saga at your local bookstore. Each new volume sweeps you along on a voyage of exploration along one of the great rivers of North America with the courageous pioneers who challenged the unknown.

Here's an exciting preview of the next book in Bantam's unique new historical series

≈   RIVERS WEST: BOOK 4   ≈

The Powder

by Winfred Blevins
Author of THE YELLOWSTONE

*On sale next summer,
wherever Bantam Books are sold.*

≈   **CHAPTER ONE**   ≈

Scratch-scratch-scratch!

Elaine flinched, and turned over toward Adam. His face was perfectly relaxed in sleep, and sweet—he hadn't heard a thing. She shook his arm. He didn't move.

Scratch-scratch-scratch!

Dammit. She resented the way he was sleeping anyway. She lay here awake and edgy, flat on her back, to tell God's truth feeling lonely as hell on her wedding night, and in her marriage bed, with the strange smell of sex in her nostrils. With her husband grandly asleep right next to her, oblivious. She had a sore crotch, nipples that her nightdress irritated, jumpy nerves, and you name it, and he slept like a lord through the whole thing.

She shook Adam again. Dr. Adam Smith Maclean was dead to the world.

She could guess how he would report their first amorous experience—playfully and happily as a kid with a new pony. He had toyed and teased and cavorted and just plain—hell, why not say it?—rutted. He played the joyful giant all the way. (Well, he was a damn barbarian, wasn't he?) Not that he hadn't been gentle and considerate and tender—he had, as much as he could. He'd been a little amused at her shynesses, too—he hadn't tried to hide the fact that he knew his way around this territory very well indeed. But in spite of his tenderness, and her own eagerness to please, well, it hurt, and smelled peculiar, and worse, made her feel self-conscious and a little shaky and in need of a lot of reassuring. But now she lay here out of sorts and lonely, and at the same time mad and jittery and making up her mind that she was going to be damned good at this business of love-making, and he slept the sleep of the satisfied.

Scratch-scratch-scratch!

Dammit, even Indians weren't polite enough to wait all night. A scratch on the door instead of a knock—that made them Indians, and surely the doctor's charges, not hers. The agency Indians had been wretched all summer with dysentery and malaria, and often they did ask Adam for white-man medicine to help out. So tonight would be just the first of thousands of nights that her married life would get interrupted by the sick. That was OK—she wanted to be used, to give the days of her life to something. So did Adam—that was part of what she loved about this crazy Indian.

OK, drastic measures. She put a foot against his back and started pushing, hard. Suddenly he sat up on the edge of the bed. She slipped out and got a robe to put over her nightdress. "Someone's here," she whispered. She saw that he was grinning at her in the dark—he was alert. He must have been trained at medical school to wake up like that, all of a sudden. He slipped on his nightshirt—he thought wearing clothes in bed a strange custom. He lit the bitch light, and she followed him through their bedroom door and through the other room to the front door. Adam moved his huge frame not sleepily but confidently, and Elaine thought that was another part of what she loved in him, his air of competence. She had to admit she loved his size, too. It felt marvelous to be enveloped by so much of him.

Adam's grandmother, Calling Eagle. Behind her his mother, Lisette. The queenly Calling Eagle spoke softly in the Cheyenne language, too low and fast for Elaine's Cheyenne. Adam hesitated, asked something softly, got a vigorous nod and one strong word in reply, and the visitors stepped back into the dark.

Her husband turned to her. In the flickering light he looked thrown off-balance. She reached to put her arms around him, but he grasped her hands with his.

He leaned against the door jamb. "They're going home," he murmured, emphasizing the last word a little. She had the most extraordinary sensation at that moment, a sharp smell of something burning, acrid and almost painful. Later she would tell Adam that she had smelled the future in that instant.

When he looked down at her, his eyes were full of plea. "Now. But the agent has said he'll use the soldiers to drive them back."

She repeated it to herself, word by word. She felt the bizarre sensation she felt when she was told her father died, the roots of her hair burning and freezing in patches. She knew she could stand it if she didn't reach to her hair with her hands, and kept her feet wide apart and stable.

So she told herself slowly what the words meant: The northern Cheyenne tribe couldn't stand it any more at this agency. They were heading for Powder River, more than fifteen hundred miles and Lord knows how many soldiers away. Tonight. On her wedding night. And, unbelievably, she was their teacher, her husband their doctor.

"Right now," Adam said forlornly.

"We'll never make it," she rasped softly.

2

All right, it was futile. All right, it was dumb. Smith started arguing with his new wife anyway.

"Goddammit," Smith barked, "do you think being Dr. and Mrs. Maclean will keep us from getting killed?"

She had her back to him, hands on the bureau, shoulders pushed up. God, he wanted to provoke her, to make her listen to reason.

She turned to him, touched his arm, and put her head against the outside of his shoulder.

He almost permitted himself a smile. Listen to reason, indeed. She'd never listened to reason—other people's reasons. Instead she'd gone to the Hampton Institute to teach Indian boys. Then traveled west to visit the Cheyenne and Arapaho Agency, then talked the church into sponsoring a day school there, then talked them past her unmarried state and inexperience so she could run it. She was wonderfully stubborn.

He was born a Cheyenne. She'd chosen to be here, and he loved her for it.

But he argued anyway. Feeling dumb, he held her stiffly and repeated the arguments he'd already used. The Cheyennes would be fugitives, at war with the United States. This was Indian Territory, a hell of a distance from Powder River, way up in Wyoming and Montana Territories. Soldiers would fight them all the way, out of Fort Dodge and Fort Hays and Fort Laramie and Fort Robinson—hell, he didn't know all the forts they might come from. People would get killed, white people and red. And by God, Adam and Elaine Maclean would have no immunity to getting killed.

And then the simple, practical considerations. His job was to doctor, hers to teach—they'd be walking away not only from their paychecks but their duty.

Some of it he didn't tell her. He couldn't imagine her trekking across the country for weeks and months on a horse, her belongings on a pony drag, her privy the bushes, her bed—her marital bed—crowded into a tipi with Smith's family, her meals puny and full of dust, her life bitter as alkali and cold wind. He didn't say, either, that she was too precious to him, that he could not risk her life at the hazards of war.

God, but he loved her.

Christ, it was awful.

3

Elaine lifted her head off her husband's shoulder. If he thought Elaine Cummings would be intimidated, he had another thing coming. We Cummings women, flinty New Englanders, ardent abolitionists and suffragists, do not quail at rough going.

She stepped away from Adam, looked into his eyes, and told him in an unmistakable tone. "They're our people." She took a deep breath. Her husband was a good man, but in some ways not grown up. "You can't walk away. I won't walk away."

She let the words hang. She decided not to add what else she knew—that he secretly yearned to go on this adventure, and yearned for her to go with him. More important, he wanted to go home, to the Powder River country, and make his life there. *Home.* She turned to the bureau and started putting the rest of their few clothes into a canvas bag. He would see they had to go.

4

Smith saw the set of his wife's shoulders, and slowly nodded. He turned and took down his Winchester from over their bed. He had lived this life—had been on the run, had taken scalps, had held a dying man in his arms—and she hadn't. He hoped she would stand up to it well, and not hate it too much. Inside, he had to admit, he could feel stirring a part of himself, a wild part he only half-welcomed. It sang out, Let's fight like hell.

Elaine looked over her shoulder at him and took the canvas bag out to where the horses were waiting.

Dr. Maclean admired her. She was stronger than he was, and wiser, and more devoted.

5

Half an hour later, past midnight in what was not yet Oklahoma, Smith made a last-minute check of his cabin for medical supplies. He'd packed his pocket surgical kit, cod liver oil, alcohol, chloroform, one tonic, one astringent, one emetic, laudanum, and some extract of smart weed for the dysentery—he didn't have any more quinine, and would just have to hope no one came down with malarial fever. These were entirely medicines he'd brought with him from the East. He'd be damned if he'd take agency stores and give the Army an excuse to arrest him for theft. He didn't see anything else he could take, or needed, since his people mostly rejected his kind of medicine anyway.

He took a last look around the cabin. Elaine was outside, mounted, with Calling Eagle and Lisette, ready to go. Smith put in his copies of *Gray's Anatomy* and Hartshorn, and grabbed for *Apple-Blossoms*, the book of poems Elaine had published when she was at the Harvard Annex, the Harvard for women. It brought memories flooding into him, memories of Boston, and of meeting Elaine, and hearing her read her poems and discovering how much cultured people admired her.

My God, look what he'd almost left behind. His ivory balls. His old friend Peddler had taught him to juggle, and he'd found these three billiards balls in a pawn shop. They were perfect for his big hands. He used them for a kind of mesmeric relaxation. In fact, it was after a session with his ivory balls that he knew—simply knew, without question—that he must ask Elaine Cummings to marry him.

Smith took a last look around the room. Their bureau, the drawers hanging out, empty. The bitch light, its wick barely flickering—he blew it out. The chamber pot. The iron bedstead, their one luxury, its shuck mattress now stripped of sheets and blankets. He thought of the loving they had done on that bed just hours ago, and felt his loins stir.

He stepped outside, stuffed the last few belongings into his saddle bags. They had to leave the wagon, which wouldn't stand the rough country ahead. They had to leave the tent, which would have given them privacy but was Indian Bureau property. He looked at Elaine. She was perched on her sidesaddle. Though she was a good rider, the sidesaddle seemed. . .

Hell, what had he gotten her into? From Boston, the center of civilization, her family, and her way of life, to . . . what?

His life. He looked around at his mother and grandmother. The Cheyennes had spent Smith's whole life getting swamped by the white man. This red-white fighting had even killed his father. And his brother. Now he was throwing his wife into it. Christ. He was scared, and the fear tasted vile in his mouth.

He swung into his saddle and looked sideways at Elaine. Hanging there on the side of her horse, in her long skirt that hid the horns her legs used to do the work of riding, she looked like an old-fashioned daguerreotype of an ideal New England lady. He felt a skin-prickly rush of want for her.

Calling Eagle clucked, and they moved out.

≈   **CHAPTER TWO**   ≈

Elaine looked at Little Wolf's face in the moonlight, and wondered what he was thinking. Was the chief having second thoughts about what he had done? It was a grave face, blighted by small-pox scars and lined by responsibilities.

Little Wolf was the Sweet Medicine chief, the carrier of the sacred bundle Sweet Medicine had brought to the Cheyennes, and so first among the other four old-man chiefs of the Tsistsistas and the Suhtaio, the two strands of people who camped together and made up the Human Beings. One other of the forty-four was among the Cheyennes fleeing tonight, Morning Star, also called Dull Knife. Elaine thought he was the most beautiful man she'd ever seen. Elaine had worked with the two of them all summer, and thought them extraordinary men, devoted to their people and deserving of genuine respect.

Elaine, Smith, Lisette, and Calling Eagle also waited for the people to come walking stealthily through the darkness. Calling Eagle had told them how Little Wolf and Morning Star threw the gauntlet in council yesterday afternoon, while Smith and Elaine were being wed.

They told Miles, the agent, that the people had to go back home—the chiefs had repeated those words all summer. They reminded Miles of the promise made at Red Cloud Agency, that the people could come back north if they didn't like the southern lands. They spoke in a measured way, regretfully and firmly.

Miles said, also sadly, that if the Cheyennes tried to leave, the soldiers would drive them back to the agency. As a promise that they would not run off, the agent asked that they turn over ten young men as hostages.

Ten young men. They didn't have a hundred men of any age left. Silently appalled, Morning Star said he would speak to the people about it, and left to go to the camp. He knew he was walking out of that council for the last time.

Camp was temporarily in a valley among some sand hills in a corner of the reservation where the women could dig roots, for they had nothing to eat. Since the army was fearful that the Cheyennes would flee for their homeland, they had horse soldiers and cannon on both sides of the little valley, the far-shooting guns trained down on the quiet lodges, not lodges of fine buffalo hides but of pathetic, rag-tag canvas.

After Morning Star walked out of the talk, Little Wolf made one further request of the agent. To the ears of the people it was a forlorn request: "I have long been a friend of the whites," he said. "The Great Father told us that he wished no more blood spilled, that we ought to be friends and fight no more. So I do not want any of the ground of the agency made bloody. Only soldiers do that. If you are going to send them after me, I wish you would first let me get a little distance away. Then if you want to fight, I will fight you and we can make the ground bloody on that far place."

The people hoped the agent would hear both the friendship and the soul-deep resolution in Little Wolf's words, would hear that the people knew they might die going home, and faced that prospect with an inner-smiling acceptance.

To them it was clear: Stay in this bad country and die of disease, or strike out for home and live or die like human beings. It was an easy choice. Surely, they thought, if the agent Miles truly understood that, he would not send the soldiers after them—he would leave them alone. Surely. Was he not a man, with human feelings?

As he spoke those words to the agent, Little Wolf felt their uselessness. Miles was decent and sympathetic, but he didn't see. He thought the people should adapt to the new life the white people had chosen for them, farming, school-going, learning new gods, feeding on white-man handouts. He thought they should just forsake their own way of life as a remnant of the past, the way a snake sheds its old skin. Accept life entirely on white terms.

Little Wolf hid his impatience. Miles had no idea that the Cheyenne people had to live as Cheyennes or not at all. He didn't know that their way of life had been brought to them from the powers by Sweet Medicine and Buffalo Calf Woman. He didn't see the importance of fidelity to the sacred arrows and the buffalo hat. So he didn't realize that once the holy ways were abandoned, the good life gone, pride and honor given up, a Cheyenne could find no joy in living. Little Wolf had to suppress his contempt for such a man.

The Sweet Medicine chief was glad the people felt these issues so profoundly—they made Little Wolf's eyes wet with pride. Now they chose to start acting like Tsistsistas and Suhtaio again. They would go to the Powder River country. Or toward it. We will walk north like Tsistsistas and Suhtaio—Human Beings, Little Wolf declared over and over, and if necessary die like Human Beings.

He added his motto: The only Indian never killed is the Indian never caught.

That night, as Little Wolf stood afoot beside the mounts of his friend Calling Eagle and her family, he waited with fear and admiration to see the first Human Beings starting on their journey.

He knew they had to sneak out of their camp. The soldiers and cannons were close, and ready. If they saw the people leaving, they would shoot. So the people would be walking quietly, even the children, and keeping to the moon shadows.

Back in camp, as Little Wolf had started out ahead, a young man played a song on a love flute, partly to cover the small noises of moccasins on earth and stone, and to make the night seem normal to the soldiers' ears. The chief thought of the northern Cheyennes creeping up this canyon, young and old, weak and strong, infirm and healthy, many bearing heavy loads. He loved them.

Little Wolf looked at his old friend Calling Eagle. He wondered if Calling Eagle felt as he did at this probable catastrophe—exhilarated.

2

How had they come to such a state?

The thousand Tsistsistas-Suhtaio led by Little Wolf and Morning Star had come in to Red Cloud Agency a year and a half ago, in the spring of what the white men called 1877. As the soldiers intended, the Indians were starving.

These Cheyennes had been on the Red Cloud Agency the summer before, but they had gone hungry—the agent at Red Cloud never seemed to have the appropriations promised the Cheyennes. In 1876 they left the agency for their summer hunt, and barely missed the Custer fight in June. All that summer before, but they had gone hungry—the agent at Red Cloud never seemed to have the appropriations promised the Cheyennes. In 1876 they left the agency for their summer hunt, and barely missed the Custer fight in June. All that summer and all that autumn Little Wolf and Morning Star's people got chased by the soldiers, just like the Lakotas and Cheyennes who did kill Yellow Hair. Because of the pursuit, they never got to make a proper buffalo hunt, so they spent the winter hungry. In the spring, they considered their empty bellies, and the white man's promises of food and a reservation in their country, the Powder River country. They came in to Red Cloud Agency.

That was when they discovered that they had stepped into the web of the *veho*, their word which meant both spider and white man. General Crook, whom the Cheyennes fought and admired, argued hard for them to get an agency in Powder River country, but the Great White Father said no. He said these Cheyennes must join their southern relatives at the agency in Indian Territory, far to the south.

Now the northern Cheyennes said no. They knew that country, and didn't like it. So the officials at Red Cloud Agency cut off their rations.

After a little starvation, the Cheyennes relented. They would go and see the new agency on the Canadian River, on the condition that if they didn't like it, they could come back. Blue-coated soldiers escorted them on the seventy-day journey to the south, and only three or four dozen Cheyennes slipped away and went back to their homeland, the Powder River country.

Right away the two old-man chiefs, Morning Star and Little Wolf, saw that the new agency was no good. The southern Cheyennes did not have enough appropriations to feed themselves, and the whites proposed to feed everyone, including nearly a thousand new Indians, without increasing the rations.

The old-man chiefs went immediately to the agent, Miles, and told him they were going back to Red Cloud Agency before the snow flew. Then the agent said, for the first time, that if the Cheyennes left, the soldiers would drive them back.

THE 1990

LOUIS L'AMOUR

C A L E N D A R

THE 1990 LOUIS L'AMOUR CALENDAR showcases thirteen full-page, four-color paintings by master Western artists whose work brings to vivid life the men and women who tamed the frontier and shaped the nation. Each painting was created as cover art for either a beloved Louis L'Amour novel, short story collection, or Bantam Audio cassette adaptation of his fiction—and has never appeared as calendar art.

Accompanying the painting highlighting each month of 1990 is a favorite passage from the story the art illustrates, personally selected by the author's daughter, Angelique L'Amour, whose hardcover book, *A Trail of Memories: The Quotations of Louis L'Amour,* available from Bantam, is a national bestseller. Her selections recall the always unforgettable experience of reading the work of Louis L'Amour.

The centerfold map spotlights key locations from Louis L'Amour's more than one hundred books.

☐ 34730-6 $7.95

ELMER KELTON

THE MAN WHO
RODE MIDNIGHT

☐ 27713 $3.50

Bantam is pleased to offer these exciting Western adventures by ELMER KELTON, one of the great Western storytellers with a special talent for capturing the fiercely independent spirit of the West:

☐	25658	**AFTER THE BUGLES**	$2.95
☐	27351	**HORSEHEAD CROSSING**	$2.95
☐	27119	**LLANO RIVER**	$2.95
☐	27218	**MANHUNTERS**	$2.95
☐	27620	**HANGING JUDGE**	$2.95
☐	27467	**WAGONTONGUE**	$2.95